better & better

Feel the width: natural organic whole hand-crafted Bristol-sourced pen-fresh literature for sensitives, with no added sugar, artificial preservatives, flavourings or oil-based pharmaceuticals. High-fibre, low-salt, calorie-neutral, non-dairy, hypoallergenic. No animal was hurt. Ingredients: aqua, fibre, glue, ink, naturally derived concentrates. May contain traces of nut.

Better & Better has no publicity budget and relies on word of mouth to find its audience. If you approve, therefore, dear Reader, please speak up, pass on, give stars.

Best before 24.02.2217

Frieda - German visitor

(Kevin = ex)

Georgina   Will (brother)   Joni (sis
                  Renée Letty Henry   ) kids
     Maureen (mum)   Eve
                      Larry (dad)

     (Jim father)
Joni (daughter) Charlie (son)

Nick - old friend / opened the box

HOW TO
MAKE
LIFE

Sarah Ménage

bb

bb

First published in paperback by
better & better 2017

ISBN 978-1-911362-00-5

All events and persons portrayed are fictional.

Printed and bound by CPI Group (UK) Ltd, Croydon, CR0 4YY

FSC
www.fsc.org

MIX
Paper from
responsible sources
FSC® C013604

The environmental cost of printing this book will be further offset by the
planting of six walnut trees in its honour, undertaken by Frank Drake, as
part of Bristol's Moveable Forest. Trees absorb greenhouse gases, clean
the air and deliver oxygen, while creating soil, food, shelter, shade and
loveliness.

A CIP catalogue record of this book is available
from the British Library

For my family,
those gone, those going,
and those to come

ACKNOWLEDGEMENTS

Dozens of people supported me in the writing and making of this book; I give all of them my warmest thanks. Some are friends, some family, some acquaintances; but being none of these, the first was all the more generous: Charlie Lee-Potter gave her time and expertise for free and added a shimmer of kudos to the novel by allowing me to quote from her detailed and incisive critique. I'm also grateful to Laetitia Rutherford who agented my first novel and encouraged me to write this one. If not for her, it wouldn't exist.

Hans Kroon became a great new friend during my first two years of writing it, and consistently boosted my morale. Mary Hayes never referred to it as anything but a 'best seller'. Bec Monks has encouraged my writing over a period of at least ten years. Writer Nick Riddle professionally checked early and final proofs and listened to hours of writerly angst and joy, some of which I also shared with writer friends Trevor Coomb, Kate Firth, Wendy Buonaventura and Heather Tweed. Heather has been a particularly enthusiastic champion, and so has my lovely friend Dawn Gordon. As well as Mary, Bec and Nick, the following also read earlier drafts and made comments that I responded to in some measure: Clive Hammond, Jo Walters, Jude Groves, Will Gibson and sister Kate Wilkinson. I especially enjoyed Kate's running commentary; it must be the happiest writing experience I've ever had – to be read at the same time as editing – me on the sofa tapping away, she on the comfy chair, occasionally snorting with amusement, occasionally silently absorbed, occasionally saying, 'I don't get this bit'.

Editor Jacqui Easby made a few dramatic cuts, most of which I bore. Any errors of any kind are my own, but Natalie Haupt reduced them by checking my French and German; Dr Robert Knight (he helps you to understand, he'll do everything he can)

– another generous stranger – answered questions and made a few suggestions about post-war Europe; and Mark Beswick from the Met Office gave a factual basis to my weather memories of that notorious summer of '76. Excellent musicians Andy Davis (guitar, bass), Simon Fish (drums, percussion) and Rach Hall (string arrangements, violin) played on some or all of 'How To Make Life Nice', 'The Glass Girl' and 'Love In A Wet Climate', which were offered as crowd-source rewards, and the following people bought them, helping to fund the first print run and launch party. I've chosen to list my backers alphabetically by surname then first name, which means that cousins, siblings and spouses may be listed together. I noticed that usually the man came up first, and was going to reverse the whole list to correct this anomaly! Tradition prevailed. You may notice that some of the below are so good I've named them twice.

A special thank you to:

David Alexis, Toby Beaufoy, David Brown, Sarah Brown, Wendy Buonaventura, Michael Cech-Lucas, Sara Cech-Lucas, Trevor Coomb, Julian Dale, Marion de Berker, Isabel de Salis, Kate Durrant, Karen Ellison, Jo Fenwick, Tim Fish, Justin Gibson, Sasha Gibson, Will Gibson, Sue Glennie-Smith, Dawn Gordon, Jude Groves, Caroline Hagen, Gillian Harris, Felicity Harper, Mark Hatwood, Mary Hayes, Jill Longman, Hans Kroon, Mags Mackean, Ginetta Martinez, Alistair Mchardy, Jenny Ménage, Jeremy Ménage, Nick Ménage, Bec Monks, Murk Muller, Bruce Niddrie-Webb, Caroline Niddrie-Webb, Jules Perry, Ann Remmer, Nick Riddle, Nicky Thomas, Simon Prestwich, Shirley Smale, Joanna Swan, Heather Tweed, Rina Vergano, Sophie Walpole, Diana Wilkin, Kate Wilkinson.

I am immensely grateful to good people who work for six life-enhancing (and life-saving) organisations: Penny Brohn Cancer Care, Macmillan Cancer Support, the National Health Service, the Lido, the Performing Rights Society, and Equity.

Thanks also to Sue and Patrick Glennie-Smith for hosting the launch at their beautiful cosy café in Clifton, The Primrose, and to Nick Moss for letting the room of my own.

Lastly I wish to thank friends and family who are not already mentioned above, including the inimitable Frank Drake, photographer, tree planter and provider of many a consoling vin rouge or rooibosh au balcon. Most especially I thank our splendid son Seamus, for his generosity, tolerance, appreciation and moral support.

How to make life nice? Without the kindness of strangers and friendship from kith or kin, it would be impossible.

SJM December 2016

MAKE THE BEST OF A BAD JOB

Georgina had emailed her daughter Joni, just to let her know where she was and what she was doing and for about how long. She had tried to phone Charlie on his mobile, but they'd exchanged texts instead of talking:

How are you? All's well I hope, including revision etc. Not sure how long I need to be here, but do call me any time on mob or landline. Take care. Lots of love, Mum xx.

ps You can come if you want. Weekend or half term? You might like books, war memorabilia etc. You could sleep in small front room. Take care. Lots of love, Mum xxx

He had replied: *Entriguing but I'd prefer to stay here thanks,* and signed off with a smiley face. Well, of course she didn't want to interrupt his school work or social life. What had she been thinking? What an absurd suggestion that a seventeen-year-old boy might like to waste his free time in this mausoleum!

Yes, it would prob be a bit boring. Btw, it's 'intriguing', with an I. Smiley face and one kiss.

Every hour or two she went to her laptop to check for incoming emails, glad that her parents' landline and broadband were still functioning (although her parents weren't). No news was good news. And she carried her own mobile with her at all times, making sure it was constantly within earshot, in case one of the children needed her, not because anything bad might happen.

Even if it did, Georgina was immune to bad luck, and would like to think she could treat those two imposters Triumph and Disaster just the same (though she hadn't yet had enough of Triumph to fully test herself). When bad things happened, she got on with it, whatever it might be, because she believed it was one's duty to make the best of things, and refused to waste precious energy on complaining or brooding or entertaining any kind of nasty thoughts.

In this spirit she had sailed through the ups and many downs of her career; and almost as smoothly braved the death of her mother and then her father, and in between these commonplace tragedies, weathered the nasty dose of breast cancer fate had thrust upon her. Cheerful was her default mode, and she had been a positive kind of person for as long as she could remember, long before emerging into adulthood from a peaceful and protected childhood in the middle of this prosperous rainwashed country of ours. Perhaps it was an overhang from her parents' generation, with their stiff upper lips and Dunkirk spirit. Or perhaps it was a result of her privileged, character-forming education. Or perhaps it was the character she'd been born with, written indelibly into her genes.

Her career was no cause for regret. She had used her talents and her time on more important things, such as family and friends; and if in fact she had wasted them, well, it was her own fault, on the whole. The deaths of her parents were regrettable but unavoidable events which had happened at about the usual time – you can't expect to live half a century without losing someone you love. And she told herself that the cancer was a useful and necessary wake-up call, emphasising that she must enjoy every second of however many seconds were left to her. If she hadn't had cancer she wouldn't be taking such good care of herself, and if one had to get cancer, hers was definitely the best cancer to get. Furthermore, if it was her destiny to die sooner than she wished, well she'd had a happy childhood, wonderful schooldays and a jolly nice life, and no-one could ask for more than that.

There were other things, however, that she did not so readily understand.

She didn't understand why Charlie had decided to live with Jim, his father, or why Joni had chosen such an uninteresting boy to go to Peru with, and then been so angry at Georgie on the day she left; not realising that the five months before they would see each other again was a gaping chasm of time, assuming of course that they would see each other again, which none of them could now take for granted. After that she would go to university, and things would never be the same again. It was a point Joni had incomprehensibly missed.

She didn't understand why the architecture firm whose reception she had organised for over ten years had 'let her go' while keeping the assistant she had herself interviewed and chosen. Was this last-in-last-out lay-off policy normal or just? And why was fate so wayward that Georgie had received the news of her dismissal two little weeks after her father's funeral, and on the same day that Kevin had finally accepted that their five-year relationship was over? There was something efficient about this concurrence of losses – a sort of buy one get one free, she supposed – but it wasn't fair.

Why her parents had moved to Bristol was yet another mystery; leaving their spacious historic red-brick house on the outskirts of Stratford-upon-Avon, with its outdoor swimming pool, its swing, its climbing frames and elm tree stumps, and replaced all that with this crumbling Regency terrace on a busy main road through Clifton? Though admittedly somewhat stretched by tourism, Stratford-upon-Avon had still been a pretty town in those days, while Clifton used to be decidedly down at heel. And why had they then insisted on staying long after it stopped being convenient and when they couldn't really afford it any more, and as a consequence lost half of it to tenants and then to buyers, and had to cram their entire material world into half as much space? The sensible thing to do would have been to sell up, set light to the rubbish or stick it in storage if they really couldn't face losing it (though they were about to lose a lot more than a few dusty old souvenirs), and buy a nice bungalow in Brighton or somewhere. Georgie could imagine Maureen and Larry in a bungalow by the sea. They'd have been cosy and happy, amongst one or two special ornaments and photographs. They could have gone for walks along the coast, and watched waves splashing against rocks. They could have breathed in good lungfuls of fresh salty air, lived on fish, lived a bit longer probably – fish, sunshine and fresh air being major allies in the fight against degenerative disease. (These three were all on her own list of Staying Alive.) But instead, her mum and dad had been cooped up with redundant objects and papers, slaves to asthma, coughing and sneezing and prone to flu.

By the time they started getting properly ill they'd moved into the dingiest dampest part of the property, where one room was stuffed to the girders with furniture they had no use for and boxes of stuff they never looked at. It was the basement, but they called it the Garden Flat; it was the garden that had drawn them down to it, that and the fact that you didn't need to climb anything to go into or out of it. By then her mother's stroke and her father's arthritis precluded any gardening and the outside had turned into a wilderness of brambles and ivy. Georgie sighed as she stared through the French windows at the greenery, wet and darkly glossy in the winter sunshine. She must do something about that. And about everything else – the boxes and the furniture. It belonged to her now – to her and to Will, her brother, who was too busy and too living in Brussels to help. It was lucky, really, that she had nothing else to do; and none of her bewilderments was worth fretting about. Life was too short!

The shortness of life was something she did understand. No, not the why of it; only the fact of it. Which was why the flat must be cleared and dealt with as soon and as quickly as possible.

So she had locked her personal things in Charlie's bedroom, got in a lodger, packed two suitcases, left Salisbury and driven to Bristol to sort out the family pile. And here she was, sleeping in her parents' bed, which was a weird thing to do, although it didn't feel weird.

'It's weird,' she said aloud to herself. Hearing the word made her shiver. The sheets smelt of the way her mother used to wash them, of wood and roses and cleanliness – even though Georgie had washed them herself. They were as smooth and comforting. It was probably the bed Georgie had been conceived in. Her parents didn't like waste.

*

The landline rang. It was Will, snatching a few expensive seconds between wealthy clients.

'Geegee! How's it going?' he asked, energetically.

'It's a bit strange to be here alone,' Georgie admitted. 'I keep expecting Daddy to come in and ask me what on earth I'm doing.' She hesitated. She wanted to explain it better, that she kept forgetting that he'd gone; and that their mother's feminine essence also imbued every corner and cranny, and seemed to linger in the air as a kind of nameless fragrance. But Will would think she was talking about ghosts. He'd dismiss her feelings as wishful nonsense.

'Oh hang on, I've just got to answer this.'

Georgie laughed. That was so typical of Will. He'd rung her, but still she must wait. She heard him speaking to his caller, promising to ring back in two secs.

'Hello? Gee? Look I feel guilty letting you cope with it by yourself. If you could only wait for the summer holidays Renée and I could come across and help. We'd be more than happy to.'

Georgie was afraid that help was not the right word. 'I just want it done, Will. And I've got nothing else on my timetable, except working out what to do with the rest of my life.'

'Oh Gee.'

'It'll be good! It's the right thing, honestly.'

'So how are you getting on with the dungeon?'

Georgie took a deep breath. 'I've been inside and counted the boxes, but I didn't open any.'

'So what's the damage? I mean, how many?'

'They've got both our desks in there you know? Mine's upside down on top of yours, which makes a kind of poignant sense. Counting all of them, including the biscuit tins – at least a hundred and fifty-seven. I thought I could manage four a day, starting tomorrow. That's only five weeks. It's not too bad.'

'Well you know my feeling about it.'

'Yes, I know.'

Will's feeling was that they should hire a house clearance

firm and ditch the whole shebang without even looking at it; because what they hadn't missed in over twenty-five years they weren't suddenly going to miss now. It could go up in flames for all he cared, though that would be messy and dangerous. But Georgie felt it simply wasn't on. She could too clearly imagine her father's response. 'How could you let these vultures pick through our private history with their mingy greedy price-of-everything-value-of-nothing minds!' She could see him as if he were right there beside her, trying to hide the moisture in his eyes; laying on the guilt.

That was her stated objection, that and the suggestion, more persuasive to Will, that the boxes might conceal a fortune in historic documents or whatever. Her real objection was somewhat formless and unexpressed. It had to do with a vague fear of family secrets and a wish to keep them hidden; prompted by something her father had struggled to tell her just before he died, which was something she couldn't possibly think about yet. His last words, attempted words, had left her with a horrid whispering anxiety about his life, and if any related difficultness or horridness were lurking in this shambolic heap, she was keen to find it quickly, before anyone else did, and wipe it out.

Her own childhood journals were in there somewhere too. She couldn't remember what confessions and secrets she might have scrawled in them, she only knew they were to be exhumed and shredded. Nothing unpleasant must be left to burden the children.

'As long as you're sure,' Will said. 'And if you change your mind, just let us know. There's no hurry. The house market's still rubbish.'

'We ought to be using it really. It's a terrible waste.'

'To be discussed anon dear sis.'

'Why did we live here anyway Will? Did you ever get it? And why did they keep our desks? It's heart-breaking.'

'Gee, I've got to go. Phone's ringing. Talk soon, ok? Buzz me anytime.'

*

She set about freshening up the atmosphere. The front sashes were stuck closed. They must have been like that since they were last painted. Ten years? Twenty? She scored and levered her way through the paint with a knife, and had to climb up onto the window sill to apply enough force to pull them apart. The outside smelt even worse than it smelt indoors – it was dank and freezing cold. She didn't dare look in the coal bunkers. She knew there'd be living things in there; she'd need to be fully clad in some sort of rubber suit before venturing amongst them. No wonder she and the children had never been invited to stay. There wasn't room anyway.

After wafting cold air through the rest of the flat, she cleared a space in the lobby, delineating five areas in five categories: Bin, Recycle, Sell, Charity, Keep.

At last, she was ready to drag the first of the boxes from the front room into the theatre of operations. She was a lucky person, she thought, so whatever she was meant to find would come to her straight away. She steeled herself and opened it with trembling fingers. The dust was as thick as dirt. She coughed as it billowed into the air, invaded her throat and lungs and stung her eyes.

The first two boxes were full of bills and cheque book stubs and receipts, for shredding. She dwelt for a while on the price of fuel. The winter gas bill for 1983 had been 22 pounds and 32 pence! Then she noticed their move from British Gas. 1985, the coming of privatisation. She could see at a glance how this coincided with a dramatic rise in the quarterly totals, but it wasn't exponential, as the more recent rises seemed to be. Their living space had diminished as their costs had increased. And maybe the weather had not been so bad.

The third box contained, amongst other documents, school reports collected in year order in a transparent folder filed next to Will's. *Georgina shows great promise. She has worked hard and deserves success. We take a great interest in which direction she will proceed as she has the ability to excel in almost any field.*

She flicked through them noting the As and A minuses, Goods, Very Goods and Excellents. *A natural linguist. A passionate debater.* Far from chucking them, she ought to frame them. She'd always wanted some laurels to rest on! She invented another category – Think About Later.

If you could choose any age in which to be a fly on the wall which would it be?

I wouldn't choose to be a fly at all or on a wall but if I could be a person visitting any age I would choose the Regency as long as I didn't have to be a maid. Any other age would be interesting. I might like to go to the future out of pure curiosity. Though it would be dreadful to find out what was going to happen because you might find out something really horrible for example you died before you had a career or a family. What I love about the Regency times are the elegant fashions in clothes and houses beautiful unspoilt countryside travelling by horse and pony no pollution or noisy cars or oil on the beaches or advertisements everywhere you look. There was more beauty. Candlelight is more romantic and beautiful than electric light. You would follow the seasons. Girls didn't have to go to school but would learn how to draw and sing and play piano. They read books and wrote and received letters full of news and had grand balls. People were more polite to each other. But for living instead of just visitting it is more comfortable now than ever before with central heating for example and also more convenient and not such hard work and faster to travel to places. Also it is easier to talk on the phone without having to see people so if I could have my own pony and not have to go to school I would certainly choose to live in the present.

Some good points, Georgina. Please ask me about paragraphs and commas. Sp. visiting.

She was hungry. She decided to open one more box and finish for the day, exactly on schedule.

The top layer consisted of a newspaper, yellowing where it had been folded round a silver framed photograph. Georgie picked it out, carefully unwrapped the photograph and smoothed out the paper. The photograph was a black-and-white one of a child on a swing – a fair curly-haired girl of about eight, wearing a patterned skirt, a plain jersey, ankle socks and sandals. It wasn't a good photograph, just a snap really, washed out and on the slant, but the girl was laughing, and the halo of light around her curls made it rather lovely. Georgie guessed the clothes could come from anywhere between about 1930 to 1950. The newspaper was much later – *The Times* of 1986. She scanned the articles in the hope of finding anything relevant to her or hers, but found only that the whole thing had become sacred and significant through its sheer antiquity. It amazed her how dated was its appearance, though 1986 didn't sound anything like old. Thatcher was running things. Prince Andrew was marrying Sarah Ferguson and the Queen was, as ever, the Queen. Georgie would have recently moved out of Bristol and been working as a temp in Chelsea, she realised, drinking at the French House in Soho, listening to Blondie. Oh, actually, yes, she thought, it was long long long ago. Before she'd even met Jim who was going to impregnate and marry her. Before the birth of beloved children. Before she'd known who she was or what she wanted to do with her life, though in fact she still didn't know and hadn't done it anyway.

She didn't like to dwell on that idea. This was going to be a hard job if every moment of her past was going to parade itself in front of her eyes, to mock and taunt and suggest unpleasantness. So she must be quick about it; she must be decisive and strong-minded.

The paper didn't give a clue as to who the girl was. Georgie examined the photograph more closely; finding nothing, and unwilling to extract it from the frame to examine its reverse, she put the photograph in Think About Later and the newspaper in Recycle, then reconsidered and replaced the newspaper in Think About Later too. It might be significantly related to the photograph, she thought. It was difficult to tell unless she read the whole thing and there were Marriages, Births, Christenings and Deaths to wade through, of which Death was the most probably relevant section.

The girl might be a stranger, as her father had occasionally bid at auctions, and was so hopeless at discarding anything whether he wanted it or not, he may well have acquired alien memorabilia just because it was in the same lot as a certain book he admired. Or perhaps he'd liked the frame. She didn't recognise the frame.

Georgie proceeded, beginning to feel the pressure of time. Under another layer of paper, she found a box of dominoes. The dominoes were in perfect condition, solid wood with cream-coloured bakelite. She wondered whether bakelite was biodegradable. Probably not, but they were beautifully crafted, as if from ivory, and still usable. The box was the original, with a drawing of the dominoes, a boy a girl and a cat printed on the front, and scribbled on with crayons. She put it in Sell. She or Will might have been the scribbler; or it could just as easily have been Maureen or Larry. How strange that was; now her parents were as much children as they were old, now they were every or any moment of their lives – a kind of Everymaureen and Everylarry. For a flickering instant she felt motherly towards them. She hoped no-one had caught it for the crayon. The horrid contrary idea of a Nomaureen and a Nolarry flashed so fast through her consciousness that she hardly noticed.

One of the things she consigned to Think About Later was itself a box: a shiny mahogany oblong with dovetail joints and sunken brass handles, so beautifully fashioned and with so realistic a patina that it must be at least a century old, maybe two. It was locked but when you shook it you could hear something rattling inside – something light, but heavier than paper. Georgie was desperate to know what was in it. Someone had tried to break in; it was damaged around the lock and on the bottom, where someone had tried to lever the panels apart. She went for the lock herself, first with a pair of eyebrow tweezers and a hairgrip, then following video instructions she found online, with a paper clip. Now, every time she passed it she gave it a shake. It was like a Christmas present, for a Christmas that would never come. She'd take an axe to it eventually, she thought. A box you can't open isn't a box at all. It's just a block.

But here was a very ordinary plastic one, labelled, in her

mother's rounded schoolteachery handwriting, 'Treasures'. She was excited. Whatever secret was hiding in this mess might emerge at any minute, and wouldn't necessarily be shocking or nasty.

Everything inside was wrapped in kitchen towel. Treasure was a misnomer in some cases, like the jointed wooden dog whose parts were held together by elastic. It was mounted on a small wooden pedestal. If you pressed the bottom in and out, it made a barking noise and the dog collapsed and recovered. It was missing two legs, but its tail still wagged. The dog had gumption, Georgie thought. She rescued it for inspiration. She had owned such toys herself but doubted if you could still buy them – it afforded too innocent a pleasure, demanded too little attention, or contravened some boring health and safety rule. Not to be played with by anyone under four years old.

The silver-plated cigarette case and the solid silver spoon were genuine treasures. The former was no longer any use, because the silk lining had deteriorated. The latter looked older still. The bowl was an odd shape, and the handle was twisted and decorated with a wheatsheaf, or perhaps a tree, where it flattened out. Georgie had never seen a spoon like it. She knew nothing of heraldry, but admired the crest. She'd polish it and use it. Keep.

The most treasurable item was a large gold pendant containing a miniature portrait of a young woman, locked behind a concave oval of glass. Her blue-eyed face was fringed with fair curls, and her lips formed a shapely crimson smile, the same red as the ladylike bloom on her cheeks. Georgie wondered if doubleness of chin had been an attractive feature at the time. High bosoms, she supposed, have always been. There was nothing else in the picture but sky, of a delicious blue that kissed the eyes and made one glad.

It was amazing that a plaited specimen of hair, preserved under glass on the reverse of the portrait, was smooth and sleek and still as flaxen as its painted counterpart. It was the colour Georgie's used to be, which was unusual for English hair, so she had often been told. It had the look and texture of hair from Scandinavia, people said.

Nothing in the object identified her. But she had existed. She had been real. She had sat one day for this portrait; two hundred years ago, judging by the hairstyle and bodice. She had chosen which dress to wear, and paid attention to her looks. Georgie stared at those two blue eyes, a speck of light in each hinting at some deep intelligence, coming through a window in some building somewhere from the same old sun. For a few moments she was captivated by her gaze, as if in communion, as if she knew this woman right down to her bones. It was odd – a comforting recognition, a kind of family love.

'I see you,' she whispered. 'Lucky you, in your unspoilt world with your pony and your balls!'

'And my inconvenience!' she imagined the retort, delivered with a merry smile.

She realised that the young woman was actually extremely old – at least two centuries old – and wondered if, when she reached that kind of age herself, any likeness of her own would have survived, and would it ever catch the eyes of a three or four times great-granddaughter or third cousin several times removed or whatever it was? Next time she was in front of a camera, she decided, she'd send a glance to posterity.

She looked up and around at what she had achieved. It was taking too long; things were spreading over the floor. She was making a worse mess than the original mess. And it was wasting time getting involved with the really old stuff. How could that possibly have any relevance? If she wasn't careful, this two centuries' worth of accumulation was going to drag her backwards, swallow up her own few precious years and bury her. She batted away a faint sense of panic, and went out to buy some nice new boxes.

She struggled with herself over whether to ring Jim, and lost the battle, as usual.

'Is Charlie there?'

'Hang on.'

She relaxed. And waited. She heard noises in the background. Jim's voice returned.

'He's having a shower.'

'Is everything OK?'

'I don't know how we manage it but the world goes on without you.'

'Have you heard from Joni?'

'No.'

'Nor have I. Should we worry?'

'No.'

'It's been two weeks.' Georgie regretted her slightly whingeing tone. Jim reacted with impatience.

'I'm sure she's fine. She'll call us if she isn't.'

Georgie wasn't reassured, but she was pleased he'd said "us".

'I'm happy that you said "us".'

'D'you think she only calls you?'

'No, I meant "us" not "me". Not you, I mean.'

'You seem to think I have no input.'

'No, I think the opposite. *You* seem to think *I* have no input.'

'Georgina I've got things to do. But I'll let you know if Joni calls, OK?'

Perhaps it was her fault that they couldn't communicate?

'Jim, I think it's great that Charlie wants to spend time with his... marvellous dad.'

'Georgie, I've got things to do.'

Ah, he'd called her Georgie and not Georgina. Hooray!

'So how are you? How's work?'

Jim was a composer. He told her about his new contracts, and how rehearsals were going for a performance in the cathedral of his latest choral fantasy, and that an old piece of his was being considered for a washing powder ad, and that one of his students had made it to the semi-finals of Cambridge Young Composer of the Year; and Georgie enthused and agreed that your luck might turn on a sixpence and success came in sideways when you were least expecting it.

'Are you wondering how I am?' she asked eventually.

'How are you?'

'I'm fucking fine, thank you. Bye-bye.'

She didn't understand what on earth had come over her. Not very polite Gee.

Oh, here it came again! The sudden gush of heat, in her breast and shoulders and neck, rising and all-pervading, flashing into her cheeks and forehead, under her hair, and bursting into sweat. She hauled off her jersey, and fanned herself with a photograph.

Five minutes later she was shivering, but she'd had enough of the jersey gymnastics. What she wanted was a cardy; a warm layer she could take off and put on again several times an hour, without scratching her face or mussing up her hair or wearing herself out. That was the point of cardies, as she'd only recently gathered, having only recently been thermally challenged. The fashion move from jersey to cardy was inevitable, it seemed, like the drift from scarlet through the blues and greens towards beige. It was foolish to resist it, you might as well resist the incoming tide; but for now she could borrow one of her mother's. When Maureen had died, her father had simply avoided the question of what to do with her clothes. They were all still intact, still in the flat somewhere, along with his.

'Borrow!' she thought sarcastically. 'I promise I'll give it back!'

The wardrobe smelt of lily of the valley, of dust, mothballs and furniture polish. And it smelt of the past because it had always smelt of these things. She was shocked to feel a sense of guilt on opening it. Its contents were secret and forbidden, more so even than those of the letters she had read. Clothing is more intimately personal, perhaps, being of the body not of the mind. She saw a summer dress she remembered – a full cotton smock hand made and worn by her mother sometime in the seventies when such things were briefly fashionable. It saddened Georgie that her mother had kept it long after she could have worn it, and that no-one would wear it now. She took up the flowered cotton in her hands and buried her face in it, stroking her cheek with the cloth that her mother had chosen, cut, sewn and worn, that had touched her and moved with her. She breathed in its scent as if she might smell her living mother, but it was faintly chemical, it was only an object after all. She let it go, smoothing out the crease she had given it.

And that was when, with a shock of recognition that made her gasp, she saw the cello case. 'Oh my God,' she whispered, staring in disbelief. 'Oh my God, they kept it.' Without ever mentioning that it was there. Expecting her to retrieve it? Willing her to ask about it? They kept it in a place where they might see it every day, but Georgie never would.

She reached down for the handle. Awkwardly she manoeuvred the case out of its home amongst shoes and bags, tugging it between dresses and jackets, polythene sliding over polythene, coat hangers jangling. The case was in perfect condition, just a little dusty. She rested it on the floor, tentatively undid the catch and lifted the lid. There lay the cello like a sleeping beauty, patiently waiting for its moment, beside the bow which was still secure in its velvet loop, though it had lost some hair. Gently she lifted the instrument from its coffin. She drew one finger down the glossy burnished surface of its belly, and let it rest on the fattest string. The string was rusty, but it murmured – bottom C, very flat. She adjusted the endpin, sat down on the bed, wedged the cello's wooden body between her thighs and hesitated. How long ago? It must be thirty-five years. Oh so many! No it couldn't be so many! The knobs creaked as she adjusted the tension of the strings, gingerly testing each with a finger tap.

For a moment she thought that nothing would come to her hands. Silently she decided she must lay it down, she must forget again what she had already so studiously forgotten. But without her willing it, some unconscious force came to her aid. Something touched her left fingers and placed them against the strings, something leant against her right arm and encouraged the bow across them. Sounds came out, scrapey and ancient, but singing, just about.

It was the first tune she had ever played properly, taught by someone who had taught her so many things. It caught at Georgie's heart, confusingly. She hadn't thought about that someone for a long, long time.

'Full fathom five, thy father lies. Of his bones are coral made. Those are pearls that were his eyes. Nothing of him that doth fade but doth suffer a sea change into something rich and strange. Sea nymphs hourly ring his knell. Hark! – now I hear them. Hark! – now I hear them. Ding dong bell. Ding dong ding dong ding. Ding dong ding dong ding. Ding dong ding dong ding. Dong bell.'

Through decades of rust the cello's plangent tones called everything back to her, all at once and as it was. The pinks and creams of her bedroom, her dolls, Silas the bear, the dark wood flooring and the home-made rug, the view from her window of silver birch and elms, her satchel, annuals, fountain pens and dog-eared exercise books, French and Latin, the smell of talcum powder and lemon soap, the wobbly landing, the polished wooden staircase and the front hall full of coats and hats and wellies, the glass shelves, the kitchen table, the Welsh dresser, parquet floor, bookcases, sofas, huge sliding windows and the garden, the apple trees, the pool, the summerhouse. Will.

Her mother, her father, fixed in that special time and place. Swimming in gold, drenched in heat.

She could picture it all so clearly it seemed absurd and impossible that it had gone. And that strange person had gone – blotted out of memory.

She laid the cello carefully back in its case, and knelt down beside it, wrestling with feelings she couldn't name.

WORK HARD

All day at school Georgina had seen the letter so clearly in her mind – she had even opened it in her mind, trembling with nervous anticipation – that she couldn't believe it wasn't there. No. Propped up on the glass shelf in the kitchen where she had imagined it were only brown window envelopes that looked like bills, and a flyer from some carpet cleaning service: *Much Ado About Rugs.* Her disappointment was like a big hand squeezing her innards. It made her want to puke.

It was a warm day for the end of March and the first day that year she'd really tasted spring in the air and felt sap rising in her heart. Through her smeary spectacles, she'd seen daffodils and primroses along the banks of the river Avon, and birdsong had welcomed her in the morning. As well as all this, it had been a not appalling day at school. Though hockey had resulted in a nil-nil draw, Miss Wandle had commended her grit, which made up for the fall and the scrape. And she and Fi and Jan had caught the giggles in Scripture, Jan so badly that she wet herself, which made it an utter scream. Georgie sniggered as she pictured Jan's comical expression, furiously pointing down below, and mouthing 'I wet 'em!' as if it had been an achievement and she was proud of it. It was ridiculous they were wasting time doing Scripture anyway, as they weren't going to be examined on it.

She dumped her satchel on the kitchen tiles and switched on the kettle. Her knee was still sore. She crouched over to examine the injury and was wondering whether to clean it and put a plaster on it, when she noticed the sound of voices coming from the back garden – her mother's and another one, girlish but croaky and speaking with a foreign tune. She peered out through the kitchen window. Her mother was sitting in a deckchair by the swimming pool talking to someone on the lounger, which was facing away from the house.

She was annoyed. Tea would probably be late. She ambled disconsolately into the sitting room while the kettle boiled. *Wish You Were Here* lay on the record player. It was Will's. She'd wanted to buy it herself but he'd beaten her to it before she could save enough. That's because he worked on the boats at the weekend, but she wasn't allowed to work at the weekend, unless it was prep. She didn't know whether it was because she was younger, or because she was a girl. It wasn't because she was doing 'O' levels, she knew that, because Will had worked as well as doing 'O' levels the year before.

She looked at the picture on the front of the album: two men in an empty concrete landscape shaking hands, one on fire. And on the back, a man without a face, with his foot on a suitcase and a record in the opposite hand, or where the hand was missing, by deliberate mistake. Brilliant! She took out the record and put it on and went back to making coffee.

She wished her mum wouldn't keep buying the creamiest milk – you always had to shake it and the bottle top always smelt rancid. And why did they have to keep changing fridges? The new freezer was too big for the larder – it was one you could put a whole person in. They didn't need such a big freezer. They only had a big freezer because the next door neighbours had one. Her mum and dad wanted her and Will to have all the best things in life, she supposed, then make them feel guilty about it. It was very tedious.

Someone had put an empty vodka bottle back in the fridge door. Georgie left it there, tutting about the idiocy of wasting electricity on emptiness. She helped herself to three chocolate digestives then put two back in the tin, one at a time. She carried the biscuit between her lips while she went back to examining the grazes on her knee, thinking she'd enjoy it properly when she'd dealt with the hurt. Gradually she became aware of her mother's voice calling from the garden.

'Geegee, darling, is that you? Come and meet Frieda!'

Georgie rescued her biscuit and took her coffee round through the sitting room, out through the French windows into the bright, slanting sunshine.

'You filled the pool,' she said as she noticed clean sky-blue reflections where there had been runnels of dirt.

'It's been so warm today, we thought we ought to make the most of it.'

Georgie screwed up her eyes. 'It's cold now, though,' she said.

Her mother's face was red, flushed with alcohol and sunshine. She was wearing a summer dress and matching straw sunhat. Something about her clothes made Georgie feel upset. She had tried too hard to be smart, and her bare arms looked white and flabby against the navy blue. There was a flower in her dark dyed hair. Her lips were a different colour.

The strange girl was lounging in a bikini and a cardigan, displaying long slim goose-pimpled legs, and tanned feet in scruffy flip-flops. Her toenails were painted gold, chipped. Her long fair hair was uncombed, her fringe too long. She looked as if she'd been put together in a hurry, so that her arms and legs and hair were pointing in the wrong directions and not glued on properly. Her real expression was hidden behind huge sunglasses, but she was smiling broadly, showing a lot of crooked teeth between her pale-pink lipsticked lips. Georgie thought she must be one of her mother's social projects, but didn't understand why she'd been dressed up for, or why Maureen had copied her lipstick. A smell of suncream and sweat lingered in the air and Maureen's transistor radio was competing with the hi-fi, Dave Lee Travis chattering against the background of music coming from the house. *Shine on you crazy diamond.*

'Geegee, darling, this is Frieda. Frieda's going to stay with us for a while.'

'Stay with us?'

The girl made no effort to sit up, but smartly held out her left hand, so Georgie had to go up and round and bend down to her level, and lay her hot mug on the garden table before she could shake it. The hand was welcoming and warm. She squeezed

Georgie's tightly, in a way Georgie knew that her father would find acceptable. No slippery fish, this – a firm, positive, useful handshake that could cement something meaningful between two people. A flash went off in her heart – of anger and jealousy and hatred and indignation. Nobody had warned her they were having a guest, let alone asked her permission.

'How do you do?' Frieda asked. She said it as if she were asking for instructions, which made Georgie let out a snort of laughter, spitting biscuit crumbs.

'Oh drat. I have said it wrong? Please excuse me.' The girl laughed at herself, but forgivingly, as if she were telling off a kitten or a bunny rabbit for being adorable. She took off her sunglasses, and the skin beneath her eyes creased. She was older than she seemed – at least twenty-five, Georgie guessed. She'd expected her eyes to be blue, but they were dark brown, almost black, that looked unusual agains the colour of her hair. So it was probably dyed. Her face was an unusual shape too, long with high cheekbones. She had freckles, but people would probably think she was beautiful, even so.

'How d'you do,' Georgie said.

'That's right,' Maureen explained. 'It's polite.'

There were two empty glasses on the table and an empty glass jug. They were part of a set that wasn't used, because it was expensive and a wedding present and never to be broken. Georgie guessed that vodka had been one of the ingredients of their drink. 'No punch left for me?' she asked.

'Oh Gee, really!' Maureen beamed. She snapped her plastic shades back over her spectacles. 'You've got your coffee. But Frieda says you can get terribly addicted to that stuff you know.'

'More addicted to *that* stuff I'd've thought,' Georgie said, drily.

'Now get along with you!' Maureen gestured with a flap of her wrist. She was in a ridiculously good mood, playful and pissed. Georgie hated it right to the inside of her bones. Her mother was usually quietly preparing a meal at this time of day.

'You have a wound?' Frieda asked, creasing her forehead as if it were a major catastrophe. Georgie looked down at her knees, red raw, specked with blood and dusted with dirt. Her grey socks were rolled down to her ankles. Her shoes needed cleaning.

'I skidded in hockey.'

'In hockey?' Frieda looked at Maureen.

'It's a game.' Maureen explained. 'You hit a little ball with a stick. You score goals.'

'We have the same, yes, hockey. The same word.'

'Did you score any goals, darling?'

'No but I set some up. Fi's hopeless; she missed every single one.'

'Perhaps you ought to shoot yourself, then, instead of passing to her?' Maureen suggested. Georgie was annoyed by the advice. She gave her mother a meaningful stare.

'You want me to shoot myself?'

Frieda laughed very suddenly and very much. 'That is a good joke, isn't it?' she said. To have spotted the witticism pleased her exceedingly. Germans weren't supposed to have a sense of humour, Georgie thought.

'This is Will's record isn't it?' Maureen asked.

'He won't mind. What's for tea?'

'I think he would mind, you know.'

Georgie left them to themselves and went upstairs to her room. Biology: The life history of the potato. English: *Cider with Rosie* depicts the end of an era. Discuss. History: Was Hitler responsible for World War 2? Maths: Tangents and logs.

She found it hard to concentrate, but concentrate she must. Her life goals were well within reach as long as she carried on getting As and A minuses. The plastic alarm clock tick tocked impatiently away beside her, prodding her to study, but her thoughts kept wandering outside, wondering who the stranger was and where she was going to sleep and how long she was going to stay and if this was a precedent, and her mother was about to set up a boarding house for alcoholic mongrels she would have to be nice to. She heard her mother lamenting the end of the vodka. When Will clattered in through the front door she watched out of her bedroom window to see what his reaction would be.

What she saw was peculiar. Frieda was sitting on the grass with her back to Maureen who was affectionately sifting through her hair, as if she were looking for nits. It turned Georgie's stomach. Maureen didn't touch people. Not since they were toddlers. But this was the odd bit: at the sound of Will's 'Helloooo!', the girl jumped away like a startled cat, and resumed her place in the lounger. Maureen, flustered, shot her a strained smile, as she called Will outside and performed the politenesses. Frieda stood up to shake his hand. She tossed her hair about. They were all extremely amused about something. Then Will put his hands in his pockets and went into some fascinating monologue. He took his leave with a charming little bow. Then he was bounding up the stairs and, a few minutes later, bounding down again.

Georgie went back to her prep, but now it was even harder to concentrate. She felt queasy, so queasy she might have to skip school next day. She left her textbooks and lay down for a bit.

When she next looked out it was growing dark. Her mother and the girl had come indoors, leaving the huge garden empty and shivering. The smell of fish and chips drew her downstairs.

'There you are, Gee!' her father shouted, blustery and excited. He was juggling newspaper packages and plates, still wearing his suit and raincoat. 'You've met Frieda, haven't you?' He grinned, his spectacles slightly misted from the indoor warmth. 'Come and help distribute the grub.'

Maureen had been too busy welcoming the visitor to do any shopping or cooking so she'd phoned Larry at the office, and he'd bought food on the way home, with fresh cream cakes as a special treat. Georgie laid the dining table. Frieda's presence unbalanced the arrangement – there had to be two on one side. Georgie ended up sitting by Will and opposite Frieda, who was all dressed up now in hippy floaty orange and gold things. Will had changed too and Georgie felt silly in her school uniform.

There was much jollity about the Englishness of fish and chips, and ecstasy about having cream cakes even though it wasn't anyone's birthday. It would ruin Georgie's diet. They even opened a bottle of cider. It would be a very merry unbirthday, Maureen exclaimed, and Frieda obligingly laughed. The conversation was stilted as they settled into eating. The weather was mentioned of course, especially as it had been rather nice. Frieda was asked by Larry about her journey and the weather at home and how her family was. This produced short utterances from the new girl such as, 'very well, thank you', 'yes, it was not too cold,' and 'I was comfortable, thank you.' Nobody raised the subject of who the hell she was or what she was doing there. Will quietly sipped his cider, leaning back in his chair and looking at his glass, his thick dark hair flopping onto one side of his face, revealing not much more than a pink cheek.

Georgie helped herself to less than her fair share of chips, and allowed herself only a modest second helping. She picked the batter off the fish then ate it anyway. A similar thing happened later with the cream and chocolate on her eclair.

Conscious of a lull in conversation, she realised that Will was staring at her, and searching for a way into their usual family repartee. 'I didn't see you at the bus station this morning, Pud?' he finally said, with glee. 'I thought you must be skiving.'

'I went the long way round. I let you win seeing as you had the car.' Larry was teaching Will to drive, and being driven by him into Stratford in the mornings.

'So you went on your bike?' Maureen asked.

'Well I missed the car, and the bus.'

'Were you late for school then, darling?'

I can't help it if I have to go to the best school in the area which happens to be nine miles away in a completely different town, instead of the perfectly decent one two yards up the lane, Georgie thought, but Maureen and Larry were staring at her, as if to say 'criticising your school and your parents' decisions is very bad manners in front of our guest.'

'I only missed Assembly,' she shrugged. 'It won't make any difference to work. It was such a lovely day, I wanted to look at the river and the daffs.'

Will scoffed. 'Oh dear Reverend Mother, the river and the sky and the wild flowers were so beautiful I simply couldn't get to chapel in time.' His prissy accent and passionate falsetto voice would normally have tickled Georgie, but she didn't feel like encouraging him in the presence of a stranger. 'What are we going to do about Georgina?' he sang. Recognising the tune, Frieda finally had an opportunity to practise her English.

'*The Sound of Music*?' she chirped. 'I am of the exact place where that film was made. Made? Filmed?'

'Yes,' said Will. 'Dad said.'

'Really?' said Georgie.

'Made or filmed,' said Maureen, encouragingly, as if she were teaching in kindergarten. 'We loved that film, didn't we Georgina?'

'Salzburg is my town! I have seen them making it!'

'Gosh how wonderful!' Maureen trilled. 'Which bit were they doing? Which scene?'

'It was "Do re mi". They were in a... Like a car but with horses.'

'A cart.'

'A carriage.'

'It was ever so funny. They did it many times.'

'Sehr funny,' said Will, leaving the table suddenly and heading for the record player. 'Sehr komisch, nicht war, Pud?'

'Will! Where are your manners?' Maureen tutted, looking outraged, then sighing with exaggerated indulgence. 'Do excuse him Frieda.'

Georgie tried to catch his eye, to see if he was mocking the girl, but he was too intent on showing off.

'Hey Georgina, lay off my records, will you?' he shouted. 'Where is it, we simply must listen to the yodelling song.'

He rummaged in the record cupboard, carelessly strewing LPs over the floor and pulling the one he wanted too roughly from its sleeve. He let the stylus drop without finesse, so the track began with a loud scratch and the music was enveloped in hiss. *High on a hill was a lonely goat olay odelay odelay ho ho.*

'Oh dear, this is incredibly nostalgic,' Maureen said. The alcohol had made her sentimental. 'They were little. You must have been about six and seven, you two. It must be nearly ten years ago. It seems so recent. What on earth happens to the time?'

'That is correct,' said Frieda, suddenly downcast. Her voice went quiet and she stopped eating. 'For me this brings also bitter memories.'

That put a spanner in the fragile machinery of their conversation. Nobody knew what to say or do now they couldn't pursue the topic of Frieda's whirl amongst the stars. Admitting you were sad simply wasn't on. That's *not the way we do it here* thought Georgie. It was dreary and wet and stinky! Ditto being a scaredy cat. Ditto loneliness, frustration, anything weak. Cross was OK as long as you weren't ugly about it, but sad was right out. No, no – embarrassment was the only horrible emotion you were freely allowed in this house. Georgie's insides squeezed in agony, as Julie Andrews and her little tribe jauntily yodelled away in the background, because Will didn't have the nous to simply go and take it off again.

Maureen was the one who had created the atmosphere and it was she who must rescue everyone. 'Oh dear, oh dear, what a lot of long faces we have don't we!' she exclaimed suddenly, choosing Georgie's face for her special attention which for a change Georgie would have preferred to have none of. 'Chin up Geegee darling!' she said brightly, as Georgie grimaced and mugged, and then, in an effort to create a diversion, and as though it had only just occurred to her, 'Oh by the way we thought you could let Frieda have your room until we've sorted something better out. We knew you wouldn't mind.'

For a few seconds Georgie was speechless. 'Better for who?' she asked rudely, without thinking. There followed another deadly silence. She stared at her plate, smeared with chocolate and cream.

'Don't you mean "whom"?' Will said.

'Excuse me, I need to get down.'

Georgie left the table without looking at anyone, hoping it would be assumed that she wasn't feeling well, as it's perfectly reasonable to leave the table if you have the sudden urge to vom your entire meal.

Her father found her upstairs in her bedroom, sullenly packing her satchel. He hovered at the door, then entered and sat down beside her on the bed.

'Georgina, I'm disappointed,' he whispered. 'Can't you be gracious to a guest? We didn't want to stick her in the box room on an old camping bed, with all our odds and sods in there.'

'But why does it have to be me?' she asked quietly. 'I don't want to be with the odds and sods either. Why couldn't Will give his room up?'

'Because we don't have time to clean it.'

'But why is she here?' Georgie ventured to ask. 'Why didn't you ask us? Or even tell us?'

'She's here to teach you German. Think how your German is going to improve! And the cello. She plays cello and piano. She's very clever. She studied at the Mozarteum in Salzburg, now that's saying something.'

Oh, da di da, that's saying something, thought Georgie. She couldn't look her father in the face.

'My German's OK,' she said. In fact her German was top of class, though he didn't seem to value this achievement, or any of her others. He could have agreed. Or he could have contradicted her and said that her German was very much more than OK, but he said nothing. 'I don't especially want to learn German anyway,' she went on bravely. 'Who wants to sound like Hitler?'

Her father gasped as though she'd stabbed him. 'That's a disgraceful thing to say.' His voice softened. 'That's not even worth listening to.'

Georgie felt sorry, but now she was being carried on a mood of defiance she couldn't seem to change it.

'You ought not to judge things without being in full possession of the facts,' he said, in a tone of perfect reasonableness, more and more quiet.

'But you haven't told us any facts,' Georgie countered with equal reasonableness, keeping her voice as measured and gentle as his. 'What are the facts? How long is she going to stay, for example? I've got my 'O' levels. Where am I supposed to go? How am I supposed to finish my prep?'

'She's here for a short holiday, that's all. Your prep won't suffer, I promise. You know you're lucky to have a room of your own, don't you?'

I know, thought Georgie. You had to go to boarding school. You had to sleep in a dormitory. You had to go through the war.

'It's a pity you can't offer it with pleasure, to someone who needs it more than you do, at least for this one night.'

Well, it's a pity Will can't offer his, or you can't offer yours, Georgie thought but couldn't say. The idea that Frieda should sleep in any of their beds seemed disgusting. She buckled her satchel and got up, preparing to leave the room in a huff.

'Where are you going?'

'For a walk.'

'It's dark. Do be careful won't you, Pud?'

Not that you care, she thought, thumping down the stairs.

'I'm fifteen, not five.'

Her school coat and uniform were pitifully inadequate in the evening chill. She walked round the block of houses, looking down mostly, at her dragging feet. She was Saint Georgina now, tormented and outcast by her own family. Nobody cared. Nobody loved her. She must bear the whips and scorns of time, unwanted and abandoned! There was no moon so the lawns were black, and the neighbours' front rooms looked cosy and light, flickering through closed curtains.

When she got home the dishwasher was washing dishes and the television was on. Frieda's rucksack was now lying in the front hall. It was made of fraying canvas, covered in old cloth badges – Köln, Venezia, Amsterdam, New York. This girl had been about a bit, lucky thing. Stratford-on-Avon must be one of the missing pieces in her collection. Georgie took off her coat and hung it by her hat, then didn't know where to go. Her father appeared from the drawing room. As he opened the door she heard the others laughing.

'Mummy thinks you deserve an explanation,' he said, gently closing the door. 'William was put out by it too but he was more polite. Come to the study.' He ushered her into his special room and sat down at his desk, pushed aside a pile of letters and papers, and picked up a blue envelope covered with scrawlings and crossings-out and a foreign stamp. As he spoke he tapped the letter on the desk, but didn't open it or let her look. He frowned. 'Frieda's father did me an invaluable service at the end of the war.' He looked briefly at Georgina to make sure she was listening. 'And if it hadn't been for him you wouldn't be here. So when we got a letter saying that Frieda was coming to visit Shakespeare's home town, we rejoiced. We invited her. It's very little to do in return, believe me. She wants to see where Shakespeare was born. And that's a pretty wonderful thing to want to do.'

'But why didn't you tell us?' Georgie murmured.

'Well, it was a surprise that she arrived today, I didn't know myself until your mother phoned. The letter was delayed, it was redirected from our old house. We would have told you. Of course we would have told you. But you were at school. And then you were here.'

Georgie felt ashamed, even though it wasn't fair. 'Did her father save your life, then?'

The question seemed to puzzle him.

'You said we wouldn't be here if it hadn't been for him,' she explained.

He nodded. 'Ah. That's true. Well, in a manner of speaking he did save me, yes.' He took both her hands and smiled with his mouth but not his eyes. 'He restored my faith in people.' He looked down again, and deep lines formed in his forehead, as though he couldn't decide whether or not to pursue the topic. Georgie didn't really want him to. She saw that he was biting his cheek. She looked up at the shelves of boxes on every wall and read their titles, written in his intelligent flowing script: Superannuated Cheque Stubs, Slides '63-'70, School Reports, Miscellaneous Shakespeareana, Rubber bands and String. 'No, no, I can't talk about it,' he said, eventually, much to her relief. 'I wasn't much older than Will, you know. It was...' He pressed his lips together and looked at her with a dreadful seriousness, shaking his head, unable to find an appropriate word. 'Unspeakable,' he whispered eventually. 'I hope to Christ you never have to go through such a time.' Then he puffed it all away and was smiling again. 'Let's think about the days ahead. It's going to be Easter soon. Come and talk to Frieda. She won't let you give up your room anyway. She's too well brought up.'

Georgie felt that as a reprimand, but couldn't contradict it, seeing as he was the one responsible for bringing her up less well, if that's what he meant.

After such an encounter she didn't know how to join in all the fun going on in front of the television, so she simply went up to bed without saying goodnight to anyone, dragging a horrible weight of responsibility. She'd made her father sad. She wondered if he'd said the same things to Will, but somehow knew that their conversation would have been lighter, different.

After a while she heard a knock at the door. She pretended to be asleep, dreading any more seriousness from her father, but the knocking came again, insistent, though quiet. Perhaps it was her mother, coming with some kind of comfort or appeasement. She switched on the reading light.

'Come in.'

The door opened onto Frieda in silhouette. Georgie instantly hitched up into a sitting position, inwardly shrinking. She couldn't see properly but her glasses were out of reach.

'Georgina. Guten Abend.'

'Guten Abend,' Georgie said shyly in return. Frieda closed

the door, silently advanced, and knelt down by the bed, too close, as if she had something private to say, while Georgie embraced her knees, and covered her shoulders with the duvet. Frieda was smiling apologetically, but Georgie couldn't manage to smile in return.

'It is a shame you had no warning of my coming.' She spoke in whispers, intimately, as if the air had thickened, enclosing them in a small cell of electric light. 'I do not want to make a disturbance. Ich fühle mich schrecklich. Do you understand?' She clutched her fist to her chest, and Georgie nodded. 'I do not know why your mother and father wanted to give to me your bedroom. That is nonsense. I will be most happy in the other room. I am very thankful to stay with you.'

The girl looked so wretched, Georgie wished she'd been kinder. 'But will you be able to sleep on the camping bed?' she whispered, hesitantly.

'I am able to sleep anywhere.' Frieda raised her eyebrows suggestively. 'When I know you better I will tell you where I have been able to sleep. Good night now. Schlaf schön. In English that is?'

'Sleep well,' said Georgie, 'sleep tight.'

'Tight?' Frieda, giggling, made an O with her mouth. 'Yes, we are tight.' She leant over, enveloping Georgie in a strange mixture of smells – lemon and BO and batter and alcohol. Georgie, flinching, was about to warn her against bugs biting, but wasn't sure of the German for bug or the conjugation of beissen. Frieda might take it seriously and be worried. No, it definitely wasn't worth getting into.

She realised Frieda was drunk, and glanced at the door, wondering if she was bold enough to simply go and open it and usher her out. But she was too slow. Frieda hung her head on one side, with more to say.

'Because I shared sadness with your mother.'

The sentence didn't seem to connect with anything. Georgie stiffened. She held her face in neutral, trying to make it clear that she wasn't interested.

'Yes. It made you uncomfortable. That funny song made me think of it. It was when my mother told me her story.'

Georgie shrugged curtly. 'That's OK.'

She lay back on her pillow, shifting away to increase the distance between them and signal that the conversation was over; but Frieda was oblivious, and hadn't finished saying goodnight yet. All of a sudden she was calling Georgie 'Liebchen' and zooming in for a parting kiss – not just one, but one on each cheek, all that long hair creeping over, and no escaping it. Flustered and speechless and peculiar, Georgie nodded again, and Frieda shot her a huge smile, an unfathomable wonky-toothed smile, before retreating. Georgie didn't know if the smile was kind or mean. It could have been friendly, or it could have been patronising. It could have meant, 'you're a silly little girl and I have the power here now'.

She slipped away, and the door closed, and Georgie rubbed her face as if she'd been smeared with slime.

She took a long time to sleep that night; her skin crawled with guilt and her cheeks tingled with the memory of those kisses. She listened as one by one the others went to bed. In the early hours she crept into the bathroom to wash her face, and then listened on the landing to hear if Frieda was managing to sleep on the uncomfortable bed.

But it wasn't fair, was it? It wasn't fair! Was it?

She wished her father hadn't said those horrible things. She wanted that conversation, and Frieda, to go away, and the sooner the better.

Their holidays were usually two weeks, so a short holiday would probably be one. One whole week of her! But how was Georgie supposed to get better at German and cello in one week?

Over the weekend she became aware of movement and change and things being carted about, and she gradually realised that Will was moving out of his bedroom to let Frieda sleep there. A plan had been hatched, without Georgie's knowledge. Will and Larry had been to Coventry to buy nice Habitat things for the summerhouse: maroon bean bags and blinds, paper lampshades, a coffee table and an electric heater; and Will was going to sleep there on the camping bed until a new sofabed was delivered.

Now it would be out of bounds to Georgie! Why couldn't Georgie sleep in the summerhouse? Why couldn't Georgie have Will's room for that matter? She should at least have been asked. She hoped everyone understood that she couldn't help carry things, but she was afraid she had prep to do. She shut herself in her bedroom, but heard Will tramping excitedly up and down the stairs, and watched from the window as his whole seventeen-year-old world was transported in boxes and suitcases down the garden to his new private den.

She went through her scales to make sure everyone knew how busy she was, but had hardly begun when she was interrupted by the sound of tentative knocking at the door. She stopped playing. She was sitting on the end of her bed. Lined paper scrawled with coloured notes and school text books and exercise books lay all over the floor, and behind her on the bed were felt tip pens, music, books and her open diary, which she rapidly shut.

'Come in,' she said, hoping it would be her mother or father wanting her help. Unfortunately, it was Frieda, standing with one hand in a back pocket and her weight rocked onto one leg, her head hanging to one side as if to make herself accessible or sympathetic or vulnerable or something.

'You are a good worker?' she said, sizing up the scene. Georgie thought she was referring to her absence during the operational manoeuvres. The casement window was open. Georgie's pink checked curtains stirred in the breeze and the loose window stay creaked against its frame as Frieda closed the door.

'Would you like my teaching?' she asked, playfully. 'Your father has asked me to help.'

Georgie smiled and shrugged, too slow to think of any polite excuses. 'OK.'

'May I sit down?'

'Of course.' Georgie waved at her desk chair. 'Natürlich.'

Frieda rewarded this German offering with another of her enormous friendly smiles. 'Ja!' she exlaimed, arranging her long loon-clad legs. 'Ich muss auch Ihnen Deutsch beibringen, oder? Verstehen Sie?'

Georgie understood, not only that Frieda was referring to her obligation to teach German as well as cello, but that she was using the polite form of the word for 'you'. What she couldn't tell was whether that was a charming thing to do, or merely servile – sincere or nauseatingly coy. The word 'echt' came into her mind. Echt means genuine, real, trustworthy. Was Frieda 'echt' or was she an 'ersatz' like the chicory coffee her dad once told her soldiers used to drink? Georgie must be on her guard; she didn't trust all this niceness. In a heroic effort to reciprocate, however, she said, 'Du durfst mich toten.'

Frieda's face went through a variety of expressions very fast and very clearly, beginning with shock, graduating to surprise, then through mild amusement to explosive hilarity. 'You give me permission to kill you?' she said, unable to supress her laughter.

Georgie went red and looked away, pretending to smile at her mistake. 'I meant you don't need to be polite.'

'Yes, to kill you would not be polite I think?'

Georgie agreed, grinning like an idiot to cover her shame.

'The word is "duzen". Du darfst mich duzen.' She laughed again, more tenderly this time, perhaps realising that Georgie was embarrassed. 'Oh that does sound ever so funny. Du darfst mich duzen,' she sighed with pleasure. Georgie had made a joke in German. Marvellous! 'Also,' said Frieda, 'ich werde dich duzen. I promise not to be polite to you. Jetzt aber, zum Cello. So. What do you play?'

'I'm just doing my scales.'

'What about a tune? Any tune you like.'

'I don't *like* any of them.'

'No?' Frieda's face fell. 'You don't like any tunes?'

'Not the ones we have to do.'

'Have to do?'

'Müssen.'

'For the exam? No, no, for me you must play what you like. That is an order! What you love. Or don't play.'

Georgie paused. This was a new idea. She doubted she'd be capable of playing anything she loved as she wouldn't want to mangle it. 'Well, there is a tune I love, but I'd rather listen to someone playing it well than scrape through it myself.'

Again Frieda looked mortified. Her emotions were so absurdly exaggerated, Georgie thought. Anyone would think someone had died by the way her brow drooped and her eyes were shining. Georgie had better do something to rescue her or the poor thing was going to blub, but she was damned if she'd spoil her favourite tune, or even share it.

'Well, I quite like one that goes something like this,' she said, settling on something less personal. She forced herself to sing, her voice shaky and frail: 'Full fathom five, thy father lies, Of his bones are coral made – '

'I know this tune. It is beautiful. Sehr schön. Gut gewahlt. I think if you start on an open string it will be best.'

'I don't know it.'

'You can try by the ear?'

So now Georgie was expected to perform! This was torture! In her own room! Her hands sweated and her knees trembled as they clutched the cello. She tried desperately to hide her awkwardness, but she knew it was plain. She got through the first line before Frieda cut in and gestured that Georgie should pass her the instrument.

First Frieda played the line herself – with smooth clear intonation, starting with a sharp angry low 'full', lyrically caressing 'father' and trailing into silence on 'lies'. Then she got up and ushered Georgie onto the free chair, made her sit straight, arranged her knees, not at all minding which bit of her she was touching. She was very free with her touching, Georgie thought, but didn't know how to object without being rude or unkind. She didn't like it that the door was closed.

Frieda took her place on the bed, not sitting, but stretching back as if she owned it, with her legs akimbo and her head resting in her arms. She stared at Georgie, as if to estimate her worth.

'To play a simple thing well. This is our work. If you can play this one line with meaning, then you will learn something. Full fathom five thy father lies. You must think what that means. You must let the cello speak it for you. You must put your heart and soul into the cello.'

Frieda's English had miraculously improved. At the same time she wasn't smiling any more. She looked miserable. Georgie braced herself in her best cello-playing position, earnestly conjuring an image of her father, drowned and lost forever at the bottom of the ocean – an image informed by the vilest scenes from *Jaws*, which more than anything made her feel ill.

'It is there between your legs, this gorgeous musical being,' Frieda went on, 'waiting for your heart and soul to flow into it.'

She looked into Georgie's eyes with an intensity that repelled them and made her insides squirm.

'You must play,' she paused, poutingly savouring the word 'play', and leant forward to tap the top of Georgie's thigh, 'from there.' Georgie looked up. 'From your cunt,' she explained, fixing her with a look.

Georgie was confused, shocked.

'My can't?'

But Frieda merely stared, and her expression was eloquent. It said 'you heard'. The tremor of an eyebrow said it, and the huge black wells of her pupils, and the crescents of white beneath each dark iris – all conveyed a depth of feeling that suddenly upset Georgie, and made her wish with all her heart to please the girl. For a fleeting moment she was pinned in time, lost in looking, as though they were soulmates, connected by some awful emotion, something you could only describe as pity. A second later, the magic evaporated. Self-consciousness returned, and she felt Frieda's eyes as invasive and alien. Oh, how she wished she could endure that gaze! But Frieda was too strong and Georgie could only submit. She shrugged, as if she couldn't care less, but had forgotten how to shrug naturally.

She cursed herself for choosing something so hard. It reminded her of the time they'd had to choose a topic in French. The rest of the class had studied cheese, wine, perfume, films, but for some reason unclear to herself, Georgie alone had plumped for revolutionary politics and the wonderful efficiency of the guillotine.

She took a deep breath, balletically positioned her right arm, placed her fingers studiously and correctly on the bow, and began; again and again and again she was made to play the same line. She did her best, of course, she always did her best, but instead of the required love and grief and resignation she could muster only nervousness and sickness, and she did indeed communicate these feelings to the gorgeous instrument between her legs. Every tone sawed under her skin to the joints. Every note was a crucifixion of wavering correction and overcorrection. And all the while she was feeling judged, as if Frieda were mocking her innocence, highlighting her foolish, naked virginity. This screechy noise was the song of her vulva! She imagined Will having a field day with the situation, if only he knew about it. She hoped to God no-one else was listening.

What about 'The Hokey Cokey!' Or 'Lillibullero!' Or 'My Old Man's A Dustman?' Why the hell couldn't she have chosen perfectly decent song like that?

EMBRACE CHANGE

Daylight would evaporate the damp; fresh air would blow off the dust; and as for inconvenient memories, well, there wouldn't be any Stratford ghosts haunting Clifton's streets. To escape from the dig and walk about a bit was therefore a must.

Georgie shut the door on it all with a sigh of pleasure, but as she retraced her old routes and reviewed her old stamping ground, she sensed that the past had followed her outside and was clinging to her like a shadow. If she looked upwards away from the tarmac and the steel, up towards the gold stone walls and wrought-iron balconies, she could imagine, staring down at her from a long window, a girl with a fringe of curls, dressed in high-waisted muslin. Then she would look down again to picture what the girl could see – a world of carriages and carts and horses and dogs splashing through mud and puddle-filled ruts, of hurrying figures in peculiar clothes, with not a single bicycle or car amongst them – before imagination faded, and memory took its place.

In the late seventies Clifton had been scruffy and bohemian, and so full of the world it was like being abroad. It was a place where you could buy a house on an artist's income; you might see someone dressed like Biggles riding a prewar Harley Davidson with a sidecar; or be invited to a fancy dress party by a stranger in a tatty pub whose eccentric landlord would chuck you out if he didn't like the cut of your jib. You might see someone bungee-jumping off the suspension bridge. There was a greasy café on the corner of York Street where you could get egg and chips for a few pence. On a lucky day you could spot Cary Grant on a yearly visit to his mother. On any day you could get a parking place if you were lucky enough to have a car. Some might have called it seedy. The proud Regency terraces were crumbling and peeling, divided into makeshift flats which housed a few musicians and students, none of whom could afford to drive, none of whom was financed by any war-mongering prime ministerial Daddy. Where bombs had fallen had been obvious then, because the newer buildings stood out against their historic neighbours like cheap ugly fillings. There were even some remaining areas of dereliction, and places where nature, ruthless and wild, had reasserted herself between concrete and mortar. Now the contrast was more blurred as modern blocks looked badly weathered and dowdy, while old buildings had been freshened, repainted and repointed; and all of them, old as well as new, were highly desirable highly expensive residences, fighting for parking space with gift shops and cafés, everything waxed and trimmed and surgically enhanced to put on a good show for the visitors. A different kind of person lived there now, too – aspirational, power-showering, label-conscious, four-by-four owners who needed fancy kitchens – she could tell by the quantity of discarded cupboard units – people who made fuck-off stacks of money, people who were more ambitious and more canny but perhaps on average not quite so interesting. Clifton had lost its creative heartbeat. It had turned into a tourist destination, which made it quite like Georgie's hometown.

The change had begun at about the same time as she'd arrived there in her late teens. Just as people began to clear out their old fittings and smarten up their old buildings to sell them, other people had realised that the old fittings looked better in the old buildings and wanted to buy them. Antique stalls and estate agencies popped up together like mushrooms. Then came the coffee shops and the cars. Soon after that Georgie had left it all behind.

Nowadays a few useful independent shops remained: Reg the veg, a butcher, a couple of delis and wine shops. And the library was hanging on by a thread – opening three times a week without much to offer in the way of books.

The change in the open-air pool epitomised it all. Well, there had been no café at all in the olden days, just a tuck shop selling sweets and fizzy drinks. Where now there was a restaurant, there used to be a sun terrace, packed with bodies, half of them supine as they scanned the sky for sunshine, smoked and stared at other bodies. There used to be a diving board and a deep end. There was chlorine and splashing about and larks – shouting and squawking and laughter. Anyone and everyone would congregate there, not necessarily for the water. It had attracted a younger crowd, some of them school kids bunking off, just as she had done herself in the end. It used to be a bit of a pick-up joint, she realised, as she hadn't realised then. It wasn't any more, so she thought.

In spite of its polish and smartness, Georgie wanted to try it out. After Good Relationships with Family and Friends, Exercise came second on her list of Staying Alive, after all, with Vitamin D coming in close behind. It would be good for her body to expose it to the elements, and good for her character to expose it to public view. She hadn't exposed it to her own view yet.

Since the operation, she'd contrived to dress and undress without observing herself. She had taken one sorrowful glimpse of her bruised distorted bosom, the livid wiggly line of the cut messily stuck together with paper stitches, the patch of blue dye, her skin stretched and gathered around it as though it were lifeless inelastic fabric; and had decided not to look again. To think that this breast, once pretty and plump, had been so attacked and demolished; a breast that had been admired and kissed had attracted something so evil and rebellious; a breast that had nourished and comforted her children, that had supported and furthered their lives had then threatened her own. This generous loving thing had betrayed her; it might betray her again, and if so she might lose all of it and the other too – or lose her life. So close to her heart, she had been betrayed! And by a scourge which cursed the primal source of human nourishment – the feminine, the giving, the precursor of love.

While the scars were sore she couldn't bear to wear a bra with any metal part – with underwires or strap adjusters or hooks and eyes. All that upholstery seemed suddenly absurd and trashy. Only one-piece stretchy camisoles would do, made of soft kind material she could pull over and forget about. Even when the soreness faded, there would be sudden shocks of pain from nerves damaged by the knife, reminding her to be vigilant, to honour the danger beyond. She would press and search in the mysterious depths for another deadly lump, which could be lurking amongst all the normal lumps and the strange new densities of healing tissue.

Until her own breasts had been threatened like this, she had been innocent of their power. She had taken them for granted and similarly ignored anyone else's. But now, everywhere she looked, she saw cleavages exposed, cleavages announcing the presence of a sexual being, cleavages selling things, cleavages asking to be clicked on. She saw men looking, men being automatically drawn to them. Her own femininity was in question. It seemed that breasts were an essential part. It seemed she could not be attractive to a man without the full complement.

But she was lucky, she told herself. She had already attracted a mate, she had fed her babies, she had no need of breasts any more; it didn't really matter. And she hadn't lost her hair or been made sick by horrible drugs. She'd got off easy, so far. And she was damned if she was going to let that bastard cancer stop her swimming in public when women with far more difficult experiences might even parade their losses on the internet. How brave they were! 'How brave I used to be!' she thought. 'But I wasn't so fearful, then,' she argued, while knowing it was no excuse. On the contrary, without fear, there would be no need for bravery. It was time to face herself. The unseen was what scared her. She must simply see it and know it.

She moved her mother's full-length mirror in front of a window, so that the light would fall directly on her body. She undressed, as usual, without looking. Then she advanced as if she were a predator and her reflection was prey. She had to pounce on herself, delay was fatal, or she might lose the opportunity and put herself away again. She put her hands over her eyes, to maintain the advantage of surprise. Then 'Woh!' she flicked them apart and there she appeared in all her naked truth. Well, she was still a woman, there was no doubt about that. Her outline asserted the fact, with its comfortable layer of fat, rather too comfortable actually. She wondered how it was possible to look untidy in the nude. Admittedly, her knees were lumpier, her thighs and tummy thicker than necessary, and her hair was a bit of a mess – in a once-short cut that had grown out in all directions and was now a patchy mix of silver grey and brownish blonde. She made tidying gestures, as one often sees others doing in public places, achieving nothing, as one sees others achieving nothing.

When at last she dared to pay attention to her damaged breast, it looked all right really – much less horrid than she'd imagined. The blue patch had shrunk, you could hardly see the scars, and the flesh had somehow rearranged itself in a valiant attempt to match its partner. They were almost a pair! She could probably get away with wearing an ordinary swimsuit instead of something with extra padding or coverage.

Her mother might have one, she thought, making for the chest of drawers. Not in the top two – knickers, socks and tights. The next one contained bras and thermal vests. Her mother had suffered so from the cold. It caught Georgie's heart to see them there with their hint of lace. Under the vests were hot water bottle covers and a gingham tablecloth and a comb – which must have fallen there accidentally, as drawers had often been left open after the stroke, and things often fell from surfaces.

It wasn't so long ago that her mother had been alive, right here in this room, and Georgie might have used that comb to neaten her hair, desperate to restore her appearance to one of normal Maureenness – less strained, less lopsided and bony. She and her father had taken it in turns to keep watch, as Maureen's breathing became ever more rasping and laboured, and the bedroom, in which she insisted on remaining, turned into a junky's nirvana.

It took about five days for her to descend beyond retrievability, but all that time contracted into one fast slide in Georgie's mind. What she remembered most strongly was their last clear exchange of words. Maureen, with a constipated expression as if she were about to wrestle with a sentence, which she often did since the stroke had destroyed her natural lyricism, suddenly said, in four clear words, 'What about the future?'

Georgie had calmed her: 'It's all right Mummy, there's nothing for you to worry about.' But Maureen had sat up straight and gestured with her head.

'Outside?' Georgie had asked.

'Yes!' Maureen had said, as if it were absolutely obvious.

Georgie had stared through the window at the brambles and weeds.

'Prune!' said Maureen.

'Prune?' asked Georgie. 'Do you mean "prune"?'

Sometimes her mother used perfectly the wrong word, with perfect confidence, such as 'shelf' for 'Christmas' or 'blue' for 'banana'.

'The future! Prune the future!' She seemed adamant and desperate.

The fuschia, she meant. Georgie knew that now. At the time she hadn't got it, but her answer had passed muster.

'It is a little out of hand,' she had agreed. The future certainly had been, and still was, a little out of hand.

On her deathbed, her mother had looked ancient, like a medieval saint, as if she had grown more sacred and holy with each passing year, and with the passing of life had reached a pinnacle. Only on its release had her glorious thousand-year-old soul fully revealed itself.

Georgie had never imagined losing her mother. Once or twice as a child she'd wept at an unwanted vision of her father's death. But her mother's? Never. It must have been unthinkable. Impossible. Always there. Peepo!

As her mother had been present for Georgie's first breath, so Georgie had witnessed Maureen's last. There was a rightness and symmetry in the arrangement. Of course, Georgie hadn't known it was the last breath until she'd waited in terrible suspense for the next, and in those moments her mother must have crossed a kind of no-man's land between the borders of living and dying. Ceasing is a process, she thought, as becoming is. You live a good while before you start to breathe; perhaps you die a good while after stopping. On the other hand, perhaps you die a good while before stopping, if as in Maureen's case you lose every part of yourself by slow degrees.

Tee-shirts were in the next drawer – all the same make, bought from some mail order catalogue, but different sizes and colours. And the bottom drawer was a medley. Unmatched pyjamas and pyjama bottoms, slips, nighties, cotton wool and – yes – two swimsuits, a bikini and a pair of trunks. The bikini was a beautiful turquoise blue, dotted with orange roses.

She couldn't recall ever seeing her mother in it. She wondered if Maureen had bought it for Joni, but although it looked unused, it didn't look new. Maybe she'd bought it for Georgie long ago, and never given it to her. Too late now, she thought, but because she was being brave she tried it on, before she could sensibly squash the notion and save herself some disappointment.

It didn't fit in any way. She laughed to see herself looking so awry. The cups were the wrong shape and full of air. Bits of her body were oozing out of them in all the wrong places. The waist was too tight, but the bottom was too loose. The tightness twisted and tortured the skin of her belly, which lacked the will to resist or fight back; and the laxity about the buttocks simply gave her a dangerous flappy feeling.

She flung it aside and tried the larger of the two swimsuits. She admired herself in it. She thrust out a hip and put her arms out in the attitude of a posing model.

Suddenly, her mother was staring at her from beyond the glass. For a moment she even felt like her mother, as though Maureen had taken a little break from heaven or hell and was borrowing Georgie's body, just for a sec, to remind herself what it was like to be alive. Georgie stood and stared, empty-headed but full-hearted, mesmerised, enjoying the moment. For however long it was, she was her mother. Yes. She actually was her mother. She and her mother were one being. This was far more than the sensation of a presence in the room. It was a presence within, and in that blissful state she felt expanded and light; she felt her body could house any spirit she called to it; she could be anyone.

Or did that mean she was no-one?

The idea shocked her. Then something flickered to the right of her gaze. She swung round to face its source. Nothing was moving. There was nothing strange to see. Only the room, and its inanimate collection of useful objects – the bed, the wardrobe, books, chairs. She heard rustling, like clothing, like silk against silk, or whispers whispering a repeated phrase. She strained to listen. 'Reach for the unreachable' it might be saying. 'Reach for the unreachable.' Perhaps it was a mouse, scuttling in the hollow between the walls.

With a rush of fear she snapped back into reality, quickly stuffing the rejected items back in the bottom drawer.

The Clifton pool had been transfigured! Today it was salubrious and professional. Tasteful and glassy. No longer a mere pool but a low-chlorine Lido, generously supplied with shower gel and shampoo, none of which contained aluminium or parabens! It had a sauna and a steam room and a hot tub, and outdoor changing cubicles, furnished with individual showers! As a gesture towards conservation, old bits of signage, like DEEP END and ENTRANCE, had been lovingly salvaged and used as decoration, tokens of the past which gave the place a frisson of familiarity and pleased Georgie peculiarly.

She gloried in covering her nakedness in cool air and hot water as a thin sharp wind rocked the curtain and swirled round her ankles, and the scent of orange and cucumber from her neighbour's ablutions mixed with garlic and smoked pheasant wafting over appetisingly from the kitchen. As she emerged she saw wind rippling the surface of the pool, which glinted under a sky splashed with blue. The water looked like crinkly polythene wrapping stretched across the dark blue tiles. A thin veil of steam hung over it.

The dress bag shielded her from public view until she stowed it. Then, feeling transparently naked, she decided to hide in a hot room for a while.

The wooden enclave of the sauna was empty except for a man on the top shelf, who was sitting with his legs outstretched, staring out of the window at the swimmers. He turned to glance at her briefly. Something about his face nudged her memory, but too vaguely to mean anything. Most people looked familiar to her these days, as if she'd seen examples of every type, and nobody could surprise her any more.

She sat in the far corner and sank into herself and the dry heat, letting it press in from all sides. She imagined poison oozing from her pores, her flesh loosening and falling off her bones like well-cooked chicken. Cleansing her body would be like clearing the house, she thought; it was all purgation, all necessary to keep nasty illnesses at bay, and to welcome in the next exciting phase of life.

As sweat began to flow, and a certain pheromonal atmosphere mingled with the smell of the heater, she found herself thinking about Kevin, and being glad. Theirs had not been a model relationship. It had involved too much bickering and not enough sex, and had been too mutually dependent. It had been a marriage in essence, without the expense of the wedding or the divorce. They'd been near to each other long enough for a psychological entanglement to occur; probably some chemical attraction bound them, which was why separating had been so tricky, separating for good. 'For good', she thought, resolutely. Yes, it would be for good.

She opened her eyes and viewed her legs plumped out on the wooden slats, and the double bump of her waist. So what if Kevin had consumed her last drop of sexiness, she thought – sexiness was rather a nuisance. There'd be no call for it now, anyway, because in proportion to losing her appeal, she'd grown too fussy; apart from the usual stipulations that he be the right sort of age, intelligence, education, culture, values, views, tastes and politics, he must be honest, fair and kind; he must have no dependent children or manipulative ex-wives; no dogs, cats or hobbies; no phobias; he must be no sort of artist, including writer; he mustn't look at porn. He mustn't look at other women full stop, at least not in her presence, that was so humiliating. All right, he can look but not stare. Kevin used to stare, claiming it was for art. No. No sort of artist. He must be utterly loyal.

Well, that was clearly hopeless – all the loyal men were being loyal – to women who had hoovered them up a long time ago. She might as well have stayed with Jim, especially as she'd done rather badly out of the divorce – making concessions wherever possible, to spare the children.

So she was probably going to be alone from now on, she thought, seeing as she hadn't met the right person after several decades of meeting people; and she was absolutely going to love it! She was perfectly happy in her own company and if the erotic side of her life was over, well it was no great loss. Yes it had brought her the blessings of motherhood and the occasional five minutes of bliss, but it had also brought longings and frustrations, and irritations and complications. Rejections. Infections! It also meant having to faff about in front of mirrors and spray on a smile and act a touch less bright than she was. Once she'd thoroughly discarded all that sexual fuss and fiddle-faddle, she could be her uncomplicated self again, her real core self – the one she'd been before hormones had risen up to enslave her, when her passions had been simple and easily satisfied – chocky! Mivvies! sparkly things! ponies! butterflies and ballet! – and to be ravished in bed was to revel in the smooth touch and fragrant scent of clean sheets, with a hot mug of Horlicks in one hand, and a jolly good book in the other! She loved clean sheets! Why would she want them rucked and sweaty? More rucked and sweaty, rather, than she could make them all by herself.

Being single again was going to be just great! Her age wouldn't matter. Her looks wouldn't matter. She didn't care who saw what, and in a minute she was going to parade her semi-naked self before a 360-degree audience, and not give a trembling middle-aged toss! She was free at last! Free again!

That word 'free'. There was something faintly disturbing about it.

Frieda. Yes, of course. Frieda was the name of the Austrian girl.

She swivelled and lifted her legs, stretching them out so they were pointing towards the man in the window. Suddenly it came to her. His name simply landed in her mind, like a conker.

'Nick!' she said, before she could stop herself. 'Are you Nick?' She regretted her more exposed position.

The man turned towards her as a bewildered stranger, and slowly transformed into a surprised and playful friend. Politely, hesitantly, he asked, 'Georgina?'

'Well done!' Georgie contracted her stomach muscles and moved her arms together, at the same time as trying to look relaxed.

'Gee. My, my...' The stranger-come-friend carried on staring, dumbfounded, smiling. His face was lined and a bit jowly, what was left of his hair was liberally sprinkled with grey, but his Nickness was intact – he was still all there, and still himself. His strong shoulders and long limbs. The parallel lines down each cheek. His friendly eyes. Yes, she'd always loved that habitual expression of disbelieving amusement. Loved it!

She said, 'So, you're still in Bristol?' at the same time as he said, 'So, you're back in Bristol?' They laughed and he gestured that she should go first.

'Oh well, my mum and dad have died and I'm sorting out the house.'

He face fell. 'I'm so sorry.'

'Yes, it's hard actually, harder than I thought. Well, I didn't think, that's the trouble. So. Regrets...' She grimaced, as if to say, 'they're nothing really'. 'But how are you? And yours?'

'I'm fine thanks, we're all fine. My mother's in sheltered accommodation. She's OK, but – ' Here he said something unintelligible, as he dragged his hand across his face, 'And my dad had a heart attack about,' he puttered, 'it must be about ten years now.'

Georgie nodded, and Nick nodded too, with a rueful look. There was no need to ask if the heart attack had been fatal, and Georgie couldn't think of how to phrase the question anyway.

'So what have you been up to? How long is it? It must be – what? Getting on for thirty years?'

They'd been the same age then, so they must be the same age now, she realised, but he looked younger, and somehow gave out a younger impression. He looked out of her league, in fact, which simply wasn't fair. Of course, a man her age, if he were free, would look for a woman much less her age, regardless of wisdom, experience, and whatever else you were supposed to gain. And what was even more unfair, the woman wouldn't mind.

He smiled warmly, and to add to the warmth he touched her bare foot as it was the only part of herself within reach.

'I have something to thank you for, Georgina. This is good – an opportunity. I did what you suggested. And it was – ' he searched for a superlative, ' – the best decision I ever made.'

'Really?' Georgie had no idea what he was talking about.

'You've forgotten! How funny. But what you said completely changed my life. You were so wise. You knew me better than I knew myself.'

Georgie wished she'd known herself so well. Looking at him now she couldn't understand how she had lost him. She must have taken him for granted, in the days when there was plenty of choice.

'What? What did I say?'

'You said I must get off the hamster wheel – '

It was impossible that she'd said anything about a hamster wheel.

'Which was selling insurance. You remember that?'

'I think so.'

'And do what I really loved. Which was gardening. I'm a gardener, Georgina. Because of you. And I've never looked back.'

'How wonderful.'

'It is. And I married Shirley Patterson.'

'OK.'

'You remember her?'

Georgie shook her head.

'And we have two beautiful girls. Rosie and Jenny. One's at Oxford, and the other's in Canada.'

'How fantastic.' How fantastic it was, she was thinking, that he'd mentioned his wife without having to be asked, demonstrating his loyalty, and at the same time demonstrating that, unfortunately, he was unavailable.

Or ex-wife. He wasn't wearing a ring.

'What about you?'

He took his hand from her foot and leant back, while Georgie wrapped up thirty years in less than thirty seconds.

'I have two too.' She laughed at the sound of it. 'A pigeon pair. Charlie's seventeen, Joni's nineteen. My girl's away at the moment on a gap thing. In Peru. It's awful. I really miss her.' She regretted saying 'pigeon pair'.

'So how's it going? The sorting out? Horrible job.'

'Well it'll be marvellous when it's done.' She took a breath, needing extra energy to be cheerful about it. 'And I do feel as though I'm meant to be doing it, though I don't understand why. You see I know with all my – whatever it is that knows – there's something hiding in there I'm supposed to find – something significant, something meaningful and important – so I'm looking for it, but I don't have any clue what it might look like, or mean, or be. I mean it could be anything. Just a memory even. But I'm certain there's something valuable in amongst all the rubbish, and it's me that's supposed to see it.'

He looked confused and she realised she must sound absurd. She was talking too much and too fast and too enthusiastically. She didn't know why she was confiding in him. 'It's probably nothing valuable in terms of, you know, money.'

He tensed his bottom lip and nodded. 'Sounds exciting, your task. Good luck with it.'

They fell silent as two young women entered. One left the door open. Nick shot Georgie a bemused look as she got down to shut it. She felt suddenly raw.

'Ooh sorry,' said the latter of the women. 'Anyone mind if I chuck some water on the heater?'

No-one minded. Scorching steam billowed into the enclosed space. Georgie put her hands over her eyes and thought about Joan of Arc. She moved down to the bottom bench. It was still too hot, but she couldn't leave.

'So where do you live now?' she asked, braving the burn.

'This you won't believe.'

'Won't I?'

'I live on a boat in the docks. The Buccaneer.'

'Gosh. How romantic.'

'Romantic and a pain in the arse. You wouldn't like it.'

'Wouldn't I?'

They laughed.

'Ooh, this is too hot for me,' Nick said. 'I'm going for a dip.'

Georgie was pleased; he'd said: 'I live on a boat' not 'we live on a boat', and he'd pretty much ignored the girls. She waited for a while after he'd closed the door, then followed him, smiling at them in case they felt responsible for driving her out.

The water shocked her toes and legs, then slapped her in the chest, piquing her scars, but was beautifully refreshing as it rushed over the rest of her skin. Without goggles she had to breast-stroke upright, like a novice, while Nick performed an elegant freestyle, half-submerged. At each end he glided, ducked and made a professional turn, so there was no further opportunity to talk. She wished she'd told him she was divorced.

Eventually she managed to collide with him on her way back to the sauna. He was carrying a towel, on his way out.

'Let's have a coffee or something before you go?' he suggested.

'I'd like that.'

They were standing face to face, half-naked, dripping wet.

'Um. How good are you at remembering numbers?' said Nick.

Georgie hesitated. She thought he'd meant they should have coffee there and then, before she left the pool, not before she left Bristol. Nick laughed. 'No, not your strong point, I remember. Or we could just arrange to meet now? This café? When?'

Georgie was again disappointed and confused. She thought he meant they should meet now, not arrange now. And she was actually pretty good at numbers.

'Well, timewise I'm completely free.'

Their wires were crossed and she kept using bizarre expressions. And she was going to have to wait. She wished she hadn't said 'timewise'. She was free in most senses of the word. She wondered if she could actually say that, but took too long about it.

'How about Sunday? Three o'clock?' he said.

'That'll do nicely. I'll see you then. Here. Then. Great.'

'Gee. It's so good to see you.'

'Likewise.'

He gave her a warm smile and then he was gone.

Likewise? That'll do nicely? Oh dear!

Georgie wondered what had happened to end their intimacy. Perhaps she used to have unrealistic ambitions, and he hadn't been good enough for her. Perhaps it was the insurance; she hadn't liked him to be selling it. But it was good really, it was all good. Otherwise no Joni or Charlie or Rosie or Jenny.

Family love. That's what was really important. She'd always known it, but perhaps she needed to be reminded; perhaps she needed to appreciate it more fully, and perhaps that was the meaning behind this strange tipping point in her life.

BE KIND

I hate Will and I hate Mum and Dad and I hate all my friends and I bloody hate school too. It smells of disgusting bleach and sloppy cabbage, and I hate the sight of it and the sound of its bloody bell. I have two absolutely huge revolting spots on my forehead and my legs look like gigantic white logs of German sausage. I'm bored. Bored bored bored bored boredy boredy bored. BOREDOM. OMEBORD. BEDROOM. MOREBOD. MOORBED. REDBOOM. ROODBEM. I'm even bored of this now. I'm so bored I want to cry, but I've forgotten how. I can't make the tears come out. I put them all in a box and swallowed the key. That's the way to do it! Smile! Smile! Even though you're faking it cos nobody's gonna know. I'm even a failure at crying. It's an absolute crime to be bored when people are dying of starvation.

I wish I could feel the same as I used to. Breathing in I am aware of the view from my window, my forlorn elm trees and patches of blue sky. Breathing out I am aware of my pen nib flashing silver. Breathing in I am aware of hair tickling my forehead and the waist of my skirt too tight. Breathing out I am aware that I am wasting time. Breathing in I am aware that my heart is beating faster. Breathing out I am aware that I am anxious because I am wasting my time.

What peculiar creatures we are, strutting about on our hind limbs looking down on the world, like walking bellows. Billions of us draping ourselves in weird bits and pieces of cloth, doing funny things to our hair. And what about that one? What's it like to be her? Or him, or him, or her? And where's the justice or sense in anything? How do you measure? The only possible justice would be for every one of us to live every life; to be each dot of consciousness, to feel its pain and pleasure, and think its thoughts and wade through all that time.

But I am only one dot of consciousness, with my little pain and my little pleasure, and my irrational thoughts and my wasted time.

I want to see the world before it gets blown up. I'm really sad when I think about starvation and war and atom bombs. I can't bear to watch the news. Plus I haven't done my bleeding Latin revision. I leaked at school and had to walk around with loo paper sticking out of my pants. I've lost my appetite. I might have a worm.

Everyone in my class wears nylon tights. It's only me and Linda and Harriet still in socks and they are obviously social spastics. I don't know why I keep changing my mind about what I want and what I think. This is excrement and vom. Tomorrow I'll be ashamed of it. I don't really hate anyone. In fact I love someone.

Matthew was the boy she adored these days, now she'd given up on David Bowie. She still loved Michael Palin of course, and would probably love Ilie Nastase again once Wimbledon was underway, but she'd maturely and resolutely accepted that it was hopeless loving anyone on the wrong side of a screen. Matthew's chief advantage was in being 3D. Solid flesh and liquid blood. 4D if you added the dimension of time – yes, he wouldn't be much fun as a statue.

She'd written his name in Greek all over her rough book. Ματθαιο. It was a week since she'd sent her letter to him. She wished she'd been braver and simply rung him up and asked him to meet her somewhere, but hadn't dared to be rejected by telephone. This slow rejection by being ignored and repeatedly disappointed was infinitely more enjoyable. In fact, it was perfectly exquisite.

She loved everything about Matthew – his fair boyish hair and broad shoulders, his athleticism, his seriousness, his sudden bursts of outrageous laughter. He was in the year above Will. He drove to school in a purple Mini. She loved the way he looked when he was drunk on lager – as she'd seen him once at her best friend Jan's party – tousled and intimate and capable of dark ideas. She longed to stroke the hair away from his neck and sink her teeth into it. She longed for him to recognise her true nature, that she was more than just Will's clumsy little sister. One of these days he might see her missing the school bus, and give her a lift.

Ματθαιοσ Ματθαιοσ *You would be so nice. I can imagine how you will touch my cheek with your strong sensitive fingers, and how you will breathe on my eyelids, and lick my lips, and slowly kiss my neck further and further down. Everything will be all right once I've got to Oxford or Cambridge. I can't wait. I'll join Footlights. I'll meet a brilliant intense and passionate man who will stare at me with soulful eyes. He'll take me punting with people like Evelyn Waugh and Michael Palin and we'll drink champagne in Elysian fields. It's not fair that boys don't have to pay for tampons. The human race relies on periods so everyone should pay. Will keeps buying the records I want. Frieda. I'm not going to even write down what I think about that vile person. Nobody seems to care how I feel, though I suppose they must do, seeing as I care about them.*

Georgie read over what she had written, admiring her handwriting. It was huge and arty – with a new kind of 'a'. She began to doodle. Then she sighed, opened her satchel and took out her ruler and pencil case. She drew up a timetable for revision – six weeks neatly spaced and measured. She would start in the Easter holiday, she decided. She would work out arithmetically how many hours to devote to each. She would invent a colour coding system with her Tempo pens.

The house was empty again, tea would be late again. This was becoming usual. Georgie didn't like coming home to an absence. Even though she didn't much talk to her mother, she would feel somehow settled and safe knowing she was there, and that the second half of her day had begun – the better part. And she was used to hearing Will coming home, always a little later than her. In a vague subconscious way she would notice the sound of the door rattling and slamming, and then his heavy high jumping upstairs to change immediately out of his school uniform. No matter how much she was concentrating on homework, or how deeply interested she was in *Blue Peter* or *Nationwide*, she would know he was home. But now he went straight to the summerhouse, avoiding the front door of the house altogether. She only gradually became aware of music coming from the garden.

She decided to go and talk to him.

He'd locked the big glass window. She pressed her face against it. 'Let me in, cretin!' she shouted.

He unfastened the window and slid it aside.

'Who said you could have the bloody hi-fi in here!' Georgie complained. 'What if I want to listen to something!'

'This is mine! I bought it myself, you four eyes.'

'Oh.'

'Listen.' He turned it up to its full volume and back down again. Georgie was impressed. 'It's for my party,' Will said.

'You're having a party?'

'Yup.'

'But my birthday's sooner than yours. Why can't I have a party?'

'I don't know, little Pud. It's just one of the many unfairnesses in life that you'll have to get used to, won't you?'

A world become one. Of salads and sun. Only a fool would say that.

'What do you think about F?'

'Frieda?' said Will, pretending she was insignificant and uninteresting.

Georgie nodded, curling her upper lip which clearly demonstrated her own feelings.

'About her or of her?'

'Anything.'

'Well, she's fairly pretty, I suppose. She can't help being a kraut.'

'She doesn't seem to do anything. I thought au pairs were supposed to clean and things like that.'

He shrugged. 'Mrs Russell cleans. It's clean enough. Anyway, I thought she was teaching you Deutsch. Wir müssen Deutsch sprechen, nicht war? Ve heff vays of mekking you ze Deutsch talking!'

Georgie smiled wanly. 'She's painting the bathroom, Will. How come she's allowed?'

'It was getting a bit tatty.'

'But she's drawing cherubs and birds and things. She's being *creative*.' She pulled a face. 'How long is she going to be here? She's going to ruin my holidays.'

'Don't moan at me, moan at Mum and Dad.'

Georgie harumphed. She wanted to ask him if he had any notion about the 'invaluable service' Frieda's father had done, but wasn't sure if was a secret and would rather maintain her special position if so.

'But why d'you think she's here?' she asked innocently. 'Did Dad explain anything? Don't you think it's rather queer?'

Will shrugged. He didn't seem at all curious. Obviously, he didn't mind so much.

As she left, he whistled and she turned round. 'Don't mention the war!' he shouted. She laughed raucously, gratified by this sign of allegiance. He slid the glass door shut and she saw him through it, playing an invisible guitar.

She decided to be in the sitting room while she waited, pretending not to wait. She couldn't settle down to homework not knowing where her mother was. Now she had no access to Will's records she had to rely on her own – mostly singles. She played 'Rebel Rebel' over and over again, increasing the volume until the speakers squealed in agony.

It was nearly six before her mother returned, with her new pet. 'Hello darling!' she shouted in an excited sing-song voice. 'Come and see what we've got!'

For tea, Georgie thought she meant. She followed them into the kitchen and watched as they emptied their carrier bags of shoeboxes and tissue-paper packages. Nothing that looked like food. They'd run out of Shakespearean attractions to throw money at, she surmised, so they'd been visiting boutiques instead. She wondered how come Frieda could afford it and hoped she wasn't being paid for doing absolutely nothing useful.

'I chose something for you, Georgina,' Frieda said. Georgie was embarrassed. It was like being told a joke: she would have to enjoy it, whatever it was. Putting her face in the appropriate expression, she took the slim package and carefully peeled off the sellotape. It was a silk scarf, in green and gold.

'Thank you,' she said. 'It's really nice.' She didn't know exactly what to do with it, so placed it clumsily behind her neck, and allowed Frieda to arrange it for her. Frieda smiled seductively, biting her lip and leaning her head to one side in a pensive attitude, lightly touching Georgie's hair and neck as she adjusted the scarf. 'I wanted you to have something feminine and beautiful,' she said.

'I don't think it goes with the school tie,' Georgie said, blushing. She felt gawky, and didn't like her appearance being assessed or admired. What did Frieda mean by her needing something feminine and beautiful? That she was masculine and ugly? How dare she? And who cared anyway, about looking like anything in particular?

Frieda glanced round at Maureen, to show off the scarf arrangement, but Maureen was busy unwrapping her own gifts.

'Oh, yes, Maureen has followed me, look,' said Frieda.

Her mother was admiring a minuscule piece of colourful swimwear.

'A bikini?' Georgie exclaimed. The idea horrified her, but she didn't say so. She hated them being together all the time, fussing over each other's clothes and accessories and behaving like best friends. She'd seen them holding hands! Imagine that! Your mum holding hands with a girl!

'Frieda helped me choose, didn't you, Frieda? We got everything I need for the summer.'

'It's feminine and beautiful, isn't it, like your scarf? Sehr hübsch?'

'Und sehr expensive,' Maureen joked.

Frieda explained to Georgie. 'My Grossmutti says that one cannot afford to buy cheap things.'

'Eh?' Georgie grimaced. She was imagining Frieda helping her mother choose. Did she go into the changing room with her or what?

'They will not be good quality. They will not last.'

How long was a bikini supposed to last? Georgie wondered, if you were already over forty!

'Hey Geegee, darling. Chin up! You look depressed!'

I've got a right to be bloody depressed, thought Georgie. When did you last take me shopping? You didn't even bloody help me buy a bra! She just smiled. 'No I'm fine. Just a bit knackered and hungry.' Daddy was bringing tea, she was told. To Frieda she said: 'Thank you for the scarf,' and went upstairs.

She closed the door against the smell of art hanging about on the landing and lay upside down on her bed, in a position which allowed her to look through the side window at the silver birch trees. She saw glimmers of green decorating their spindly branches and solid white trunks, caught by lingering rays of the late afternoon sun. Through her other window she saw the elms on the other side of the house, still black skeletons. She loved to look at the trees. When they'd first come to this house their soft sounds had frightened her. She used to imagine she was hearing the ghosts of crying children. It was such an old house. Her father had reassured her, it's only the trees, and they'd stared out together at the dark world, at leafless branches trembling in the wind. Those were the days before she understood that ghosts were nothing more than a load of unscientific bollocks.

She heard Frieda messing about in Will's room next door. She was singing the song Georgie had chosen! As if to show how hauntingly beautiful it ought to be, in comparison to her own piss-awful rendering. It made her uncomfortable, unrelaxed, as if she herself were the stranger. She might have to meet her at any moment and put on a different face. And she didn't like it that all her personal things were on display in the bathroom; that Frieda might go poking around her hair removal cream or cotton wool pads. And that her bedroom door had no lock on it. Suddenly she thought of her pocket money, hidden in a piggy bank behind some tee-shirts in the wardrobe. And of the diary on her desk.

She heard a knock at the door.

'Hello?' Georgie looked at Frieda upside down.

Frieda laughed. 'Bist du müde?'

Georgie yawned as an answer, it went with the word, 'ja, jaaaaah.' She sat up and swivelled round to face Frieda, to be less vulnerable.

'Trotzdem. Wir müssen üben ja? Freitag hab' ich nichts von dir gehört. 'Stehst's?'

'I think you mean I should be practising cello. But I've got heaps of homework to do, I'm afraid.' Georgie glanced over at her desk, at the neglected exercise books, the closed pencil case, a satchel full of text books lying accusatively on the floor.

'Ach so. Man sagt, "Arbeit allein macht nicht glücklich." 'Stehst du?'

'Work alone doesn't make you happy.'

'Man muss auch spielen.'

'One must also play.'

'Du könntest Deutsch mit mir sprechen, ja?'

'Ich kann.'

'Könnte.'

Ah, yes, könnte, the subjunctive form. Georgie smiled inside.

'Ja, ich könnte,' she agreed, grateful that Will was not in the room. She felt a tickle of amusement in her guts, and in response her mouth twitched gently at the corners. The girl was obsessed!

She wanted to be alone until it was time to eat, then either watch television or be alone again afterwards. She certainly wasn't up for another go at giving birth to 'Full Fathom Five'. *Ich will alleine sein* – she framed the phrase mentally, I want to be alone, it chanted loudly in her imagination, in the voice of Greta Garbo, but she couldn't bring her mouth to form the words in any accent. I could but I won't. 'Ich könnte; aber ich werde nicht!' Nein! Nicht! They were as hard to say as No and Not.

Oh the relief at the sound of the front door opening and Larry arriving with supper! Maureen had been too busy to do any cooking as was now usual, so Larry had come home via the deli and the baker and the greengrocer. This was Georgie's cue to go and lay the table, a perfect excuse to escape from Frieda's suffocating nosiness. She sidled awkwardly around her lurking figure, explaining that she had domestic duties.

As she passed Will's room, now Frieda's, she glimpsed a floor scattered with clothes and magazines. She regretted not shutting her own door properly, thinking again of the diary and the mean things she'd written.

Her mother was in a marvellous mood. Spending money had made her happy. At the dining table, she'd normally be quietly listening; now she couldn't contain herself, chatting about what they'd done and what they'd seen, going on and on about how brilliant Frieda was at playing the piano, how they could give a little concert perhaps, with wine and nibbles, and invite the Priestleys and the Bretts and the Trevors, as they hadn't had a party in ever so many years, and how Frieda was going to teach her to play too and she'd been learning German words, wie geht's, entschuldigung, bitte, danke, wieder. Georgie glanced over at the piano, which had functioned as an oddly shaped and rather cumbersome shelf for displaying ornaments and photographs, but it was indeed open, and there was indeed open music resting on the stand showing that it had probably been played.

'Georgina, you haven't been practising!' her mother said suddenly. 'Frieda says you have a natural talent and you must nurture it.'

Frieda smiled at Georgie and she blushed.

'She has a good intonation and good spirit. She makes a very beautiful sound.'

'We never hear it,' Maureen sighed.

'I don't want anyone to hear!' Georgie protested.

'Talents are to share, are they not?' said Frieda. 'It will help you in the examination.'

Georgie looked pleadingly at her mother. 'I think Georgina's decided not to take the cello exam this year, haven't you darling? So you can concentrate on 'O' levels.'

'Yes.' Georgie looked round at Will. She imagined he might make some jeering comment and was gearing up to counter it, but he was merely chewing, gazing across the table at Frieda, though she wasn't about to say anything. She realised that her father was also staring at Frieda, in some trance of admiration, while Frieda was studying her plate, hiding behind a curtain of hair, but somehow glorying in every single person's attention. Georgie looked back at her mother, detecting a brief moment of confusion shrugged off in a weird smile.

'You can only do your best,' Maureen said, but Georgie could tell she was thinking about something else, something she'd just observed and didn't think much of. There was a peculiar atmosphere, as though they were playing a game, where the conversation and what was really happening were two different layers.

'They're changing the grading system so grade 1 and grade 2 are going to join up and be grade A,' Georgie said, though no-one was listening. 'So it's impossible for me to do as well as Will.'

'I don't know why you need to compare yourself to Will all the time,' said her father. 'His record is unbeatable. You can't get more than a run of eight ones whatever you do. So you're bound to be disappointed, aren't you? If you constantly compare.' He looked back at Frieda, falsely grinning. 'What does our guest think? An independent view.'

'You'll probably get top marks anyway, won't you?' said her mother. 'Oh this one's such a silly, always underestimating herself,' she confided to Frieda.

'No I don't.'

'If it will be easier you can work less,' Frieda suggested brightly, at which everybody nodded and smiled.

'The point is, does it matter if they're As or ones?' Maureen said with unadulterated joy.

Georgie felt suddenly impatient. She wasn't getting through.

'Of course it does! It devalues the top grade doesn't it? Der! Plus it means that Debbie Needham's going to do as well as me too, which is ridiculously unfair. I'm better than she is in every single subject except Maths. Including hockey and tennis. And athletics.'

'Georgina I'd prefer you not to be rude to your mother.'

'I'm sorry.'

'You both got prizes last year though, didn't you?'

'I know, but she got the lanyard.' And she gets all the good drama parts, Georgie thought. And she's got millions of boyfriends and billions of clothes. 'I thought at least I could beat her in the things that matter, you see,' she explained.

'What is the lanyard?'

'It's a thing you win if you're good at sports. A decoration, like a badge,' Georgie explained to Frieda. 'You wear it round your neck, like a noose.'

'Noose?'

From everyone's reaction Georgie saw that she'd plunged the conversation into morbid nastiness, but Larry changed the subject before anyone had time to explain what you usually do with a noose. 'I'm hoping you can help me with something, Frieda,' he said. 'One of my clients, Maureen you know him, David, he sells cars. He needs some promotional photographs. He thought I could take them. Remember, Maureen, we showed him our slides of Mallorca. So he thinks I know how to hold a camera. They want pictures of the cars, of course, and Stratford in the background, of course, and some blonde dolly bird sitting on the bonnet.'

'Of course,' said Will.

'So naturally I thought of you, Frieda.'

'Dolly bird?' Georgie spluttered.

Maureen made a kind of quacking noise, supposedly a laugh. 'I think Dad was using the term ironically, darling. Geegee's very women's lib, aren't you, dear?'

'Yes, thanks.'

'She read *The Female Eunuch*, didn't you?' Maureen grimaced.

'We also have this in German. *Der Weibliche Eunuch*. I have also read.'

'We should be treated equally, that's all. You wouldn't ask a blond man to sit on the bonnet would you?'

'I'm not sure,' said Larry, 'It probably depends on the car.'

Will laughed.

'I would like better to sit in the car than to sit on it,' said Frieda, with her usual cute humour. 'Then perhaps I may drive it?'

Georgie ignored Frieda's flirtatious smile and tried to catch Will's eye, but he was determined to avoid her glance. He didn't look in her direction until Maureen had followed Larry into the kitchen to help him locate the pickle, at which moment he brazenly glared at her, smirking, with one finger placed on his upper lip to indicate a Hitler moustache. Georgie snorted. She couldn't help herself.

Frieda looked from one to the other, questioning. Will instantly adopted an expression of innocent neutrality, as if he were perplexed by her confusion; but Georgie was not so quick. Hilarity had gripped her round the belly, she couldn't let it go without another snort bursting through her nose, followed by a choked explosion of loud giggles.

'What is so funny? I do not understand,' Frieda asked, smiling uncertainly.

Georgie released another breathful of laughter before sighingly reassuring Frieda, without actually facing her, that it meant nothing. She concentrated furiously on the dining table; so primed for laughter she didn't trust herself to move. Oh, it was such painful pleasure! She stared at the looping patterns on the wood, counting each swirling line. Will, aware of her discomfort and relishing the opportunity to exert his power, mercilessly pressed on with his veiled references.

'I really bombed out at school today, Georgie.' She could imagine his face, full of mischief. 'But I've done a jolly good blitz in the summerhouse so that should earn me a few medals.' Georgie scanned her brain. Churchill. Hitler. Holocaust. She couldn't think of any way to join in, and she wouldn't trust herself to say it anyway. 'Who do you think you are kidding Miss Georgina?' Will sang. By biting her lower lip she managed to relax her face into a serious expression. She wished her mother and father would return. They were taking a jolly long time with the pickle. They must be having a conflab about something, something to do with Frieda, probably. Then Will excused himself to go to the loo. Blatantly he Nazi saluted her and goose-stepped out of the room. It was impossible not to laugh.

'I'm sorry,' Georgie said, letting it all out. 'I'm sorry. It's from a television programme. It's not really funny.'

'Krieg. Ja. I understood it. He talked about the war.'

Frieda's mouth still smiled, but her eyes were sad. Georgie's heart plummeted. She felt suddenly sick of herself. She asked Frieda to pass the butter and silently helped herself to another slice of ham. Will returned, now humming the Dambusters theme. Georgie tried to quieten him with a hard look, which he didn't seem to notice.

'But I am not German,' Frieda said, with force. 'Meine Mutti ist aus Ukraine. Mein Vater ist aus Österreich.'

'Dein Farter?' said Will. In spite of herself, Georgie couldn't help responding to the wicked twinkle in his eyes. She willed herself not to laugh. She thought, I will not laugh, I refuse to laugh. If I laugh now I will die tomorrow. All the while her diaphragm was shaking and her face was going red and she was absolutely on the point of wetting herself. Frieda hadn't finished. Her voice came loud and sharp.

'Ich bin Österreicherin! Ich war nach dem Krieg geboren! Es war nicht mein Krieg!'

The trouble was that she *did* sound like Hitler. She slammed her hand on the table so that it rattled.

'Die Nazis waren das Ungeziefer!'

Maureen was suddenly there in the archway. 'What's happening?' she asked, alert to a change in mood. 'Georgie what is Frieda saying?'

'She says she was born after the war,' Georgie said, quietly swallowing, her forehead twitching in bewilderment.

'Yes?'

'So it wasn't her fault.'

'Well of course, it wasn't! Whoever suggested otherwise?'

Concerned, confused, Maureen set the pickle on the table and now they found out why mentioning the war was a bad idea. No matter how anyone tried to leaven the atmosphere it was dense and oppressive. Although Frieda returned to normal, and said some kind things to Georgie about school, Larry didn't even smile. And after supper Georgie felt obliged to humour Frieda by playing cello instead of watching television. She expected her to hear it and come knocking. Nobody came.

We're allowed to make jokes, she thought. That's just the way we do it in this family. I have to put up with being teased, so why shouldn't Frieda be teased? And Will was much worse than me, anyway. It wasn't my fault.

At bedtime she knelt down and prayed for forgiveness.

RELEASE YOUR CREATIVE DAEMON

Upon waking, she was often confused. In her dawning consciousness, as she realised that her dreams were only dreams and didn't need to be finished now that she was in the actual world, she gradually regained her co-ordinates, imagined her relationship to other objects, and prepared to negotiate the translation of her body from a horizontal to a vertical existence – that evolutionary moment in her day which more and more resembled the crawling of fish onto land. She would think she was in bed at home in Salisbury; she would think that Charlie was in the room next door needing to be woken, that the loo she was about to visit was off the corridor to the left, and that the kitchen was downstairs waiting to be switched on to provide cups of tea and breakfast. It was a shock then to open her eyes onto light coming in through a different window from a different direction. Her mind would whirl drunkenly, unhinged and unsteady for a few seconds while she realigned herself and remembered all the other things that were actually true and actually present and actually belonged in her present world. Oh yes, of course – her mother had died, her father had died, her children had gone, she must sort out the boxes and clean away the past.

Then one morning she thought herself somewhere else entirely.

It was dark, early, about four o'clock. She woke suddenly, under a great pressure which bore down on her chest and seemed to be trying to squeeze the air from her lungs. She saw, vividly and with her eyes stretched open, a glowing white face immediately in front of her own, intently returning her gaze. What she saw she felt as a personality, a woman with a history and an agenda. She felt a hand urgently clasping her own. As if for an eternity she lay rooted to the bed, quite unable to move, staring and staring as slowly, quietly, the vision dissolved, and she realised that she was holding her own hand, and the marks on it had come from her own nails. Slowly, quietly, she let her breathing settle down and at last was brave enough to relax. She felt stunned, as if someone had given her a beating. She wanted water, but couldn't summon the energy to move just yet. She wanted to change the bedclothes and dry herself. Sweat had trickled between her breasts, the sheet was clinging to her back, and she desperately needed to relieve herself.

The room was dark. Too dark to see. But as she imagined what she was about to do, she imagined quite another place. There would be cold water in a blue floral china jug, a white flannel and a matching bowl placed in front of an oval mirror on a fine red mahogany dressing table positioned to one side of the window. In the corner nearest the door would be an oak chair with a chamber pot under its hinged seat. A chest full of fresh dry linen and handkerchieves would be standing at the foot of the bed. A glass would be sitting on a mantelpiece above a fireplace in the opposite wall, beside the glass a small decanter of red wine. A Persian carpet would protect her feet from the wooden floorboards.

Next she was sinking, sinking, gathering speed.

She staggered out of bed, wildly aiming for the chamber pot, stumbled over the bedside table, and found herself lying on her ordinary plain-cut carpeted floor. The pain shocked her into a more wakeful state – a sharp bony pain in her shin, a more subtle throbbing in her ankle and a freezing chill over her whole naked body. She moaned and then, because moaning wasn't enough, she shouted, angrily, 'OW!' as if the energy of her voice would drive away the unusual atmosphere in the room, as well as the pain. She cursed, 'Fuck, Willy, Bugger, Piss, Shit!' crawling and groping her awkward way to the bathroom. In the humming electric fanlight, pissing at full throttle, she saw that she'd skinned her shin. The injury needed soothing, after which she washed, put on a dressing gown, stripped the bed, turned the mattress, remade the bed, and refilled her glass of water. By the time she was lying down again a blackbird was singing outside her window, and she could sense the first dim fingers of dawn touching the curtains. She heard the church bell strike six. The atmosphere was heavy, dreadful. Her shouting and activity had not dispelled it. She thought she could smell ash and burning, interlaced with something sweeter like pot pourri. She opened the window to try and clear the air, but though the morning garden was cool and moist, it stank of rotten things.

She turned the light back on and gave up any idea of sleeping.

She didn't feel like reading. On the contrary, she felt an urge to write; so she settled herself at the kitchen table with a cup of tea, scrap paper and a pencil. Sleepy words tumbled from her brain – staccato nonsense at first, as if a throat were clearing; followed by verbs and conjunctions, a voice making sentences, making sense.

1812. Violence and discontent. Bad weather and poor harvests. Port closures, trade embargoes, rising prices, bankruptcies, riots... King mad, Prime Minister assassinated, Prince Regent a despised dandy, waster and rake. Common folk, robbed of their common land by enclosure acts, are now being robbed of their labour by machinery. Weavers are rebelling in the North. Croppers are rebelling in the Midlands. Britannia, her constitution failing by these woundings of internal organs, and exhausted after quarrelling for twenty years with her haughty and unruly sister France, now begins a bloody argument with her brother America! The future of the fleet is in jeopardy! Civilisation itself is in the balance.!

Yet I, meanwhile, am happily ensconced in my uncle's country mansion, surrounded by luxury and expensive taste and content as any girl of five and ten can possibly be. I write letters, read novels, sew, sketch, play piano and cards, and walk about the shrubberies, just as I have done for the last five years, blissfully ignorant of what is happening in the wider world, and stupidly blind to what approaches in my narrow one.

She wrote until her hand was tired, and her tea stone cold, then read it, as a stranger might. It was the beginning of a story. She had even given it a title: 'Value Family'. She felt elated and relieved as though the words had been struggling to get out and all she'd needed to do was to let them flow through her hands.

Value Family. Yes she did. Charlie and Joni and Jim, and Will and the little ones and Renée. And those past, they were also family. And Kevin felt like family too. It was about time she heard from one of them.

Just as she was thinking of them all, the phone rang out, zapping her brain, flooding her with excitement. It was amazing the way that always happened – you thought of someone, they rang. It was a deep connection beyond understanding! A gossamer thread in the fabric of human consciousness!

But it wasn't Charlie or Joni, and it wasn't Kevin either, ringing up to apologise and protest his undying adoration as he usually did after a period of missing her. It was her kind friend Sheelah. Georgie exaggerated her surprise to compensate for the disappointment.

Sheelah wanted to help. 'It's a tough thing picking over your father's rubbish, so close to cremating him,' she said. 'It's part of the mourning process, of course. I felt exactly the same when my mother died.' Georgie imagined Sheelah, with her beaming face and tiny purple plaits and the wireless phone tucked in between her chin and ample shoulder so she could make a list or prepare a meal at the same time. 'Oh, the things I had to do! Cleaning hair out of the hoover, can you imagine? There were her teeth on her side table. And all her lipstick and eyeshadow unused. But I thought, if it goes to charity it's going to help people and d'you know, I honestly felt my mother's spirit agreeing with me. I could feel her in the room, saying "yes".'

'Oh Sheelah, I've been feeling the same sorts of things, and this morning something really strange – oh it's hard to explain...'

'You just can't appreciate what it's like until it happens to you can you?'

'True.'

'Georgie, listen! I've seen the perfect job! Well I've seen a couple actually. '

Georgie congratulated her, assuming Sheelah would find the time and the energy to do both.

'Not for me Gee, for you!'

'But this job's going to take at least another month, Sheelah, maybe two.'

'It's an organic farm. Admin, dealing with customers and veg boxes. Brilliant! You could do that standing on your head. So good ethically too. And the other one's delivering flowers. You just need a clean licence and a car.'

'I'm getting rid of the car, actually. No I can't apply for anything at the mo. I've no head space.'

'I could drive you. It's no trouble.'

It was difficult, but Georgie refused the offer and reversed the direction of the conversation eventually. Sheelah wasn't so good, she said, but she was praying and meditating and chanting, and as she was certain these measures would accomplish something, they probably would. Georgie wished she could do that sort of thing herself, she said, but not so enthusiastically that she might have to.

There was still nothing from Charlie or Joni. No text, no email. Nothing in the inbox but cosmetic surgery and Mediterranean cruises. That's because she'd given away too much information and the internet knew her birthdate. Didn't the internet have enough information? She supposed it was preferable to being ambushed by default Thai brides, though horny sluts and penis enlargement were still slipping through the sieve.

'Chin up Gee!' she told herself. 'Don't let it spoil a lovely day! No news is good news. It means they're both getting on fine.'

Value Family. She cast her eye over her writing, but now the words looked like spider trails, meaningless meandering threads.

She tore it in half and half again, and threw the pieces into Recycle. How could she think of adding any more rubbish to this mess?

'Kill your darlings!' she exclaimed with a sigh, instantly wishing the phrase away. It was bad magic. It reeked of guilt. 'No, please don't. Please don't kill my darlings!' But even in the negative it sounded ominous and worrying, and a twinge of something horrible slipped in behind her smiling face. 'Please keep my darlings alive, alive and well.'

As she passed the muddle on her way out to meet Nick, her eye was caught, as it kept being caught, by a fluttering at the edges of her vision. She turned her head as quickly as she could, hoping speed would catch it out. Her glance fell directly on the locked box.

She didn't know how she knew this, because she had never been all that interested in antiques, but somewhere along the line she'd learnt that the Georgians had loved furniture that was ingenious and surprising – wardrobes that morphed into beds, tables that grew and shrank, bureaux, cabinets and chests with secret drawers and false bottoms in which which you might conceal a fortune.

That's the one, she thought.

NE REGRETTES RIEN

She was slightly early for her rendezvous with Nick – too keen for company, which didn't bode well. To appear nonchalant, she'd dressed down and hadn't bothered to do anything special to her hair or face. He'd already seen her half-naked, she reasoned. But now she was regretting this casualness; being cooped up and conversational with a flatful of ancient relics was making her look as haggard and tired as the relics themselves – as if she'd been infected by their age; and men were, after all, such credulous dunces when it came to assessing women. Nick might have taste and discrimination, but he was still male, hampered and governed by testosterone. At least, she hoped so.

A pile of semi-digested Sunday papers offered nothing to grab her interest, so she was alone with her thoughts while she waited, which wasn't necessarily a good thing. An idle mind let foolish thoughts rush in. Thoughts about Frieda for example, thoughts with a touch of family guilt about them, which she simply didn't want to entertain.

Other solo customers had laptops and tablets and smart phones to distract them from the here to a now elsewhere, while she was apt to slip away and wade about in the there and then.

She had to admit that Will had assessed the situation accurately. In fact, he was 'right': she wasn't progressing at the rate she'd expected to; she was getting too involved. Every little thing – every object, every piece of paper – was connected to some memory, to some feeling, to some idea, some thought that would kick off a train of thoughts. You couldn't just recall something once and that was the end of it. The memory would reverberate for a few days and catch you unawares, demanding that you did something with it. Told someone, for example, wrote it down for example. Otherwise it would go round and round knocking against the insides of your skull, getting louder and louder like an angry child demanding to be heard.

She checked her own basic and not-at-all smart mobile to make sure that it was still on, that she still had signal, and had still received no messages. Though it certainly wasn't boast-worthy equipment, she kept it out on the table, in full view and full earshot, ready. It was her only link to the rest of her life, and somebody might need her. Somebody must need her eventually. If not, that was a wonderful thing, she told herself. It meant she had taught her children to be independent. She had completed her parental task and passed with merit! Though perhaps not distinction.

She stared out of the window at the human aquarium, soothed by the rhythm of swimmers ploughing their liquid furrows like huge multifarious fish. It helped to quell her growing excitement. Excitement might be unhealthy. If her heart beat too fast, it might run out too soon.

She saw Nick before he saw her. She gave him a little wave and he rushed to her table, full of energy. In his open-necked linen shirt, he looked cool and fresh and ready for something. His thinning hair was wet, he smelled citrussy, and there was colour in his face and brightness in his grey eyes. Georgie presumed he'd just had a swim.

'Hello! Am I late? I'm sorry I'm late! I'm not usually late!'

'I'm early,' Georgie blurted, absently pocketing her mobile.

On his initiative their greeting was enhanced by a kissing, which wasn't too embarrassing. This kissing business! It had certainly become the done thing, but Georgie wished there could be some general agreement as to quantity. She let herself be led by Nick, who came in for a second hit which she graciously received, managing to resist saying 'how terribly continental!' though the words were dancing desperately on her tongue. He sat down, they ordered drinks – green tea for Georgie, one of her many anti-cancer measures, expresso for Nick, though he didn't seem to need it. He put his elbows on the table and leant into the space between them.

'So.' He simply stared and smiled for a few moments. 'How are you?'

'I'm very well thanks,' she answered, not entirely truthfully. 'How about you?'

'I'm good,' he nodded. 'I'm good, thank you.'

Georgie's heart sank at his use of the word 'good'. She wondered how much more Los Angeles he'd be speaking. But language changes, she reasoned. Manners change. Otherwise we'd still be grunting and barking at each other, wouldn't we? And clubbing each other on the head and carting each other off by the hair. On impulse she grabbed a hank of her own, as if to see whether it was strong and long enough to support her weight.

She listened to him telling her about his work. His special interest was educational; he was going into schools and showing children how to grow things.

'It's really great getting them to realise it: you plant a seed, you grow a plant. It's incredible. They find it miraculous, which it is of course. And I love working with them. The admin's a bit, you know, and all that side of it,' he made a sour face, 'you've got to tick a few boxes and turn a few somersaults for the authorities, and some of the teachers are a bit wack, but the kids, wow. I think this up-coming generation is fantastic, don't you? My kids are! I bet yours are too. They're very different from us, don't you think? So much more confident. More in touch with their feelings. So much more savvy. They get stuff. Like Rose for instance, she simply decided she was going to spread the word of Shakespeare, got her A levels, no fuss, no nagging, went to Durham, got her degree, got a job. She had it all worked out. She's filming it too. Look her up, she's on Vimeo, Rosie Dendrum, fantastic films. She's acting and directing. And Jenny's going to be the same. She knows what she wants to do, and she's fearless. Really great girls, both of them. I'm so proud. Though I don't know if I deserve so much of the credit.'

As there was enough of a gap, Georgie thought she might

as well get the information she required while the topic was hot.

'No, the credit goes to your wife!' she said, more archly than she meant to. 'At least I presume you're married?'

'Oh God, no. No, no, no. God no.' He started laughing. 'Did you know Shirley?'

Georgie shook her head. He nodded his, and sighed, as if he were about to recount some anecdote involving a pit full of boa constrictors.

'No we got divorced a long time ago. I wouldn't have the boat otherwise.'

There was a thick pause. Georgie felt a hot coming up. She hoped he couldn't see it. She removed her cardigan with acted insouciance, annoyed that it stuck at the elbows so her routine included at least five sideways wriggling movements instead of the usual two.

'I've been talking too much,' he said, adopting a more confidential attitude. 'It's because I've realised what you did for me. It's you I've got to thank for the whole way my life is at the moment. God, if I were still working for Mutual Adversity! It doesn't bear thinking about! So thank you Georgina. Thank you from the bottom of my heart.'

'You're welcome,' Georgie smiled, still struggling with her knitwear. She felt like a fraud as she wasn't at all sure she'd been the one responsible.

'So tell me, how it's going? How long d'you think you're going to be here? Do you know what you're looking for yet?'

An image of Frieda flashed into Georgie's mind, but caution slammed a lid on it, like the snapping shut of a cello case. The box she couldn't open was her only promising find.

'Actually I've got something you might be able to help me with. You're a practical sort of chap. Can you pick locks?'

Nick was taken aback. 'Oho, well I've been accused of many things, he he, but yes, I could probably have a go. Whose door?'

'Not a door; it's an old wooden box. An antique. It's incredibly frustrating. I can hear it rattling but I've absolutely no idea what's inside it. It's firmly locked and you can see where people have tried to get in.'

'What kind of rattling? I mean rattling like silver or rattling like a chess set?'

They both started laughing.

'Yes, it's just like Christmas. No, it sounds like,' she thought for a while, of all the things she'd already imagined, 'postcards and pencil sharpeners. Light inconsequential things. But light things could be consequential couldn't they?'

'Paper money? Share certitificates? House deeds?'

'It's probably a few stamps and tiddleywinks. There's definitely something hard in there.'

'Stamps can be valuable. Think of that film – what was it – *Charade*!'

'Whatever it is, I'm desperate to see inside. And it can't be impossible to open the thing. Will you give it a whirl?' Georgie cringed at herself. Whirl!

'Have you thought of taking it to a locksmith?'

'Yes, of course, but I don't want a stranger with me, in case. Well, because I don't want anyone I don't know to witness whatever discovery I might make. Or not make, which would be just as bad. I'm up the road. You could have a go now if you've nothing else to do.'

She regretted the suggestion even before it was out, as she knew the flat wasn't presentable. But it was too late now; he was eager to help.

While they finished drinking, she asked after mutual acquaintances, in case he had newer news than she did: Jeremy, Chrissy, Nina, Jo, Tim, Annie, Brian – she had to rack her brains for their names; she hadn't seen any of them in over twenty years and recalled only sketchy aspects of personality, habits, looks, jumbled together in abstract collages. 'Petite, shy, dark, lots of jewellery, guitarist boyfriend,' for example, or, 'propped up the bar at the Dug Out, early dreadlock adopter,' or 'bent anaesthetist, blue eyes, donkey jacket' or 'sandals, Genesis tattoo, beautiful feet'.

'Most of my friends are dead, actually,' he said suddenly.

'Oh, no.' Georgie exclaimed. 'Why?'

'Because they died.'

'Oh! We're getting on, I suppose. Well I am.'

She expected him to make the usual remark about not looking as old as she was, and prepared herself to brush it off with flirtatious surprise and bashful thanks. Or at least he might remind her that he was slightly older. Instead he broke some terrible news.

'It was Jon's funeral a couple of months ago.'

It took a blank few moments for Georgie to register who Jon was. She realised with a mental thud of regret.

'Oh, no.'

Jon had been the hilarious one. The one who would start the party and keep it going. The one who wore dazzling Hawaiian shirts before they came back in fashion, and platform heels after they'd gone out; who introduced them to the mescal worm; who played every instrument he touched; who was adorably faithful to an adorable little woman called Minky; and whose dearest ambition was to wallpaper the inside of his house with the entire fifth series one-inch Ordnance Survey map of England and Wales. He had it all except Anglesey. He was always smiling. Always stoned. Georgie sighed. 'I suppose I might have known. What was it? Drink or drugs?' She wondered if he'd ever found Anglesey.

'Yes, drink mainly. He was one of those unrepentant drinkers. Nina told me he was in hospital waiting for a liver transplant when everything started to fail at once and he died within a week. He was drinking right up to the last, she said, whisky from a ginger beer bottle.' He laughed, shaking his head. 'Typical Jon.'

They agreed that Jon had died a happy man, but walking back to the flat, Georgie was left with an uncomfortable feeling she couldn't define. Something to do with her own intimations of mortality, which she didn't mention.

*

She prepared Nick for the state of things before launching him into it. She switched on the light, and as his eyes adjusted he said, 'I see what you mean.' It was not presentable. All along the wall of the front corridor were boxes, cardboard and plastic, large and small, red, green, white and brown. They were piled high on a parade of furniture: two chests of drawers, followed by bedside tables, cabinets, shelves, folding chairs. All the accumulated outside stuff, which should have been hanging from pegs, was bundled and stacked against the opposite wall on a pair of dining chairs: raincoats, hats and scarves, with wellies stuffed underneath. A rusty bicycle was hanging from the wall, draped in cobwebs. Georgie noticed it herself as if for the first time. It made her feel sick, as if she'd tasted the rust.

'It's awfully dark in here, isn't it?' Nick said.

'Yes. It's like a cave. When it was built they thought it was all right for the servants I suppose. But now these dark flats are worth a fortune. Did you ever come here?'

'You did introduce me to your parents once.'

'D'you remember them?'

'They were charming. Your mother was dainty and kind. Pretty too.'

'Was she? I suppose she was. I never realised.'

'Well, why shouldn't she be, with such a daughter?'

Georgie felt the pleasure of this gallantry without commenting. She stored it away like a secret jewel.

'And she loved her roses. And her Jameson's,' he went on.

'Blimey, you knew her better than I did.'

'Your dad was the serious one, wasn't he? But I made him laugh once.'

'They were both fairly serious.'

'Something satirical about Thatcher, probably, before we knew what was coming.'

'I don't remember.'

'But they lived upstairs didn't they? Didn't you have more floors?'

'Our Great Aunt Ruby had the whole house. She lost the

upper floors then Dad sort of continued the trend.' She sighed, regretfully. 'He was good at everything except money. Anyway they partitioned it off. It was Will's idea. Will my brother. I don't think you knew him?'

'It's not ringing a bell.'

'No, he would have been at Oxford when you were around. Winning prizes. Unlike me, doing nothing and going nowhere.' She realised that in her present life she was still doing nothing and going nowhere; Will was still winning prizes, for that matter.

Nick didn't know what to say, and Georgie kicked herself for being so embarrassingly negative. Now he might imagine she was depressed or defeatist or some awful thing.

In the well in the middle of the flat where there used to be stairs, there were half-emptied boxes, and untidy avalanching piles and groupings of every possible category of small object. Toys, files, letters, cards, crayons, ornaments. Bills. Scrap books. Patterns. Half-finished knitting, and half-balls of wool.

'Ooh look at this,' she said, thrusting a paper into his hands: a loose poem of her mother's she had come across with the patterns. 'Talking of not knowing my mum.'

TEAR-OFF SLIP

"I/We
Shall/shall not be….

What?

(I shall be drowned
and no-one will save me).

Coffee, and chit-chat camaraderie
Among the haloed ones
The
Matching-shoes-and-handbag set

Who do the cricket teas;

Whose scruffy sons associate
With scruffy mine.

"Please
Indicate ...."

"The system of timed interviews
Used, as in former years,
To minimise the queues ...."
Will slash will not
And parents will slash will
Not so much as they would like
"Be free to circulate"

Rather, will circle warily
Each master's desk,
As sharks premate;

Or, as the unblinking pike,
In seeming leisure,
Bask by the shallow bank
And wait
To strike.

Nick read it, nodding inscrutably.

'But look,' Georgie explained. '*As sharks premate.* It makes no sense. Is there such a word? Premeditate. She must mean premeditate. So look at the letters you have to insert to make it work. EDIT. It can't be a coincidence. That's a find, don't you think?'

Nick raised an eyebrow, confused.

'Well, she loved crosswords. It's an instruction from beyond the grave, you see.'

'She meant you to find it and edit it?'

'Some such thing.' Georgie replaced the poem on one of the piles. 'It's organised, but not obviously. I do have a system.' She rapidly pointed in various directions. 'Keep, Chuck, Sell, Charity, Recycle, Think About Later.'

She showed him the wooden box and he admired its beauty. 'I can see what it needs,' said Georgie, 'it needs something metallic about this long,' she demonstrated the length of her thumb. 'With some sideways bits sticking out like this.'

Nick smiled, knowledgeably. 'That's a key,' he said. He asked her to find paper clips and tweezers and a hammer, and while she rummaged around in kitchen drawers and bathroom cabinet and toolbox, he put on his spectacles and examined the problem. He asked for some light; she fetched an anglepoise, realising as she arranged it that this had been her very own, a birthday present she had inexplicably desired and loved, then casually defaced by writing Ματθαιοσ on it in indelible ink. She watched Nick in the spotlight, as he shook the box and observed it from all directions, slanting his head this way and that as he peered into the brass hole. He asked for some card. She found him a postcard. He slipped it between the edges of the top and bottom of the box. His hands were practical and strong, but sensitive and articulate too. He asked her to hold the box, jiggled, poked, eased, fiddled. He held his tongue between his teeth as he performed these operations, a fierce wrinkle of concentration appearing above the bridge of his nose.

She didn't see how he managed it, but suddenly, as if it were simple, obvious and straightforward, it was done, it was open!

Disappointment! There was nothing in it but broken parts of itself. A layer of worn green baize and a faded red ribbon.

'It's a writing box!' Georgie said. It smelt of ink and mouldy paper.

Nick read the brass lock fitting. 'Patent Bramah. Well, that's why you couldn't open it. I've heard of Bramah – he was a genius. He invented the flush toilet, you know, in seventeen something or other. The lock's probably the best thing about it, and now I've decommissioned it. Well, it must have already been broken actually.'

He handed back the tools, and then looked at the card: a painting of the Grand Canal. 'Turner,' he said. 'Painted at about the same time as this box was made I should think.' He held it out to her, but as she took it, he wouldn't let go. 'We should've gone to Venice – you and I – together,' he said. His expression conveyed a disturbing complexity of humour and world-weariness.

'Ah, "should have". That's a construction I never use,' Georgie said, too fast for her own good. He would misunderstand. She shouldn't have said it. 'It doesn't help,' she went on, in an effort to undo the damage. 'Best not to dwell on alternative histories. Because one thing's for sure, you can't change the past. No. You start from now. Onwards and ever upwards!'

There was such a lull in conversation that the phrase seemed to echo. Long enough for Georgie to realise that you can't always go on. You can't always go up. There comes a point where you descend. There comes a point where you reach a wall.

She offered him a drink but he had to be off. He kissed her once only this time. They didn't arrange to meet again, but Nick said he'd see her soon, and she agreed, so that wasn't too bad, was it, she thought.

His going made her solitude all the more palpable. The stillness and quiet of it. The clicking and ticking. Her disconnection from the faint sounds of life elsewhere. He'd brought energy and warmth and movement into the grave.

Cave, she meant. Cave.

She started humming, to move a few molecules of air and lighten the atmosphere. Full fathom five thy father lies. No, not that one, Gee.

Somehow she was still holding the postcard, as if a wiser part of her thought it was important. She looked at the painting, its delicious liquid gold and blue, the busy little figures, the cirrus clouds. She turned it over and read what she'd written – what her father had read.

The date was two years ago, April 2009: *Dear Dad, We're staying in a v reasonable tiny flat 5 mins from the Rialto, eating fresh fish and veg from the market & drinking vivid orange Aperol and Prosecco! Yum! Tons of people everywhere simply stare and smile, including us. Weather glorious, sparkling. Take care, love G xx* Kevin had added his name.

The postcard failed to mention the arguments in the market over what to buy and who would cook it, or the sheer volume of Aperol they'd drunk, and how much it had cost, and the hangovers they'd endured afterwards, or, of course, Georgie's own local weather system, which had not been glorious. Those were innocent days, before cancer and everything, when she still had a dad to write postcards to.

She wondered what had gone wrong between her and Kevin, and what had gone wrong between her and Nick – just now, twenty-five minutes ago, and before, twenty-five years ago.

She put the postcard on top of Think About Later and surveyed the scene. Three weeks' solid work and she'd gained almost no ground in her march towards solving the problem. She'd found nothing worth finding. Will would be coming before long. She wondered if she could force herself to admit that he was right and let him win. Really they should get professional help. They were free to make their own decisions; did they need to honour the wishes of permanently absent relations? Could she let go of her wish to please her father, now nothing could please him any more?

The last time she'd seen him had been there in that very room. She had tended him his last two days and most of the last night as well, with Joni's help, and then Will's. Charlie had already said his goodbyes.

To think about it was almost unbearable. Georgie wished she could do the whole thing again, better. She'd ask better questions. She wished she'd asked better questions. Why had she been so dim? So dumb?

'Why didn't I ask better questions?' she asked herself aloud. She was answered by the sigh of a curtain, and the creak of a floorboard in the flat above.

*

'Do you want water or do you want to move?'

'Nnnn.'

'Do you want water?'

'Nnnn.'

'Do you want me to move you?'

'Nnnn.'

'I can't tell if you're saying yes or no. Can you squeeze my hand if you mean yes?'

A faint tightening of pressure.

'Can I do anything for you?'

Squeeze.

'Are you in pain?'

Nothing.

'Are you thirsty?'

After a pause he croaked. She put the cup to his lips, tipping it gently as he sipped. His head flopped back against the stack of pillows when he could manage no more.

'Would you like some music?'

There was no answer.

'Would you like me to leave you in peace?'

'Nnnn.'

'You'd like me to stay with you?'

She remembered something that had happened when she was five months pregnant, the first time. Jim was away. She'd been visiting Bristol and had taken a cycle ride on her old bike. She'd gone too long without water or food. Agassi was winning Wimbledon. She had come back and sat on the settee and fainted. When she regained consciousness her father was sitting beside her holding her hand. She was wet. Her body had leaked. A doctor had arrived, taken her temperature and told them to give her sweet drinks. It was thought she might lose the pregnancy. But she didn't lose it. She kept it, oh yes, she hung on to that pregnancy with all her might. She'd felt faint and frightened but just the touch of her father's hand had kept her in the world.

Now she held her father's hand in one of her own, and stroked it with the other. It was a dead weight, already stiff and shiny, but still alive just then. Still alive.

'Nnnn.'

'Are you trying to say something?' *Geegee you bloody idiot, what do you think he's trying to do?*

Squeeze.

'What's it about?'

No answer.

'Oh. Um. Is it something you need?'

No answer. Still, no answer. Quiet breathing, a deep frown.

'Is it information? Something you want me to know?'

Squeeze.

'Is it about...?' Georgie sighed. It could be about anything. Perhaps he was worried what would happen if he died.

'Is it about the house?'

'Nnnn!' He was angry with that suggestion. Impatient. Georgie felt hurt.

'Is it about people?'

Squeeze.

'Do you want to see Will? He's coming. Will's coming, Dad, he'll be here later this evening. He's on his way. Will's on his way.'

Larry's breathing became faster and more laborious.

'Who is it about then? Is it about you?'

Squeeze.

'But it's not anything you need. So. Um. Is it about your life?'

Squeeze.

'I love you Daddy. You've been a wonderful dad. I'm going to miss you.'

Squeeze. 'Nnnn.'

'Is it that you love us?'

Squeeze.

Again his breathing became louder. She hadn't got the answer.

'I don't know what it is! What can I do for you?'

'Sh sh sh sh sh.'

He opened his eyes, pleading, contrite. Georgie shook her head, bewildered. 'Well, you've got nothing to apologise for, so you can't be saying sorry.' She stated it as a fact, as part of her reasoning, part of her reaching for a different explanation, the correct explanation, the ten out of ten, the one that would win a golden star.

'They. They. They. They.'

'It's all right Daddy, don't worry.'

She thought of saying 'everything's going to be fine', but she couldn't bear to lie to him. Instead she said, 'I hope you feel better soon.'

She was sure he had tried to say sorry. When she dared to remember it, she was certain. But what could he possibly be sorry for? Something she couldn't bear to pursue, even in her imagination.

She poured herself a glass of organic low-sulphite red wine, to go with a small square of organic fair trade 85% chocolate. These might help to stop the cancer coming back, she hoped. If not, *tomorrow's tangle to ye winds resign!*

She looked at the mess. So there was nothing in the antique box. No, that would have been too obvious. Whatever she was meant to find was somewhere else in this jumble of bits and bobs and odds and sods. She would have to carry on searching. It wasn't about honouring her father's wishes, anyway. It was about understanding them.

DRINK IN MODERATION

Oh frabjous day, callooh callay! a) School was breaking up for the Easter holidays, b) She was meeting Fi at the Duck, and there was an exceptionally high chance of Matthaios going there, c) a and b were enough.

She kicked her grey skirt against the bedroom wall, and after it her tie, blouse, low heel lace-ups and socks. She would never wear that tie again! It had been strangling her for five years, and over those years, in a project of quiet and steady rebellion, she had pulled out its threads, sometimes a red one, sometimes a black one, until nothing but a few bits of warp remained. She retrieved it and casually dropped it in the bin, wrapped herself in a dressing gown and went to have a bath, softly singing the songs they'd murdered on the bus home: 'Daisy, Daisy...'

Frieda had given them a sky on the bathroom ceiling, with bulbous clouds and golden cherubs and a seagull. Georgie did her best to ignore it. She had to admit the girl could paint. In fact, if she were being really honest, she had to admit she rather admired it. The cherub peeping above the mirrored cabinet seemed to be winking at her, and made her feel smiley inside.

By setting the chair at the right angle and standing on it, she could view and assess her nakedness. 'Fat!' was the disappointing verdict. The cherub agreed. But there was nothing to be done, and anyway, she was becoming womanly, and becoming a woman who preferred the pleasure of food to whatever pleasure there must be in being thin. Pippa Burchill, in her opinion, had gone too far in the opposite direction – you could see her ribs. She envied Debbie Needham's kind of slim, but she was actually pleased with the roundness of her own breasts and the pink sensitivity of her nipples and the curve of her hips, though boys didn't appreciate those things. She longed for a boy to kiss her everywhere. She could imagine so clearly how stupendously gorgeous it was going to be!

She studied her face. It was a shame about the specs; she did look better without them, but seeing was obviously more important than being looked at. She refused to wear make-up. Make-up was traitorous to the female sex, she believed. It meant sucking up to men, which was not on. Skirts and high heels likewise, though she allowed platforms because boys wore them too. The spots were retreating, but she noticed with horror that a wrinkle was forming underneath each eye. It made her heart sink, that she should be ageing at fifteen! She didn't think any of her friends had wrinkles yet. And now she regretted her hair. Her fringe was too short. She kept trying to grow it, but kept getting annoyed with it flopping over her face into whatever book she might want to read.

She decided on the lavender coloured cord flares and purple gingham smock over a grey flare-sleeved cotton top.

And now she was ready there was nothing to do but wait.

Thursday

Dear darling heart-stoppingly gorgeous Matthew, I may well be about to see you and hope we can talk of serious things, intense, poetic, profound things. I wish you'd bloody replied to my wanking letter. Wank is the worst word I can think of, although wanking isn't the worst thing. Bloody's nothing – like damn. Fuck is as bad as bloody used to be say 10 years ago. Balls bugger and sodomy are not as bad as that even. Bestiality etc is worse, but you can't spit it out. I think cunt is a horrible word, clit is too hard to say and cock is base. I don't mind prick. The worst possible expression I can think of is 'Jesus wanks'. I still love Jesus in a way because I remember how I did when I was little, but he has to be beautiful. So does Mary. I wouldn't feel the same if he had a big red nose or squinty eyes. Which is superficial and vain and not fair. I sometimes wonder if the gospels are right and I'll go to Hell. What if what happens after you die is whatever you expect to happen?

MENU for after life

1. Eternal happiness – a loving ecstatic embrace of all loving human souls including my family if they're dead.

2. Eternal orgasm – extreme sensuous and intense pleasure, with someone you adore.

3. Eternal contentment – a soothed mind, pleasant appreciation of all things in the universe, and that it is all right, means something etc

4. Life like this on earth but without any horribleness. Keeping all senses but only feeling a variety of pleasant and agreeable things – beautiful music, delicious food, clean sheets, soft cosy clothes, rapturous smells. Keeping all intelligence but mind serving a fruitful purpose and for the good of everyone. Keeping all the physical abilities of a human, but muscles used constructively and regularly and only for good. Plus the acquirement of a few extra abilities like flying, staying underwater without drowning, seeing into the past. Other people but only being kind and interesting.

5. Perpetual excitement in anticipation of an event, because usually that's more enjoyable than the event itself. It wouldn't necessarily be frustrating if you didn't realise the event wasn't actually going to happen.

I was going to order number 1 and feel noble in preferring that to number 2, but actually I'd rather like number 3. I wouldn't mind being satisfied as to the purpose of the universe. In fact I should be most interested to know, please. I can't help thinking that anything eternal would be boring. I'm bored of this now. And Heaven isn't a fair idea is it if some people go to Hell? Bad people can't help being bad. I'm pathetically nervous. Oh I hope with all my heart I have something wonderful to write on the next page!

She wanted to leave the house without anyone noticing that she was dressed up, but what do you suppose, she was intercepted by the ever abundant Frieda and her despicable compliments.

'You look nice,' she said, as expected.

'Thank you,' said Georgie, awkwardly covering a wave of disgust.

Frieda cocked her head to one side, and looked her up and down in a most disconcerting and intrusive way. That was the moment when Georgie noticed a flash of gold at her throat, and saw, instead of a cross or crucifix, a six-pointed star. Confusion swamped her. It might as well have been a swastika – she would have been less surprised. Immediately she thought of how she and Will had teased her, scouring her memory for anything stupid they might have said.

Frieda was staring at her expectantly, waiting for an answer. Georgie hadn't been paying attention. She listened to the mental echo of her question: something about make-up.

'Um. I don't wear make-up.'

'Nor do I, except for meeting special people.' Frieda made a face as if 'meeting' meant something rude. Georgie went red and looked away. 'Let me help you with it,' she went on. 'You have not enough care, feminine care.'

'No, honestly.'

'From Lawrence, yes, you have the male side, but your mother is too busy with Will.'

Lawrence? Nobody called her father Lawrence – not even Maureen. The sound of it made Georgie cringe, as though Frieda had a special intimacy or preferential rights, as though she'd stolen a piece of him for herself, a deep part that Georgie didn't even know about. She wanted to feel resentful, but was still upset about the Star of David. Perhaps it was just a piece of pretty jewellery.

'At the same time Will wishes more from his father,' Frieda went on, twisting her mouth as though she could hardly contain her amusement. 'You each have what the other wants. It is a dilemma. If only you could swap.'

Georgie hadn't a clue what she was on about. 'We don't believe in make-up,' she said, abruptly extracting herself from the encounter. 'I'm eating at Felicity's!' she howled to anyone who might be listening, and made her escape.

Fi was wearing lipstick and eye-shadow and mascara, and something glittery on her cheekbones.

'I'm being ironic,' she explained sheepishly, though Georgie hadn't accused her of anything. 'You're letting the side down – me and all other girls and women,' she was thinking, but she couldn't possibly say anything nasty. She was painfully disappointed. If her own second-best friend was going to betray the female sex what hope was there? It was too bad that Fi was pretty. She knew how to dress too. Under her cream-coloured furry textured jacket she was wearing a shiny black dress, and tiptoeing on shiny black-and-white platform shoes. She'd done something interesting to her hair too, to make it curly and springy. Georgie's only hope was to be the clever one, the daring one, the funny one – though none of these qualities helped much with getting boys. Pretty trumped it all.

'I'm only enhancing what's there. You wouldn't sell your cleverness short, would you? You'd try and get top marks. Anyway,' Fi whispered, as they entered the pub, 'you don't look eighteen, and I do. So I'll get the drinks.'

Georgie submitted to her logic, but felt humiliated. She fumbled in her pockets and handed her a fifty-pence piece. 'Snake bite,' she said.

'A pint or a half?'

Georgie looked at her as if to say, 'are you incredibly thick?'

Fi brought back a pint for Georgie and a dry Martini for herself and they sat with their backs to the wall and a good view of the door to the lounge bar. Georgie told Fi about Frieda and Fi commiserated. She said she used to have an au pair who hoovered and babysat for them sometimes, so she understood.

'It's all right, she'll go away eventually,' she reassured her. 'Does she flirt with your father? Or your brother?'

They were pissed by this time, and laughed too loudly.

'Actually you know, I think she's from Lesbos. She keeps,' Georgie tensed her body and screwed up her face, 'touching me!'

They agreed that this was exceptionally revolting.

'It *is* flirting, and she even touches my mother!'

Fi went to the bar for a second round of drinks.

Georgie didn't want to think about Frieda any more. She took advantage of the gap in conversation to launch the subject of boys. Georgie loved necks, shoulders and tallness. Fi loved small bottoms and strong chests. They both loved wickedness, artistic talent, Levis and the smell of Brut. They hated boys to be keen or wet. They agreed that they would marry for money, or it wasn't worth marrying at all. Georgie said she wanted hundreds of children and Fi said she'd like two cats and a dog. Georgie said that owning a cat or a dog would disqualify a boy whatever else he might have.

'Number one, he's got to make you laugh,' she said.

'Number two, he's got to make you come,' Fi responded, slamming down her glass like a judge's hammer and squealing with delight.

Georgie heard the pub door swing open, and her eyes strayed over to see if Matthew was arriving at last. It wasn't him, it was a woman. But her disappointment turned into alarm as she realised that the woman was Frieda – a glowing, eyelashy, painted Frieda – looking over her shoulder, and simpering.

'Oh I don't believe it, that's her!' Georgie hissed. 'What, has she followed me?' She bent over her glass, hoping to make herself invisible.

Fi gasped. 'Crikey, she's ever so beautiful. I see why you can't stand her. And that's your dad isn't it?'

Georgie looked up. 'Oh my everlasting God, what's he doing here? I'm going to be Uncle Dick.' Fi gave her a face full of alarm. 'Get me out of here!' Their fear dissolved into helpless giggles as they headed for the Ladies.

Georgie sat on the loo seat, wondering how she was going to escape without being noticed. 'Was my mum with them?'

Fi said she hadn't seen.

'I don't hate her, Fi. Not hate. I think she's Jewish, you know. I don't know how.'

Fi told Georgie to wait and nipped back out. Georgie looked up and around. High up in the wall was a tiny window, decorated with spiders' webs. She wondered if she could fit through it. The idea made her chuckle, and the chuckle made her want to chuck, that and the smells of urine and mould.

'I have to report that Matthaios has arrived,' Fi said on her return. She'd brought the drinks with her and handed Georgie the rest of her pint.

'You're joking! He's here and I can't go out because of my bloody dad! That is the absolute end of the world.'

'Your dad's gone outside. Your mum's not here.'

Fi suggested hiding in the public bar, then they could lure Matthew and his friends to join them.

'Good plan,' said Georgie.

She ended up waiting alone, as Fi went to get the boys; it was too risky for Georgie to be in the lounge bar because her father or Frieda might come through again at any moment. She sidled up to the window and, sure enough, there were Frieda and her father, sitting on the terrace wall, huddled in coats, avidly talking. She didn't like how close they were to each other. She didn't like how they were copying each other's gestures, and how her father's smile was shy and apologetic. He was probably practising German, she thought, and embarrassing himself. She wondered what on earth it could be about, and why her mother wasn't there. It was Friday; her mother had choir practice or the Women's Institute or flower arranging or something. Perhaps they were talking about the photographs he was going to take of her. It gave her a feeling of hurt and panic she couldn't understand or articulate.

She ignored the looks she was getting from strangers, she ignored the chatter and shouting and laughter that excluded her, and focused on her booze. She'd swigged it by the time Fi came back and was beginning to feel rather pissed off, until she saw Matthew and his mate Rowan following behind.

The rest of the evening went a bit blurry. She drank another pint, at least one, she was sure of that. And they laughed a lot. And Matthew talked to her. He was very interested in who Frieda was, and what her dad was doing out with her alone, nudge nudge wink wink, and all four of them, or at least two of them, thought it would be hilarious to sing *Deutschland Deutschland über alles* and *O Tannenbaum* and to Nazi salute and goose-step along the dark streets of Stratford.

Matthew had gone. Fi had gone. Georgie was alone with Rowan.

'I'm staying here for a bit,' she told him. She sat down on the pavement. The street was whirling. She lay on her back and looked up at the black sky, full of moving stars. She could feel the hard damp tarmac against her shoulders and wet seeping through her hair.

'Come on, I've got to get you home.' A kind male voice.

'You go home. I'm going to sleep.' Oh no, oops here it comes, aurghaurggh, arf, argh, arf. She turned over and puked on Rowan's shoes. How ghastly, how miserable, yet how ordinary it was, for sour soup to be gushing spastically from her mouth, for tears to be squirting from her eyes and her back to be shuddering in cold agony. Her body was doing it, not herself. She spat the last of it into the gutter.

'That's better,' she told the shoes.

Next she was saying goodnight to a shoulder and an ear. Next she was in her bed. Next she was lurching for the bathroom. Next it was morning, and her head felt like a dried-out coconut, in searing pain.

Her father didn't summon her until the afternoon. She was struggling through a late breakfast of ricicles when he popped his head round the kitchen door and said, 'I want a word with you in my study.' I want a word with you. The phrase alone was knicker-wetting. She'd heard too many teachers and other people's parents using it. She didn't think she'd done anything so wrong, apart from getting home late. Perhaps it was nothing to worry about. She emptied her remaining mush down the disposal unit and laid the bowl and spoon in the dishwasher. Perhaps he was planning to explain what he and Frieda were working on.

No such luck. She knew from the tone of his 'come in' what kind of punishment lay ahead.

'Georgina. I'm disappointed in you.' He spoke quietly, mildly, as if he were telling her about a day in the garden, which made his meaning strike all the more deeply and with a keener force. 'Actually the word "disgusted" is nearer the mark. Ignorance you can be forgiven for, but not for deliberate stupidity. Not for unkindness. That I simply will not have. I thought better of you.'

'I'm not unkind,' Georgie protested, in true innocence. 'How am I unkind?'

'You know perfectly well. This nonsense about the war. What on earth are you thinking?'

Yes, that was a bit mean, but it was Will as much as me, she thought. In fact, he had most definitely started it. She began to say so, but stopped herself, as she wouldn't be believed. Will was better at hiding his bad behaviour.

What she'd really like to say was: 'What the hell were you doing in the pub alone with Frieda?' She felt sure that his wrong-doing exceeded her own. Actually, she'd like to say: 'What the fuck were you doing with the fucking au pair last night?' but she couldn't mention it in any way, because she shouldn't have been there to witness it.

'I want a lock on my door,' she said quietly, looking away from her father's sad face.

'No.'

'I want privacy.' She said this more firmly, but still without meeting her father's gaze.

'In this house we trust each other. We knock. That's the way we've always done it, and that's the way we'll continue to do it. We don't need to change anything to accommodate Frieda. How would she feel? As though we didn't trust her.'

'Will has a lock.' The undeniability of this fact emboldened Georgie to look up again, to confront him directly. She felt her mouth turning down at the corners.

'You know perfectly well that's because he has an outside door.'

A flame of fury shot through Georgie's guts. Why should Will have the outside door? He always takes preference! He always comes first! He always gets away with every possible thing and I never do and it's absolutely bloody not fair!

'Well Frieda is an OUTSIDE PERSON!' she yelled, turning and leaving without excusing herself or saying goodbye. She had never shouted at him before.

She slammed the study door and stamped up the stairs,

knowing she was behaving like a child, yet also knowing that it was impossible for her to behave any other way. It was like being sick or catching the giggles – her body was doing it of its own accord. She slammed her bedroom door too, though less effectively because the carpet was too close to it; then she dragged the dressing table against it to bar intruders, its mirror swinging to and fro and knocking painfully against her chin. The music box which held her jewellery – plastic necklaces and rings, leather wristband and clay beads – toppled to the floor and part of its spinning ballet dancer's arm snapped off.

She threw herself on the bed, and lay there dry-eyed, though her mind was boiling, by turns mortified with shame and petrified with rage, as she desperately justified herself, and hated Will, and despised and loathed Frieda, and wanted to shoot something or throw something or shout at someone. Fuck you all! Fuck the whole bloody arseholing miserable shitty cunty bollocksy sodding bleeding rubbishy wanky tripey lot of you!

She thought of putting a fist through the cello, but didn't want to hurt her knuckles. Instead, she moved the dressing table back to its original position, gathered up her baubles and glued back the ballet dancer's arm. She sat quietly in the light of her anglepoise and wrote.

VALUE FAMILY

In the vast waters of Georgie's structureless solitude, Will's visit was going to be the first stepping stone. The next would be a visit from Sheelah, and after that the job would be finished and she'd be safe on the other side of it.

How slowly time passes when you want it to pass! It reminded her of waiting when their father was dying. Will's arrival then had made everything seem less frightening and more as usual; their father's death had become a shared burden – a burden somehow more than halved. Now she was hoping for a similar effect – Will's simply being there would bring a different perspective into the building, as if he might open a hidden window and clear away the gloom and the clammy atmosphere of the place. He wouldn't be sensitive to its weirdness. He wouldn't feel oppressed by unidentifiable smells emanating from nowhere, or hear voices whispering unintelligibly in his ear, or wake in fearful sweats feeling observed, or notice little darting movements happening in its corners and darknesses. He wouldn't notice because none of it was actually happening, was it? No. It was all the invention of her own tired mind, her own silly nonsense. More than that, he would straighten out her confusion over Frieda. His memories would be more accurate and more prosaic than her own. He was sure to demonstrate the folly of her peculiar hunches. Her common sense was hoping that Will could persuade her uncommon sensitivity to stop fretting about it and go home.

He rang to let her know that he was planning to come with Renée and the children too, and they were going to spend the rest of the week in Wales and make a little holiday of it, so now, with elation and dread in equal measure, she looked afresh at her surroundings as though through Renée's eyes, and began again to rearrange and polish things in preparation for the visit, knowing, however, that it was hopeless trying to achieve a standard that would meet with Renée's approval, and aiming merely to prevent an instant repulsion.

Although she felt uncertain about Will's motivation in bringing Renée – or, more accurately, about Renée's motivation – she was sure to enjoy their stay. As she waited in Arrivals, she vowed to see the best in her sister-in-law and would even refrain from being a typical irritating aunt, unless Renée gave her permission, although it was going to be difficult as she simply doted on the little ones. She wanted little ones of her own, was the truth. How strange that little ones for her would be grandchildren. The generations were already out of synch.

'Henri! You big boy!' she squawked as she spotted the compact foursome emerging from customs. 'You'll be as tall as your Daddy soon, won't you? Tu es si grand, un si grand garçon, n'est ce pas?' She hadn't seen the children in at least two years because Will had come alone to Larry's funeral.

'Hello Auntie Georgina,' said Henri, as if he'd been rehearsed. He ducked from Georgie's touch.

'Et quel âge as-tu maintenant?'

'I have six years old.'

Eve was sitting glumly in a push chair, swaddled in a tiny red duffle coat, her fair hair scraped to one side and held with a slide. 'Bonjour Eve,' Georgie trilled, to little effect.

Renée offered both cheeks one after the other, accompanied by a frozen little smile. Her skin was smooth and cool like ivory, Georgie thought, though perhaps less cruel. In comparison to Renée's efficient impeccability, she always felt herself to be scruffy and untucked. The coiffure, the couture, the maquillage were all spotless and effortless. Her clothes said 'quality', confidently but not too loudly, not in any vulgar way. Renée was going to be too sexy for the second-hand 2CV, Georgie realised with an inner qualm. She wondered where on earth you could find such stylishly cut casual wear. Not in any shops she herself frequented, certainly. This was clothing in a different league, supported by a salary she couldn't conceive of. How could such elegant little pumps bear any walking or carrying; how could anyone keep everything so clean and uncreased, and at the same time be in charge of two children with the usual children's fidgetiness and slobberiness; how could anyone maintain such a high shine up close to infant impulses and excretions? Will had always fallen for these distant foreign beauties, and usually had the means to secure them. In contrast, he looked a little ruffled from the trip, slightly greasy and sleepless, though it would only have taken an hour and a half from door to door. He let go of both suitcases to give Georgie a proper bear hug. 'Ah little sis! I don't see you often enough!'

'I know. We mustn't always meet at funerals.'

'Let's have a look at you!' He held her at arms' length and studied her face. She was grinning absurdly, she couldn't help her feelings overflowing. 'Fully functional!' he said, 'That's what we like to see.' He frowned. 'How are you though, Gee, really? Well?'

'Fine. I miss Charlie and Joni and the house is a mess, that's all.'

She knew that his concern was about cancer, and dismissed it with a smile and a shrug. She offered to push the pushchair, to which Eve submitted after the slightest fuss. When they got to the car, Renée offered to sit in the front seat, leaving Georgie and Will to manage the luggage and the push chair and the children. Renée adjusted her limbs to fit the available space and snapped the seatbelt across her chest, then laid her left hand ready on the dash board, as if it might control the car. She kept it there for the entire drive, answering Georgie's queries with monosyllables. Will, busy in the back and deaf to their conversation, could contribute nothing, so little was said until Georgie dropped them off at the hotel. Renée, appealing to Will, said she needed longer to recover from the trip and would prefer to spend the evening there and come to the flat the next day. Of course, they wanted to take the opportunity of some time alone, wining and dining while the little ones were in bed. This was their well-earned holiday, after all.

To round off her evening, Will intercepted Georgie's presents for the children, so Renée could make sure they were suitable.

'Will?' Georgie said, before she left them. 'You know how when you start sorting things out and tidying things up they get worse to begin with?'

Will faked concern. 'Gee, what are you telling me?'

She said she'd see him tomorrow.

They arrived next day, all dressed in different outfits, rested, refreshed and ready for lunch. Georgie beckoned them up the muddled corridor and noticed Renée casting a cool eye over its contents as she advanced, ahead of Will and the children. Something caught her interest. It was a discoloured drop-leaf table half-hidden beneath a box full of games equipment and curtains. She stopped and examined what she could see of it, perhaps imagining how it would look restored and French polished, how it might grace the drawing room, or how much it would fetch at auction.

'Mahogany?' she asked, addressing Will.

'That belonged to our Great Aunt Ruby,' said Georgie. 'Our grandfather's sister, on Dad's side. All the oldest and best things came to us through that route, didn't they Will? Including the flat.'

She led them to the larger and fuller of the two front rooms and opened the door, feeling a quiver of anxiety now Renée and Will were actually present, in case they were about to discover something valuable or interesting, something she'd missed.

They stood in horror, surveying the scene. Renée gasped, wrinkling her nose at the strange smell that greeted them, the sweet musty dusty smell of history. Will sneezed. The bed Georgie had once slept in was turned and upended. Boxes were piled onto shelves and other bits and pieces of furniture. A person-width gap led to the window.

'I see what you mean,' Will said.

'They used to have more space,' Georgie explained to Renée. Her heart started racing as she scrutinised the medley from yet another new perspective. Just as she feared, Renée spotted something intriguing, registering her discovery with an emphatic 'Ah!'. She removed a glove and gingerly advanced, while Georgie looked along her beeline towards the dull glint of metal poking out of a box. Renée plucked the thing from its neighbouring items with a fastidious finger and thumb. It was a fork.

'Plaquée,' she said, quickly replacing it. The word sounded rude.

Georgie's relief was audible.

She finished the tour by ushering them towards the old stairwell, and showing what she'd achieved in the way of organising everything into piles. 'And this one's for immediate dumping,' she finished, triumphantly pointing out a collection so small as to make no difference one way or the other. 'I'm finding such treasures!' she enthused. She selected the vintage collapsible barking dog as an example, showing it to Henri and Eve, who were unimpressed in spite of her vocal contributions.

'Toys need to be in the original box,' Renée complained. She extended a slender hand towards the object, and Georgie gave it to her. 'It has been played with.'

Georgie agreed.

'It is broken, and not very clean.'

'True. It's not for putting in your mouth is it?' Georgie joked, amusing nobody. 'Speaking of which, let's have lunch! Then we can work out how to proceed.' Will and Renée shared a meaningful glance. It somehow suggested they'd already worked out how to proceed.

The kitchen was cramped and crowded, but with a little imagination in jigsawing differently sized mats, and a little effort in seeking out appropriately sized chairs, Georgie had managed to arrange five places at the dining table. Will presented her with a bottle of Bordeaux and Georgie thanked him and asked him to do the honours while she brought food to the table.

'Bit strange to drink with fish, but who's complaining?' he said, cheerily averting any such comment.

'That's perfect for me,' Georgie said. 'I'm afraid I can't justify white wine these days. It doesn't even contain flavonoids.'

'Flavonoids,' Renée said.

'They're good for cancer,' Georgie explained. 'I mean, good against cancer.'

'I hope you can justify champagne!' Will said. 'We bought some duty free as a present. For you, for another time.'

Georgie declared that champagne required no justification and thanked them again, effusively, noting Will's diversionary response to the rude word she'd used, and vowing not to spoil anything by saying it again.

He rinsed and dried and filled three wine glasses. She was surprised that he also poured a little into Henri's plastic cup, mixing it with some bottled water he produced from their enormous travel bag. Unfortunately the children didn't want to join them and would eat none of what she had prepared with them in mind.

'They don't even like bread?' she asked Renée, as Will distributed raisins and bananas and crisps, and equipped them with plastic plates and plastic entertainment.

'Don't worry, we can give them some proper food later,' Renée assured her.

While the grown ups ate, the children sat on the kitchen floor with their snacks and an iPad each, so the adult conversation was accompanied by recorded exclamations and comic jingles. Georgie wondered whether her gift of books had been deemed suitable. She opened a second bottle of wine. Again Renée and Will shared a glance. Georgie chose to ignore it. She reminded herself that it was rare for the family to be together, it was an occasion to relish and cherish. She looked fondly down at Henri. He was growing more and more like Charlie, and it gave her an exquisite pang to recall how her son had looked as a little boy – a little boy she could carry in her arms, who would hold her hand. Who needed her. Henri's seriousness, his focus and determination, covered shyness in the same way that Charlie's used to. He stroked the iPad with practised dexterity, and every so often leant over to help his little sister. Eve, too, was cute, in her sulkiness.

'They get on well,' Georgie said, dreamily.

'Oh yes,' Will agreed. 'We do what Mum and Dad did; we've never let Eve take any of Henri's special attention.'

Georgie queried his assertion with a confused glance.

'It's fairer, seeing as the younger one knows no better; so you get no jealousy,' Will explained.

Renée smiled complacently, but the information and all that it implied gave a severe jolt to Georgie's equanimity.

'Henri looks just like Charlie at his age,' she said, trying not to betray any hint of outrage. 'Isn't heredity amazing!'

'Oh not at all,' Renée said. 'Henri looks like my mother. He is the spitting image.'

'In one respect he's dissimilar I hope,' Georgie said, again arousing no humour.

'Eve too looks like my father, and a bit like myself I think,' Renée continued.

'She is as beautiful as you,' said Will fondly, and Renée's lips twitched into what was meant to be a smile.

Georgie had reached a limit of tolerance. She wasn't going to let Renée hog the genes as well as everything else. 'Eve looks like you, Will, with her dark eyes and her curls. His hair was much wavier when he was little,' she told Renée. 'Mum kept one of your locks, Will, did you know? It's in there somewhere.' She flung out an arm in the general direction of Think About Later.

'Oh that is disgusting!' Renée exclaimed, still smiling.

A sip of wine quelled Georgie's surge of indignation. She regretted mentioning her mother's sentimental gesture. It was secret, precious and private, not to be judged, least of all by someone of Renée's sensibility. 'So how are we going to get on with the job?' she said to Will.

'A trip to the dump?'

'There's not enough for that yet. We might as well wait until there's a car full. We don't want to waste any more of the earth's resources carting the stuff about.'

'I'm sure we can make it up to a car full. And there's certainly some obvious stuff in the corridor. Do any of us play hockey or cricket any more?'

The suggestion gave Georgie a mouse squeak of anxiety, but she agreed, as she could think of no reasonable objection, though it occurred to her that Henri or Eve might one day take to sport. Sweat pricked her brow, and she felt her shirt clinging to her back. She took off her cardigan, worried that now her choice of deodorant contained no nasty chemicals it didn't work very well, and that mixed in with the tea tree and geranium might be traces of lizard or rhino. Her face was glowing; she was sure she looked ridiculous.

'But before we get on with that, Gee, Renée has a proposal.'

Georgie looked at Renée. Renée looked at Will. 'You explain,' she said.

Here it comes, thought Georgie – what they've been planning and discussing for me behind my back. She'd suspected something of the kind, and felt herself resisting before she had any idea what they were going to say. 'Well it's simple, really. There's no point in selling while the market's so depressed. It can only get better.'

'I disagree with that for starters. Nobody knows what the market's going to do.'

'It can't get worse.'

'I disagree. The whole system could collapse at any moment. Banks could fail. Bombs could fall. Hurricanes. Floods. Nobody knows whats going to happen.'

'Gee, our idea is to invest a small amount in it to make it a really lovely place to live in and let it out until things have improved. We wouldn't ask you to contribute, but we'd have to get back our investment. Say we put in fifteen grand. We'd collect rent until we broke even, allowing for inflation and loss of interest of course, then share it after that. It would probably only take a year. Maybe two. Depending on how much work needs to be done.'

Georgie knew her answer and didn't know how to say it

politely, as she'd had very little practice with this particular word: 'No.' She uttered it without frills. 'No.' It was quite easy, after all.

'Well, think about it. We're not proposing to make any extra money over you. It's just to bide our time. And we couldn't let it as it is.'

'No.' Georgie shook her head. 'No.' She was getting the hang of it.

'Gee. What don't you like about the idea? You can't say no without even considering it.'

'I can say what I fucking like, thank you.'

'Georgina, really! The children!' Will chided facetiously. Renée made it clear that she was shocked, but said nothing.

'Oh, honestly, they've heard "fucking" in the playground, haven't they? Charlie and Joni heard all sorts of words. It hasn't ruined them.'

'Georgina, come on, now. Behave yourself.'

'Fracking then. I can fracking well say what I fracking like. You don't have to listen. You never have done, anyway.'

'Qu'est-ce que c'est le fracking Papa?' asked Henri.

'That's totally unfair, Gee.' Will's jovial smile was beginning to congeal.

'What is the fracking?' Henri tried again.

'Welcome to the world. Life is unfair. Whoever thought it was anything else? You just didn't notice because you were the boy, and you were the first, and you kept all the special attention.'

'Maman. Papa. What is le fracking?' Henri persisted.

'C'est une méthode pour extraire du gaz naturel,' Renée explained. 'Mais ce n'est pas bon. Pas bon pour la Terre.'

'And the younger one knows no better,' Georgie carried on. 'No, I didn't even notice, myself. Frieda was the one who noticed.'

'Frieda?' Will was stricken. He gasped as if the name had winded him.

'You remember Frieda.'

'Not easy to forget.'

'I've been reminded of her because I found some stuff.'

He seemed suddenly worried, and looked at Georgie with a face full of questions.

'What's wrong?' she asked.

'I just wondered what you'd found.'

'My cello!' She laughed. 'My cello, that was going to make me an international star. Play it from your cunt!' She laughed again. 'Oh dear. She was right. I should have played from my cunt.'

Will's jaw tensed and he looked sheepishly round at the children. Henri was paying attention. He appeared to be seriously bewildered.

'Zere is no such word as can't,' he protested.

There followed an awful silence. Georgie realised she'd drunk too much wine. Renée's face was a picture of fury, tight, tense, rage burning in her eyes. She won't age as well as I have, thought Georgie, unkindly, but actually she would probably age much more attractively and easily, seeing as she'd have access to high-tech cosmetic procedures, no moral scruples and no shortage of funds. She'd be one of those perpetually glamorous women, letting the side down.

'OK, we're all getting a bit upset. I think we'd better do this another time,' said Will.

As a novelty, Renée took charge of the children, allowing Will to hang back for a quiet word with Georgie before they left. He made sure they were out of the door, before venturing to speak.

'I don't understand why you're so adamant, Gee. Isn't it in your interest to make the most of the place? I thought it was generous of Renée. We won't be benefitting. No more than you, anyway.'

The true answer was that Georgie didn't understand either. But she told him, 'It's my right. I've spent my whole bloody life being steamrollered, Will. Because I'm nice. And I'm sick of being nice. Why should I be if no-one else is? I'm not going to be bloody nice any more, that's all.'

Will was uncomprehending. His jaw was set.

'I'm here alone. I think about my life,' Georgie added, as if it made any sense.

'I'll come back later,' he promised. '*Sans famille.*'

But how could he ever be sans famille? He *was* famille!

It was dark by the time he returned. He couldn't stay long, he said, he just thought they needed some time alone.

'Have you sobered up?' he asked, jovially, not in a way that could offend her. He asked Georgie if she had any wine opened and accepted a glass of red, sighing exhaustedly as he sat down with it on the nearest appropriate horizontal surface.

'I haven't thought about Frieda since... God,' he trailed off. 'Renée was a bit jealous, you know.'

'Really?'

'Anything can trigger it. She thinks you don't like her.'

'That's ridiculous, I like everyone.'

'She thinks you're distant.'

'*I'm* distant?'

'Yes, but it was Frieda's name that upset her.' Georgie cleared a space for her own bottom and sat down beside him, listening. 'When we were first together we had to work through my entire romantic history before she accepted my overtures, and that particular name wasn't one I'd shared,' he said confidentially. He shook his head, as if he didn't understand any of it. 'So she thinks I've withheld something.'

'There's no reason you'd mention her is there? You were seventeen.' A new idea occurred to her. 'You weren't – ?' an item, she meant.

Will shook his head, with a regretful little smile. 'You know why Frieda left?' It was half a question, half a statement. He was hiding behind his lawyerish slipperiness and ambiguity.

'Not really.'

'But why do you think?'

Georgie said nothing.

'You've no idea?'

Georgie did have an idea but she didn't want to explain it.

'You must have an inkling. Or something,' he went on. 'Come on Gee, you're so full of theories usually.'

'All brontosauruses are thin at one end...'

'Much much thicker in the middle and thin again at the other end.'

They laughed.

'Well I suppose I thought it was because she behaved so disgracefully and was a bad influence on us.'

Will was quiet. He looked away.

'I've started to wonder if she fucked up my life, Will. Or she inspired me to fuck it up for myself. I might have gone to university or had a career or... Instead of throwing it all away in a selfish greedy fit of... Hedonism. Which I'm not sure now I even enjoyed.'

Will gave her a deep look. He nodded, but not for no or yes – she knew he was deciding whether or not to say something. His lips tightened before he came out with it.

'She was pregnant. She had to go back home.'

Georgie took a moment to process the information. 'Oh. Of course. Why didn't I think of that?' She hadn't thought of it because she'd always felt herself somehow responsible for Frieda's sudden departure; qualms of guilt clouded all her recollections of that time. 'How did you know?'

'She told me?'

'She told you?' That was something Georgie couldn't easily picture. 'Pregnant how? Who by?'

Will shrugged. 'No shortage of suspects.'

Gravely Georgie examined his expression, looking for further information.

'Not me, your honour,' he said with emphasis.

'But why would she tell you and not me?'

Will shrugged.

'What did she do about it?'

He shrugged again.

'Did she go home to have the baby, then? Or to have an abortion?'

'I know nothing,' he said, attempting to revert to their televisually referential patter. He was downcast by the conversation. He looked as if he wanted to say something else about it but changed his mind.

Georgie felt a tug at her guts, and the usual sudden flush of blood and heat invaded her chest and face and neck. She couldn't tell Will what she was thinking. It was too horrifying an idea, connected with her anxieties about their father's last days alive. She didn't want to dwell on such a ghastly possibility.

'Let's go and look at this rubbish, then,' she said.

They moved into the old stairwell and Will hovered in front of the mess with his hands in his pockets, not knowing quite what to say or do.

'I'm worried you're not really getting on with it Gee. Look at this, for instance, you've got to be able to let go of this.' It was a cracked china saucer, decorated with letters of the alphabet.

'It reminds me of Stratford.'

'Do you want to be reminded of Stratford? You're usually so... Forward-thinking. Interested in the present. And the future. You did say that it would take five weeks. That was four and a half weeks ago.'

'Something happened that I didn't like. Something connected to that.' She tried to explain it: on coming across this apparently innocuous object her reaction had been instant, explosive, as if the saucer had screamed at her *Look out!* 'I just can't grasp it. I get the memory, a little kind of flash like a photograph but it's not a sight, it's feeling and a smell and something to do with cup cakes. What is it? What is that? You don't know do you?' She sighed. 'I've almost got it but... not quite. It flickers just out of view.'

'If it was something you didn't like, why do you want to remember it? Anyway, it's probably completely trivial. Someone telling you off for dropping it or something. Childhood is full of such tiny injuries and insults.'

Georgie thought about it. It had a ring of truth.

'I don't think you're getting enough sleep,' Will said quietly.

'No. Well, that's the hormones. Or lack of.'

Will knelt down and shuffled through some of the objects and papers in Keep. The miniature painted lady caught his attention. 'Who's this?'

'I don't know. An ancestor? Isn't it beautiful?'

'Is it worth anything?' He wrinkled his nose as he turned it over and saw the plaited hair. Georgie thought she'd better come clean.

'Nothing here's worth anything monetary. Don't you remember they took everything to be valued on the Antiques Roadshow? Mum was really disappointed. It's just junk really. In money terms.'

'I don't think she's beautiful,' Will said.

'Oh.' Georgie felt disappointed, seeing as the portrait resembled herself, she thought – herself as a young woman, at least. Not that it mattered any more, how she'd looked as a young woman. 'But it's a beautiful object,' she argued. 'The painting. It's exquisite. Just think, having to make do with that instead of a photo. Somebody gave it to someone as a love token. She existed! He existed! And our existence might depend upon their having met. Oh, and talking of photos,' Georgie scrabbled amongst a heap of papers and files and found the framed girl on the swing. 'You don't know who this is, do you?'

Will studied it, with a blank look on his face.

'D'you see any likeness?' Georgie asked.

'Not really. Gee, your imagination is on the move. How could you possibly see any connection.' His exasperated confused expression suggested that she was making no sense. 'They're alike in that they're both female human beings,' he conceded.

He hadn't understood. Could he see a family likeness in the photograph, she meant. Or was she a complete stranger?

'Why can't you see the value in all this?' she said.

'I just don't, Gee. I can't bring myself to engage with it. I want to help but I also want to live! And breathe!'

'How can we just throw it away? If we do it'll go to landfill.'

'Well, Mum and Dad are landfill now, aren't they? It's a curse, this bloody stuff. Simply looking at it drains your energy.'

'Yes, it's true. And it's come to me to expiate it.'

'Let bygones be bygones!'

'Well I understand that phrase differently. I thought it was about patching things up and forgiving people.'

'It is, Gee. It is! Forgiving and forgetting.' He gave her a warm smile and put his arms round her. It was funny to realise how the annoying brother she'd always known was actually this strong, reliable middle-aged man. She felt like a child in his embrace; he'd somehow managed the transition into adulthood more convincingly than she had. And he was a father, and he was family. She felt a wave of emotion threatening to overwhelm her, and automatically clamped down on it; she might be able to contradict him, she might even manage to be angry, but she certainly couldn't be weak on him.

'I don't agree that it's about forgetting,' she said, as he released her. 'Remembering is important, or you repeat your mistakes. You never learn anything, you can never plan anything. You live in a limbo of nothingness like... like an Alzheimer's patient, or a baby, or a fish. They live in the present, don't they? But grown-ups have to be prepared. Like boy scouts.'

She interrupted herself, realising she wasn't convincing him, she was merely amusing him, and he wasn't going to argue.

'I want to be an aunt to them, Will. They're my family too. It's terrible I can't simply give them a kiss or a present. And Henri does look like Charlie, don't you think so?'

'Does it matter?' Will laughed at the absurdity of her concern. 'Well, actually, we were going to ask you to come and babysit for us this evening. Huge favour. We thought it'd be nice to go out on the town. D'you think you could?'

The hotel bedroom smelt of Paris. Two open suitcases spilled their contents over the spare chair and the bed, and delicate colourful things were hanging in the open wardrobe. Will had donned a silk suit, and Renée was wearing a silver coat and pointy grey court shoes. When Georgie arrived, the children were already combed and clean and wearing perfectly exquisite pyjamas.

'Ooh look!' she said to Eve, 'you're covered in little ladybirds!' Eve stared. Georgie thought better of commenting on Henri's little tigers.

All she had to do was tuck them up and be there in the adjoining double bedroom, where she could enjoy her fill of television, mini-bar and the tapas Will had ordered especially for her. Renée gave the children a kiss each and said they were to 'speak English to your Auntie Georgina. And go to bed when she says so.'

'Oui maman,' said Henri.

The children accepted their parents' departure with scarcely a squeak.

Georgie was pleased to find the books she had given them on the windowsill in their bedroom. Later she discovered the wrapping paper in the bin in the master bedroom; the presents had been opened carefully by an adult, but they hadn't been hidden or discarded; an English alphabet for Eve, A Roald Dahl story for Henri. She offered to read to them.

'Maman says we can play,' Henri said. He pointed at a case of toys beside the bed, a heap of plastic – ugly articulated creatures, Transformers and cars. Eve was already cuddling a panda and dandling a doll by one leg, flipping it from side to side so that it gurgled.

'OK, you can play for a little while,' Georgie said. 'For thirty minutes. Then I will come and say goodnight. Trente minutes. Puis dormir, oui?'

From the next room she heard the noise of electronic games, and went to investigate. Eve had learnt how to drag an image of a blob of cream onto an image of a cake, and was being rewarded with a tinkling bell and the voice of a woman exclaiming 'Délicieux!' Henri was dexterously manoeuvring an image of a hamburger round an image of a race course to the sound of cranking gears and screeching brakes. The little cook; the little racing driver. There was nothing to be done about it. Georgie smiled at them, and went back to her olives and wine, automatically rescuing the wrapping paper, to be added to Recycle.

'Time to sleep now!' she sang when she next looked in. Eve was already asleep. Her iPad had slithered off the bed, and the panda was again firmly stowed under one arm.

'Please may I have a glass of water?' said Henri. Georgie obliged, indulging his delaying tactics.

'Careful not to spill it now,' she said, putting it on the further side of the bedside table.

'Please may I have my mug?'

Henri got out of bed and fetched a mug from the travel bag, which was resting in an armchair in the corner of the room. Georgie poured the water from the glass into the mug.

'Time to sleep now,' she said quietly. 'Eve is already asleep, look.'

'Une berceuse.'

Georgie leant over to kiss him. He recoiled.

'Une berceuse.'

Oh dear, Georgie didn't know what it meant.

'Qu'est-ce que c'est une berceuse?'

'Daddy sings to us.'

'A lullaby!'

While Georgie racked her brain for a song she might have sung to Joni or Charlie, Henri began.

'*In ze house on Colly Saker all ze gold you ever need,*

'*Pearls and jewels gold and silver, all ze gold you ever need.*'

As she listened to the mispronounced words, delivered with such pain and seriousness in his clear, resonant, beautifully pitched voice, she felt a surge of unaccountable emotion. It was a song her mother used to sing. Its simple melody and lilting rhythm recalled her to the safety and cosiness of her own childhood, and behind Henri's voice she imagined an echo of her mother's, shy and light, but mesmerising. Georgie

sang along with him the words as she remembered them, while
Henri quietened and closed his eyes.

'In the house on Colley's acre Molly's mother sowed a seed
'Buried for her daughter Molly all a golden girl could need
'Pearls and jewels gold and silver nothing could the girl want for
'Sewn inside her little dolly, Molly keeps her mother's all.'

Will's boy had given it a slightly different emphasis, and her
own version might not be the original, she realised. It was a
Chinese whisper, changing as it passed from parent to child – a
quivering thread of connection, something of her mother that
lived on, and was changing, as all living things must change.

It lulled the boy to rest, but Eve woke up and her soulful
dark eyes glared at Georgie, from behind a tumble of fair hair.

LOVE THE ONE YOU'RE WITH

'Wash your hands before you look!' shouted her father. It was the first thing he'd said to her since their little talk.

Georgie ran her hands under the kitchen tap and dried them on a fresh tea-towel. The envelope was on the dresser. She opened it carefully, taking out each photograph by the very edges, then balancing them on her other fingers so there was no possibility of greasing any even if she'd dipped her hands in butter. She made sure to keep them in their original order, in case it meant something.

Frieda in shorts and flip-flops and sunglasses, Frieda in black and white, Frieda in colour, Frieda beside the car, in the car, on the car, striding, leaning, lying, smiling, laughing, pouting, with plaited hair, with loose hair, with bunches, by Shakespeare's birthplace, by Anne Hathaway's cottage, by Hall's Croft, by willows and swans and blossoms and daffodils.

Georgie didn't care whether or not they were artistic or well composed. She hated them. She closed the envelope and returned to her new place at the dining table wondering what to say. It was teatime so she was imprisoned by the necessity of eating, and couldn't avoid the interrogation. This was their only family time; the only time they actually had to speak to each other. Her father was at the office all day, Will was working on the boats and her mother was forever out with Frieda. She'd spent the first few days of the holidays in blissful loneliness, looking for Matthew on her bike when books bored her.

'Well?' said her mother, brightly.

'They're good.' Least said, soonest mended.

'Come on, Gee, don't be a spoilsport.'

They're amazing. They're fantastic and marvellous and wonderful and fabulous, she thought. 'I said they were good,' she said, with a shrug.

'We'd appreciate an honest opinion without actual unkindness, as always, I hope,' said Larry.

'I don't mind the ones where she's in the car. But why would you ever be *on* a car? I thought we agreed that she wasn't going to be *on* the car. It's ridiculous. And why shouldn't it be a boy? Why shouldn't Will have done it? Or Mum?'

'Jealous! Jealous! Jealous!' Will quietly sang his usual taunt.

'Frieda is here, Georgina. Please don't "she" someone who is present. I'm sorry Frieda, we brought her up to have better manners.' That was Maureen.

Georgie boldly continued. 'You wouldn't see a politician lying on a car telling everyone to buy it, would you?'

The lull in the conversation meant they were considering the possibility, perhaps imagining Margaret Thatcher or Harold Wilson in such a light at such an angle. It wasn't so absurd.

'Or anyone with any self-respect. A novelist or a film director. Anyone intelligent.'

That comment must have been beyond the pale because the silent embarrassment that followed was unbearable. Frieda had been quietly concentrating on her food. She had a way of doing everything that was a kind of performance. Everyone was watching and she knew it. Her hands were expressive and delicate, and she moved them slowly and gracefully, even peeling an apple or cutting a slice of cheese. She put down her knife and looked around at her audience.

'I agree with Georgina,' she said, at last. 'Did I not say it? But Lawrence has persuaded me.' She shrugged. 'I am sorry, Georgina. You are right. Those should not be used.'

She said it firmly and seriously, and now they all took notice and wondered whether Georgie had a point after all. Larry raised his eyebrows, but said nothing. His mouth went into a straight line. That was when Georgie noticed the unshaven shadow round his chin. Will shut up singing and shoved half a sticky bun into his mouth, and concentrated on chewing it, a hint of pink showing on each cheek. Maureen noticed a mark on the table-cloth and went to fetch a sponge to soak it out.

For Georgie it was a triumph; something like that had never happened before. Never had she had an ally in her struggle against the weight of family opinion. Here was a little taste of recognition, slightly marred by guilt. She looked over at Frieda without moving her head and Frieda shot her an encouraging meaningful smile which struck her in the heart like an invisible dart of love.

From that moment onwards, everything changed. Now Georgina wanted to practise cello. She wanted to practise German. She wanted to be heard going up and down her most difficult scales or spelling out her vocabulary. Frieda would knock at the door. 'You would like help?' And Georgie would say, 'Ja, bitte. Danke schön.' And they would converse exclusively in German until they stumbled upon a word Georgie didn't know.

She could play Full Fathom Five from full five fathoms. She could play Bach, Elgar, Schönberg if she liked; she could play anything! Sometimes she felt as if the bow moved without her assistance. She took the cello downstairs to the living room and played with Frieda's piano accompaniment, while her mother looked on with undisguised pride in a way that made Georgina want to laugh and sing and puke all at once.

She neglected her 'O' level subjects.

When she told Frieda her hopes about the life she would lead in Oxford or Cambridge, Frieda smiled and shrugged as if to say 'maybe'. In German she told her how she had slept under the stars in the Gobi Desert. She had watched Niagara Falls. She had picked grapes in France and apples in Israel. She talked of the hippy trail to Nepal, as if the names on it were sparkling charms strung around her wrist: Istanbul, Damascus, Baghdad, Tehran, Kabul, Lahore, Bengalores, Kathmandu. She showed Georgie her 'Davidstern', asking for help with the clasp, in a motion and tone suddenly awkward and naïve. It had caught in Frieda's hair, and Georgie, in an aura of honoured embarrassment, fumbled to unscrew it, unable to avoid causing a pain she knew must be exquisite. 'Echtes Geld,' Frieda announced proudly, dangling it in her fingers. She said, as if it were in some way connected, that her sister Angela was the angel of the family, so she herself must be the devil. She made horns from her index fingers and held them against her temples, and, locked by her gaze, Georgie noticed again the crescents of white beneath each dark iris. She was such a slippery person! You couldn't tie down your thoughts about her. She had the exuberance and openness of a child, but the authority of someone who had lived a zillion years. And more importantly, far more importantly, she cared. She cared.

One day, Georgina looked at her carefully organised timetable with its precisely measured lines and strict forty-minute allocations, each separated by a narrow five-minute break. She saw that she was six days behind on Physics and Chemistry, three days behind on Biology, she hadn't done a stroke of English or Maths and her French and Latin were fading away behind the German. She began a Tippex job, then decided just to start again from now, with a clean sheet of paper, this time including periods of music and German conversation. Biology became Bio, Physics Phys as she pincered the subjects into smaller and smaller gaps of time.

On Bank Holiday Monday the sun shone from a cloudless blue sky. Maureen was helping run a stall at the WI fete in aid of a Nigerian school they were sponsoring. She was packing butterfly cakes and flapjacks into Tupperware containers, rolling up red, blue and white bunting and chatting brightly about all the arrangements. They'd covered every eventuality except the possibility of broad sunshine. They'd put a canopy up for the brass band and hired a tent for tea and cakes. Maureen wondered aloud whether they could unhire it and save a few pounds, though perhaps it would be just as useful in the provision of shade and coolness. How she loved the smell of a marquee and grass and cakes and tea! It made her think of weddings! It made her proud of England! It made her think that summer was on its way and the world wasn't so bad. Did Georgie want to come? No? Did Frieda want to come? She imagined it might be a bit dull. It was aimed primarily at children and older people. There was a clown and throwing the ball into a loo and a jumble stall and a craft stall. She mustn't forget to take the apple juice! Wasn't it funny how teenagers were in a class of their own? You gave up childish pleasures at twelve or so, then you rediscovered them twenty years later. Perhaps when you had children of your own. She herself liked nothing better than to guess the number of smarties in a jar, eat cakes, pin the tail on the donkey. Such simple pleasures! One of the members had written a book and was signing copies. Maybe she would bind her poems up and see if she could raise a few pence out of them at next year's do. Frieda had inspired her. Do what you love!

While she was emitting, Larry was packing his camera bag with rolls of colour film. He'd been asked to photograph the event for the monthly newsletter. He was beginning to feel like a professional.

Georgie took Frieda for a walk across Shottery Fields and into town, along the river to the Bancroft Gardens. Now the world and his wife were out, everyone in tee-shirts and bright colours, smiling and chatting, full of humour and energy as they watched Morris dancers and fed the swans and hovered around the theatre, stumbling into each other as they asked for directions with monstrous cameras strung around their necks. Maureen used to bring her and Will to this stretch of the riverside, Georgie told Frieda, when she was young enough to be in a pushchair. They would stand right next to the water throwing stale chunks of bread, some of which she would eat herself. She used to like the rusky taste and the texture of the crust. It made her feel sad to think of it. As if she had lost her childhood there – it had simply drowned in the river all those years ago.

'Do you want to be a child again?' Frieda asked, studying her face as though she must be mental. 'I really do not.'

Georgie shook her head. 'I'm looking out for a certain boy,' she said, shyly. Frieda perked up, instantly interested. 'He drives a purple Mini.'

'Who is this?' Frieda asked.

'Matthew. He goes to Will's school but he's in the year above. And my mum goes to the same church as his mum.'

'How does he look?'

'Tall and fair. And strong. He's good at rugby. And he's funny. He makes me laugh, anyway.'

'That is good.'

But there was no purple Mini amongst the rows of Vauxhalls and Morris Minors and Fords. Frieda spotted one or two tall fair men in the throng of Stratford-gazing humanity, but not Matthew.

On the way home they took a different route, which went past his house. The Mini was parked outside. Georgie, feeling exposed and absurd, hardly dared to look up from the pavement. She was desperate to know which curtains were open and, giggling and awkward, she asked Frieda to look for her. She knew that Matthew's bedroom window was the upper left. He might be there. He might be there with someone. She wondered if she would ever be on the other side of that precious glass. Frieda suggested simply ringing the door bell and asking if he were in.

'You must, what is it? Take the bulls by the horn, ja? Komm! Komm!' she urged, grabbing Georgie by the wrist as she undid the front gate and strode up the garden path. There was a porch to the house, and a stained glass window in the door. Georgie had done this sort of thing as a child – rung a stranger's doorbell and hared off out of view as a dare, dread and excitement swimming in her belly.

'His mum knows you, yes?'

'Not very well.'

Frieda rang the door bell. Georgie pulled her hair forwards from behind her ears, adjusting her fringe so that it fell into her eyes. She stared at the red tiles beneath her sandals. She heard footsteps and the click of the lock, and bravely looked up through stripes of pale brown as the door swung open. It was Matthew's mum, in an orange checked dress and fawn cardigan, peering with a quizzical guarded expression through ugly black-rimmed spectacles. She didn't look at Georgie straight away, and didn't recognise her.

'Is Matthew at home?' Frieda asked.

Matthew's mum looked from one to the other, irritated by Frieda's boldness. Her face softened into a faint smile.

'Georgina? Hello there! No, Matthew's doing his Duke of Edinburgh. And you must be Elfrieda. Maureen's mentioned you.'

She offered her hand, and Frieda shook it, saying, 'Frieda.'

'I'm afraid I can't offer you tea.' There was no explanation.

Thank goodness, thought Georgie.

'Shall I tell Matthew you called?'

'Yes,' said Frieda. 'That would be very nice of you.'

'Thank you so much,' said Matthew's mum. 'I do hope we meet again soon. Goodbye now.' She stepped backwards into the murky front hall.

'When will he return?' Frieda asked quickly.

'Wednesday,' she was told. 'Goodbye now.' The door closed.

'Fotze,' hissed Frieda. Georgie giggled. Frieda looked back at her as they went down the garden path and through the gate.

'It is true,' she said under her breath. 'She does not want to share her son with another woman. We have to make a plan. We have to meet him when she is not there.'

Frieda asked her what Georgie had done so far to win him. Georgie didn't mention the letter. She said, 'Nothing much, except meet him with friends in pubs.' She added that Will might invite him to his party.

'Perfect! That is your opportunity.'

'I can't wear make-up or tarty dresses or high heels or anything,' said Georgie.

'But you must,' asserted Frieda.

'I don't believe in all that,' Georgie tried to explain, embarrassed. 'It's sort of against my principles, you see. I don't want to kowtow to men. I refuse to. It's not fair. They don't wear make-up do they? They don't have to wobble about on heels to make us interested in them. They don't have to wear silly uncomfortable knickers and squeeze themselves into corsets and do peculiar things to their hair and pretend to be stupid.'

Frieda stopped walking and studied Georgie's face, confused and amused at the same time. 'Why not?' she said simply, with a wicked smile.

When they got home they had the house to themselves. Georgie suggested raiding the larder for alcohol. She found half a bottle of white wine and some vodka and orange juice in the fridge and mixed it all together in the glass jug she wasn't supposed to use. It was warm enough for a swim. She dashed upstairs to put on a swimsuit. When she came down she found Frieda, already changed, but emptying a bag of make-up onto the kitchen table. Lipstick, eye shadow, mascara, nail varnish, a fountain of little plastic and glass containers clattered onto the wood.

'I want to paint you!' she announced, wielding an open lipstick.

Georgie retreated with a scream of hilarity. 'No!' She wrestled with the French windows and was out on the terrace hopping and skipping towards the pool pursued by Frieda, who was brandishing the lipstick as if it were a tiny gun.

When her mother and father arrived home, Georgie and Frieda were sunning themselves dry by the pool, quaffing Gewürtztraminer cocktail. Instead of glowering at Georgie, showing her disapproval without explicitly expressing it, which would be normal, her mother laughed like a maniac at what they'd done. She fetched a glass and joined them on a lounger, in bare feet, announcing that she had some Campari and could fill the Soda Stream if they ran out.

Phew, what a day she'd had! They made nearly five hundred pounds. It was a record. The mayor's wife had come and distributed raffle prizes. Maureen was one digit short of winning the champagne. Her butterfly cakes ran out in thirty minutes. There wasn't a crumb of anything left. Maybe she'd make a few dozen more next year, though of course the marvellous weather must take some of the credit. She'd never known such a dry spring. But wasn't sunshine overrated? She did enjoy a bit of rain now and then, especially now the garden was beginning to flourish. Had Georgie seen the crocuses this year? There was an enormous patch by the apple trees. It looked as though they'd multiplied. Wasn't it wonderful the way they hid under the soil and suddenly appeared just when you thought winter would never end?

Georgie didn't know what had got into her mother. It was almost like happiness. Fi's opinion was that she had a lover, which Georgie said was utterly out of the question.

'She doesn't have the time,' she explained. 'Frieda's always there.'

But Larry was also turning into a different person. He had given up the razor and his greying hair was creeping over his ears and beyond his collar. He was wearing different things too, even to work. He'd bought a wide tie with flowers on it for the office, and a Hawaiian shirt for home. He and Maureen had kaftans. Maureen had chosen white, which you could see through if she wore the wrong colour underwear. Larry's was purple. Purple!

'Can you imagine having a dad in purple?'

Fi had commiserated. 'It's better than having no dad, though,' she said, referring to the fact that her own father was never home because he was too busy making scads of dosh, buying and selling wine. 'Perhaps he's got the hots for your au pair,' she added. 'It's rather sweet. Although maybe she's interested in your mum.'

Georgie laughed, but afterwards she felt a horrible dragging sensation in the pit of her stomach. It couldn't be possible, she told herself. It was a completely disgusting idea. Trust Fi to come up with it, judging other people's parents because her own mum and dad couldn't keep their knickers on.

Georgie wanted to go with Maureen and Frieda to see Shakespeare's birthday celebrations. She found Frieda in the bathroom, leaning over the sink, plucking her eyebrows, as the golden cherub looked on.

'Doesn't it hurt?' she asked.

'Yes!' Frieda said. 'But you have good eyebrows. You do not need to help them.'

Georgie raised them, as she looked at herself in the mirror behind Frieda. She'd never known there was such a thing as a good eyebrow. She touched one, and felt the ridge of brow underneath her fingers. 'They're for protecting your skull,' she said. 'The best eyebrows would probably be the thickest.'

Frieda laughed. She took up her lipstick and Georgie flinched, anticipating another attack.

'I am going to be pretty for Shakespeare,' Frieda announced, pushing out a pearly pink knob, and opening her mouth in a garish expression as she expertly applied the colour. Round the two little cusps, along into the edges. She pressed her lips against each other and dabbed them with a piece of tissue. 'You can borrow if you like?'

Georgie declined, with a self-deprecatory shrug. She envied Frieda's ability to ignore the principles of feminism whenever it suited her.

'I wonder why it's better to have pink lips than ordinary lip-colour lips,' she said.

'It is cool,' said Frieda, pushing them forwards as she spoke. 'Boys like it.'

'Doesn't it taste funny? Why would having whale blubber on your lips make a boy want to kiss them?'

'There is Austria. There is England. Boys are another country. You have to learn another language and another – what is the word? Etiquette?'

'Why can't they learn ours?'

'Boys are limited. As the stronger peoples, we have to forgive them.'

The stronger peoples. Georgie liked that.

The pavements were full, soldiers and police were out in force, excited chatter filled the air, and people waited, milling about behind the barriers. The procession was heralded by a brass band and Maureen cheered with patriotic fervour as the beadle emerged into view, a proudly corpulent man dressed in a Georgian red coat, peaked hat and white stockings, leading the way for local dignitaries, a few token well-behaved children in school uniform, and ambassadors from Afghanistan to Zambia. Blazers and boaters, cocked hats and plumes, smart dresses and suits, kimonos and turbans, wreaths and posies! As little groups peeled off to stand beside their allocated flagpole and painted wooden shield, with Great Britain at the top of Bridge Street in the shadow of Barclays Bank, Maureen, Frieda and Georgie took up a position close to Austria. A hush fell upon the street as the hour approached, then the trumpets blared, the flags unfurled, the band struck up and the crowds cheered and clapped and snapped. The procession reformed and moved on. Next stop was Shakespeare's birthplace and then the Holy Trinity, to his grave. Georgie and Frieda began to shuffle in that direction, and suddenly Matthew was approaching them, looking hugely happy. He nodded in recognition. Georgie felt suddenly alive, and suddenly conspicuous.

'What are you doing here?' she shouted, stupidly.

Her mother turned round amidst the hooting and cheering, and, seeing Matthew, thrust out a friendly hand.

'Hello! You're Judy's son aren't you? I'm Geegee's mother, Maureen.'

Georgie wanted to crumble and vanish into the dust under their feet. Matthew agreed that he was Judy's son and politely shook Maureen's hand, then Maureen introduced him to Frieda and Frieda to him. 'You know my daughter already, don't you?' she added.

It was all wrong. Georgie should have done the introductions.

Maureen said her feet were tired. She'd seen the flags and she wanted to go home, but 'you young things can do whatever you like can't you? Georgina, have some money in case you want to buy, I don't know, pasties or snacks or something.'

She put two pound notes into Georgie's hand, betraying a hint of regret that didn't match her good will and generosity, and for a moment Georgie felt uneasy. Maureen's parting was like a warning, as if they were about to do something heinous and unforgivable.

Matthew suggested they all go to the Duck for a drink, so they extracted themselves from the thickest part of the crowd and hurried in the opposite direction to make sure of getting there before any tourists. As they arrived, Georgie handed the notes to Frieda. She asked for a vodka and lime and dry roasted nuts, and bagged some seats in the sunshine while Matthew showed Frieda where the bar was.

They took an unbelievable age about it, so long that Georgie began to wonder what they were up to. But when Frieda eventually emerged, carrying two wobbly pints of Guinness, the kindness of her expression evaporated all suspicion. There must be a long queue. It was a busy day. 'I forgot what you said,' she apologised, then ran back inside with Georgie's repeated order. She returned with a vodka and lime but no nuts. Georgie was famished.

'He has met some friends,' Frieda said, settling herself into one of the chairs Georgie had commandeered, taking a good gulp of the black beer which left a rim of foam on her upper lip. 'So,' she smiled excitedly, 'he is nice! You chose well.'

Matthew was very charming and apologetic when he finally appeared. He explained that he had some business to do with an old primary school mate of his. He tapped the side of his nose.

'Ah ja!' Frieda said. Georgie didn't understand what they meant.

He had visited Salzburg four years ago, he said. It was a little like Stratford in many ways – instead of the theatre and the birthplace, they had the Haus für Mozart and Mozart's Geburtshaus. 'They sell these Mozart chocolates, don't they?' he said. 'Can you imagine Shakespeare chocolates?' They jeered at the very idea.

'Milk of human kindness chocolate?' suggested Georgie. It wasn't taken up.

She tried a few times to enter the conversation but had to content herself with admiring Matthew's neck and cheekbones, and loving the way the breeze lifted his fine babyish hair, and the sound of his voice, and his infectious laughter. At least she could gaze at him without restraint. On her second vodka and lime she piped up and made a few more jokes, to better effect she felt.

As she and Frieda walked home she said she couldn't help feeling that Matthew was more interested in Frieda than in herself.

'Oh, not at all. When a boy doesn't look at you. That is the good sign,' she said, and then, contradicting that notion entirely, she added, 'Perhaps it is because I am feminine.'

'Hübsch,' Georgie said, with resignation.

'It is the make-up, clothes, shoes. You can do the same. Feminism means to be free. You don't need to do as you are told by anyone. Not men, not women.'

The stronger peoples. To be free. Georgie felt a rush of excitement. The future seemed huge and wonderful and blindingly light, bursting with untold possibility.

I belonged to that generation which saw, by chance, the end of a thousand years' life... to the scream of the horse, the change began. Georgie lounged on the sofa flicking through 'Cider with Rosie', conscientiously noting passages to quote in her long overdue essay. *Meanwhile the old people just dropped away... Our Mother was grey now, and more light-headed, talking of mansions she would never build.*

A knock on the French window startled her. She looked up from the book and her imaginings, to see Frieda, beckoning with one finger, holding another to her lips to signal that Georgie should be quiet. Her expression of irrepressible humour and excitement was too intriguing to resist. Georgie looked round to check that no-one was watching and went out to see what was up, following slowly as Frieda darted barefoot over the lawn and dodged behind the summerhouse.

A rusty old dustbin was standing there amongst brambles and nettles. It was smoking. Georgie advanced to look over its brim. Magazines and twigs had been thrust randomly into its hollow. It smelt of paraffin.

'We burn our bras,' whispered Frieda. 'I first!'

Georgie watched in wonder, as Frieda wriggled and twisted, pulling a little pink flowered bra from under her cheesecloth shirt.

'No!' said Georgie, 'Don't!' She started laughing.

'Come!' Frieda flung it onto the dustbin, with an exuberant shriek, and there it lay, half in, half flopping over the side. A weak flame licked its edge and retreated, ignoring it. They were both laughing now, and Frieda began to dance, hooting like a red Indian.

'We need to push it further in!' Georgie said, looking for a suitable stick to use as a tool. She found a rotten bit of trellis, wormy and splintered, and with it she poked the bra. She looped one strap over the end and lifted it, but then collapsed in giggles as she failed to place it in a better position.

'It's like fishing!' she screeched through her teeth. The weak flame began to gain confidence, guzzling into the edge of a newspaper. As it flared up Georgie hung one bra cup in the flame. Finally it took, the edge glistening black and blue, filling her nose with the stench of scorched cotton and something else synthetic and putrid.

'Now you!' shouted Frieda.

'Votes for women!' shouted Georgie. She handed Frieda the stick and removed her own bra in a similar fashion. But she hesitated. She quite liked her bra.

It had been difficult to buy. She'd had to do it on her own, with no moral support. No-one had even suggested she needed one, as she grew and grew, well beyond the 30 or 32 double A her friends had started wearing months or even years before. Hockey, athletics, running for the bus became embarrassing and painful, with just a vest and a blouse and a tie between her burgeoning adolescence and the outside world. She'd waited and waited for her mother to inaugurate her into the mysteries of womanhood. The day never came. One morning at breakfast before Will and Larry came down, Maureen had said, quickly and quietly, as if it were a matter of shame: 'It's about time you got yourself a bra, isn't it, Gee?'

So she had gone alone to a department store, lost and bewildered amongst a morgue of headless amputated busts and torsos scantily adorned with lace and satin. She'd pretended to look through the boxes, though she didn't understand the drawings or the numbers. Finally a nice lady offered to help. She took her into a changing room and measured her through her vest, delicately and kindly, and with the no-nonsense attitude of a nurse who has seen hundreds of naked bodies and takes no particular interest in your own perfectly normal specimen. She smelt of freesias and wore pink lipstick. Her hair was dyed and permed. She wore pearl earrings. '34 B,' she said, rolling up the tape. 34 because Georgie had a strong broad back, and B because that was how far she projected from her rib cage. The lady disappeared and brought back four different bras. Georgie tried each one. The lady pulled and adjusted the straps, digging her painted fingernails here and there, looking on with a studied frown. She asked how each one felt, and Georgie wasn't sure because they all felt strangely confining and uncomfortable. Together they settled on a cream broderie anglaise cotton, with a double row of hooks and thick adjustable straps. It cost two months' worth of Georgie's pocket money. She paid in change. She had no idea if it was a reasonable price.

There it went onto the flames beside Frieda's, which was now properly scorched in large black patches. Frieda's was pretty, diminutive, designed to be seen. Georgie's looked practical and old-fashioned; it was meant to do a job without expecting any reward or compliment. The flames tickled its edges then one flame beat the others, flared and smouldered and took charge. Her innocent cream-coloured bra was edged in black and red. She felt unutterably sad. It hadn't done anything wrong. It wasn't anything to do with male dominance. On the contrary; it represented Georgie's first act of independence.

LOOK AND LEARN

She hadn't expected *Recent correspondence* to contain anything interesting, mainly because she'd imagined it might contain recent correspondence. It wasn't recent, not any more. The top layer was innocent enough, though poignant. It didn't prepare her for what lay waiting in the depths.

A Christmas card to Grandma and Grandad, for example, signed in childish writing by Joni and Charlie, aged about six and four, she guessed. Her little girl's hand, her little boy's hand had made these very marks. Charlie's kisses were plus signs. She kissed them. The card smelt just as old as everything else. This was the sort of thing you had to get rid of immediately or it would become more and more difficult to do, the more the date of its creation receded out of memory, out of reach. She probably had samples of their handwriting at home, she reasoned, and from every dolly-step stage of their development.

But this was special because they had chosen it, and they had written it to her parents, and her parents had died.

The word 'dead' was one she was not yet prepared to use about them.

Recycle.

A bundle of airmail letters from herself, tied up in wool. They dated from the eighties, sent from all over Europe and South America. There would be descriptions of her visits and tales of what she'd done. She might like to be reminded. Her grandchildren might be interested. Or Will's.

Think About Later.

She came to the next item with astonishment and disbelief, followed by a murmuring sense of karmic felicity. Here was a birthday card to herself from Nick! *The* Nick! From Nick all those twenty, thirty-odd years ago! A painting of roses spilling out of a watering can, and inside, written in black ink that had blotted onto the facing card, 'May this be your best day so far, and may all your days be so, love Nick.' She'd searched for him online, without success, and here he was in her hand!

Keep.

She couldn't with honesty claim that this day was her best so far, though it wasn't over yet. There must be a best day so far, she supposed, idly mulling over what it could include. Friends and family came first to mind, then food, wine, music, dancing and interesting conversation. And the sea she added mentally, passing over an old postcard from Bude, and wondering about another trip to the Lido, and whether a best day ought to include a sexual encounter, or at least a swim.

More birthdays and Christmases. Here was a card from Will and Mitzi, Will's first wife, but he had signed for both.

And here was one from Maureen to Larry dated after the stroke. She saw with a pang her mother's disintegrated handwriting – she had signed her name with as much patience and difficulty as the children, in huge clumsy letters.

Remember. Regret.

Recycle.

A letter from an address in Islington, in Will's efficient scrawl, dated 9 November 1987:

Dear Mum and Dad
This letter will surprise you. I have been seeing a counsellor, and have decided to get in touch with you about something which has for many years enraged me. The hope is that bringing it out into the light will resolve some of my bad feelings...

Georgie's heart fluttered with anxiety. She ought to put the letter back where it was and simply ask him about it. Or simply shred it. Or forget about it. But the damage was already done, her eye had skipped down the page of its own accord, and seen a word she couldn't possibly ignore.

...I have thought long and carefully about how to say this, and there isn't really a way that avoids hurting anyone, so I'm just going to write how it was from my perspective and hope that you'll forgive me for being so blunt.

I'm sure you remember Frieda? She was not an easy person to forget. We were in love, very much in love. I was besotted, and she returned my feelings. I was nearly eighteen by the time she left, and old enough to make my own decisions, but I was influenced by your disapproval and allowed you to separate us.

She probably was too old for me, she probably wasn't all that good for me, but it was up to me to find that out, not up to you to force the issue. I think that if I had pursued our affair to its natural conclusion, either we would now be happily ~~married~~ together, or I would have been able to let go of her image, which has haunted me ever since. This thought makes me feel very bitter towards you. I don't understand why you did it, and can only assume that it was some kind of misguided jealousy.

I have never met anyone else who made me feel as special as she did and I believe that your actions ruined my prospects of ever finding love.

Yours
Will

Georgie's guilty feeling soon faded as an angry one bubbled up to take its place.

For one thing, Will had lied to her, pretending he'd had nothing to do with the girl. And then, it was disgraceful to blame their parents for her leaving, when he knew perfectly well she'd left because she was pregnant – for which it now looked as though he might be responsible!

November 1987 was around the time of his divorce from Mitzi – who had been a little like Frieda in that she was pretty, blonde and Teutonic, and most unlike her in that she was a cow and a half, and losing her had been a jolly good thing as far as everyone but Will had been concerned. He must have been confused and upset and searching for excuses, she reasoned. He couldn't have meant it. She wished he'd signed off 'with love' or 'all my best'. How cruel it was to have been so cold!

As she looked up from the letter, deeply submerged in these

cogitations and boiling feelings, something flashed at the edge of her vision. She scanned the hall and the stairwell. All was as usual. She looked again at the letter.

It was the word 'jealousy' that had struck her. She couldn't properly comprehend his insinuation. Was he suggesting that their mother was jealous, because of her motherly love for Will? Or did he imagine that their father was jealous, because he had feelings for Frieda? Or was it both?

She wondered whether Will knew that this letter had not been destroyed, and whether he'd considered the possibility that she might find it. She wondered how it had been answered; whether the problem had been resolved. She tried to think back to those late eighties, if she had seen Will and her parents together, whether there had been any ill feeling between them. Of course, it must have eventually been resolved, simply by time passing, which was how Maureen and Larry usually dealt with things.

Distracted, she looked up. It happened again. A movement of something in the hall. She clambered to her feet and walked towards whatever she had seen. Behind a pile of books was something bright. It was the glinting of a mirror – another piece of Great Aunt Ruby's elegant but neglected furniture. From its precarious position she lifted a swivelling oval glass, pitted and misty, attached to a box base, with drawers. The drawers fell forwards as she lifted it, disturbing a pile of books, and something heavy dropped out onto her bare foot.

'OW!'

Lying beside her foot was a key. She leant the mirror against the wall and picked the key off the floor. Its handle was a simple brass oval, but the blade was of a peculiar design – crenellated, like a tiny coronet. It occurred to her that it might belong to the writing box, since Nick had commented on the unusualness of its lock. The writing box was now under a pile of files, but she didn't need to move them to test the key. It fitted. It turned. Something clicked, and she was overcome by a deep sense of satisfaction. How typical that she didn't need it any more, but how wonderful that the lack of it had brought Nick closer into her orbit.

She left the key where it belonged – it seemed the safest place – and went back to tidy the fallen books. The top one had broken its back. She knelt down, tutting, and gathered together its loose pages to fit them neatly back between the book's frayed cover boards. She noticed a few smaller and yellower pages that had been torn from a different book – one so old that the esses looked like effs. The subject matter made her gasp. It was pointed, shocking.

CHAP. LV11 OF A SCHIRRUS AND CANCER.

'This difeafe is often owing to people of fuppreffed evacuations;' she read, 'hence it proves fo frequently fatal to women of a grofs habit, particularly old maids and widows, about the time when the menftrual flux ceafes.'

By 'gross', I suppose you mean 'fat', she thought. Which is simply rude.

'It may likewife be occafioned by exceffive fear, grief, anger, religious melancholy, or any of the depreffing paffions... Sometimes the disease is owing to an hereditary difpofition.'

'Hereditary difpofition' and 'depreffing paffions' were both underlined in black ink. Belladonna, hemlock, wort, mercurial pills, and frequent blood-letting were prescribed, but then:

'Should the tumour not yield to this treatment but on the contrary become larger and harder, it will be proper to extirpate it, either by the knife or cauftic. Indeed, whenever this can be done with fafety, the fooner it is done the better. It can anfwer no purpofe to extirpate a cancer after the conftitution is ruined, or the whole mafs of humours corrupted by it. This however is the common way, which makes the operation fo feldom fucceed. Few people will fubmit to the extirpation till death ftares them in the face; whereas if it were done early the patient's life would not be endangered by the operation and it would generally prove a radical cure.'

The pages were covered with worrying stains, suggesting that an extirpation had been tried within spitting distance of them. No anaesthetic when esses were effs, she thought. Oh dear me, no. Not even chloroform.

Opium was mentioned but only in relation to the end game.

She spared herself a full description of the difeafe, skating over such words as 'pain' 'ftench' 'haemorrhage' and 'convulfion' and letting her eyes rest at last on some useful advice:

'To avoid this dreadful diforder, people ought to ufe wholefome food; to take fufficient exercise in the open air; to be as eafy and cheerful as poffible; and carefully to guard against all blows, bruifes, and every kind of preffure upon the breafts or other glandular parts.'

'Eafy and cheerful' was also underlined.

'I *am* easy and cheerful,' she argued, aloud. 'How dare you?' She snapped the book shut. 'Didn't bloody work, sir, did it?'

After these excursions into the olden days, returning to the present moment was like coming up from the bottom of the ocean. The change could be a shock, confusing and disorientating, as if you were being decompressed. Time turned elastic. She would find that an hour had passed in a few minutes, or the opposite, she'd be surprised at how early it was. And she'd easily forget about the ordinary things she needed to do – simple things like eating or even going to the loo.

Now she'd gone and lost that letter of Will's. She retraced her steps round the flat and found it where she'd started, beside the mirror, on its own little oblong of floor. She left it there. It was to be thought about later, but sooner than the things in Think About Later. It could be the start of a new pile: Think About Sooner.

As hours passed, she found nothing to add to the category. The letter took priority. Every time it caught her eye her feeling about it changed, but she couldn't turn it into a pleasant one. No, there was something horrible about it. Sadness imbued every line: Will's sadness on writing it, her parents' sadness on reading it.

Never mind Geegee! Relief was on its way. Sheelah was

Georgie's most practical friend. She wanted to help lift and carry things. She meant well, and could be trusted not to gossip about delicate family information. She would share Georgie's concerns and absolve her of guilt and breathe fresh air into the crypt. In Sheelah's company, everything would be twice as easy and twenty times as cheerful.

VALUE FRIENDS

It was typical of Sheelah to arrive well ahead of the arranged time. Always her energy was directed ahead, her generous weight streaming through her toes, as if she were about to spring forwards to retrieve a stray ball. She gave the impression of being purposeful and determined, an impression in no way contradicted by the quilted jacket and riding boots she wore or the purple hair wisping out from under a bowler hat.

She gave Georgie a big, cold-cheeked, warm-hearted hug.

'Goodness Georgina, I don't envy you!' she exclaimed, as she peered into the darkness, demonstrating by her expression the gaping difference in their capacity to tolerate disorder. 'Where do I go? I mean, is there a space anywhere in my size?'

Georgie laughed. 'The kitchen's not so bad.' She ushered her further into the depths of gloom. 'The trouble is I've flattened it all,' she explained. 'It was stacked high so now I've taken things down there's more space under the ceiling and less space on the floor. I suppose I ought to get us some high chairs!'

Sheelah glanced sideways at the collapsing mess as she headed directly for the kitchen. 'Good grief, no, please don't get anything else!' she said, plonking her huge multicoloured cloth bag on the table. She pulled out two packages – one in cellophane, one in a tin. The tin was of tea; it looked exotic and Chinese; that was good, it was probably green. 'I've brought some cake. Home-made,' she announced, thrusting it into Georgie's hands. Georgie wondered how to tell her that cake wasn't on her Staying Alive list.

'It's sugar-free, dairy-free, gluten-free!' Sheelah told her.

It sounded rather cake-free.

'Everything in it is organic. High-cocoa chocky. Beetroot and carrots instead of sugar. Almonds instead of flour. A tincy wincy bit of herbal remedy, which is the bees' knees for cancer sufferers, I read it online. And golden syrup but you can't not have everything.'

'Bugger the golden syrup! I'll eat it.'

'Not sure about wine though Gee? Isn't it a real no-no for breast cancer sufferers especially? Curse of the middle class.'

Georgie looked around to locate the bottle Sheelah must have seen.

'I'm not a cancer sufferer,' she said. 'I'm a cancer survivor. I'm starting to believe that I might be around for a bit, you know.'

'Good. In which case it's essential to enjoy yourself!'

On that they agreed.

Sheelah got her bearings in the kitchen, insisted that Georgie sit down and relax and proceeded to make a pot of tea. It wasn't that easy for Georgie to relax when she had to explain where everything was and be told that it wasn't in the most efficient or most obvious place. The kitchen was still arranged to her mother's design. Georgie had never questioned it and nor had her father, that the tea strainer was in a drawer on the dresser, while little spoons were in a drawer to the left of the sink, knives were in a drawer to the right, the teapot was on a high shelf and plates were in a cupboard on the opposite side. Sheelah bustled about with more energy and sound than it usually takes to make tea.

'It's so good of you to come,' Georgie sighed. 'I think I'm going a bit mad here alone. A slightly peculiar atmosphere. Strange noises and such. And I've been feeling weird about certain memories and things I found.'

'You obviously need cheering up,' Sheelah said, thrusting a hot cup into her hands; 'and I have excellent news for you! Guess who I saw coming out of Bites with a woman in tow?'

Georgie interrupted her thoughts to cast her mind about for a suitable candidate.

'Charlie?'

'No!' Sheelah beamed, amused and dismissive. 'Come on, who?'

Georgie could think of no-one. She shrugged, bewildered.

'Kevin!' Sheelah squealed his name as if she'd just found it in a golden envelope.

The great news struck Georgie in the heart. She blew on her tea, shocked at the tumult of unpleasant feelings that had erupted in her chest, while Sheelah paced a tile's-width stretch of empty floor, explaining why she ought to be glad.

'So that seals it. You don't need to suffer the agonies of indecision any more. You'll never get back together! He isn't going to ring you up again! No more flowers or apologies or funny little drawings to tempt you. No more passionate declarations or irresistible bottles of vintage champagne! He's found his match. I didn't think it would take him long, actually, once you'd convinced him it was over. Isn't that a relief?'

'So who was she?' Georgie asked, in a casually disinterested manner.

Was her hair grey or dyed? Dyed blonde or dark or red? Was she young? Was she slim? Did he know her already or was she new? Was she beautiful? Did she have a cleavage? Where had they met? How could Sheelah tell they were together? Together together or just friendly together?

'I don't know. At least I presume they were an item by how easy they were with each other. He doesn't have a daughter does he?'

'No he doesn't have any children.'

'Oh, well maybe he wants them.'

'He doesn't want children.'

It was absurd to mind. Absurd, irrational and unfair actually, as Georgie was free herself, so Kevin must also be free. It was no concern of hers any more whether or not he wanted children or how old his girlfriend was or what size her breasts were.

'She's probably not as young as she looked,' Sheelah went on, in an attempt perhaps, to ease the pain. 'She looked a bit stupid to be honest. A bit tarty, you know. I don't get this fashion for tattoos, do you? Why would you have one on the back of your neck for instance? You could never see it.'

Georgie's heart twisted by one more degree.

'He told me he didn't want children,' she whimpered.

Sheelah wasn't paying attention now anyway, she was pacing up to the window and undoing the sash. 'You've got a garden here,' she announced. 'Very green.'

'Yes, I love the green.'

'You need to get rid of that ivy, it's poisoning the whole plot.'

'I rather like it.'

'It's going to break the wall. I'd pull that up if I were you.'

'I suppose I should do something about it. But I thought we might be selling it first.'

'The garden will help you sell it, if it's in a decent state.'

Georgie felt exhausted. She knew Sheelah was right. It's going to take years, she thought. She would never get away. She must have expressed it somehow because Sheelah hurried back and sat down beside her, issuing a stream of comforting words and noises. 'You could always pay someone else to do it,' was the bit of it Georgie heard.

Money was the sticky wicket in their relationship, and whenever it came up Georgie felt uncomfortable. Actually she didn't have enough money to pay anyone to do anything, she only had enough money to be the one being paid to do the things, but this concept was beyond Sheelah's comprehension. Sheelah had never wanted for fifty quid, let alone a tenner. It had happened to Georgie often enough, when Jim was late with his contribution or a big bill had come in. She didn't resent her straitened circumstances; she'd always felt grateful for the roof over their heads and food in the fridge, and plumbing and gas heating and electric light and all the conveniences of modern life. She compared her lot to those of women in the third world, women who had to walk ten miles for water and ten miles back, who couldn't read or write, whose dream was to own a bicycle. But when Sheelah said that about paying someone else she felt a little bit cross. Not about being poorer than Sheelah, just about Sheelah's obtuse attitude. 'I don't have much of an income at the moment,' she explained. She knew it was a mistake as soon as it was out. Sheelah had plans for her, to raise her up from her miserable subsistence.

'Now you're on your feet again...' she began.

'I'm fucking knackered!' Georgie surprised herself by asserting with what felt like great force and certitude. 'I don't have the energy to even think about getting another job, so please don't suggest anything at all, because you'll just be wasting your breath and my time.'

There was a temporary hiatus in the flow of their conversation while Georgie listened to an echo of what she'd just said, and regretted it. Sheelah didn't heed it overmuch. She let it pass, although it was highly unusual for Georgie to quarrel with her, or swear that much.

'What about your brother?' she went on. 'He can't be short of a bob or two. He should be helping you.'

Georgie just nodded, although the suggestion was impertinent. It was all too difficult to explain. She certainly wasn't going to go into Will's offer, especially not the bit about her refusal. How could anyone understand that, when she didn't even understand it herself?

'What this place needs is a good shit!' said Sheelah, waving a theatrical arm in the vague direction of the rest of the flat. 'It can't be good for you all this impacted gubbins. It's stagnating and festering. Hanging on to it all, it's enough to give anyone cancer.'

Georgie balked. She didn't like Sheelah's blaming tone, or the insult to her parents' only belongings.

'I don't know what you mean,' she said.

Sheelah's expression said, *it's obvious.* She didn't need to vocalise it.

'You mean this stuff might give me cancer again?'

'Yes, if it hasn't already given somebody cancer. You've got to let it go, Georgie. Let it go. Like a Buddhist. That's what I do.'

Georgie was wondering how to let go of her urge to punch Sheelah in the face. She observed her breathing for two breaths.

'Well, I know I should,' she said.

'You use an awful lot of "should"s!'

Georgie decided to ignore that one, though it raised her heartbeat and got a good shoosh of adrenaline pumping around her kidneys. 'And that's exactly what I'm in the process of doing,' she explained quietly.

'Don't be in the process of doing! Do the doing.'

Oh dear, that was too much. Georgie opened her mouth and heard 'I AM FUCKING DOING THE FUCKING DOING!' shooting out of it like a hard sharp blade. She was amazed at her own volume, but this time, at last, she made herself clear. Sheelah was silenced, a look of discombobulated horror on her face. 'Why d'you think I'm so fucking knackered?' An arrow swishing through the air. 'I'm letting it go, and watching it go, and feeling it go and it hurts!'

Silence.

'It HURTS!' Louder.

Silence.

'It hurts!' At this point Georgie's bottom lip began to tremble and tears pricked her eyes.

'It's all right,' Sheelah cooed, warmly embracing her. 'Let it all come out.'

The springy texture of Sheelah's arms and bosom ought to have given comfort, but Georgie refused to let it all come out. If she asked how dare the fucking bastard disdain her after all she'd done for him, how dare he take up with some mindless bint young enough to be his daughter – or granddaughter – how dare he let go of Georgie when she couldn't let go of him: if she raged against the sheer unfairness of life and death and sex, she'd simply be accused of having an ego. So she held onto the fury and the snot.

It was something to do with self-respect, that she couldn't abandon herself to someone who would judge her; even though she loved Sheelah and had been her friend for fifteen years, and had many times accepted her help.

Their meeting had set the pattern of their unequal

relationship. It had started on an aeroplane, a cheap flight to Crete, which Georgie had taken just before Charlie's second birthday, to take advantage of the fact that Joni was not yet at school, and Charlie could still fly free. She had decided to take a break from her life with Jim, but couldn't bear to leave the children with him. It was asking for trouble – it was begging and pleading for trouble, filling in a form and paying for trouble.

Jim had helped them check in the pushchair and baggage, and kissed them all goodbye at the gate. He was angry about Georgie's blow for independence, and wanted to demonstrate how she needed him, but was just as keen to get back to his sound-proofed studio, and couldn't have spared the time to join them anyway.

A nice lady was sitting by the window, four-year-old Joni was in the middle, and Georgie was in the aisle seat, with Charlie on her knee. All was fine until the engines started up. Charlie decided to get off the plane and go back home, and couldn't be made to understand that the option wasn't available. First he complained in a quiet moany sort of way, struggling to be free of Georgie's embrace. Then he began to cry in earnest, still struggling. Soothing words and sounds didn't work. Refreshments made no difference – not milk, not chocolate. The nice lady at the window turned and smiled with kind sympathy, which felt to Georgie like withering criticism. Then Charlie began to shout and scream. 'Naaaaoo! No! Daddeeeeee! Off!' Georgie, always a little nervous just before take-off, wondered if he knew something everyone else didn't. He couldn't be amused by either of the toys Georgie extracted from the bag under her seat; he wouldn't even look at his Star Wars figure, or the Lego ambulance with the real flashing light; he batted them away. He was shouting and screaming from the moment they roared up the strip and lifted into the air until it was time to undo seatbelts and people were stretching their legs and leaning on other people's seats. Joni had started up by this time, because Charlie was hogging every second of Georgie's attention. 'Mummy. Mummy. Mummy. Mummy. Gee. Mummy. Gee. Mummy. Gee. MUMMY!'

And while Georgie was wriggling and fiddling to unfasten her seatbelt, which was impossible to do at the same time as restraining Charlie, the bag beneath her seat spilled. A mug of milk and a bottle of water rolled into the aisle out of reach of her toes. A paperback book slid out, followed by a box of tampons which emptied itself around a pair of court-shod feet.

'MUMMY!'

'I'm sorry Joni darling I can't deal with it until Charlie's settled down.'

'Daddeeeeee! Daddeeeee! Off! Off!'

'Is there anything we can do?' asked the flight attendant. Georgie, sweating, twisted and in disarray, exposing midriff and bra straps, was too involved with two-year-old arms and legs to look at her.

'I don't know, I don't know what to do.' She was beginning to despair.

'Aaaarrrggh. NAAAO!'

'Mummy. Mummeeee. I need a wee wee. I need a wee wee Mummy.'

'Would he like a drink of something?'

'No,' Georgie felt her chin wobbling. Her face was streaked with sweat. 'I've tried that.'

'DADDEEE! DADDEEE!'

'So his father's not here?'

'I need a wee wee Mummy.'

'No.'

'What about a toy?'

'DADDEEE!'

Now came Georgie's own sniffles and smarting tears. Well, that was worse than all that had happened already – absolutely not the thing, especially not in front of the children. She fought to hold back the swell.

'I've. Tried. Everything. Nothing. Works. I can't. Deal. With it.'

The nice lady by the window piped up. 'Why don't I show you where the lavatory is, while your Mummy takes care of your little brother?'

'I want MUMMY!' Joni said, leaning heavily into Georgie, grabbing her arm with both hands and pulling her top further over the exposed shoulder right down to the elbow; the lemon-coloured summer top she had pushed them all round the shops to find because she hadn't had any new clothes in four years, the beautiful lemon coloured summer top which was stretched taut and cutting into her neck tore apart. That was the dambuster – that, and the lady's kindness. Georgie let it all flood out in gushing tears and guttural sobs. She couldn't help it; her feelings had been inexplicable and ungovernable ever since Charlie's weaning.

Now the window lady smiled at Georgie. 'I could hold onto your son while you take your daughter to the toilet?'

Georgie finally looked at her properly. She was about forty, fair-haired with a smudgy sort of face, blue eyes, big cheeks. She put out two strong arms and pulled Charlie firmly towards her with a 'There we are!'

'NO! DADDEEEE! NAAAAAO!.'

'What's his name?'

'Charlie.'

'Come on Charlie you're going to sit on my knee now. Just until your mummy comes back.'

'NAAAAO!'

'Thank you. Thank you so much. Thank you.'

What a relief it was to let go of him! Georgie stumbled up the aisle urging Joni ahead of her and they queued together. There wasn't room for the two of them in the cubicle, so they left the door ajar and Georgie encouraged Joni through the gap, then when she'd finished the whole procedure, explained to her that she must wait outside while Mummy sorted herself out. Georgie rearranged her face as best she could with little dribbles of water and paper towels.

By the time they returned Charlie was perfectly happy,

looking out of the window at clouds. Sheelah was saying 'and that one's like a great big bus. Vroom vroom vroom! And what do you think that one's like? I think it's like...'

'Bird.'

'It's like a bird! It IS like a bird.'

They were staying in the same hotel, and ended up spending time together: sitting on the beach staring at the sparkling Sea of Crete, or by the pool reading the odd paragraph of a novel when they had a chance. It was perfect weather – bright, hot and sunny, with a fresh island breeze. They swapped the children between them and took turns to swim. They sat outside cafés drinking ouzo and eating olives, and wondered at the sight of black-draped old ladies whiling away their last sunny hours crouched on front doorsteps. They dragged the children round the picturesque yellow stone ruins of Knossos, Europe's most ancient city, gave Joni a ride on a donkey, bought postcards and worry beads. In the evening they sat on Sheelah's balcony with a bottle of retsina, watching the sun turning the sky red and the land pinkish gold. Charlie would be snoozing on Georgie's lap, Joni sleepy and yawning but grown up and pleased with herself for being awake so late. Sheelah gave her all the attention Georgie couldn't spare. Between them they had enough for both.

She learnt that Sheelah had come alone to think about her life and make a momentous decision. She was never going to have children. She was going to split up with the man she was living with and start up a business selling jewellery on a cart in a shopping mall. She knew about enamelling and silversmithing, and wore many of her own striking 'pieces'. They were works of art, and Georgie told her so and encouraged her with admiring enthusiasm.

So right from the first moment of their meeting Sheelah had been Georgie's rescuer, and no matter how Georgie tried to return the compliment and the debt, the roles were irreversible. If she invited Sheelah to lunch, Sheelah would bring half of what they would eventually consume and flowers to boot. If

Georgie rang her to ask how she was, she inevitably wound up confiding all her own frustrations and ailments, because Sheelah would get in first with the questions. In the end she'd come to accept it and realise why it was; to allow it and to stop feeling guilty about it and even enjoy the favour she was doing Sheelah through her moments of helplessness and inadequacy.

But now Georgie felt a certain resentment about her position. She released herself from Sheelah's embrace, but gently and slowly, mulling over positive things she could say to move things on, though not actually saying anything. *It's OK, I'll be fine. I'm just a bit tired. It's just taking longer, it's just a bit harder than I thought. I'm over worrying, just missing the children...* She couldn't bring herself to say the last one; it might not be fair, since Sheelah had no children to miss.

She was still forming sentences in her mind when Sheelah murmured, pensively, 'I'm going to share something with you I've never mentioned before.'

Sensing a change in Sheelah's mood, Georgie put aside her own quagmire of feelings to make room for what promised to be a difficult confession. Sheelah pondered awhile before speaking, staring at her hands.

'I once let everything go, you know. Possessions. Home. Even my name. A long time ago. In my teens.' She hesitated, and Georgie gently encouraged her to go on. 'I joined a cult. The Gupta Dhanas. I let go of my Christian name because I hadn't chosen it and my father's name because I didn't want a name from any man. And I've never never never regretted it.'

Georgie was amazed, startled. 'Really? So...'

'Sheelah was a gift from my spiritual guide.'

'And that was a woman?'

'His gender wasn't the point.'

'No. And your surname?'

'My idea. Deed poll.'

'God, really?' Georgie didn't know what to say. It was hard to believe; that you could know someone for so long and fail to know something so essential. It made her feel uneasy. It suggested more than the kind of jokey misandry that used to pepper their conversations; something far deeper and more painful. It was a blotting out of one's childhood self, a rejection of one's family.

'I don't think I could ever do that,' she said quietly. 'I feel as if I am my name, as if I couldn't possibly be anyone else!'

'That's ego, that's attachment, you see. It's random. It's meaningless. There are plenty of other Georgina Suttons in the world. And Sheelah Wilds.'

So what, thought Georgie, but she didn't say it. She didn't want to sound flippant, but she didn't have the energy for discussing metaphysics or psychology.

'It's family,' was all she said.

'Didn't you take Jim's name when you married him?' Sheelah argued.

'I suppose I did. And I gave it back when I divorced him. I'd always felt like a Sutton. I never felt like a Burke. So...' Georgie wondered what had happened to make Sheelah kill her roots in this way. 'You're not really Sheelah?'

'I am really Sheelah.'

'I meant, what was your previous name? Or is that... too sensitive to think about?'

'Sheila Cox.'

Georgie stared, eyebrows raised.

'Yes. Sheila. So actually all I took on was a different spelling.' Georgie nodded earnestly. Sheelah sighed. 'Life is full of disappointments. But the way I look at it is this: I came to the same place by a different route. And the Irish Sheila means blind, but the Sanskrit means 'character'. Character. That's one up on blind, after all.'

Georgie doled out another slice of cake each and got up to make the next cup of tea. 'So what were these. Guptadanas, did you say?'

'Yes. Bastards, actually. A blessing I managed to extract myself. But it was a good philosophy and it's still essentially important – to me at any rate. But what's really great about it is that these sorts of ideas are becoming more and more popular aren't they?'

'Mindfulness and so on?'

'Partly.'

'What... Living simply, fasting, not being so grasping sort of thing? I hope so. We certainly can't go on as we are, can we?'

'No, not that part so much. It's to do with trusting your prayers to the Universal Spirit. The law of attraction. Whatever you think about you attract into your life. Think good things and you attract good things. And vice versa. If something bad happens to you, you've brought it in, somehow. You need it. You learn from it. It's so true.'

Georgie stiffened.

'And you can bring in good things, even material things, or a better job, or healing, or the house you want, by praying, attracting, believing,' Sheelah expounded.

'I know, you've mentioned the idea before and I'm sorry but it sounds like a pile of pants to me.'

'You should try it.'

You use an awful lot of "should"s, thought Georgie, feeling her heart rate rising and a wave of heat coming through. She made tea as she spoke, slowly and deliberately, cooling herself by loosening her collar and relaxing her shoulders.

'Of course one's attitude makes a difference, but only so far. One simply doesn't have that much power. For example, you're saying it's my fault I got cancer?'

'No, no, no it's not as simple as that.'

'According to your theory I've attracted the cancer into my life.'

'It's not as simple as that.'

'How do you interpret it, then, according to your theory?'

Sheelah looked flustered. Georgie carried on breathing deeply in, out, in, out, don't shake it all about, thinking, 'I am well, I am happy, I approve of myself,' as she carefully presented Sheelah with her tea. 'I'm just curious. How would you interpret getting cancer if you got cancer yourself, for example?'

'I just think you have to take responsibility for what happens to you in your life.'

'I agree. But what if something happens that you're not responsible for?' Georgie began speaking as if she were explaining to a two-year-old – kindly, but with the sure authority of an adult – that sometimes you slip and fall over, sometimes you can't put things back together again, sometimes it rains. 'What if it's really not your fault? What if you're struck by lightning or born an orphan with AIDS in a mud hut? Is a baby responsible for being born in a mud hut with AIDS, for example?'

'Calm down, now, Georgie, you're getting upset again.'

But Georgie didn't think she was getting upset, at least not visibly. She thought Sheelah was getting upset.

'I am calm. I just want to know if you believe that a baby is responsible for being born with AIDS?'

'No, no, not the baby.'

'No. Not the baby.'

'It must be the baby's spirit I suppose.'

'The baby's spirit?' A tiny seismic event occurred in Georgie's voice. She made sure it didn't happen again. 'I see, so it's like original sin then? A sort of Catholic thing?'

'Well, not really. In a way I suppose except that there aren't any priests. And it's from a past life.'

Georgie was breathing deeply, but her emotions didn't seem to be responding. She didn't want to shout again, but she wasn't prepared to engage with any more of Sheelah's quasi-religious nonsense.

'I'm perfectly calm.' She took Sheelah's hand and placed it against her ribs. 'Can you feel it? My heart is quite steady. Not too fast?' Sheelah's expression was compassionate, understanding. She nodded. Georgie went on, in a cool modulated downtempo voice. 'But if you believe that a baby is responsible for getting AIDS... Or whole communities are responsible for drowning in tsunamis... Or that some unknown person is responsible for a tree falling down on them in a gale, or a bomb going off on the bus they happen to take... Or for losing their job in an economic downturn, or for being in the way of a bloody great Land Rover that's veered off the road...' Sheelah's expression had changed into one more serious and defensive. 'Or that it's my fault,' Georgie paused, 'that I got cancer.' Sheelah took her hand away. 'I don't ever want to speak to you again, that's all. Tell me you understand and stay, or go, it's up to you.'

Sheelah looked down and thought about it for a few moments, and then without a word, she went. She collected her things and exited through the jumbled corridor in a sheath of silence that neither of them could work out how to punctuate. She wouldn't look at Georgie, she hardened her face.

The door banged and Georgie sat down again and finished the tea and the cake, trying to remain as impassive as Sheelah had looked. At first she thought Sheelah would come back. She wasn't supposed to have gone. She was supposed to have stayed; they were supposed to have sorted out their differences and come to a mutual understanding. Georgie told herself that they would somehow make it up at some future date. She tried to work out how she could have said what she meant in a less aggressive way. But then she would fire up again about how victims are always blamed, and how unkind it was, and how unsupportive – how little like a friend!

It upset her terribly. No matter how she breathed or relaxed or how many positive thoughts she thought, she couldn't ignore the fact that she was upset. The upset was floating about in her solar plexus like an unwanted ghost, dangerously close to vulnerable glands.

Names of things and names of people often hovered at the fringes of Georgie's thought, irritatingly out of reach. It had happened when she was pregnant and was happening again these days as one of the many gifts of the menopause. She was developing the habit of letting them go; trusting that they would pop into her mind eventually, without effort. Her upset was like that. The name of an emotion was eluding her. The word 'jealousy' popped into her mind. No it's not jealousy, she thought firmly. I don't get jealous. That's far too depressing a passion!

Think About Sooner. She reread Will's letter and moved it to Think About Later.

GO SHOPPING

What a perfect month is May! And Will's unbirthday party was going to be on the first day of that best of all months.

'Will you be flying the red flag?' Larry asked him with an air of amusement. Georgie thought it was either some kind of prohibition, as in being the opposite to a green flag, or something to do with exciting bulls, which she supposed must mean the boys, so why would Will want to do that? Either way, her father didn't seem worried. He and Maureen were going out for the evening. Will was to observe their usual rules: curfew at one, no swimming, no noise, no unruly behaviour, no smoking indoors, preferably no smoking at all. In other words, no fun. Their mother, on the other hand, betrayed some anxiety.

'What goes on at these parties?' she said. 'Do people "snog"?'

I bloody hope so, Georgie thought. She was ticking off the days. In her fantasies she was snogging Matthew in every room of the house, and in the summerhouse and behind the summerhouse. She would lie in bed and imagine that her own hands were Matthew's, that he might touch her so tenderly and cleverly. She held a picture of his lovely face in her mind as spasms of joy rippled through her body like magic.

She was allowed to invite friends, to supply girl material, she supposed, though Will's lot were too young really. Fi and Jan were coming, naturally, and Debbie Needham and Pippa Burchill. The five of them gathered together at break time to talk about what they were going to wear and Georgie felt left out. None of them had wanted to burn their bras, so she was going to have to fork out for a new one or feel like a bloody sore thumb. And she couldn't keep excusing herself from tennis either – period pains couldn't possibly last two weeks. It was no fun lying in the sick room anyway, even when you were actually ill. Staff members were forever disturbing you to find out how you were feeling, keeping you awake with their sympathy and nursing.

'What are you wearing Georgie? We're all wearing long.'

'Velvet flares and cheesecloth smock.'

'Oh nice. Without a bra?'

'I'm getting a new one,' Georgie lied.

'Nice.'

She was so behind with revision, when was she going to have time to buy a bra? And how was she going to afford it?

One evening Georgie's father summoned her to his study. She thought she was in for another ticking off. She thought it must be to do with not working hard enough, with being distracted from Academe. Far from it. He had good news, delivered with a jaunty smile. What with the smile and the beard and the hair grown so long it was curling, like the patterns in his new ties, he was beginning to look like a completely different man. He told her she was going to receive a clothing allowance, until she was earning her own money or had a university grant. She had Frieda to thank for the idea. What did she think about seven pounds a week? If it wasn't enough it could increase. 'When did you last go shopping with Mum?' he asked.

'When I last got too big for everything.'

'I'll give you some arrears then. Frieda wants to help you. She's a real cutie, isn't she? Such an angel.'

Georgie agreed. She graciously overcame her slight annoyance at having been discussed, and couldn't think of any reason to resist being dressed by an angel with an eye for the feminine and beautiful, though the word 'angel' brought back a memory of Frieda making finger horns, like a fiend. What you saw in her was what you looked for. She was an optical illusion, shimmering from one shape to the other, between Freund and Feind, friend and foe, like the young-woman old-hag picture; and Georgie couldn't see both sides of her at once, no matter how she tried.

Her excitement grew and grew. She would open a book

and not be able to read it, because her head was full of other things.

Frieda took her to shops she hadn't ever noticed – boutiques with obnoxious women in charge, who 'madamed' them but melted in the warmth of Frieda's confident broken accent and charmingly eccentric smile. She flattered them by consulting them, and teased them by seeming to consider price tags that were well out of reach. She chose things for Georgie to try, and Georgie emerged, hideously embarrassed, from behind various curtains in various garments, while Frieda's mouth pouted and twisted and she hung her head to one side and then to the other, flicking her long fair hair this way and that. At last Georgie was clearly modelling the very thing; the response was no pout or twist, but an exclamation, and a nod to the shopkeeper. The very thing was a silk halter-neck dress, in blood red. It made her think of the red flag, exciting bulls. She couldn't wear either of her pretty new bras under it, because it left her back and shoulders utterly bare. 'It hangs wonderfully!' said the shopkeeper. 'Cut on the bias, you see. That's why it's a little dearer than the others.' They added a black cotton shawl in case it was cold, the black shot through with silver threads which emerged at the ends as silver tassels. To complement the dress they found a pair of slingback sandals, nail varnish to match the colour of the dress, and a bracelet to match the silver threads.

At Saturday lunchtime she was so nervous about the party she only managed a tiny slice of steak and kidney pie and let Frieda finish the baked beans.

Frieda marched into the bathroom while Georgie was showering, but Georgie didn't mind. She'd already been seen half-naked once or twice on the shopping trip, and though at the time she had shrunk in modesty, she decided to be pleased about it because: a) losing her inhibition was a necessary step in the boyfriend project direction, and b) it was normal. None of her friends were shy about their bodies. Mostly they were slimmer, it had to be admitted, and more tanned. Fi didn't even have white strap marks, for example. Changing after Games, Georgie would sometimes feel like a naïve white blob. But Frieda had accepted, even admired her shape, and Frieda's taste could be trusted. She'd said, 'If only you have confidence you are very beautiful.' She knew about so many things.

She said she would wait in her bedroom and Georgie should come when she was dry and Frieda would help her to change.

She welcomed her with a gift. 'For you!' She handed Georgie a cat's cradle of red lace. 'Panties!' she explained, with laughter in her voice, relishing Georgie's perplexity. 'Put it on! If you wear the usual one, you can see it through the silk. If you wear nothing, it will be worse.' She made a coy face in pretence of shock.

'Where do I put my legs?' Georgie handled the item as if it might strangle her. 'Which way round do they go?'

Frieda showed her, and Georgie, absurdly, as if she were on a beach, wobblingly stepped into the object and pulled it up underneath her bath robe. She hurried for the dress, hanging on the wardrobe.

'Make-up first,' Frieda advised, 'or it will wrinkle.'

Frieda sat her down in the middle of the room where the light glared, and Georgie felt a layer of sensitive squeamishness in her skin, the pricking of goose pimples, and dampness in her armpits, while Frieda moved round the stool on her knees, choosing from her own as well as Georgie's supply of cosmetic chemicals.

She varnished her fingernails first, loading the brush with glistening red drops, and applying three precise flicks to each finger and four to each thumb. When she'd finished, she moved onto Georgie's toes, while Georgie sat with arms helplessly akimbo and hands helplessly splayed, stoically resisting the exquisitely ticklish gentleness of Frieda's touch.

'You have a dancer's feet. Arched. Hübsche.'

Georgie was going to suggest giving them back to the dancer.

Instead she accepted the compliment, without understanding it. Pretty feet? They're just for standing and walking and running on, she thought. And kicking things. You might as well have pretty knees. Her unsaid words thickened the ensuing silence.

Frieda dragged Georgie's hair out of her face, painfully securing it under a band.

Holding the heel of her hand against Georgie's temple, deep in concentration, and as minutely as if she were painting a miniature, she drew a line of soft kohl around each eye, right onto the inside of the bottom lid. It hurt. Perhaps it was supposed to hurt. Georgie soldiered the pain, determined not to betray herself. Next Frieda dabbed silver eye shadow over each fluttering lid. She mascaraed her lashes and stroked rouge onto her cheeks, while Georgie meekly observed her, noticing every pore and freckle and laughter-line in Frieda's face, gradually relaxing in the warmth of her attention, and loving it. She even loved the sweet smoky smell of Frieda's breath.

Lipstick came on last, then Frieda changed her mind. 'I did not do it well.' She wetted her thumb with spit, rubbed off the colour and blotted Georgie's mouth, before going over it again with a darker red, moving her own mouth as she did so, in reflection.

Georgie let her hair be fluffed up with a hairdryer and, as a finishing touch, was doused in French scent which smelt of sea air and orange blossom, finer and more sophisticated than the sticky musk she'd meant to wear.

At last Frieda took the dress from its hanger, with an air of reverence, as if she were preparing her apprentice for a religious ritual. Georgie solemnly slipped off the bathrobe and laid it on the stool, feeling obvious and worse than nude. Her bottom was bare, basically. The dainty unabsorbent strip of lace didn't cover much of anything, really.

Frieda held the dress open for Georgie, pulled it carefully, sensitively round her hips and over her belly, then, while Georgie held her hair out of the way and bowed her head, she tied the halter straps round her neck, tightening and releasing them so that the silk fell with exactly the right tension. She smoothed it carefully over Georgie's body, studying her face for a response. Georgie could only stare back, unsure, surprised by the ripple of pleasure she had felt, and wondering if something else was going on, something less straightforward, and more... More designed. She often had the idea that around Frieda things happened in layers, as if she were using code. Other meanings swam under the surface layer, challenging her to dive, to take some kind of risk, to do something outrageous. She brazened out Frieda's gaze, challenging her in return.

This time, Frieda capitulated. 'It looks like no underwear,' she announced, dismissing her with a nod of approval. 'Do you get it?'

When she saw herself in the mirror, Georgie felt confused.

'Put off your glasses,' Frieda suggested.

Georgie did as she was told.

'Now you can see your eyes.'

'I can't see at all,' Georgie complained, screwing up her face. She turned to look directly at Frieda, catching a disturbing moment of rapture in her expression. It was admiring, radiant, almost amorous. But of course, she was proud of her own artistry – of what she had created out of Georgie's ordinary body and face, her dull raw material.

Before they went down, Frieda gave her some advice: she must allow Matthew to pursue her. If anything she must ignore him. 'Flirt with other boys – make him jealous,' she said. Georgie thought ignoring him would be easy. No wonder she had failed up to now – she'd done all she could to attract his attention and engage him in interesting conversation.

'Maybe you will then catch another boy,' Frieda added, in that strange contradictory fashion of hers.

Everyone agreed that they had never seen Georgie looking so lovely. Even Will approved. He congratulated Frieda on his 'schöne Schwester'. Her father kissed her forehead. He said, 'be good my pretty girl,' and Maureen laughed and whispered, 'you look special,' as she followed him out, leaving them free to demonstrate their maturity and responsibility. Georgie didn't need the rouge. Nobody had ever called her pretty or special before.

People arrived – fuzzy moving shapes which Georgie couldn't identify and didn't dare to approach. She relaxed decorously in an armchair pretending to be cool, but in her short-sighted specialness she was beginning to feel a trifle isolated, and the sexy knickers were cutting her in half. Nobody was interested in talking to her, so it seemed; at least, nobody did. At last Jan and Fi arrived, announcing their presence with highly charged soprano shrieks. They didn't recognise Georgie until she stood up and touched Jan on the shoulder, eliciting a comically exaggerated response.

'GEE! It's YOU,' she screamed. 'I LOVE your dress! Hey you look FAB without your specs!' Georgie looked round the room to gather Frieda's reaction, expecting her to be pleased, but Frieda had vanished. Fi stroked the dress, in awe.

'Silk?' she asked.

Georgie shrugged.

'Phew, that must have cost a few pence.'

'It's an old one of Frieda's,' said Georgie. She didn't know why.

Jan produced a bottle of Mateus Rosé from beneath her corduroy jacket and Fi opened her shoulder bag to reveal a small bottle of rum and a bottle of red wine with a posh-looking French label on it. 'I raided the cellar,' she whispered. 'My dad'll be furious, but don't worry, he'll be too drunk to notice when he next goes down.'

'Glasses!' Jan shouted, so Georgie pointed them towards the kitchen.

The kitchen table was covered with bottles and cans, and two boxes of real ale. Two of Will's friends were leaning against the dresser cradling pint glasses, discussing with great enthusiasm the similarities and differences between Nicky Lauda and James Hunt. Georgie reached past them for two tumblers, then a third; she'd already lost her cider on a bookcase or shelf somewhere.

'Corkscrew!' shouted Jan.

'Shall we mix them?' Georgie asked, ranging the three bottles on the table.

Jan mimed putting her finger down her throat, meaning, 'No.'

'What's happened to the corkscrew?' she asked. 'Do either of you fine gentlemen have any notion?'

'We're on the ale, man,' one of them said. The three girls clocked each other and exploded with inexplicable laughter.

Georgie looked in the cutlery drawer. 'We've got loads, normally. Buggeration, they've all gone.'

'What to do?' Jan shrugged theatrically.

'We have to go on an expedition!' sang Fi. 'You first Georgie.'

The French windows were wide open and the chairs and sofa had been moved to the edges of the sitting room. Bowls of crisps and nuts had been placed on every surface, and candles, waiting to be lit. Sketchy figures were standing, leaning on furniture, and sitting on the floor. Some of the boys had brought girls. A man in a shiny suit was looking through the record cupboard, rejecting LPs.

Georgie knew nobody, and felt weird walking amongst them in her foreign clothes with her painted face and her blurred vision in her own home. She thought she ought to tell Will that two strange girls were on the sofa, smoking. They were using an egg cup as an ash tray.

Outside dusk was gradually falling. Although it looked as if it might rain again, Will had opened up the front of the summerhouse, by sliding one of its two huge glass windows fully across the other. It was almost an invitation. The girls crossed the terrace, and ventured inside. It smelt peculiarly sweet. A joss stick was burning.

'That's a bit dangerous,' said Georgie. She wrinkled her nose at the state of the room, straightening the duvet on the unmade bed so they could sit on it.

'Careful,' she said to Fi, who was about to crush Will's camera. Jan spotted a corkscrew lying next to the record player.

'It walked here,' she laughed, coming to join them on the bed. 'Oh my merry arse, look! Your brother's been busy.'

There was a square box of Durex peeping out from under the pillow.

'Might have been busy thinking about it,' Georgie said, in his defence. 'Leave it alone!'

'They're only jonnys,' said Jan. 'Nothing to be scared of.'

'Actually they're Willie's,' Fi declared. Jan hooted, and Georgie joined in, relieved that it was just a wonderful joke.

Fi opened the French wine first. 'This is expensive,' she told them, 'so we'd better enjoy it.'

She sloshed it into their three glasses.

'Let's drink to 'O' level success!' suggested Georgie.

Fi and Jan looked at each other, aghast.

'Let's drink to getting off with a nice boy,' said Jan.

'Three nice boys,' said Fi.

'Three each,' said Jan. 'Chin, chin!'

They clashed their glasses together and took a gulp.

'It's horrible,' said Jan. 'Tastes like petrol.'

Georgie wasn't sure. Her tongue felt as if it had been leathered.

'Perhaps it needs to mature,' Fi suggested. She looked at the bottle. 'No it's definitely mature. 1945, look.'

'Perhaps it needs to breathe?'

'Those grapes were growing in the war!' Jan shouted.

'Don't mention the war!' said Fi, and Georgie shushed her.

'Oh blimey O'Reilly!' said Jan, 'I don't want to drink it now. Come on, let's knock it back, then we can get onto the nice stuff.'

'Where's Frieda?' asked Fi.

'I don't know.'

'What about Matthew? Has he arrived yet Gee?'

It was dark by the time Matthew turned up, but his blazer and white flares made him instantly visible. Georgie's blurred sideways glimpses of him set her heart singing and sharpened her consciousness. She could sense his atmosphere, wherever he was and wherever she was. She wanted to bite his face. She wanted to smell his neck, and kiss him right down from neck to shoulder and lick his skin and suck his fingers. His hair was tousled, as if he'd just got out of bed – suggesting that was where he belonged.

'Hi Gee,' he said. 'Nice dress.'

In that moment Georgie went to heaven. No experience could possibly go beyond that sudden glorious tingling spurt of ecstasy. The pleasure of his compliment blanked out all thoughts. He looked her straight in the eye, and her heart was bumping so wildly she felt the silk quivering against her stomach. She didn't know what to say, so she followed Frieda's advice, turned elegantly round on her little heel and ignored him. Oopsy daisy. Her ankle collapsed and she bobbed. It was like a little curtsey, down and up again. She didn't look back. She limped away, mortified.

Jan and Fi were by the pool huddling together on a lounger, sharing a cigarette. They looked cold.

'You're smoking,' Georgie said, non-committally.

'We're not inhaling,' said Fi.

'It's cool,' explained Jan and they cackled with laughter and guzzled their drinks. They were now on the rum and Coke. Fi offered her a splash and she added it to whatever was in her glass.

'Matthew's here, looking knicker-wettingly lovely,' Georgie told them. 'I'm playing hard to get.' They cackled some more. She tried to get them to shift along but they complained that the free bit of the lounger was wet.

'Still crazy after all these years!' Jan sang along with Paul Simon in her own personal harmony. 'That's us!' she exclaimed, jubilantly raising her glass to the night.

Frieda was right that if Georgie ignored someone it might make them want her, only it was the wrong someone. It was the man in the shiny suit. He cornered her and spoke about Howlin'

Wolf and Muddy Waters and Karl Marx. His name was Andrew and he had a moustache. She half-listened, glancing over his shoulder, catching no sight of Matthew anywhere, or of Fi or Jan. In the candlelight couples were slow dancing to *Desire*, snogging and stroking each other.

Andrew told her that Labour was on the way out and the country was in for a reckoning. 'We're letting our manufacturing go, and our mines,' he explained. 'Our coal, our ship builders! What's made Britain great! Not that we are great! No, we've been a load of bastards raping and pillaging the rest of the world.' He talked about the decline in the value of sterling, the rise of the iron lady. Georgie didn't know how to extract herself. The only method was to finish her drink and say she needed to go to the kitchen for more. She waved her glass at him and he grabbed it. 'What are you drinking?'

'Wine, please,' she said meekly, escaping into the garden as soon as he'd gone.

He found her again when she was on her way back indoors. It was too cold to be outside in silk and tassels and she hadn't a hope of seeing what was happening out there in moonless dark and short-sighted mizzle. She was feeling pretty sloshed and wobbly by now.

'Why are prices rocketing through the roof?' he went on. 'It's the price of oil!'

'We've got our own oil,' Georgie said haughtily, in an attempt to close the subject.

Andrew seemed encouraged by any response. 'That should be invested, that's for the future, that's for infrastructure.'

Georgie let her eyes stray lazily over the rest of the assembled population.

'It's Scottish oil to be accurate,' he went on.

She could see two of everything now, everything blurred.

'You're really sexy, d'you know that?' he told her, putting her drink on the piano. 'Pure cheese.'

Georgie felt a wave of disgust. His face swam in front of hers and next he was grasping her bottom and had a hand on her breast, squeezing as if it contained tomato ketchup. She allowed him to eat her face because she didn't know how to stop him. Actually it wasn't too bad if she forgot who was doing it, though the moustache kept reminding her.

Somehow and sometime later she extracted herself from his slobber and made her way to the kitchen for a glass of water. There, finally, she found Frieda. Will was sitting on one side of her, Matthew on the other. Matthew was in his shirtsleeves, his face flushed and happy. Frieda was wearing a dress like Georgie's, but it was blue – a strikingly icy blue that went well with her faint tan and fair hair. Her lips were pink, her eyelids heavily covered in black shadow. She was smoking a fat cigarette, and the smoke had the same sweet stench Georgie had smelt in the summerhouse. They all laughed at Georgie for some reason, and Frieda offered her the cigarette.

'No,' said Will. 'Not for Pud.'

Frieda smiled dreamily. 'It will not be wrong.'

'I don't want cancer, thanks,' Georgie said, uncertainly smiling.

They laughed again.

'Is it a drug?'

'You could say that,' said Matthew, simpering.

Georgie ignored him. She saw on the table a torn foil packet of tablets.

'No drugs for Puddy,' Will repeated, swiping the packet.

'Those are pills, not drugs,' Georgie retaliated. 'And they're Mummy's.'

'Mummy's little helpers,' Will sniggered. 'Well we all need a little help don't we? In this wretched grind.'

Georgie stumbled upstairs to bed, hoping that her disdainful exit would act as a lure. She didn't understand what was going on, and she didn't like it that Will had opened Maureen's pills. It felt wrong. It felt like a betrayal.

She lay on her bed and watched the ceiling dance, and slumber covered her.

*

She was woken by the sound of the stairs creaking, and whispering sniggers, and a knock at the door. She waited, breathless, and was glad she had, because the knock wasn't for her, it was for Will's room – now Frieda's room. She heard low talking and the sound of laughter through the walls.

Her heart battered her chest. She couldn't bear it. She stumbled out of bed and out onto the landing, and after listening through the door, knocked. Frieda came out, enclosed in a miasma of nauseating smoke. Georgie heard Will's voice, talking to someone else, and then made out Matthew's shape in the red candlelight, bending down over something. Frieda closed the door behind her and ushered Georgie back into her own room, putting her finger to her lips to indicate that she should stay silent.

'Come to bed now,' she whispered, 'I'll send Matthew to wish you good night. He is going to go soon. Your parents are here. We must be very quiet.'

Frieda kissed her goodnight, once on each cheek. She smelt alcoholic and smokey and something else cloying like sour milk or marzipan. Georgie waited in the dark, her thoughts and feelings awhirl, curious about what was happening in the room next door and straining to listen through the wall, half-wishing to be invited in, half preferring the prospect of being alone with Matthew. She heard people leaving, and imagined with every murmur that he was at the door, that soon he'd be beside her talking in whispers, breathing the smell of boys onto her, kissing her perhaps, with abrasive lips, and touching tongues.

At about five o'clock she woke up with a head sucked dry and throbbing, still wearing her dress and slingbacks underneath the duvet. She got herself to the bathroom in time to puke up tidily, then tiptoed downstairs to fill her glass with kitchen water, because the bathroom water tasted nasty.

An attempt had been made to clear up. Bottles were standing beside the overflowing waste paper bin and the kitchen table was covered with dirty glasses and a pile of empty bowls. It stank like a pub, of stale beer and smoke. She went quietly through the sitting room to the French window, opened it as quietly as she could and stepped into the dewy garden. The sky was light, covered in creamy clouds. Strewn over the patio were cigarette stubs and empty cans. A collection of glasses stood beside the swimming pool, some still containing an inch or two of cider or beer.

The summerhouse was still and silent and looked empty beyond its half-drawn curtain. She heard a creaking noise, and the sound of Will snoring in a moany kind of way. She tiptoed past and up to her lovely elm trees. Birds were beginning to chatter and gurgle. She thought that must be the most beautiful sound in the world and these were the most beautiful trees. She rested her face against the bark – cold and moist and scratchy. Whatever happened in the rest of her world, she thought, these birds would sing, and this tree would be here and comfort her, nourishing her with oxygen while she nourished it with carbon dioxide. She thought she could feel its age and its wisdom, she thought she could feel its love. A piece of bark stuck to her cheek as she looked up to view its canopy of branches and twigs. All around her the garden was pale green and quivering. Even the silver birches were in full leaf. Only the elms were locked in their winter phase, reserved and bare. One old yellowish brown leaf from last Autumn was still attached, hanging miserably alone. She realised that new leaves were never going to spring from these old trees.

Someone had planted them over a hundred years ago.

And now they were dead.

BE EASY AND CHEERFUL

On first being diagnosed, after the shock and disbelief, something new had crept into her soul and into her bed: sheer terror. It would grab her suddenly in the night out of nowhere. It would swoop up through her body, grip her heart and jolt her awake, so that she could feel adrenaline exploding into her bloodstream, oversharpening her nerves, setting off her pulse and her muscles. It was as though a deafening bell had gone off: FIRE! FIRE! FIRE! with nowhere to run; the danger was within.

Over the weeks and months, the wounds had healed and the terror had gone away. She had learnt to calm herself down, and simply living had dispelled it; she'd lived a few months after having cancer, so she'd probably live a few more, and the months would turn into years.

But every now and then, sheer terror would rise again, bringing horrible flash-imaginings of a figure falling or drowning, bleeding or ill, tortured, smashed, screaming, in flames, worse, imaginings she fought to blank out, but fighting only made them louder and sharper. She was terrified for Joni. She was terrified for Charlie. She was terrified for herself. She knew the operation might not have been enough, and even if she drank gallons of green tea, ate mountains of cabbage, forswore sugar, rejected alcohol, juiced, exercised, meditated and relaxed with religious zeal, it was also a matter of luck. To some the cancer returns. To others it doesn't. She had seen the chances expressed in graphs, graphs with an inevitable downward slope, some sloping more acutely, some more gently to the only possible conclusion for everyone. And she knew too well that youth was no guarantee against dying. All too well. She was afraid for everyone she knew and that every farewell might be the last.

Which was why she decided to patch things up with Sheelah straight away. Their parting had not been the best, and must not be their last. It was going to be hard, but pride had no place in matters of life and death, which, as far as Georgie was concerned, meant all matters.

Sheelah took so long to answer, that Georgie nearly gave up. When she finally said 'Hello', her voice was tentative, even fearful. She knew who was calling, of course.

'Sheelah, it's me,' Georgie said, lightly, to pacify her.

'Yes.'

'I wanted to say sorry for overreacting and hope we're still friends?'

Sheelah was silent.

'I'm all in favour of positivity, as you know, it's just that... I've realised it might have been exacerbated by the thing about Kevin. I was probably in a bit of a state and I went over the top. But I'm fine now. Absolutely fine. And I'm sorry.'

'Understandably. Oh Gee!' Sheelah sighed with unnecessary sympathy, and followed the sigh with a remorseful groan. 'I'm so sorry I told you about them! I've realised it must be horrible having to picture someone you loved with someone else, however glad you are to be free. I suppose it makes your own intimacy seem less special?'

Georgie hadn't thought of that. An image burst into her mind of a curvaceous naked back, a naked bottom, blonde hair tumbling down over a bright new red-and-black tattoo, a Chinese serpent with a forked tongue, and Kevin, in an animal frenzy, moving towards and away from it. As Sheelah spoke the image intensified, like the proverbial pink elephant.

'But honestly Gee there's no need to worry. I'm sure it's all just about sex. Straightforward biology. I doubt if he loves her.'

Biology? No. That was hideous! Love was OK. Love was fine!

'And as for her, she probably just wants a sugar daddy to take her out and buy her dinner. I doubt if there's much depth to it.'

Kevin doesn't buy dinner, Georgie thought. Or sugar. And biology, biology still rankled! She could have tolerated 'chemistry', 'chemistry' she could have taken on the chin. But biology? *Biology?* No, that simply took the biscuit!

'They're probably just having fun,' Sheelah concluded.

'That's neither here nor there,' Georgie tried to explain, resolutely ignoring the word 'fun', because that would be the final cherry.

'Exactly, it doesn't mean anything and it won't last or anything.'

'I don't care, actually,' said Georgie, tongues of rage rising in her chest. 'He's no concern of mine any more is he? Subject closed.'

'It might take some time to get over it.'

'I am over it. I'm not even going to think about it. I'm free so he's free. He can do what he bloody well likes with who he likes. I don't care where he puts his anatomy. I'm absolutely fine. Ready to find someone else.'

'Yes, you might be a bit up and down about it.'

'I don't want to know anything more about her. I don't want to waste any brain cells on either one of them.'

'Quite. She's not even that pretty.'

Ah, finally, something to be grateful for. Georgie felt like flinging her arms around the bearer of this wonderful information.

'All she's got is the beauty that is youth,' Sheelah expounded.

'Yup. Yup,' said Georgie, thinking of the beauty that is youth, the very beauty she no longer had herself, and the only beauty she might once have had. 'This isn't making it any easier, Sheelah. He wasted my last good years, my last few drops of sexiness.' She paused, hoping that Sheelah would contradict her, but Sheelah was in listening mode. What is the beauty that is youth? Smooth taut elastic skin, firm breasts. Unbearable. Tight moist fanny. No, no, it's unthinkable, so don't think about it, Geegee. Chin up! No moping! 'Why did I bother being faithful?' she erupted. 'He can't have appreciated me at all, seeing as he's now content with some ignorant little tart.'

'Well, she's not that bad. He still has taste. She sounds quite posh in fact. Boarding school type, possibly Catholic. Not very bright, though, admittedly. '

Every comment was worse than the one before.

'Or she might just be pretending to be dim to concede to his masculine superiority and massage his ego. He'd love that, wouldn't he?'

'Hang on, it sounds as though you've met her?' Georgie said.

'Oh, well, there was a do.'

It turned out that Sheelah had sat beside them at a dinner party, thrown by friends of Georgie's, attended by Georgie's friends.

'So to cap it all, he's now swiping my social life?'

'You were invited. You just weren't there.'

'How could I be invited? Why would I be there? Why would I want to see her? I don't want her face on my retina.'

Georgie's veins were now flushed with cortisol and adrenaline. She knew it was unhealthy. She must breathe and relax. She massaged her neck and stopped listening, as Sheelah was cooing and murmuring with helpful understanding and advice.

'I suppose it isn't fair on you, but you can't help admitting he's sociable and charming and entertaining and nobody but we two know what an arse he can be. Even Natalie won't know his bad side yet.'

'I feel completely... Oh, I can't think of the bloody word! I might as well not exist at all!' Georgie said, again hoping to be contradicted.

'Superfluous? Redundant?'

'Exactly!'

'Join the club!'

Georgie wrapped up Sheelah's compassion as efficiently as possible by repeating the original apology, asking how she was, and arranging to get properly in touch when the flat had been emptied and she was back home. But their farewells were said in a sour key and she regretted calling; it was far better to let things go. She hadn't healed the rift, and now monstrous hot thoughts were clattering in her mind and wringing her heart and crawling through her body. Natalie. Natalie. I don't want to know her bloody name. I don't want her bloody name knocking round in my brain.

And what was that other idea disturbing her equanimity? Oh yes! It was the idea of Will very much in love, and parents very jealous. The intimations of the letter were wriggling under her skin like maggots.

Absurdly she checked her mobile inbox and laptop after saying goodbye, hoping that a message had arrived while she was speaking, as if such a coincidence were remotely likely.

Wonder of wonders, an email had arrived from her beautiful Joni! As if in answer to her thoughtless emotionalism, her ghoulish preoccupation with exes and bygones, here was a reminder of what was really current, and really important. She clicked on it, almost breathless with excitement.

Hi Mum, Great people here. Amazing times. I've parted with Sam and I need extra money. Please can you put some cash into my account? £300 should be enough, then I can put it on my card. I'll pay you back. Love Joni xx

Georgie didn't know whether to be delighted, relieved, or worried. Of course Joni needed money and of course she should come to her mother for it! She felt proud to be the provider for once. And of course, Georgie could dig a bit deeper into her overdraft – it wouldn't make much of a proportional difference, and soon rent from Salisbury would be helping. But there was no news! Nothing about how Joni was feeling, nothing about what had happened between her and Sam, nothing about what she was doing. Georgie didn't particularly approve of Sam, but at least he was male, at least he might have created an impression of protecting her treasured daughter. And Joni had been keen on him. She might be hurt, she might be enduring jealous agonies, or feeling rejected and unwanted and superfluous. Now she would be alone, vulnerable and prey to every imaginable danger, and if she was about to go and do any of the reckless things Georgie had done at her age, well, Georgie couldn't bear to imagine it. But Joni was less naïve. Joni wouldn't be so stupid, would she, as to find herself at the wrong end of a gun, wearing a bikini? Or to snort a line of khaki powder of unknown composition and provenance through a stranger's foreign banknote? Or hitch in shorts? Or ride on the back of a stranger's motorbike without a helmet. Without a helmet! It was amazing Georgie had survived so long. Oh yes, she'd been the brave one once.

Georgie hadn't started taking care of herself until she was pregnant, and then it was the pregnancy she'd taken care of, not herself. Even then, she'd been careless – the time she'd gone out on the bicycle too long without water, without enough to eat. But it didn't do anybody any good to dwell on that memory; she'd done her best, she'd always done her best, even if some of it wasn't all that good.

She spent a long time composing her reply, desperate not to interfere, wishing to express complete confidence, yet incapable of withholding annoying advice.

Dear Joni, How lovely to hear from you! Really glad you're having a good time! Terribly sorry about Sam – hope all's well now and you're not too fed up. I'll put the money in this afternoon. Let me know if you need more. Don't spend it all at once! Take good care. I'm very much looking forward to seeing you again soon. Let us know if/when/where you want to be picked up. Lots of love, Mum xxxxx

What she didn't say: Don't take any drugs. Don't catch any diseases. Cover your skin. Don't hitch a lift. Don't ride on the back of a motor bike without a helmet. Always let someone know where you are. Come home! Come home! Just make absolutely sure you come home, alive, well, happy, and in one piece!

If she missed something out, that would be the bit the bad fairy would notice. That's how spells go wrong – they are taken too literally, the fault is sought and found, the flaw is fatal. Jodi, come home, alive, well, happy, in one piece and sane. And still my Joni. My Joni who still recognises me. And I still recognise you. And I am also home, alive, well, happy and in one piece.

'I'm going mad,' Georgie said aloud. 'I'm going mad, and talking to myself is the first symptom.' She began to sing it, the Queen song: 'I'm going slightly mad, I'm going slightly mad.' She laughed at herself, then wondered if laughing out of the blue meant that she was even madder.

Had her parents worried like this about her and Will?

No.

Even when she was little they'd given her a long rein. Maybe they'd had no idea of the danger she might be in. They'd survived a war, after all. Perhaps it seemed completely safe to let their children loose for a day in a quaint temperate market town, running around in fields where alcoholic farmers prowled about with shotguns, or on building sites covered with unstable masonry and ugly machinery, or for walks after dark along roads and rivers.

It was a generational difference. Once people had more children and some of them died. Now they had fewer, they were expected to live – obliged to live. They weren't allowed to climb trees without a chaperone, or garden without gloves or watch a magnesium flame without goggles. They weren't allowed to catch mumps or measles or German measles or scarlet fever. Or polio, thank goodness. Charlie and Joni had each had a mild brush with chicken pox, that was all. They'd been spared the misery of all the other infectious diseases: the murderous headaches, the sweating and freezing and thirst, the itches and the sores and swellings, the hacking coughs, the buckets full of sick, the stink of diarrhoea, the being wrapped in clean sheets with a hot water bottle, the staying indoors instead of walking to school in the dark and cold and wet, the being woken now and then with a bowl of Scotch broth or a glass of Ribena milkshake, listening to pop music on the radio or quiet birdsong from the garden, hearing snow falling against the glass, watching the light change while Daddy was at work and Mummy pottered about downstairs, waiting for Will to put his head round the door and ask was she feeling any better.

Oh yes, you had to be quite ill in those days, to feel sure you were loved.

Sometimes, when an unpleasant idea flitted through Georgie's mind, it left lingering in its wake a feeling which hovered, unidentified, disturbing her flow until she could name it and dispose of it. It happened especially when she was tired, and these days, she was more and more tired. What was this horridness teasing her stomach and tapping her throat? Why was she chronically congested? One nostril was forever blocked, and she'd developed an annoying little cough. It was probably nothing – it was the dust in the flat, there was plenty of that, but if it travels, breast cancer has its favourite haunts: bones, lungs, liver, brain.

Somewhere deep down she knew that her anxieties were distractions from worse horrors, and occasionally she would catch a tiny glimpse of hell through the bluster and cover. When she was tired, when she was hungry, when she'd recently been burdened with the news of some new or ongoing atrocity, if her defences were down a spectacularly nasty thought might slip into her head, then what if Sheelah was right, and you could make something happen just by imagining it?

So worries are jolly useful, she thought, firmly averting her consciousness from that underworld of worseness. And it really didn't matter that Will and Frieda had been in love. In fact, love was a positive, wasn't it, between mutually consenting adults? Her mind flashed an image of 'mutually consenting adults': there were too many of them, Natalie, Kevin, joined by Will, then Frieda, Maureen, Larry...

Nick!

Yes, distractions could be pleasant too, and she might as well concentrate on something she'd actually like to happen, if only to prove the nonsense of Sheelah's magical theories. She would meet him again by chance in the sauna. They would stay on for coffee and green tea in the bar. She would invite him to look at the garden. At some point or another it would rain, and his kisses would mingle with the raindrops and his shirt would stick to his chest.

'Oh, don't be such a silly! Come on Gee! Busy, busy, busy!'

She faced her task with renewed verve, but couldn't help noticing that it was her mother's voice she had heard, coming back through her own mouth, in the way it used to do sometimes when she spoke to the children, especially when she was cross with them. It made her feel better, somehow. It made her feel safe.

Her grandparents might have said the same thing to Maureen, and maybe someone older still, from longer ago, had started it, and set it off repeating and repeating through the generations. It was a tradition in an ancestral tongue; and one that Georgie had failed to honour. Yes, she was the last of the sillies. She never applied the label to Joni or Charlie, only to herself. 'That's a silly thing to do,' she might have said to them, naming the behaviour, not the child, which was the fashion when they were little. But still. 'Such a silly' made her feel safe.

Her mother and father had a glass cupboard full of photograph albums. Now she had to deal with the box of loose photographs that hadn't made it to the albums: *Assorted Friends and Relations*.

They certainly were assorted, coming from sundry periods in history as well as various geographical areas, which couldn't be identified except as being English, or perhaps Irish, the more rural ones. Wide shots of people near generic brick-built Victorian cottages, trees, grass, a canal, a beach. Some of them were copies of the photos that had been gathered and preserved in photo albums. She remembered Maureen doing it after Aunt Ruby died, patiently identifying and labelling and compiling. Maureen had tried to involve Georgie, and now Georgie wished she'd paid attention. How strange that she hadn't been interested in these people, who supplied her genes, who had to meet for her to exist at all. To her then they had been shadows and stains. Now she could see they were shadows of real people who had lived and felt and thought and were as important to themselves as anyone ever was.

She cleared and cleaned and dried the kitchen table so she could spread them out. Friends and Unknowns she put to one side. Relatives she arranged like a family tree, if they were separate, fathers on the left, mothers on the right, and their children below. It was a game of solitaire, shifting cards, filling gaps.

Except for the pocket-sized Brownie snaps – of ladies in funny swimsuits or long parallel dresses and cloche hats, and men in flannels smoking pipes, standing beside square motor cars – the older photographs were better quality, made to last, like most old things. The studio portraits of her great-grandparents were too solid and thick to be stuck in an album, while the more recent colour photographs were floppy and washed out, unfocused some of them, and badly composed, not worth putting in an album.

The oldest was finely detailed and beautifully sharp, printed on glass, framed in a velvet-lined case peeping through an oval window cut from a thin plate of brass. It showed a mature woman, sober, strong and still. Her hair was centre-parted and partly covered by a lace bonnet. Her high-necked dress draped every inch of skin, falling from sloping shoulders that spread out into wide arms, like an elaborate tasselled shade covering a lamp. Georgie could see the veins on her left hand, in which she held a plain black book – one finger marking a page, and in the other hand what looked like a rosary. She searched online to date it. The glass image was an ambrotype, she learned – at least a hundred and fifty years old. The woman might be any age from forty to seventy. Georgie couldn't tell whose mother she might be.

Most of the photographs were labelled on the reverse in Maureen's clear rounded script. There were Charles and his wife Sarah, the Wellingtons from Leeds. He – stodgy, serious, self important, she – determined and slightly amused; whose daughter Flora had married Larry's father also called Lawrence. The Sutton counterparts were Dorothy and Thomas. She looked proud and unforgiving, he more genial and relaxed, bald and bearded.

There was Maureen as a fat baby on the lap of her mother, Caitlin, and as a young girl playing with a blurred dog. There were studio shots of her with crimped forties hair looking up and down and side to side, smiling without showing her teeth. And there she was in Kodachrome, cradling Will, exhausted, but blissful, surrounded by green.

Here were Maureen and Larry in happy retirement, sunning themselves in the back garden. And Maureen with Joni on her lap, each gazing into the other's eyes. Two years later Maureen would not even be able to sing her a lullaby.

Here was Will with Mitzi on their wedding day, an over red photograph, where everyone had big shoulders and even Georgie was wearing a hideous square-shouldered purple suit, her hair fussily flicked and layered and out of proportion to her face.

Here were pictures of her and Jim and the children, with buckets and spades, taken when they were still a unit. They looked young and smooth-skinned. They looked happy. He had a full head of dark hair then and more muscle in his tanned legs; her own hair was thick and golden without a hint or a streak of grey.

She had been so young! No grey at all! Without even trying!

The shutter closes and the moment has passed. Nostalgia is inevitable; the moment is unfixable. You catch a slice of light, you think you caught a moment, but the moment slipped away forever like all the rest. You could feel sad about a photo because it showed you as you were the day before, the minute before; and you would never ever be like that again.

Georgie's eye landed on an image that made her start, it was so lovely: a black-and-white portrait of Frieda – beautifully lit, warm, soulful. Larry must have taken it. He had captured the smooth curve of her generous open smile, and the lesser curves of her brows and eyes, echoing the curve of her cheek which was outlined in light; a beauty made all the more exquisite by its contrast to those uniquely uneven teeth, the fatal flaw. The image expressed his sheer innocent pleasure in her youth and loveliness; he had seen something wonderful, and his unacknowledged talent and skill had caught it so that others could see. It hurt her heart to look.

And there Frieda was again in faded colour, leaning against the summerhouse, wearing a stripey tee-shirt, flared jeans and sandals. The greens had gone yellow, the reds orange. This didn't look like one of her father's shots – it looked more amateurish, and Georgie sensed something in Frieda's expression she didn't like – something coy, yet intense. Maybe Will had taken it? She shuddered at the thought. What went on in that summerhouse, she wondered. There was no information from the photograph, nothing could be seen beyond the glass, half curtained-off, a black shape from which no light emerged, and no detail. It used to be a family place, full of deckchairs and garden toys, tools, pots and the lawn mower. George remembered its cool dark, the smell of grass and glue, the glinting of sunshine through the side blinds, the mark of a spider's web across the glass. It had all been pushed aside and covered with a tarpaulin, to accommodate Will. Georgie stared, but the more closely she looked at the picture, the less she could see. Frieda's face smudged and blurred into abstract shapes and daubs. She was a stain on paper after all. Georgie put her aside, troubled again by a feeling without a name.

She identified portraits of every one of her grandparents and five of her great-grandparents. She placed the best of them at the top of a pile of less good examples, or group pictures, positioning the piles according to their place in the family tree. Without thinking about it she put shots containing children and parents together in the mother's pile, so the right hand-side of her display was weightier.

Now she could look across from one to another and see

connections. She would stare, say at the face of her mother's mother – her light eyes, her thin permed hair, her defined cheekbones – then whip her eye down to an image of Joni, discerning which parts of the great-grandmother had carried through, tracing invisible links as if they were threads winding and weaving together into the tapestry of her family, with each member forming a little knot on the surface.

It took her three hours to go through the box, and then she didn't know how she ought to put them back again. She thought about taking a photograph of the display, then had a sudden urge to scan them all before they faded for good. But it occurred to her that paper and card stored the images more securely than digits on a hard drive. You could break a hard drive in a second and lose thousands. For all their lifelike sharpness and detail and colour, her recent pictures of Joni and Charlie were fragile wisps. The technology could become defunct. The electricity could fail. They were just microscopic ones and noughts.

She wondered if everything that ever existed was an expression of ones and noughts.

We're all right as long as the electricity doesn't fail, she thought. And then she realised that it was bound to, eventually; the sun itself wouldn't last forever. She remembered hearing Stephen Hawking predicting that everything in the universe was going to end up being nothing more than a random and even distribution of photons, at a temperature just above absolute zero. The temperature had struck her as being oddly irrelevant, as no-one would feel it or measure it or care. 'But don't worry too much,' chanted the machine voice, as the real man grinned, 'there's a long time to go before that happens.'

A long time, a short time, it's all a matter of time before we and all our treasured ones vanish and time has no solidity and now is always now and life itself is thinner than air and you may as well float around in it without trying to cling because there's nothing to cling to nothing that lasts so clinging is impossible and disaster will strike you from behind or sideways or underneath when you least expect it and you're almost home while you're skidding about in all directions and relations, relations especially, relations are all of it.

Brrrrr! Brrrr! Georgie was shocked out of her trance into a state of high alert. The landline was ringing. She found the telephone under a pile of vintage holiday brochures. It was Jim.

'I've had an email from Joni. Thought you'd like to know.'

'Thank you, yes. So did I. What did she say?'

'She's having a great time and she wants some money.'

'Yes, that's about the size of mine too. D'you think she's all right?'

'Of course she's all right. I notice you didn't ring me about yours then.'

'I've only just got it! When did you get yours?'

'Yesterday.'

'So you waited a day to tell me?'

'It's not a competition.'

Georgie let it go. She asked him how much money Joni had asked him for.

'Three hundred.'

'Same here. But isn't it cheap to live there? Why does she need so much? What's she buying? You don't think it could be something criminal do you? Oh God, I hope she's not smuggling cocaine or anything.'

'Joni? Georgie! Do you know your own daughter? She's perfectly competent. She's probably running workshops or starting a business or providing a village with sanitation or something. Can you simply leave her alone and let her get on with her life and be pleased to have spawned such a clever independent girl?'

He wasn't explicitly saying so, but he meant that Georgie herself was not clever or independent. There was nothing to be gained from arguing.

'She's finished with Sam,' she said.

'Yes. Good riddance.'

'You're not worried at all, are you?'

'No.'

His deadpan insouciance was a balm to Georgie's heart, as she knew he cared about Joni just as much as she did. It was perhaps the only thing they had in common, this unimpeachable, unwavering, unassailable, unconditional love for those same two miraculous people. It was the most important thing you could share with anyone, she thought, and would always be so.

'How's Charlie?'

'I thought you knew.'

'No? What's wrong?'

'He went AWOL.'

Georgie was shocked into silence. The information fuddled her brain. She couldn't connect it to any sensible scenario so it seemed for a few seconds to be impossible. Oh no, she thought, with dread. This was what she'd missed out, this was the fatal mistake. In focusing on Joni, she'd forgotten Charlie.

'What d'you mean? Where is he?'

'I don't know. He said he was coming to you.'

'Well he hasn't told me. When? When did you last see him? Did you upset him?'

'Yesterday morning. Look, don't worry, he's probably just gone to the flat. I must have misunderstood. He's taken the car.'

'That's outrageous!'

'He passed his test. I said he could.'

'Oh Jim, I can't bear this, I can't bear it! I mean. What the hell can we do?' Georgie dragged her free hand through her hair. 'Phone his friends? Phone the hospitals? Phone the police?' Jim said nothing. 'I've got to be allowed to know where he is. It's the least little thing a mother can ask! It's not fair to expect me not to worry when I don't even know where he is! Oh, I can't, I can't, I can't be a mother, it's too hard, Jim. Never mind school, never mind 'A' levels, what about his driving? Is he OK at driving? Young men drive so dangerously! The insurance must have cost a fortune. When was the car last MOT'd? He is insured, isn't he? Did you get the exhaust fixed?'

When Georgie had run out of questions, Jim sighed. 'Try the flat. I'm sure that's where he is. I'll go over there if necessary. You need to get some rest.'

Well he'd got that right. Georgie was tired. Her nights were more and more fractured and distressing. It didn't help her sleep, to know that Sleep was high on her list of Staying Alive. As was Being Calm.

She tried to control her breathing, whining a little to soothe herself. It was no use being breathless and high-pitched – she couldn't speak to anyone in that state, least of all Charlie. You're allowed to be anxious, she told herself. It was like the fear of the diagnosis, all recalled and rushing back at full intensity. I want to see my children grow up. I want to see their children grow up. I know I'm going to die. I know they're going to die too. But not yet. Please, please not yet!

She rang Charlie's mobile number. No-one replied.

She rang the Salisbury flat. Just an answerphone message – her own voice. She left a message that if Charlie turned up please would someone get in touch with her immediately, day or night.

She rang Charlie's mobile number again. Again there was no reply.

'Aaarrgghhh!' She groaned. 'Pick up the bloody phone! How dare you worry us like this!' She looked through her saved messages. The last communication she'd had with Charlie was to correct his spelling. 'Please God,' she thought, 'if you exist, please don't let those be my last words to him.'

She typed another.

Where t f r u? Worried sick. Please ring as soon as you can. Love mum xxx

And then another.

Ps sorry I swore

And another.

Love mum xxx

Mum came out 'nun' on predictive text; her anxious fingers fumbled and corrected and deleted and tried again.

'Nun?' she shouted. 'That's the opposite to Mum! Who the fucking hell wants to write a text about a nun?'

Then she waited.

SEIZE THE MOMENT

It was too hot to do anything. It was too hot to do nothing. The sun rose into an empty sky which changed colour through every tone of blue from thin pale gauze to deep dark royal midnight. It was an airless hazy merciless sky, far away from any sea breeze; it bore down upon the earth and squeezed the energy out of it. Everything was too bright. Light glanced off every angle of glass or patch of pale paint. You had to squint to avoid it slanting into your eyes and pricking them. Everything was uncomfortable. Flies tickled your cheek. Your hair matted with sweat. Sweat streamed down your sides and back, behind your ears, down your neck. Your clothes stuck to your skin and to each other. Your thighs chafed. Your knickers itched. Your mouth went dry. Your flesh burned. If you sat on the grass, flocks of ants and ladybirds would find you out and tickle you crazy. The air was thick with pollen which scratched your eyes and teased your nose and fogged your lungs and made you sneeze and cry. It was exhausting just to breathe, let alone walk, carrying nothing. Your sandals would stick to the molten tarmac and make a squeaking noise as you picked up your feet. You'd imagine windows shattering, or your skull cracking. Everyone was saying you could fry an egg on this and that – on the pavement, on the windscreen, on the seat. On *Nationwide* someone actually did fry an egg on the bonnet of a car.

There were signs on the main roads outside towns: 'You are entering a restricted water zone.' You weren't supposed to fill your swimming pool or water your roses or take a bath. You weren't supposed to flush the loo. Standpipes had been erected in the streets in case the water was turned off. In other parts of the country people were queueing for it with buckets. You saw them on the news, jolly and patient, enjoying the inconvenience because it was a change and people could complain about the heat together instead of complaining about rain, swapping stories about what had melted and what had burned. Gradually the country was bled of green. Lawns browned and turned scratchy. The earth was caked and cracked and unforgiving. Shrubs turned yellow and leaves fell too soon.

It didn't happen all at once. It started with four hot days one after the other in early June – the first blast of what was to come, just before Georgie's first exam.

She'd tried to revise in bed, but the heat made her head ache. She lay sweating under a sheet, then flung off the sheet. The cereal bowl of cold water she had brought to bed was tepid. She soaked a handkerchief in it, and laid the wet cotton over her face. After the first cooling touch it was warm and slimy within seconds, running down behind her ears and making the pillow sodden and flat. Both sets of windows were wide open, but no breath of air moved in or out. She went downstairs in her nightdress to stand in front of the open fridge, cracked some ice cubes into a glass and tipped the top one into her mouth. It stuck to her tongue. She took it out, held its gorgeous frozen coldness against her eyelids, one after the other, then dragged it across her forehead and along the back of her neck. A delicious shiver travelled down her spine, and then she was too hot again an instant later.

Quietly she opened the French windows and crept barefoot into the warm night air. The pool was flat, like a dark mirror. The level had dropped since Maureen had filled it, some of it leaking into the ground, some evaporating in the heat. She sat on the edge and dipped her toes into the water. It smelt rank, of chlorine and moss, but it was cool. She let the water swirl around her calves in a moment of solitary sensuality, and was about to climb in, on a whim, when she heard a noise. She stopped still, her heart pounding in her chest, to listen. Crickets were humming, and far away on some main road a car droned.

A hiss, 'Ssss!' came from the darkness beneath the dead elm trees, followed by a loud whisper, 'Gee! Here!'

It was Frieda, sitting on the swing, smoking. At first Georgie didn't notice Will lurking in the dark, perched on Georgie's space hopper in his pyjama bottoms and giggling quietly to himself. Georgie wondered if his laughter was malicious.

'Phew! Zu heiss, oder?' Frieda rocked back her head, exhaling upwards. 'We talk about your mother. He cannot believe, because he is so much a little boy, that Maureen is attractive. Hübsch. Do you not see?'

Georgie tried to suppress her true reaction, but her eyes widened and her chin retracted of their own accord. 'Well, Daddy does say she's well preserved.'

'Pickled is the word,' said Will, still sniggering.

Frieda offered Georgie the fat cigarette. Will said nothing against it.

The first drag was hot and choking. Georgie coughed and shook her head, and tears smarted her eyes. Frieda smiled and urged her to try again. The second attempt was merely disgusting. Nausea stroked the back of her throat, making her gills twitch and her neck shiver. Then a wave of relaxation weakened her knees and she slumped down in the grass, which seemed, in that second, entirely hilarious.

'It's horrible!' she sniggered, her shoulders juddering.

'Sh!' said Will. His shushing turned into laughter, like a train, 'Sh sh sh sh sh.'

Frieda slipped off the swing and knelt down on the grass beside her. Her hair stroked Georgie's arm and she smelt of patchouli oil. 'I try to persuade him to travel with me,' she whispered. 'When I leave here I go to Venice, and then to India or South America. But he won't come too. He is a scaredy puss.' She leaned over him, playfully and lightly singing it: 'Scaredy puss! Scaredy puss!'

Georgie wondered when Frieda was meaning to leave. She was going to miss her.

'I have plans,' Will said, drunk and wobbly. He took the smoke from Frieda and lay back in the grass, opening his arms wide as if he were opening himself body and soul to the night sky.

'Plans!' said Frieda scornfully. 'Have you plans, Georgina?'

Georgina shrugged. Her main plan was to dry her feet and go back to bed. She needed to carry on worrying about the Latin exam. 'I suppose I'm going to be a doctor,' she sighed. 'A surgeon, maybe.'

Frieda exclaimed in warm admiring tones, as though being a doctor was a wondrous thing. 'My father is a doctor,' she said. 'My mother is a nurse. It is all work. There is no time to play. So for me they wanted music. But I am more interested to travel and – ach! A piano and a cello in a rucksack.'

'You should get a guitar,' said Will. He dropped the burning stub on the lawn, and trod it down under a flip-flop before sloping off to the summerhouse, without saying anything further. Frieda turned her beauty and gentleness on Georgie, who decided to stay out awhile now Will had gone.

'You come instead Georgina? First to Salzburg. My mother will love you. Then in Venice for autumn. We shall work in a restaurant with my friend. Then we will save enough money to go to Bombay and down to the beaches where we will live for a little money like – wie die Prinzessinnen!'

'OK,' said Georgina.

Frieda laughed. 'OK! That is our plan.' She held out her hand and Georgie shook it. 'But it will be very hot. '

'I'll have to ask my dad, of course,' Georgie yawned. 'And he won't let me.'

'I thought in England when you are sixteen you are an adult?' Frieda took a purse out of her shorts pocket and began rolling another of the floppy drug cigarettes. 'I was an adult even younger.'

Will reappeared, dangling his guitar, and Georgie was disappointed. He sat down on the swing and began to tune it, smirking over his drunken ineptitude, then gave it to Frieda, who exchanged it for the purse and its paraphernalia. In Frieda's hands the guitar sounded clear and sweet. She began to sing, 'Ave Maria.' Her pure girlish voice soared into the sky, and Georgie lay back in the grass to listen. I'll just stay here until the song is over, she thought.

She gazed up at the shimmering indigo sky, splashed with stars and marbled with faint clouds, while Frieda's crystalline voice filled her ears, melting with the pure bright sounds of the strings so they became one sound, and the ground and the sky were the sound, and Georgie's body too, and everything was unconfined and forever and beautiful. What was this feeling? she asked herself, and the answer came ringing into her mind effortlessly: happiness. The sky and the ground and the stars and the song and the singing were all happiness. Latin was happiness. Exams were happiness. Her beating heart and her heavy eyelids and her cooling skin were happiness. The tune was all one note, and time had stopped. I am alive, I am alive now, she thought.

This moment is real.

This moment is eternal.

Unfortunately it wasn't quite true. The song finished and Will was calling her Pud and telling her to go back to bed. 'You need to be ready for the exam, don't you?' She knew she must, but she didn't want to go to bed yet, not until Will and Frieda did.

Reluctantly she stood up, but Frieda put the guitar aside and stood up with her.

'Tomorrow may not come,' she said simply. She took Georgie's hand and twirled her under the arch of her arm, and next they were dancing, or at least moving about, first to Frieda's humming then to Will's aimless strumming. Georgie copied Frieda's gestures, now swinging her hips, now raising her arms, now embracing and being embraced, now pulling out into a dizzying spin. The strumming came faster and louder, and ended with the sound of Will's fist banging against the hollow wood, a discordant resonance as he parked the guitar. He got to his feet and stood sheepishly aside but Frieda opened the ring to include him.

'It is a circle dance. We do it for rain.'

'Ring a ring of roses, a pocket full of posies,' Georgie sang. 'We don't want rain, though, do we? Some like it hot!'

Will refused Georgie's hand.

'Go away little Puddy, or you'll fail, won't you? 'O' levels tomorrow.'

Something made Georgie look up at their parents' window. It was open, but dark, and the curtains were closed.

Frieda tugged on Georgie's hand. 'Why go? You are free!' Her voice pitched upwards on the last word, like a spasm of ecstasy, reaching for rarefied heights. FREE! FREE?

Georgie hesitated. She stared into Frieda's eyes, smiling and unembarrassed, divining there a promise of something intimate and secret and special. She was held by her gaze as firmly as she was gripped by the hand, and felt a current flowing through the air, like heat, and her hand beginning to hurt. She glanced over at Will, who was holding Frieda's other hand. His eyes were closed and he was rocking silently to his own personal rhythm. Suddenly Frieda's face darkened. Some unpleasant thought had crossed her mind, like a cloud passing over the moon, and she dropped Georgie's hand.

'Gute Nacht meine Freundin,' she murmured, with a sigh of resignation.

Georgie nodded. She crept back indoors and put herself back to bed, with the word 'free' still ringing in her mind, disturbed by a vague sense of loss. She had failed to grasp the moment. She had let Frieda down.

The alarm clock woke her. She shut it up and lay for a while on the creased damp sheet, not wanting to move. She realised she didn't actually have to go to school. She could go anywhere she liked. There would be a fuss, of course. Phone calls would be made. Letters would be written, as letters had already been written for no good reason. People would be cross. People would summon her; such as the headmistress who had already told her to get her head down, and her father who had already told her to buck up. People would be anxious and concerned about her too, so, all in all, she might as well just go, for now, until she'd sorted out her plans; but she didn't have to, that was the important thing. She would go of her own accord, because her education was for her own benefit, not for the school or her parents. She didn't have to do well in the exam either, come to think of it. When she looked at her timetable before slipping it into her satchel it seemed irrelevant, as if it came from a different era.

In previous years at school she'd snatched moments of freedom by going to the loo or fainting and spending a while in the sick room. She'd hide under the rough grey blankets until it was boring; or she'd glory in three minutes of solitude – pulling at loose threads in her uniform, or watching hot water rush over her hands and swirl into the plug hole, or humming a Gilbert O' Sullivan song to herself: these little things could be a comfort during an escape from the classroom, somehow reminding her of a realer self, establishing her sanity in the confines of that glaringly public institution.

But the freedom she felt on that first day of 'O' levels was more profound. It was an idea; what had begun as a speck, casually tossed into the soil of her imagination, was growing strong and vibrant, choking all other thoughts and ideas, hogging the space and the water and the light, because it had such a will to live. She might climb it into the clouds.

When she entered the great hall and saw the regimented ranks of desks, the scenery for a horror play she'd seen erected year after year with terror in her heart for its victim actors, for herself she now felt fearless. She found her place and arranged her pencil case and her mascot – a tiny plastic troll with long pink hair (all the girls had them) – and sat down as if it were any old morning. She watched teachers hushed and serious, moving amongst them, passing out paper, and then Miss Greene at a desk in the front watching the clock over her spectacles, looking up from a book every now and then to survey them, catching Georgie's eye as pens scribbled and backs twitched. Freedom was something to fall back on as the clock ticked away; a life as wide as the world, unlived and waiting, sat beside her whispering in her ear.

And when everyone exchanged stories of the hellish hour they'd spent, and compared answers, and some of hers were wrong, her heart was light. What would a Latin 'O' level result matter when she was eating mangoes on a beach by the Indian Ocean? Or taking orders in a Venetian café? Or listening to Mozart in the Alps? Frieda didn't have a Latin 'O' level. You didn't need one to bite into the world and suck out its lovely juice.

Fi and Jan noticed her unusually cavalier attitude and admired it, and she revelled in their admiration. This was a new trick; she could be class clown. 'None of you could possibly have cocked it up as badly as I did,' she boasted. 'I didn't even see the last two questions. I thought I'd finished! I was doodling!' Giggling hilariously, she showed them her rude drawing of Miss Greene, and Fi and Jan laughed with her, to exhaustion. It was impossible to get an A even if she'd answered everything else perfectly, and she hadn't, and she didn't care. It was fantastic! She could be top at not caring. Next she had to not care about English and then she had to not care about Maths.

This was the rhythm of that steadily heating June. At the weekend Will would be chugging tourists up and down the Avon, Larry and Maureen would be out shopping and Frieda would often 'come with', as they called it, leaving Georgie to revise in an empty house. During the week, Will was at school, Larry was at the office, and Frieda tagged along with Maureen on her charity projects. Unless it was an exam day, Georgie usually had the house and garden to herself. She would sit in the curtained sitting room hoping her new hero, Björn Borg, would be on court, distracted from her book by the thwack thwacking of tennis and commentators' stiff-lipped exclamations. Strawberries and ice cream would lure her to the kitchen, then sunshine would draw her and her book outside. The pages were too bright to read. She'd put the book to one side and lie down on a towel in the buzzing heat, seeing blood red, gaudy orange, lime green and gold pooling under her eyelids, or minuscule rainbows vibrating on her lashes. She'd be sweating in a few seconds, burning in minutes. The cold glinting surface of the swimming pool would beckon. She'd strip off and jump in, glorying in the wash and splash of cool water sluicing over her naked skin. Silvery drops plopped after her arms and legs, and her hair streamed out like reeds. With nervous excitement, she'd imagine Matthew arriving. What would happen if he called to her or joined her? What would his naked body look like? How would it feel to be clasped to his chest, to take his tongue into her mouth?

She'd dry in the sun, change into shorts and a smock, lather her browning limbs with suntan lotion, cook herself on the towel for a while, then go back indoors for lemonade and ice, or lemonade, ice and a little shot of vodka, or for an update on the cricket at Lord's. A tall blond handsome white-clad bowler might be sauntering away from the wicket massaging his groin. He'd turn and canter to his lazy delivery. Ball tocked against bat, to measured comment and shuffling applause. She'd switch back to tennis on the other side. A hundred degrees at Wimbledon! This was England. This was summer. But it was hot! You had to enjoy it while you could. The book would follow her, indoors, outdoors, in blazing heat, or pimply shade, always marked on the same page. The sky watched, and shadows advanced across the garden, and no revision was done.

In the early evening she sometimes went for a walk with Frieda. They'd find a hidden place beside the river and smoke. There was a good spot in the churchyard where they could crouch in the long grass amongst crooked crumbling ivy-covered slabs. There Frieda taught her how to roll a joint. Once they drank a bottle of vodka, but more usually it was cider, pilfered from the larder, chilled briefly in the freezer.

'Tomorrow may not come!' Frieda said, and 'Heute!' as she lifted the bottle.

It was true. What if Georgie worried and worked and worked and worried, and was knocked over by a car on the way to school? Which would you more regret, she asked herself: that you hadn't worked hard enough, or that you hadn't had enough fun? The answer was clear. She was living in the answer, noticing every little wonderful thing, such as the low evening light gleaming yellow on the river, the pale rose colour of a swan gliding by, the freckles on Frieda's upper lip, the faint laughter curves bracketing her mouth, a dappled patch of golden sunlight gradually moving over the stone behind her back, casting distorted ivy-shaped shadows and embossing the name of some long-dead man. Or woman. Or child.

'I love him not,' Georgie announced as the last petal fell from the daisy she was plucking. She picked another and twirled it between her finger and thumb.

'You still love Matthew?'

'A bit,' Georgie admitted.

Frieda commiserated. She touched Georgie's hand in sympathy, as if someone had died.

'Who do you love?' Georgie asked. 'I mean "whom". Wem liebst du?'

'Wen liebe ich? Ich liebe – ' Frieda nodded her head, embarrassed – 'older men. Your father, for example, is a very nice man.'

Georgie screeched in horror and disgust.

'It is a different kind of love, of course,' Frieda laughed. 'My mother and father loved him and I understand. You love him also. True?'

Georgie wrinkled her nose and agreed, but she was irritated that Frieda had changed the subject to a different kind of love, as if she were hiding something.

'And I love your mother. And I love your brother, too,' she added, betraying nothing.

'I mean, whom do you love how I love Matthew?'

Frieda shook her head and her mouth made an upside down smile. 'Nobody.'

Now it was Georgie's turn to sympathise.

'Oh no! Das ist kein Problem,' Frieda smiled. 'Ich hab' geliebt und – now I am free. I prefer to be free. I love nobody and I love everybody.'

There was that word again. Free!

'We drink to that!'

They drank to freedom, and to now (that was Georgie's idea), and to Shakespeare's bones (Frieda's idea), and laughed helplessly over absolutely nothing. Maureen and Larry greeted them on their return, blissful that they were such friends, and Georgie went to bed while the sky was still light, drowsy and happy, thoughts sliding over each other and mixing in her mind with images of foreign lands and beautiful men.

'Frieda says she'll take me to Austria,' she announced at breakfast. She didn't mention the rest of it. Her mother and father looked at each other uncertainly, then smiled as if to approve. Will smiled too, in an ironic way. Georgie noticed him catching Frieda's eye and stopping himself from saying something nasty. He glared at Georgie for a second or two, open-mouthed and sarcastic, then carried on shovelling frosties and milk into his mouth. Georgie discerned a hint of pink beyond his long dark curls. She tasted the pleasure of a win.

'Johnny Mercer's kicked the bucket. More shootings in Northern Ireland. And they're still going on about "grovel",' Larry complained from behind *The Times*. 'Poor chap's apologised, that should be an end to it.'

'He's South African!' said Will. 'And they're blacks! Tell the students in Soweto there's an end to it.' He looked as though he wanted to fight about it. Larry gave him a threatening glance. Her father was beginning to look like a cave man, Georgie thought, or a grey-haired version of Noel Edmonds.

'They're talking about cricket,' Maureen explained to Frieda, with deprecation, trying to avoid any unpleasantness between the two males. 'The England captain was rude about the coloured team, though why he's playing for England I don't understand. Aren't there enough English players? What does it say about Chrissie Evert, Larry? Equal pay for the women at Wimbledon? Did you hear that, Georgina? They say they're going to boycott it next year.'

'About bloody time!'

'Rather bad manners, I think.'

Georgie was exhilarated. Things were improving on all fronts. It was just the best time in the world to be alive, and to be a girl, and to be free.

And the heat went on.

Georgie's birthday party was going to be much better than Will's. The evening would be warm and light. They were celebrating the end of exams, so everyone would be jumping for joy. She had the whole day to prepare for it, with Frieda to help. They went shopping for peanuts, crisps and bottles of spirits, and bought raw vegetables to make dippers.

She cleared her bedroom, filling three boxes with dolls and dolls' clothes, Tiny Tears, Sindy with her blonde wig, and Sindy's little sister Patch in her Brownie uniform, plastic ponies, Kerplunk, Spirograph, clackers. Blue Peter annuals and *Madeleine*. A yard of paperback books went: *I Carried The Horn, Five Have Lots Of Fun, Mary Poppins, Swallows and Amazons*. Even the Batmobile she'd rescued from Will's box was in there.

'These can go to the WI,' she said to Maureen, embarrassed at her own largesse. She helped stow the toys in the car. Maureen was all dressed up for her evening meeting, in a long flowery smock dress and Jesus sandals, her recently permed hair squashed under a big floppy straw sunhat. Behind her spoonlike sunglasses, she looked displeased about something. Georgie thought she must know about her smoking, but her fears were soon allayed. Maureen had been watching the Ladies' final at Wimbledon, she said, and was disappointed at the result.

'I'm sad for Ginny, not for us,' she explained. By 'Ginny' she meant Virginia Wade. By 'us' she meant England. Every year she hoped. Every year she was disappointed. 'We did invent the game, after all,' was her excuse for minding. It was odd, really; seeing as she'd been born in Ireland.

When Will came home from school he set up the hi-fi outside, and helped them carry tables, chairs and big cushions onto the terrace. Everyone was coming, he said, and Rowan had given him some ace cassettes he'd copied off – of new bands he'd heard on Radio Caroline. Georgie agreed that he could be the DJ. He set up a barrel of real ale on the table, and Georgie laid out the dips and snacks and the glasses they'd hired. Frieda was busy making rum punch.

'Don't do anything I wouldn't do, now, will you?' Maureen said to Georgie as she left. She seemed vulnerable and anxious in a way that made Georgie want to help her somehow. She ran after the car as it reversed out of the driveway, and knocked on the window. 'I want to keep Silas,' she shouted. Maureen wound down the window and posted Georgie's battered old teddy through, winking over her sunglasses. She'd saved him without having to be asked. He was wearing the school tie Georgie had thrown away. She was touched.

By the time Georgie's friends started arriving, her mother was safely out of the way, but her father lingered. Worse than that, he was wearing the purple kaftan. Georgie noticed with a sick sinking feeling that he was barefoot; it didn't look as though he was planning to go anywhere. Then, as if to humiliate her utterly, he started singing 'Waterloo'.

She followed Will into the summerhouse.

'Will? Is Daddy staying?'

'I don't know.' He seemed unconcerned.

'He can't stay! What are we going to do?'

'It's your party.'

'Well, I don't know what to do.'

Will shrugged. He pulled the huge curtain across the window. 'If you'll excuse me, dear Pud, I'm going to change.'

'It's not fair. He didn't stay for your party. Why is he staying for my party?'

'He wants to keep an eye on you, probably.'

'Can't you say something to make him go away?'

'Like what?'

Georgie hung her head. She thought of suggesting that he offer to keep an eye on her himself.

'I suppose "fuck off" might be going a bit far?' Will said. He glared at her and she sloped off outside.

Her father was chatting to Frieda by the drinks table. He helped himself to a glass of punch and clanked his glass against Frieda's.

'Prost!', they said together, and laughed because their voices had chimed in unison. Georgie screwed her courage to the sticking place.

'Dad, I was just wondering how long you were thinking of staying?'

He turned his earnest blue gaze in her direction.

'Aha! She thinks I'm going to cramp her style,' he chuckled. 'No. I do get it Georgina. It would be highly infra dig for me to stay. I'm going to the pictures.'

Georgie was relieved, but she didn't like the way Frieda was looking at him over her glass and behind her fringe, as if she thought nobody could see the abject admiration in her eyes. And she was anxious right up until the moment her father left, in case Debbie Needham saw him, or heard him singing. Her reputation would be finished.

'NO MORE EXAMS!' Fi and Jan blared, wielding an open wine bottle each and sloshing it directly into their mouths. Fi presented Will with a carrier bag of albums, and Jan dumped a pile of singles beside it.

'Let's get this out of the way then,' Will said with an ironic flourish, and 'Mamma Mia!' started up to a mixed reception of groans and cheers.

Although she noticed Matthew's arrival, Georgie didn't at all mind that he came with a girl, or even that the girl was tanned and skinny and had leather thonging winding all the way up her legs. Her name was Jackie. She had an American accent and everything she told them sounded like a question, as if she didn't know that she came from LA? and she was staying until Fall? and Shakespeare's town was totally far out? Georgie felt proud of this exotic guest. She poured drinks and offered crisps and was introducing the girl to Fi and Jan, when Rowan bounded over.

'Come and listen to this!' he cried, pulling Georgie away from the conversation. He grabbed the glass and bowl from her hands and plonked them on the table. Will had turned up the volume and their ears were assaulted by pumping electric guitars. *Oi! Oh! Let's go!* They skipped and twisted and pranced and leapt, not caring how they looked, jostled by others who couldn't help joining in. Georgie's dress split at the seams and she screamed out in ecstasy.

'This is the one I want you to hear!' Rowan shouted, grasping her firmly round the waist.

Hey little girl, I wanna be your boyfriend.

It was fantastic to be taken like that. His arms were strong, he held her tight and moved rhythmically, from the hip. He smelt of spice and smoke and fresh sweat. Georgie thought she had never been so happy in all her life.

Later on, as Genesis and Pink Floyd wailed dreamily into the summer night, she found herself with Rowan under Frieda's duvet. Her own bed was occupied. He asked her to undo his flies and touch him and she obliged, following his instructions meticulously, trying to do well.

'Mmmm. That's nice,' he whispered.

'Nice?' she slurred. 'At school we're not allowed to use that word. Snot precise.'

'Mmmm. Yes it is.'

'Though actualary sometimes it means precise.'

'No, no, don't stop!'

'Sboring. Smaking my wrist ache. I won't be able to play tennis.' She sat up and he pulled her back down. His mouth was hot and his kissing was impatient and intense and wet, but ever so lovely, in a way she hadn't expected. He stroked her thighs and she let him because it felt tingly and exciting. When he touched the cotton between her legs she arched her back. She imagined she was a cat, writhing under his fingers, which were reaching under the elastic now, touching her flesh, lingering there deliciously. He pulled the stringy pants to one side and she felt his penis nudging against her upper thigh.

'No, we shouldn't,' she said. He pleaded. He told her he had a jonny. Abruptly he sat up. She heard him tearing the packet open and smelt something rubbery and synthetic clouding round her nose. He kissed her again, then pushed into her once, twice, three times, more and again and again and again. It hurt, but she didn't stop him. When he'd finished she pushed him away, unsteadily rearranged the cotton and lace and tripped downstairs to join the throng outside, wanting to lose him.

'Where's Frieda?' Will asked.

Georgie shrugged. She staggered about in search of drink or dope.

It was a night remembered in slices like blurred photographs. Jan was first in the pool. One by one she was joined by others yelping and whooping. Georgie was the first to strip. Her dress was ruined anyway; she tore it from hem to armpit. Only Matthew's girlfriend followed her example. Georgie put her arms round her neck and told her she was the most wonderful person in the whole wild world.

The sky was dark and starry. A sliver of moon sank over the houses.

Then people were getting out, and the music was turned down, and everyone had gone home.

Next morning Georgie woke up to silence and pain. The house reeked of smoke. Cigarette butts and roaches littered the garden and the pool. The parched yellow lawn was a wasteland of empty cans and broken glass. A lost scarf, a pair of sandals and a shoulder bag had lain on the recliner all through the night.

Nothing was mentioned about rules being broken. The family gathered silently in the curtained sitting room and watched Nastase lose to Björn Borg. It was his last chance of winning Wimbledon. Maureen left the room, and when she returned half an hour later, her eyes were red.

BELIEVE IN DREAMS

When she dreamt of the children they could be any age, and not necessarily contemporary with each other, or together. Often Joni would be thirteen. Charlie would more often be seven. But their ages were irrelevant to what they would be able to do or understand. Joni might be three and chatting about her best friend's trip to Rio de Janeiro. Charlie at seven would be able to discuss politics and throw a mean javelin.

Georgie might be carrying Charlie on her hip, the familiar weight of him relying on her, enclosed and safe within her arms. She asked him if she should invite a friend to join them for tea. He said, yes, but he'd like a teenage friend. Oh yes, she thought in the dream, you're a teenager now aren't you? Instantly she was awake, grip-jawed and hot and alone. She felt as though her boy had been ripped from her side, tearing flesh.

After such a dream, when she couldn't see or speak to them again in the day, as was always the case now, she would sense their dream selves accompanying her. In her societyless condition, when everything about her was quiet and still, she could forget reality and lose the present moment, and ideas would cling to her like veils, blurring her vision.

These days she dreamt of them often. And she had baby dreams too, which weren't about any particular child. She'd had these baby dreams when they were very little, possibly even before they were born. The baby would usually be lost or strangely deformed, and, though she might not be its mother – she might even be a child herself – she was always responsible. She had dreams of babies the size of matchsticks. How was she supposed to care for a child so small? She would lose it under a leaf or behind a cup of tea. She would search and search and never find it again and wake up desperate to go back to sleep so she could carry on looking.

And now she was walking alone along the seashore, one step in front of the other, slowly, rhythmically, in time with the calm washing in and out of grey waves, under a great grey vault of sky, in an empty grey world. Suddenly the earth cracked open and jolted her into blackness, falling at speed in a rush of terror, and she woke, breathless and pumping blood and drenched in fear, which lingered even as she came to see that she was sitting safely in the armchair in her parents' bedroom, and the book she'd been trying to read had slid from her hands and into her lap. It was dark around her pool of electric light. She ought to be in bed but something was wrong. She remembered with a sinking at the pit of her stomach that she was waiting to hear from Charlie. She looked at her mobile. No, he hadn't texted. She dialled for last caller on the landline. No, he hadn't rung. She checked her laptop. No, he hadn't emailed.

There were so many ways for him not to be in touch!

He was probably all right, she thought, and worrying about him wasn't useful. It would do nothing to help matters one way or the other. If anything it would make things worse by disturbing her sleep and spoiling her temper. As a girl she never worried! She must have thought that the people she loved were immortal. She must have thought that life was nice.

Well, it jolly well was nice, she told herself, mostly. Parents are supposed to die eventually, and she had escaped her own end for the time being, and Charlie was probably all right.

She decided to go to bed, though she was unlikely to fall asleep except by trying not to, which was easier if she were fully clothed and uncomfortable. Nevertheless, she got undressed and cleaned her teeth and eventually flopped under the duvet in the dark.

The clock ticked. The fridge hummed. She could hear squeaking footsteps in the flat above and traffic on the street and the creaking of pipes and a rattling noise which sounded like a mouse in the wall. Light at night isn't good for melatonin levels and since her diagnosis she'd been careful to avoid it in her desire to control every aspect of consumption and in her terror of anything remotely carcinogenic. 'The odd night won't matter,' she thought, and switched the light on anyway. Sleeping was hopeless. It was going the way of all her other self-imposed prescriptions.

The miniature portrait was lying on the bedside table. She picked it up and stared at the woman and the woman stared blithely back from her two-hundred-year-old hour, reflecting in each eye that glint of a window – a window which might still exist.

'What did you used to hear in the night?' Just the clock. And early in the morning a maid might be clambering up and down the stairs. And late at night there might be voices coming from the dining room or library. A horse out on the street. The wind in the trees. The bells of St Andrews, the church that was going to be bombed, striking out the hours.

'Who are you?' Georgie asked.

She imagined her laughing, 'I'm nobody now.'

'You were somebody though, weren't you?'

Oh yes. I was as real as you are. And what happened to me will happen to you.

'What happened to you?'

That fine forehead might be in the ground somewhere, perhaps not far away. Some of that hair was here in her hands, locked behind the glass. The cross she was wearing might be in a box; Georgie might uncover it. The rest of her was dissipated and spread throughout the world, some close, some distant. A molecule from this woman's body might now be in Georgie's! – having travelled through soil and air and animal and vegetable, with other particles gathering and dispersing, becoming and disintegrating, all temporary, in process. Georgie's own body was the food she had eaten and the air she had breathed; and where was her body bound, which other bodies might she share molecules with, which animals, which vegetables? And what would happen to the bit of her that wondered?

She felt convinced there was something important to be understood in this woman's face; it seemed so familiar, she knew it so well, but couldn't grasp what it meant. It was like knowing a word or a name that flutters just out of sight, you strain at it, but you cannot speak it, you cannot bring it forth. You try, but it will only come if you stop trying. It will come in sideways, when you've forgotten you wanted it.

There was nothing to be gained by staring at her. She remained stubbornly silent, impenetrable. She wouldn't give up her secret.

Georgie got up to make herself a cup of tea, then carelessly poured herself a glass of wine instead, because an open bottle happened to be standing beside the kettle. The kitchen table was still laid with photographs. As she sat down in the half-light falling in from the hall, her eye fell on the glass photograph.

It was the same woman.

Goose pimples prickled her neck. Here was the answer to her question, 'What happened to you,' as if she'd been led to it deliberately.

The eyes had saddened, the mouth no longer smiled, the cheeks had thinned, the hair greyed, but the person was the same. Georgie dashed back to the bedroom to fetch the miniature. She placed the two pictures side by side. The colourful young girl was now voluble, simply in her contrast to the older version: she was challenging, amused, vigorous, excited; her eyes shouted out in passion, 'I defy you and I shall surprise you!' while her older self was quietly resigned, disturbed from reading the black book, which was, Georgie guessed, no novel. 'This happened to me,' she was saying, that was all.

'What then?' asked Georgie. Ay, there's the rub. What then? She'd recognised something of her own face in the younger woman, but not the older one, she realised. She was unfamiliar with her present reflection. It would shock her if she saw it glancing from a shop window or a parked car. She was a stranger to herself now.

The idea that you've lived before seems perfectly reasonable. Stretch your mind back to your earliest memories. The sky – those ever-changing blue, grey and white shapes, the fringe of the pram, the singing of birds, the sigh of the wind and patter of rain, discomfort that vanished in the smell of talcum powder and the touch of clean winceyette, voices making music that meant nothing, that moment when it came to you: oh yes, I see, this is the new place now, the sight of your hand, the sound of your name, that moment when you realised you were Georgina. You were you.

I!

Me!

You could have come into yourself like that from some other plane, couldn't you? From somewhere your mind had disintegrated into a dream.

'I'm going slightly mad,' Georgie sang to herself, again.

She fetched Great Aunt Ruby's mirror and placed it in a position where her face was well illuminated. She parted her hair in the middle and combed it neatly to either side. For a bonnet she used her mother's tea cosy. Then she studied herself, frowning and sad as she focused, to see what likeness there was, if any, holding the photograph beside her, to see its reflection next to hers. The eyebrows were similar, and the distances between features. Their chins were the same shape. Georgie's mouth was fuller, her eyes were warmer, her hair was dyed, grey at the roots, her cheekbones more prominent. We're like enough to be sisters, she thought, closer than cousins, further than twins.

It occurred to her that the mirror might have belonged to the woman. It was the right age. She might have looked in it to check her bonnet or her hair, just before leaving for the photographer's studio, or waiting for the painter to arrive. She might have lived in this very building – the walls were over two hundred years old! What have these walls heard, she wondered, through all that time?

Shouting and crying. Cursing. Laughter. Lovemaking. Music. Small talk. Weather talk. Songs. Sound waves have travelled through the bricks, disturbing the crystals. They might have left a trace so faint and tiny no-one could ever read it.

She was in the basement though; not the place for a lady. Here would have been servants cooking, carrying and boil-ing water, chopping, scrubbing, washing dishes and clothes, gossiping about their families, winking about the people upstairs.

Georgie's mind emptied out as she stared and listened.

Where the chimney was blocked in would have been a vast range sheltered by a mantelpiece; and above the mantelpiece she saw a tidy row of bells, shelves neatly stocked with enamel bins and jars and bottles of clay and glass, bright copper pans and ladles hanging from the walls, edible material suspended from the ceiling on hooks – onions, grasses, and feathered things. She could imagine the smell – raw meat, and something else more sickly, like lard or fatty soap.

Where she was lying, a kitchen table.

A cascade of hideous images crashed in. She screwed her eyes and turned her head away – from bright red rags and shining flesh, black ropes and white knuckles, the flash of steel, the crumpling of skin, a spray of blood. She heard a scream of pain, as if from far away.

Was it an extirpation?

An extirpation without anaesthetic!

Or was it a birth?

A sudden loud noise pierced her ears and made her start with a little cry.

The phone! At last, the phone was ringing! It was Charlie, Universal Spirit be praised!

'Charlie! What time is it?'

'Three?'

'Where are you?'

'I'm at home. At yours.'

'Are you all right?'

'I'm fine.'

'Why didn't you call sooner?'

'I lost my mobile.'

'What's going on? Why aren't you at Dad's?

'We had an argument.'

Georgie could imagine that. She thought it wiser not to probe. 'Well, you can't stay there, can you? As I'm here.'

'I've cleared it with Tania?' Tania was the lodger.

'You didn't clear it with me! I know you can't see me, but I do still exist, you know?'

'I'm seventeen, Mum. I'm not a child, OK?'

'No, you're not a child, but you've got school tomorrow and how are you going to feed yourself?'

That question was not worth hearing, apparently.

'My room's full of your stuff.'

'Technically speaking it's my room, isn't it? As it's my flat.'

'Except it's basically like the landlord's flat if you want to be technical.'

Georgie tutted, but he pressed on before she could comment.

'I'm going to bring it to you as soon as I can, OK?'

'It's not OK. And you can't yo-yo around from one parent to the other depending on your whim.'

'Well, you shouldn't have split up, should you?'

Georgie thought of explaining that just as he was finding it difficult to live with Jim, so had she. But she wasn't allowed to say that, because she wasn't allowed to say anything negative about Charlie's father, whether or not he ever said anything negative about her, and it wasn't fair.

'You can't bring any more stuff here, I'm up to the ceiling with stuff here.'

'OK, so I'll put it in Joni's room.'

'No, don't do that, she wouldn't like it. Can't you walk round it? It's not so much is it?'

'No I can't. Yes it is.'

'So when did you pass your driving test? Why didn't you tell me?'

'It's no big deal.'

'You can't come on the motorway. Have you driven on the motorway yet? Come on the A roads. They're more direct even if they're slower. Less petrol.'

Sigh. 'Motorways are safer than other roads, Mum. I've got to go.'

'Oh, darling, I've been really worried about you!'

'I'm fine! I wish you could stop trying to control me!'

'Control?'

Control? No, I don't fucking control anything, she thought. Nothing's up to me! Nothing's ever been up to me! I've spawned and sacrificed and skivvied and scrimped and done my fucking best and now I'm being thrown away as if I'm all used up and finished! Go ahead, chuck me on the rubbish heap! Dump me in landfill!

Rubbish heap. It was a phrase Charlie had misunderstood as a child. 'I looked for the rubber sheep, Mummy, but it wasn't there,' he'd said, presenting her with a rotten satsuma he didn't want; having trusted without question that 'the rubber sheep' was where it belonged. He must have been about five. Before the divorce. When they used to have a proper garden, with a compost heap and an incinerator, and a swing and a climbing frame.

'Look, Charlie, I was worried, that's all. I'm sorry if I swore. It's perfectly normal for parents to worry. I don't see why I should apologise for being a normal mother.'

'Why did you put all your stuff in my room and not Joni's? She's not even here and she's going in September.'

It was true. Georgie hadn't given Charlie's room the respect she'd given Joni's. But nor had he. When he'd allowed her to clean it she'd always find an odd sock or a whole tee-shirt stuffed behind the radiator stiff and stuck together with cobwebs, old cups of moulding coffee and sticky glasses on every horizontal surface, little heaps of dusty ticket stubs, receipts and coins under piles of dusty paper and torn envelopes, and the floor covered with books and comics, used clothes and odd shoes left just where they'd fallen.

'I'm seventeen. I'm not seven. You know? Seventeen-year-olds can fight in wars.'

'You can do what you like, Charlie, more or less, but if you're thinking of joining the forces I'll be very very miserable.'

'You didn't want me to go and now you don't want me to come back! I can't do what you want all the time. I'm going to bed. Good night.'

'Good night.' Sleep tight. Don't let the bed bugs bite.

She followed his example and took herself to bed; the bed that had become a rack, in a flat that was a dungeon, with random access to two centuries of her family's misery. And it smelt of a dungeon. Of crypts, old castles, damp, cold, like the inside of a mountain, the smell of sadness and imprisonment.

'Joy as well as misery, Gee!'

She tried to dream of Nick. His boat was a sauna, packed with tropical plants. Every time she lay down with him she was pricked by the same cactus. Schubert's song 'Vorüber! Ach vorüber!' began to play in her mind, then 'Ave Maria'. The music conjured a memory of Frieda, and Vienna, and Schiele's paintings, then repulsive images of Kevin and Natalie poked into her brain – skin and bone entangled with pert nubile flesh. Taunting images and haunting sounds were knotting in her mind, and the knot had a common thread. It was Death and the Maiden! *Buried with her daughter Molly.* But a maiden shouldn't die, should she? A girl should know love before loss!

She turned onto her left side, heart side.

'Sheelah's right. I do use a lot of "should"s!'

Her left side was the cancer side. She turned again, away from stabbing pains and phantom lumps. No pressure on the glands!

'Well why the fuck shouldn't I use a lot of "should"s?'

Kevin would be painting Natalie now, claiming her as territory.

She couldn't understand why it troubled her to be honest: sex with Kevin hadn't always been much cop; when he couldn't be bothered to please her, or he'd drunk too much and his passion dithered. Latterly once or twice he'd entered her too fast, and even though she'd wanted it, his cock had been a blade, a single shocking stab that made her cry out loud and push him away.

Biology. So Sheelah had said. The word was wounding. The

man must be hard, the woman wet. Otherwise it simply doesn't work. The human race depends upon that crucial combination. Biology, not love. And she had probably finished with all that.

One of her first responses to the cancer diagnosis had been to delete any lewd photographs from her hard drive. It took priority over her last will and testament. She wanted to spare posterity. But the face recognition software had retained one. Her computer had seen a friend in Kevin's penis; had cropped and preserved it for future reference in case she forgot; and she'd kept it because it made her laugh to see it there detached and confined in its own miniature square, taking up its position in a grid of grinning strangers picked out from the crowd, with its own leering expression of ashamed disgruntlement. It was a joke she hadn't shared. Such is the accidental nature of documentary history; and yet, all that endures is significant, just by the fact of its endurance.

LOOK AFTER YOUR TEETH

If reading is listening to the past, then writing must be speaking to the future. Hello future! What are you like? Am I there?

The genes for love have a better chance of survival because the babies whose parents care about them have a better chance, that's all, so nothing means anything. I am extremely miserable and I don't know why. I thought love was everything, but all it is is sex and survival. You get attracted to the person who'll make the best babies with you, because of their pheromones or because they look exactly the opposite to your family. And men don't care so much about the babies because they might be carrying someone else's genes.

Wednesday

Pay no attention to above drivel! Everything is tickety boo and hunky dory! Whoever you are.

Thursday

I'm sick of Frieda and Will going off together and doing everything without me. Yesterday I shouted at them to wait but as soon as I came downstairs they'd already gone. So I had to go on my bloody own as per usual, even though it was my idea. Later I found out they'd met up with Matt. Well, if she is carrying on doing sex with Will, at least that's better than my other idea – I'm a bit worried something's 'going on' with Matthew and Frieda, even though she told me he's not her type. It's rubbish and tripe. It's absolutely downright unfair. Daddy was cross too. He said 'what the HELL are they up to?' Almost as if he was jealous, as though Fi was right about him. So if they carry on like that I'm going to tell him about the drugs. I wouldn't mind but they're always doing it without me. Why shouldn't I do it too? They're my lungs!

Saturday

It's hot. It's so hot I

Friday

*

Tuesday

I found out something cringingly horrible. At Will's party, Jan and

Fi PAID that boring politics bloke to get off with me. As if it was some wonderful gift!!!!!! They are not my friends any more. So there's nobody left to cheer me up except Rowan, and he's getting annoying, ringing me up all the time and saying he's in love with me. How unutterably childish – but he's only two months older than me so what d'you expect? Why does it have to be Rowan and not Matthew anyway? Why is the world so mean? Rowan Heywood. ROWAN. NOWAR. OWARN. Georgina Heywood. I suppose the reason that 2.4 is the average number of children is that people want to have at least a boy and a girl, but even if they have two boys or two girls, most people don't want three. If everyone went on trying until they had at least a boy and a girl the average would probably be nearly 3. Except some of them wouldn't ever succeed. Even if they really wanted a boy and a girl people would probably give up at about four and one of them would probably turn out gay or lessy, especially if they were boys.

The other thing I found out is that Fi told me Frieda went to the pictures with Dad. I am extremely fed up about it. It was my party! He didn't even tell anyone! And of course it was probably an X film. He should have taken Mum at least. And Fi and Jan always want to make a dirty joke out of everything. They are so childish.

I wonder when I stopped believing in God.

Excuse me smudging this, but my hand is sweating. I'm wilting. I can't even bear to go out in it any more.

Thursday

My mind feels squirty and dissolvy. Usual teeth falling out nightmare and the crying child which I haven't had for ages. Ugh. Locked up and trying to get out. I thought I could hear it banging on the door.

Saturday

I have bought an absolutely brilliant rucksack! Frieda and I had ein fantastisches conversation about what to take. Espadrilles, walking boots, high heels, flip flops, sunhat, suncream, sunglasses etc. skirt, dress, Levis, shorts, pants, obviously, tights, bikini (need to buy) (when I've lost a bit more weight). Bras (pretty). Toiletries inc make-up and refresher pads. Towel. Water bottle. Sleeping bag. Shoulder bag, purse, travellers cheques, Schillings. Passport. We're going to get an Interrail ticket for Europe and buy our tickets to Brazil from Austria because I haven't told M and D the whole truth yet. Jumper. (Rain?)coat. We're going to Austria first –

Salzburg then Vienna then the cottage in the mountains, hence walking boots, then Venice!!!!! Hooray! I'm so ridiculously excited I could die. In fact, it's so brilliant I'm worried I actually will die before it can be able to happen.

She'd been expecting to find these adolescent outpourings at some point, and read the last entries with a certain sense of relief. The journal had been hiding in a box packed when they moved house in 1976 – a time capsule, unopened since then. It looked like someone else's handwriting, someone else's life.

She took everything out of the box and placed it around her on the floor. Her plastic alarm clock and plastic adjustable calendar, discoloured. Her mangled school tie, with its embroidered name tag. Her collection of egg cups. A Spanish doll, a French doll, a glass horse. A medal for coming second in the Warwickshire County Athletics 200 metres sprint. Little decorated sweet tins containing drawing pins and paper clips. Strips of instant passport photos of herself mugging and laughing with various friends – Jan, Fi, another girl whose name she'd forgotten. There was a strip of Rowan, shyly smiling for her, *To G with love from Ro* with a heart drawn in biro on the back, then a strip that came as a shock, of herself and Frieda. In the first shot neither of them was ready – Frieda was startled and looked vulnerable, while Georgie was looking away, neutrally making herself comfortable. It was intriguing, because Georgie had always thought of Frieda as self-confident and experienced. Oh no; Georgie was the one who looked solid and sure. Frieda's fragility was clear to her now. Her face was open, transparent. She looked hunted, that was the word. As if she thought the light would eat her. She didn't even look as wise as Joni.

In the same box were collections of stickers and cards of pop stars, football players, space rockets, birds and animals, that had come free with ice lollies and sweet cigarettes.

When England won the World Cup, Georgie was only six, but she'd collected all the players and World Cup Willies. She knew the footballers' names and had been sure that England would win. She was determined they would; by watching and cheering, she could do her bit. The whole family watched the final, forsaking the paddling pool and sitting round the black and white telly with crisps and pop. The Kinks were in the charts, lazing on a sunny afternoon. The Beatles were on the news, and later that summer everybody was singing about a yellow submarine.

She'd wondered how come she should be so lucky to be born British, the best in the world, with its friendly bobbies and swinging London and the Commonwealth, whatever that was, where black people jumped up and down in bright clothes for the beautiful queen. *The Wizard of Oz* soundtrack was one of her favourite records then. 'That's a horse of a different colour!' and, 'There's no place like home!' She couldn't remember how the subject had cropped up, but her mother had told her that, no, *The Wizard of Oz* wasn't English. How could she understand it then, she asked; it didn't sound foreign. But then, who knew Woolworths was American?

Oh dear, what a painfully gradual disillusionment it was to learn that Britain didn't always come top. Cowboys and Indians were American, Tom and Jerry were American. Apollo was American. And the Royaume-Uni had fallen far far behind in Jeux Sans Frontières. But never mind; the British were jolly good sports!

The night of the moon landing she was nine and Will was ten. Will boasted that he was going to watch it, and Georgie pleaded and pleaded to be allowed to stay up too. She got out of bed every time she was tucked up, and set up such a wail and a noise, 'It's not fair! Just because he's a boy. Why shouldn't I be interested in the moon, just because I'm a girl?' And for once it worked. It was a wonderful exciting night. Afterwards they ate baked beans on toast and guessed what was going to happen next. Georgie thought there'd be machines to help you do sums. Will thought there'd be machines to do everything, so nobody would have to work. All the buildings and the roads would be white. We'd go on holiday in space and wear shiny clothes that you wouldn't have to wash. We'd eat pills instead of food. We'd have rockets on our backs and just be able to fly wherever we wanted. Maybe we wouldn't even need rockets because we'd be able to beam up from one place to the other like in *Star Trek*. We might even be able to travel in time. Maybe we'd come back to now.

Those were the days when she'd think and think and think about infinity and eternity, and hope that if she thought hard enough she'd be granted a vision. It was something to do with circles, she thought, because they don't have an ending or beginning, and it was something to do with other dimensions. She used to sit by herself, straining to picture spheres in four dimensions, imagining colourful shapes swirling out like spirograph patterns.

Robert Kennedy's assassination had happened on that television too. It was before colour, before they could afford an older house, when they lived on the Bridgetown estate. She'd known nothing about him except that he'd been shot and everybody cared. She liked the look of him in the photographs. She felt as if she loved him; it was desperately important that he live. He was still alive at bedtime so she kneeled beside the bed and prayed. 'Dear God, please don't let Robert Kennedy die! Please please please make him be all right!' When she woke up and learnt that the prayer hadn't worked, she went to the loo so she could cry in private. Will would have teased her if he'd known. Georgina remembered that death as others remember the death of his brother. Or Martin Luther King's or Lennon's or Princess Di's.

Further down in the box was a sketch book, an exercise book full of stories, and right at the bottom a polythene folder that was really too big for the box. To extract it she had to dig her fingernails down the sides. The corners of the box were lined with dust and the whole thing smelt of damp.

The polythene contained a letter signed by Miss Dunn.

She remembered Miss Dunn. A woman who talked too slowly and too much. She used to teach Biology and liked to add to the curriculum snippets of knowledge gleaned from her own personal corner of the animal kingdom. 'When you lose a tooth that's it, you can't have it back again. Look after your teeth and you'll keep them your whole life. I still have every one of mine!' She used to display them in a crocodilian smile. 'Not a single filling!'

Georgie wished she'd listened. But no, she'd liked the sweet cigarettes and the lollies and the stickers and cards too much. Thank goodness she hadn't passed that on to the children. Joni and Charlie's teeth were all present and correct.

She wondered where Miss Dunn's teeth were now. They might still be in the world and still without fillings. They might still be biting and chewing things, though that was unlikely. A woman who had never had toothache or children – what did Miss Dunn know of life?

Dear Mr Sutton

We are very disappointed in Georgina's recent change in attitude and thought it best to let you know this by letter as there will be no parents' evening before 'O' levels begin. She has the potential to do very well indeed, and could pursue any career she desires, but it will be difficult to recover from a poor set of 'O' level results, especially in her 'A' level subjects (which she has, however, yet to choose). We were expecting her to be inclined towards Medicine, and certainly presumed she would apply to Oxford and Cambridge.

We can do nothing but advise you, and hope that you will be able to urge her to readopt her characteristic high level of effort and achievement.

Yours faithfully

B. C. Dunn

My characteristic high level of effort and achievement, thought Georgie, slipping it back in the box. There were Will's 'O' and 'A' level results. All ones, all As. Where were hers? Not treasured and kept. The 'O's were the first exams she had ever flunked. On a whim she retrieved Miss Dunn's letter and ripped it into tiny pieces which she sprinkled into Recycle like confetti. She never wanted to see those words again, words that had dismayed and disheartened her father, that had sealed her future.

She remembered being summoned to the Headmistress's office, whose large panelled door was imagined to conceal a kind of verbal torture chamber; and the threat of a visit beyond it would make the girls hysterical with fear. Georgie had gone there on wobbly legs. She was over-conscious of them because she'd folded the waist of her skirt over twice to shorten it, but she was damned if she was going to bow down to tyranny and unfold it.

She'd waited in the hall, on a hardbacked chair, within dark warped wooden walls bedecked with paintings of illustrious men and women. A vase of flowers occupied the middle of the space, posed on a fancy curvy-legged table. Every surface was varnished and dustless. A grandfather clock ticked, loud in the silence, and as the minute hand reached its zenith, it jingled. She didn't know why she'd been called. It might be bad news from home, good news from the school. Perhaps she'd won the essay competition: 'What would you like to do with your life?' She'd been brave and original and concise, which is what they said they wanted. She'd proposed that since nobody knew how much life they had ahead of them, it only existed in the past and the present, so doing something with your life meant doing it now; so instead of writing an essay, she'd better just do what she liked.

As no-one came for her, and no-one had told her how to proceed, eventually she went up to the door and knocked, and was commanded to 'come in!'

Miss Crawley looked up from her desk over a pair of spectacles with a cord hanging from each side. 'Ah, Georgina Sutton. What's happened?'

Georgie shrugged anxiously. 'I don't know.' She realised she hadn't won anything. Miss Crawley lost no time in introducing the topic.

'Well I expect you know that Heather Blewitt's been a
ninny and got herself a bun in the oven, which perhaps is an
appropriate result from our front runner in Domestic Science.
But *you*. Georgina. You, Georgina. Consistently the top of the
class. Do you know how intelligent you are?'

Georgie had not yet had any chance of getting pregnant,
worse luck. She looked away from Miss Crawley's accusing face,
at the Persian weaving beneath her feet, wondering where the
deliberate mistake was and whether it was otherwise perfect.
The room smelt of lavender-scented talcum powder and old
books. Miss Crawley blathered on. 'Our girls in the top stream
are the top nought-point-one per cent in the country. And you
come top in that stream. That makes you one in 30,000 as I'm
sure you can work out in a spit.' Actually no, she hadn't worked
that out, and everybody is one in 30,000 and what was the word
'top' actually supposed to mean?

'You have a duty. To yourself. To your parents. To society.
Let Heather Blewitt be an example! Please?'

Georgie waited, still looking at the carpet, and the glossy
wooden boards it was lying on, wondering if the interview was
at an end.

She had come here as an eleven-year-old, to be dissected
and assessed; bright-eyed and keen, her hair freshly combed
and tied in bunches, her hands smelling of soap, her spectacles
gleaming and clear. Asked if she'd had any problems with the
entrance exam she'd said, 'I didn't know how to do fractions.'
The Headmistress had folded her hands on top of each other
and leant forwards. 'If you take an orange and divide it into
three pieces what fraction is each piece?' The answer seemed
too obvious. Georgie hesitated. 'A third.' She thought it would
be ridiculous to divide an orange into three. You'd normally
just divide it into its own segments. You'd never guess a third
without doing that first. 'And if you halve each piece, how
many do you have?' 'Six,' Georgie said. But it would be messy
and sticky and the six pieces would not be fair and she wanted
to suck her fingers and wash her hands just thinking about it.

'That's correct.' The Headmistress had smiled. 'You don't have a problem with fractions.' She seemed like a kind woman. She'd given her a column of ticks and let her pass.

Now her forehead was pitted and cross. 'You are taking stupid risks with your future by behaving as you are. And this slovenly behaviour isn't making you happy. Not that happiness is the be-all and end-all, no, of course, happiness is no reason for doing or not doing anything.'

Georgie didn't know what she was talking about. Of course she was happy. Happier than usual! All she'd done was to forget a few preps and not listen in class, arrive late, skip lunch, wear mascara, miss the school bus home a couple of times, and wear boots and black tights instead of grey socks and flatties. The happiest girls were smoking in the loos and getting shagged.

'Shall I tell you this? Yes I think I can presume upon your confidence. I could have been a doctor myself, you know. Then when I was about your age what d'you think I went and did?'

Georgie looked up, her head still set low. Miss Crawley's eyes were wide and her lips were pressed together into a contemptuous line.

'I fell in love.'

She said it as if she were doling out dunce caps and the word 'love' meant a puddle of cow's piss.

'I had to claw my way back to any kind of successful career.'

Georgie wanted to know more. It would be good for a laugh with Jan and Fi. She waited quietly, encouraging the torrent to continue. But then Miss Crawley looked away, suddenly saddened, and appeared to be wrestling with some sort of speech impediment. The moment stretched intolerably, bewilderingly. Georgie could neither move nor speak.

When at last Miss Crawley recovered her composure, her face had changed. She stapled up her reminiscences with a short sigh, and a look of benign resignation.

'It wasn't worth it. Believe me.'

Georgie did believe it. She was grateful to see Miss Crawley's face relax into something approaching a smile.

'Now, pull up your socks, take off those ludicrous stockings and get your head down. 'O' levels in three weeks!'

The mention of 'O' levels provoked a rush of nervous nausea. Georgie looked Miss Crawley in the eye, emboldened by their moment of intimacy and the glint of humour in her expression.

'I don't know if I want to be a doctor. I don't know what I want to be.'

The woman appealed to her God in disgust and exasperation, as if not knowing what you wanted to be was quite the most idiotic thing she'd ever heard of.

'Off you go!'

Ah! Georgie was free, and in six days she'd be sixteen! Then she could do whatever she bloody well pleased and Miss Crawley and her sad bloody secret could go to hell.

Georgie had never told anyone about that strange meeting.

School! Echoing corridors, clattering crockery, the smell of cabbage and loos, incinerators and ink, old plumbing, wallpaper painted in sick, cream yellow, sage green and violet grey, Father Eternal ruler of creation, creaking wooden stairs, high ceilings, long sash windows, break, hot chocolate in plastic cups, buns, blackcurrant licorice, shivering in grey skirts, the bell, the giggles, headlice and verrucas, bunsen burners and newts, Gallium in tres partes divisa est, Bic biros, fountain pens, poster paints and collage, j'ai un frère, j'ai douze ans, tennis racquets, hockey sticks, rancid airtex shirts, mouldy rubber-soled pumps, flannel knickers, chapped legs, prize days, blazers and boaters.

Glorious days! If only they hadn't upped and left and come to Bristol, Georgie might have settled down and done her best again. The 'O' levels were a blip – a little tear that had been allowed to gape and fray until it was unstitchable.

'Why did we have to bloody move?' she asked the air, and her mind formed a phrase as if the air were answering: 'I want to go home!'

It had been even worse for Will, having to start a new school in the middle of 'A' levels. But somehow he'd taken it all in his stride. He'd joined the debating society and was elected captain of the first fifteen rugby team in the first term. In the first week! He'd even had time to pull pints, so he managed to earn a few bob into the bargain, something Georgie would never have been allowed to do. Again, she didn't know if that was because she was younger or because she was the girl.

Now she knew that Will must have been missing Frieda. Maybe that was why he'd thrown himself so frantically into his new life. She'd missed Frieda herself, she supposed. Perhaps they all had, in their different ways, and each had mourned privately, because sorrow was something not to be spoken of.

'Stickers etcetera give to Henri. Ornaments, tins and egg cups to charity. Medal.' She sighed. 'Landfill I suppose. Or should I wear it to show everyone I nearly won something once? What's it made of? Feels like metal. I'll put it in with the tin cans. Sheet music? All paper to be recycled. Or played. Not that I can play these any more. Hmmm. Must stop talking to myself. Georgina, stop it! Stop talking to yourself! All right then. Ha ha.'

She wound up the clock, and set the date and the day on the calendar. She admired the egg cups – a collection of souvenirs from family holiday destinations. She recalled her favourite: one from Mallorca that had come with a matching mug and bowl, like a little family. It was missing. The set was missing. She realised the box had been raided, leaving rough marks where there should have been sellotape.

'Who's done that then?' she asked, outraged.

Diary. Georgie picked it up and flicked again through its biro-crinkled pages, thinking that whoever had opened the box had probably read it. 'It wouldn't have been Will. So it must have been Mum or Dad. Or both.' She laid it to one side. 'They shouldn't have! It's outrageous! Always interfering! How dare they?' It suddenly occurred to her that they wouldn't have needed to wait until it was in the box. Perhaps they'd read it sooner, when it was innocently lying on her bedroom desk.

There had never been a lock on her bedroom door. Will might have read it, then, the teenage Will. Frieda might have read it! Anyone who had ever entered the house might have read it.

Rowan might have read it.

Georgie felt a pang in her chest.

'Oh well, it was his fault if he read something he shouldn't. Everyone knows diaries don't tell the truth.' Only a partial truth, a passing truth. 'People don't necessarily know what they feel anyway.' But you don't know that when you're sixteen.

She looked at the black and white foursome of Rowan. He was a darling. Why hadn't she seen what a beautiful sensitive boy he was? 'Oh Ro. I'm sorry. Please forgive me?' Why hadn't she loved him for introducing her to the gorgeous mysteries of adulthood? Why had she taken his beauty for granted? Why had she not passionately welcomed him when he'd come to Bristol, especially to see her; instead of being ashamed of him, amongst her new city friends. She'd called him a yokel. She wondered what had become of him, and before she knew it another wave of confusing emotion was swelling in her breast, and her mouth was trembling and her eyes were stinging.

'Buck up Geegee!' she told herself. 'Don't be such a silly. It would've had to stop sooner or later, wouldn't it? Otherwise I'd never have had the children.' She blew her nose. 'That's what you get for wantig to blub, a bloody bugged up dose. Daargh. It's all this stuff! This bloody stuff is stuffig me! Why am I doig it? I'm fed up with it! I'm fuckig fed up!' She ranged her eyes over the little heaps of objects and papers, still, quiet and unconcerned. For a few moments she felt a strange kind of peace in her relationship to it all. If she left it just like that, perhaps time would stop.

She thought about the distances everything had travelled to get there, the variety of people that had owned these things and passed them on, trails and chains leading inexorably to here, to now, to her. She realised that this particular configuration of stuff must be the unique result of an almost infinite web of small occurrences and changes, so that it could only be exactly like this because everything leading up to it had been exactly like that.

'What, does that have to include, say, Genghis Khan? Would this lobby look precisely like this if Genghis Kahn had died at birth? No, no, bad example, he's too important, of course it wouldn't. What about an ordinary person? Or an ant? If an ant that didn't die at birth had in fact died at birth, would this lobby look precisely like this?' She thought the death of an ant might at least change a corner of it, for a moment forgetting her own much more significant contribution.

An ant? Or a sperm or an egg? she went on in her reverie. Little things make all the difference. Maybe the universe is a hologram, she thought in a spasm of excitement. Maybe all of everything ever is contained in every tiny little bit!

Suddenly there was subsidence, a loud noise and a toppling. The mirror she had balanced against the wall somehow fell forwards onto a collection of small boxes she'd just exhumed from the front room, and her nerves exploded at the disturbance. She shouted at it. 'Leave be alode!'

She was hungry and tired, and hadn't got dressed yet, though it must be noon. The bedroom clock had stopped. 'Dab!' Her mobile had run out of charge. 'Bugger!'

What do you eat when you live alone? You can cook whatever you like! You can cook special things using alternative ingredients because you're suddenly very fussy about what goes inside you. You can cook with organic soya cream and organic coconut oil, and organic rice and quinoa! Oily fish and colourful vegetables! First of all you cook too much, and you're forever storing leftovers in little bowls covered with saucers then throwing them away. A quarter of a cauliflower. A collapsed third of vegan shepherd's pie. A third of a can of beans. And you buy too much because so many things come in pairs. You're forever wrapping a chicken breast or a trout in cling film, then postponing eating it because you had it the day before, then forgetting about it, then throwing it away; or putting whole seeded potatoes and sprouted onions in the compost. Then you skip the odd meal because there's no-one reminding you to eat. You might as well just have a sandwich. You might as well just have a salad.

She opened a tin of sardines and ate them from the tin with a fork, walking from room to room in her underwear looking for a space to sit down. The only clear space was at one end of the bed. 'Not very good manners, Gee. Slovenly behaviour. Standards droppig. Dropping! Ing. Ing.'

One of the sardines broke as she was posting it into her mouth. It balanced on her chin, dribbling olive oil. She slurped it up, making a disgusting noise. But what did that matter? No-one was watching or listening. She wasn't being recorded or monitored, was she? 'But I'm watching, aren't I, so buck up!' she said to herself, and then, 'Yes but who are you to tell me what to do when I'm on my own?' It's probably not a good thing to insult yourself though, she thought. 'Actually, it's not a great thing to be having such a conversation. It feels mad! It feels mad, I tell you!' This turned into a little song, as she took the empty sardine tin to the kitchen, rinsed her hands and ate a banana. 'Banana, potassium. Fish, omega threes.' She put the exercise books on the bedside table 'Now what? Dressing needs to happen. I need to get out.'

Later, she reinstated the mirror, and looked disapprovingly at her reflection.

'Stop it!' she said. The concerned lined sad person who looked back at her had the air of the woman in her photograph, the woman she fancied was the mirror's original owner. The resemblance frightened her. 'Stop scowling!' she shouted, as her mother used to, even before she knew what it meant. 'I'm not doing anything,' she'd complain, scowling even worse. Only later did she learn to smile on demand. 'That's better!' Everyone say cheese!

She took her smile down to the docks for a breath of air, vaguely on the lookout for a boat called The Buccaneer.

LISTEN TO THE PAST

That feeling of being followed. Casually you look behind, say as you cross a road, and only half see the figure that pursues you. Your curiosity becomes unbearable. You turn to face your stalker, regardless of embarrassment. No-one is there.

Ever since arriving at the flat she'd felt it – out of doors followed, indoors led. It was an illusion. A mirage. She was learning to deny the sensation and had almost succeeded in resisting the impulse to turn and check, when she was blessed by a sudden incarnation. It happened in the local newsagent. Georgie was casting a cynical eye over the headlines, knowing she wasn't going to buy anything, when a fragile but somewhat accusing feminine voice interrupted her musings.

'It's Georgina isn't it?'

The sound of her name was a jolt. She turned in shame and shock, expecting to be ticked off. The lady smiled, instantly dispelling such a notion.

She was delicate and silver-haired. Her eyes were like bright pins, and her powdered pale skin was criss-crossed with expressive lines. A green silk headscarf framed her face, above a beautiful camel coat decorated with a spray of tiny diamonds.

'I'm an old friend of your mother's,' said the lady. 'We used to meet at the rink. Then later it was the WI.'

Georgie was astonished and gratified to hear Maureen spoken of, and with such a sense of recency. It made her mother more real, somehow; that there were unknown witnesses to her existence, that she was carried in memory, traced on other minds.

'Gosh, really?' she responded with disproportionate enthusiasm, betraying the added pleasure of having been recognised. 'I've found something in a box just yesterday about that. It looked as if it was really good fun! They're closing it now, though, aren't they? For student flats?'

'I haven't seen her for a while,' the lady said.

'No. She's um... Died. I'm afraid.' Four years ago, Georgie could have added. Not all that recently, but she still wasn't going to use the word 'dead'.

'Oh I am sorry. Yes, well I did assume, although she was very young.' The lady grimaced and looked down. 'I'm not what I was myself.'

Georgie tried to think of some useful comments, like, 'she had a good innings,' or, 'it was a good way to go,' or, 'it comes to us all in time,' none of which seemed appropriate; only two of which were true. The lady dealt with whatever internal commotion she was dealing with then looked up with a rheumy but penetrating gaze.

'I remember you too, you were secretarying weren't you? She was worried about you. But you've turned out all right?'

Georgie was surprised by the idea of her mother's worrying. 'Oh yes, thank you, I'm fine,' she said. Apart from the divorce and the bereavements and the cancer and the menopause and the redundancy and Kevin and losing the children, she thought. Not losing them, but they're not being at home any more. 'And the children are fine. Joni and Charlie. Joni's nineteen, Charlie seventeen. Yes, they seem fine.'

'I don't buy newspapers any more,' said the lady, gesturing at the rows of exclamatory headlines and exposed body parts. 'There's never any good news is there? It just goes straight to recycling.'

Georgie agreed. 'Oh, they're relentlessly horrid aren't they? I look at the headlines sometimes. I don't watch it either. The important things come through, I find.'

'Newspapers hacking telephones. Tsunamis. Civil wars. What about unusual acts of kindness? Or people saving lives? Or people loving each other against all the odds? Ordinary people, not just celebrities or Royals.'

'And why the celebrities *are* celebrities, who on earth knows?'

Georgie said, thinking 'these days' but not saying it. 'Why are the Royals royal for that matter?' she went on, turning back to gauge the lady's response.

'It's all about selling things, these days, isn't it?' the lady said, as if to agree. She opened the shop door and gestured that she was about to leave. 'Are you coming through?'

Georgie followed her, glad of some human engagement. They were going in the same direction and walked along together for a while as traffic trundled past, Georgie slackening her stride to keep level with her. She was still thinking about bad news and wondering why people would want to buy it.

'I've been here a long time though,' the lady said.

'Here?'

'I was born here. This is my front door. I wondered, would you like some tea?'

Georgie felt she had things to do, people to see. 'Well I...' But what did she have to do, actually? Put some bits of shopping in the fridge and empty some more boxes. And she had nobody to see but herself, as she didn't seem able to engineer a meeting with Nick, in spite of having drunk four green teas in the Lido café, and twice circumnavigating the docks. The old lady's expression implored her. Perhaps this chance encounter was an important event in her day; keeping her company might be one of those unusual acts of kindness. 'Yes, that would be lovely, thank you,' she said, finally.

The lady passed Georgie her handbag while she struggled with the front door key then led her into a light airy flat on the ground floor. The walls were papered in pastel flowers and butterflies, covered with gold-framed prints and photographs.

'So you've been here – ?'

'Eighty years,' came the reply

'Gosh.'

'I haven't seen any reason to move. Not yet. My granddaughter wants me to, but I've put my foot down. I'm going out in a box.'

The lady hung up her coat and led Georgie into the sitting

room, motioning that she should sit down on the sofa, an old model which toned in with the lady's classic clothes – her beige skirt, flowered cotton shirt and bottle-green cardigan. She wore pearls. Georgie felt scruffy in her jeans and jacket, as if she might defile the furniture. She hesitated in the middle of the room, wanting to offer to help. There ought to be a bell and a maid; or Georgie ought to be the maid, she felt. The lady departed and, while she was tinkering about in the adjoining kitchen, Georgie admired the prints. One was a panorama of Bristol, drawn in the mid-nineteenth century, she guessed. Temple Meads was there, on a ribbon of railway under its massive hangars. The right side of the picture – the east side of Bristol – was sooty and black, thicketed with chimneys, under clouds. On Brandon Hill there was no Cabot Tower. Tyndall's Park Road went through a park. Tall ships filled the harbour and were dotted all the way up the Avon, alongside Clifton with its patches of green, its arcs of Georgian terraces, and its grey cliffs and suspension bridge. She identified her own house amongst the intricate rectangles.

As the lady entered with a tray Georgie moved some books along the coffee table to make a space for it, placing Matisse and Cézanne carefully on top of *Country Interiors*.

'I saw you looking at the panorama. Isn't it wonderful? They must have done it from an air balloon. Copied from photographs, but they couldn't snatch a photograph so quickly in those days.'

'It's fantastic. I love it that you can see this terrace on it.'

'Yes, well, it's been here since 1791, this place.'

Georgie pretended to be surprised.

'One of the first terraces built, this, you know. After the mansions. And it was all new then. After the Civil War there was nothing left. All burnt down by Prince Rupert to starve the besieging Roundheads. But guess what survived?'

Georgie smiled. She shook her head to show that she had no idea.

'A tree. And we mustn't let it go. It's one of the oldest in Bristol. It's outside the new hospital.'

'The private one.'

'Yes. God rest the NHS. It's a chestnut tree, and I've been reliably informed that it's getting on for four hundred years old.'

'That's amazing!' Georgie's jaw dropped. 'It was already ancient before this was built.'

'Oh yes. You know, I don't think of this place as being all that old. It's only two-and-a half-times me!'

'It rings a bell, 1791. Should it?'

'Declaration of the rights of Women. Mozart's death. The first slave revolt in Haiti.'

'Gosh, your history's good.'

'It's from the Wikipedia. My daughter printed out the page for me. Now you be mother, my wrist is a little shaky with the teapot handle. I can manage the kettle all right.'

Georgie poured the tea first and then milk, sensing that she might have made a faux pas, but knowing that caring about it would be even more faux. As she settled back and looked over the room, her eye was caught by a recent photograph of two children.

'Are these your grandchildren?'

'They're my great-grandchildren.'

'Oh sweet! Great-grandchildren. What must that be like?'

'It's absolutely tremendous. They're even more special than my grandchildren, because they're special *to* my grandchildren.' The lady looked radiantly proud and happy, as though a light were shining through her papery skin. 'It multiplies.'

'I'm sorry, I don't know your name,' Georgie said.

'I'm Eileen.' She gestured at the photograph. 'And that's China, and that's India.'

'OK.' Georgie nodded, unable to resist raising her eyebrows.

'Fashions change in everything don't they?' Eileen smiled.

'So you're the same age as my mum would be. So you were nine at the beginning of the war?'

'Fifteen at the end of it. That's right. And what a coming-of-age that was.' Eileen sighed, forgivingly, not regretfully. 'We were quite lucky to get through it really, you know. The incendiaries came over here.'

'Really?'

'Oh yes, some of these roofs caught fire.' She leant forward, relishing the memory. 'We were got up in the middle of the night. I'll never forget it. Sirens everywhere. A great red glow over the town. My father was away. My mother and my little brothers, we all went down to hide in the Anderson shelter. We were pleased to use it! It was very exciting.'

'Weren't you scared?'

'Not really. I just assumed we'd be safe. '

The conversation paused. Georgie was imagining how frightening it must have been, comparing it to the safety and security of her own childhood. Then Eileen went on, as though she were recalling a history lesson, careful to get it right.

'November 24th 1940. That's a date I won't forget. The moon was out. They could see the river and they followed it and dropped their bombs. You can't black out the moon can you? Or the river.'

Georgie shook her head, ponderously. The river was like an artery or vein, she thought, leading all the way to the city's heart.

'You don't have a Bristol accent,' she remarked.

'Oh well, the family was from London originally,' Eileen explained.

'I often wondered why we came to Bristol. We were perfectly happy in Stratford. But they did end up loving it here didn't they?'

'Everyone does. It's got character.'

'Yes, I loved it myself eventually.'

Again the conversation paused. Eileen was staring into the distance. It didn't seem right to break her concentration. At last she looked at Georgie and spoke.

'You know, your mother thought there was something buried

here that was meant for her. Something left by the family. She found something in the loft, a book, a diary – something like that. Where you used to live.'

'In the loft where we used to live?'

'Colley Acre. Colley Acre, that was it. This land here is Colley Acre, where all these buildings are. She came to look for it. Her heritage.'

Georgie was struck. Her mother's heritage. But her mother had been born in Ireland. Surely this was her father's heritage. How generous women are to assume their husbands' family histories, she thought, because their children's heritage matters to them as well as their own.

'Colley Acre. That does ring a bell.'

It was no bell, it was her mother's gentle singing: *In the house on Colley's acre.* She looked where Eileen had been looking, through the back windows and onto the terrace garden. 'Did she find it? Whatever it was.'

Molly's mother sewed a seed, buried for her daughter Molly all a golden girl could need.

Eileen shrugged. 'Maybe they got the wrong house. Maybe they didn't look very hard. It was just a feeling I think.'

'A feeling.'

'I don't know. I... I can't remember.'

Georgie let her eyes rest again onto the view from the back window, the lullaby still sounding in her mind.

'So in the war, was everyone digging for victory?'

'We did. Of course. We liked the fresh vegetables.'

'All the gardens?'

'All the gardens and the communal garden too. That went a bit wild for a time. Everything went a bit wild in the sixties. It's nice now though isn't it?'

'It's beautiful, yes. Especially now things are coming up.'

'They've been coming up for a long time. We got daffodils in January.'

Georgie sipped her tea. She thought of the ivy, choking everything. 'Ours is a bit wild,' she admitted, politely side-stepping a conversation about climate change in case it was too depressing.

'Your parents couldn't do much with it I suppose, later on.'

'No.' A weight of guilt came thundering down on Georgie's heart. 'We should have helped them more.'

Eileen just smiled.

Georgie had emptied her cup and Eileen seemed tired.

'I should go,' she said, getting to her feet, and Eileen stood up too, to see her out. 'It's been really lovely talking to you,' said Georgie, 'Do come round to me, won't you?' She realised it was absurd to venture such an invitation. There was no possibility of receiving Eileen in the midst of such unwelcoming disorder, and Eileen would neither be so rude as to turn up unannounced, nor so bold as to use a phone number she must have overlooked for at least four years.

As Georgie passed through to the hall, she noticed on the sideboard two china figures she knew she'd seen before. They were unusual, both of black men, one playing a violin, one kneeling, looking heavenward with a Bible on his knee. The Bible said BLESS GOD THANK BRITTON ME NO SLAVE. 'I recognise these!' Georgie said. 'Thank Britain indeed! Thank Britain for trading slaves in the first place! Yes. I must've been here before. Maybe I came with Mum one time.'

Eileen chuckled. 'You were always wanting to get away.'

Georgie felt embarrassed that she was getting away now. She began to say something, but Eileen noticed her consternation and laughed. 'Don't worry, I don't mean it. Your great aunt left these pieces to me, you know; I'd always admired them. This too.' She picked out a lacquered pill box from the display, and hesitating a moment, handed it to Georgie, who held it to the light to admire its decoration of finely painted urns and vines.

'Pretty! It feels like bakelite.'

'Much older, can you see there's a date and a name scratched in it?'

Georgie squintingly made it out. 'Agh, I can't see close with my lenses in. Eighteen-hundred and something. Bollescote? Bottescote? Manor. Hmmm. Interesting.'

She began to replace the object, but Eileen stayed her hand.

'It's yours. Perhaps it's your family seat.'

Georgie wanted to refuse. I have enough stuff, she wanted to explain, but it was impossible to reject Eileen's generosity.

'Well, thank you, that's really kind. Thank you.'

She committed her last view of Eileen to memory, wondering whether they would meet again. It cheered her to know that you could be happy and independent and sociable and proud and beautiful – yes, you could be beautiful too, even if you were over eighty. Provided you were provided for, as Eileen so clearly was.

'What a wonderful elderly lady!' she said to herself, carefully avoiding the words 'old woman'.

Something of this encounter encouraged and heartened her. When she got home she went to the bedroom and stared out of the back windows onto the rambling weed-filled green green garden – green of all shades and depths. The old walls were a foot deep in ivy. Shrubs at the bottom had grown right over the garden gate. The lawn was just a patch of moss in the centre, crying out for light. Ivy roots had crept into it from all sides. The only glimmer of any other colour came from a straggle of dandelions, straining for insects. It was a slugs' paradise. A robin leapt up and flew off, and returned again and again to the same spot in the ivy. It was building a nest.

If something were buried out there she'd need more than a spade to get to it. She'd need some proper professional gardening help, from someone conscientious, someone kind, who would leave the robin's home, and rescue her mother's roses and jasmine and honeysuckle before it was too late.

She googled 'Bottescote Manor': A Palladian conference centre, gym and health spa facility, surrounded by manicured greenery, furnished with shapeless sculptures. It was the backdrop to someone's wedding, its main hall walls covered with old paintings of men and women in fancy costumes.

Events, Private Hire, Golf, Retreats, Gardens in Glory, Shop, History:

Bottescote Manor was built in 1743 for Samuel Glover, financed by his estates in Virginia. In 1762 it passed to his son Sidney Glover, who added the Henry Holland portico in 1773. In 1787 it was bought by munitions dealer Jonah Sutton.

Sutton! 'It *is* ours!' 'Jonah Sutton, munitions dealer,' she read on. 'No, no. Must be some other load of Suttons.'

Inherited by son Lionel in 1847, ceded to son Gilbert in 1848, and in 1869 sold to corset manufacturer James Heale, who, in turn, passed it to his son Robert in 1894.

'Ha! What about the daughters?'

During the First World War the stables were used as a hospital. During the Second World War the house and surrounding buildings were requisitioned for use as a barracks. Throughout this period it was owned by the Heale family until Winifred Heale bequeathed it to the local council in 1956. Maintained by the council until its sale in 1997, it was refurbished with the help of charitable donations (1978-86) and used as school, then as an Adult Education centre. In 1997 it was acquired by hedge fund ASS, and is now managed by UK Health plc. Ghosts are reported: the 'girl in gold' is said to bear a resemblance to a painting of an unidentified young girl which was found in a damp corner of the stables during the restorations, and has been attributed to Sir Thomas Lawrence. Painstakingly restored along with the rest of the property, it now takes pride of place on the first landing.

She clicked on the hyperlink 'unidentified young girl', hoping to know her. Up she came, dressed in glimmering yellow satin, with a cocker spaniel sprawling elegantly beside each foot. She was posing in front of a misty undulating English landscape complete with trees and cattle and sheep and no other person. The green blued as it stretched to a distant spire on the horizon, where it met a rampantly swirling pinkish-grey sky.

'That's my girl!' Georgie whispered, though she didn't really believe it.

*

She lugged *Ancient Correspondence* into her theatre of operations and left it there for a moment to investigate the oak record cupboard that had been hiding behind it. Once this had been the very thing – the pinnacle of modern British style! It was still full of records – LPs on the bottom shelf, EPs and singles on the top – announcing their presence by that special whiff of cooked vinyl and polythene which made her think of the word 'gramophone'. They were lined up in no particular order with tiny lettering on their spines: JS Bach, Elgar, The Rolling Stones, The Beatles, Mozart, Paddy Roberts, Ravel, John Lee Hooker, Miles Davis, Beethoven. Pink Floyd. There was *The Hissing of Summer Lawns*, her first own Joni Mitchell record. 'Don't interrupt the sorrow,' she sang to herself. The tune alone spoke to her of that particular summer or her mangled memory of it. Yes, yes, she could well imagine the lawns had hissed in complaint as they browned and shrank that year! It occurred to her that it was also Frieda's year. The contents of the house were intent on reminding her.

Blue was there! And *Diamond Dogs* and *Waterloo* and *Still Crazy After All These Years*! Most of the albums belonged to her parents, some were Will's. Well, he didn't want them any more; it was her turn now. But here was another one of her own, her very first LP, the soundtrack to *Barry Lyndon*. She'd emptied her piggy bank and bought the whole album for one single track. She parted its open edges, and reached into its slithery inner sleeve, which stuck to the vinyl with static. It used to fascinate her, this magic in the air, how it lifted her hair, even the tiny hairs on her arms, stroking her without touching. Balancing the central hole on her middle finger, steadying its outer edge with a thumb, she studied the grooves and patterns and recalled how she used to read their code, anticipating how they might sound. Now she couldn't remember what any of it meant. She wanted to listen. Somewhere here was bound to be a record player. She stood and surveyed the room, catching a glancing reflection of her own sudden movement in the glass of the cupboard door. It stopped her breath and she waited a moment to recover.

'You're scaring yourself, you silly! It's only you! It's only me!' Oh, there was her mother's voice again, calling her a silly as she used to; as though she were calling through the glass and Georgie might just climb across and join her on the other side of it.

The music system was wedged underneath a coffee table. She sidled painfully between folding chairs, cases, shelving and box piles to reach it. As she extracted it from its cosy corner, a dented ping pong ball and a knitted bear came with it. Dust and cobwebs were smeared all down her jeans.

It was all there – turntable, cassette deck, amp, speakers, even the stylus – and all the connecting wires were intact, though everything was coated in dust. Beside it there were pocked carrier bags full of cassettes, broken plastic and stray paper liners, and several Sony Walkmen of different vintages, including a CD player, which looked incomprehensibly older and scruffier than the rest. Some of the cassettes were radio recordings – *Radio 1, Just a Minute,* – some were duplicates of the records. Her heart sank as she noticed another two cardboard boxes stuffed full of recorded videos, their scribbled labels naming all the television programmes her parents had never had time to watch. Yards and yards of magnetic tape. It could have tied them to their chairs and strangled them. Amongst them were commercial videos and DVDs too, and a set of Linguaphone Chinese nobody had learned.

'I despair!' she shouted out loud, suddenly overwhelmed by the sheer quantity of entertainment, the hours and hours, and days and days, of jokes and chat and information and drama she was never going to enjoy.

There was no room to set up the sound system in the stairwell, so she hoisted it into the kitchen where she cleaned and assembled it, with one speaker on the dresser and the other on the fridge.

'Women of Ireland' was the track she wanted to hear – a

harrowingly beautiful tune she remembered falling in love with, or falling in love along with. She had listened to it over and over again, lifting the needle and resetting it, lifting and resetting it, to everyone else's irritation.

A hiss and a crackle introduced the tune, played at first by a single lonely fiddle. It conjured the contours of a landscape of bleak peat-covered hills and glowering skies. The fiddle was joined by an orchestra, as textured and rich as technicolour, then the high whistle joined in like a spirit cry. The sound was full and resonant – better quality than she was used to.

'How odd of me,' she thought, 'to want to hear something so sad.'

It took her back to those strange limbo days, a couple of weeks at the beginning of September just before they were torn away to new lives in Bristol – the last of their days in Stratford. After her awful 'O' level results. After Frieda left. At around the same time, the family had acquired Aunt Ruby's things and Maureen had become involved in them.

Georgie played the track again. The music seemed to grip her lungs and pull them groundward and gave her a yearning sensation she couldn't attach to anything.

A few days after Frieda had gone, some men came to cut down the dead elms. Georgie remembered the sound of the saws, rasping through the early September afternoon, and the chomping of a machine which consumed the branches and sprayed them out as fragrant dust. Looking on, she had felt that an era was over. The world would never be the same again.

It had been so. The world never was the same again, and nor was she. A spirit of Enterprise had come marching into everyone's lives, shackled to the spirit of Greed; wide-shouldered, big haired twins, guzzling expensive champagne, snorting coke, pogoing to punk, spinning to synthesizers, sliding shinier and shinier surfaces under flatter and thinner and more and more sophisticated screens.

'Oh!' she heard herself moaning. 'How I do long!' But she didn't know what she might be longing for.

She remembered the moment her mother had looked up from her photograph albums and said, 'We are women of Ireland, you and I.' In her selfish bubble of hurt and remorse Georgie hadn't listened. All she could say was, 'I'm of England.' She regretted that now. Maureen had wanted to talk about Cork. She would have told her things that could never now be told.

'How I do long to be home again!' she intoned.

Her ties were coming loose. It wasn't Salisbury she was yearning for. It couldn't be Bristol, seeing as she was already there. Perhaps it was her own birthplace she longed to reclaim; for wherever she might fall, and however it might change, she would always have been born in Stratford. 'And being born is the most important moment of a life,' she thought. A contrary idea flitted momentarily across her mind, but she ignored it because at precisely the same time as she was thinking these thoughts, her eye fell upon a file labelled 'Stratford'.

Goose pimples rose along her arms.

'Don't be absurd, Gee. It's not even a coincidence. I've just reached a certain seam in the... Whatsit. Geology.'

She opened it to find poems and letters:

Pope's Mill
it was called, when I was a child
though I cannot remember it at work
with sacks of grain,
but marvelled at the placard
bearing the high-water mark
of those unprecedented floods before my time
when field and river became one
great clumps of trees were islanded and householders
shored up their homes
with sandbags.

Now it has gone;
I witnessed its demise.

A noise
as of distant bombs
and gunfire answering
drew me towards the choking dust
where men
protected by their helmets did their worst.
Only an ivy-covered wall was left,
Then perished with the rest.

Once I would stand
and gaze
in fascination at the weeds
the streaming hair of green girls drowned
or wade
as far as I could dare
testing for shingle with each bare
footstep
and wondering
at the elemental force.

Not all the water tumbled down the sluice
in sunlight,
the mill-race drove
mysteriously underground,
finding some hidden place to spend
its energy,
then reappeared to laze
between the arches of the bridge.
And, drop
by drop, was it the same
or not the same?

It has been tidied out of all recognition;
For shame the sign
'Great Danger – Queers' has been erased.
Expensive flats reflect

their unimposing images. Smart ranks of locks and weirs
have caged the flood.

Only the name 'Mill Lane' remains,
that gateway to the Seven Meadowland
where buttercups would gild
my sandals on a solitary walk.

Yet wait
Before the bulldozers rape all
and pave the last vestige of my golden age
and the wild unicorn fades into the woods of myth
And listen carefully
for holy and enchanted still
a voice reverberates
as water thunders through the chasm
at its own free will

Keep.

Georgie remembered the weirs. That smell of detergent. That roar of water. She, too, had waded right into the river, and felt the bottom of it, surprisingly disgustingly soft, not like the hard sandy shelf she was expecting; the water had been thick, green smelling, unrefreshing, and weeds had wrapped around her ankles.

Oh, she had wanted a baptism! She had hoped for relief from the heat! But it was a river to gaze at, not to touch or enter. That day she'd lost a thimbleful of innocence. It was dangerous to remember, and dark as that murky water, but she was drawn inexorably down.

The letters were still in their envelopes. Most were addressed to Stratford and redirected to Bristol. One was from Salzburg. She swallowed her queasiness at seeing the postmark, and, steeling herself against any possible sentimentality, opened it and read:

Konigstrasse 8, den. 22 Nov 1977
Lieber Will

Thank you for sending the money but why do you not reply? Please write to me. I would prefer from you a letter than all the money in the world. I look for a letter every day, so every day I am sad. I love you.

Mina needs more than money. She needs a father's love. If only you could send me that!

Please please write to me.
Yours with love always
Frieda

Georgie was stunned. Her hand fell.

'Will! You fucking lying... fucking lying bastard!'

Nervously she sifted through the other letters looking for another from Salzburg, wanting a sign that Frieda had been answered.

She found an earlier one, undated, with an illegible postmark:

Konigstrasse 8
Lieber Will

I have a healthy baby girl and she is named for you, Wilhelmina. Now I am a mother, I love you more. Thank you, thank you my dear William. Please come soon.

Yours with love
Frieda

And two more in a similar vein, but more resigned enclosing two faded polaroids. A baby. A little girl.

'Oh my God, she looks like Eve!'

Georgie stared for a long time at the solemn little face. It was deeply familiar. In demeanour, in form and in feature she was as like Will's daughter as another daughter ought to be.

'This is my niece! Oh yes, that is another niece!'

The girl's dark eyes and corrugated forehead betrayed an air of bewilderment, as though she had only just been planted in the world and didn't particularly care for it. Her dark hair was tied in jaunty bunches, like daisies sprouting from her head. She was wearing a brightly patterned jumpsuit, and the jolly style of her costume seemed to jar with her personality – mini Greta Garbo dressed as mini Carmen Miranda.

Why had Will failed to write back; why had he not gone to her; and how the hell had he managed to send money when he must have had so little to spare? He'd only been eighteen! He was about to be a student on a grant.

With a spasm of guilt she remembered Will's letter to their parents, blaming for interfering. So Larry and Maureen must have taken charge of the whole affair, persuading him to forget about it and carry on with his career.

She wondered how on earth they had covered it up. She herself had been in the house when those letters had arrived, but Larry would always have been first down and first to the post. And Will had been away at Oxford.

It dawned on her that Will knew nothing of this child, and had never received these letters. Otherwise they wouldn't be here; he would have kept them, or, more likely, destroyed them.

She needs a father's love she read again. Not *she needs her father's love*. Georgie stretched her mind back to her scant German. Would it be normal in German to leave out the possessive qualifier? In French you say 'la main', 'le pied' – 'the hand', 'the foot' – not 'my hand, my foot.' But in French, German and English you own your father. My father. Mein Vater – mein Vater – the words were resonant. She could even imagine them in Frieda's own voice. Would Frieda not have written 'she needs her father' if Will were the child's father? Of course she would! She was desperate!

Georgie looked again at the polaroids. The baby certainly did resemble Eve, but then, all babies look alike, she told herself.

'No, they don't! All babies look different! Babies look like their dads!'

Some lines of Goethe came into her mind. *Wer reitet so spät durch Nacht und Wind? Es ist der Vater mit seinem Kind.* 'Who rides so late through night and wind? It is the father with his child.' It was one Larry had loved to declaim.

She fell upon her diary, as the phrase chanted in time to her heartbeat. 'It is the father with his child. It is the father with his child.'

Frieda went to the pictures with Dad and *dirty joke* and *Daddy said 'what are they up to?'* He probably wants to join in.

'No. No. No. No. No,' she said firmly. 'Don't be a silly, Gee. I've thought it before and I've dismissed it before. Daddy would not have gone twatting about with Frieda. I know it looks suspicious, but there's not nearly enough evidence to convict him.' The idea was not a new one, and though she'd so far avoided following it through, now it had her by the neck, and wasn't ready to let her go. 'He would have had the opportunity, I agree. But not the means, no. Infidelity wasn't his thing, was it?' That wasn't entirely true, and Georgie knew it. Larry had indeed committed the 'odd peccadillo' which Maureen had pretended not to know about because it meant nothing. 'I wasn't paying him enough attention, that's all,' she'd told Georgie, years later. 'It's all right now. Most marriages are a bit spotty, you know. On both sides. Nothing's ever perfect.'

'Not this girl, though, Daddy. It's not fair on Will.'

Georgie scrabbled through the box of loose photographs and found again her father's black-and-white portrait of Frieda – lost, needy, yet amused – her expression was complex and appealing, but somehow hurt. Frieda looked so young and defenceless to her now – a woman-child hoping to be attractive, hoping her adoration was mutual, her adoration of the man behind the shutter. Georgie was kneeling on her heels. She dropped the photograph and hugged herself and bent over. What upset her most was the contrast between Larry's artistic portrait and Will's amateur snap, and the difference in Frieda's attitude. Her dear brother hadn't stood a chance; his innocent longing had been trampled and slain and mocked by a selfish middle-aged fantasy.

'I can't bear it. '

Everything slotted into place. Her father's deathbed apology. Payments received. A reason for moving house, so they couldn't be found. Will's incomprehension.

'Why didn't they destroy all this?' she appealed to nothingness. 'Why have I got to know it?' And then she thought, 'What about Mum? Did Mum know?'

'Does she know, Dad, does she know?' she shouted at the air. 'Mummy! What do you know?' In the dead silence that followed the phone rang out and Georgie shrieked in surprise.

She picked it up, half-expecting to hear Larry or Maureen, answering her question. It was a man with an Indian accent.

'Good afternoon to you, Mrs Sutton.'

'Mrs Sutton? I'm sorry, this isn't Mrs Sutton.'

'Is... Mrs Sutton at home?'

'She hasn't been home for a while, I'm afraid.'

'Because our information is telling us that a person at this address has recently had an accident. It may possibly be a different person?'

'Yes, because... Mrs Sutton's... died, you see.'

'I see. I am very sorry, madam.'

'Where are you?'

'I am sorry, madam?'

'Are you calling from India?'

'I am not permitted to say exactly from where I am calling, but in Bristol I can see that the weather is most unsettled today, isn't it?'

'Is it?'

'Oh yes, certainly. And is there anything else I can help you with?'

My father's just knocked off the au pair my brother was madly in love with, and landed me with a little sister I've never known. That's my recent accident. 'I'm terribly sorry,' Georgie said. 'I wish I could help. I mean, I wish you could help.' She wondered if the man was paid any more than commission, if she'd deprived a family of income by not being Mrs Sutton –

who certainly had had an accident – and what the weather was like wherever he was on the surface of the globe.

'I am sorry for your loss,' he said. 'Have a nice day please.'

'It's not a loss, it's a gain,' she told herself, fumbling with the receiver.

She sat down in the kitchen and, shoving some piles and files out of the way, put her hands firmly on the table to still them, 'Phew! Calm down now. Everything's going to be OK. Water under the bridge. Not my problem. Think about it tomorrow. Chin up Gee! This won't do! Phew! Whoo! A cup of tea, that's what's needed in moments of crisis. A good old brew.'

She thought of phoning Sheelah, but that was impossible. She would only be able to call on Sheelah when she didn't need to.

'It's not such a bad thing anyway. Quite normal and natural really. I have a little half-sister, that's all. Unless she belongs to Will, then it's another little niece. One or the other – and it doesn't really matter. Mina. Pretty name. She must be... about thirty-five.'

In her mind she ran through everyone she loved, but nobody could be called on; she was too far away from everyone and had been too out of touch or didn't know them well enough to be weak on them, or to confide this peculiar news. She couldn't rely on Jim or Kevin. Jules and Paula hadn't forgiven her for splitting up with Kevin on their Christmas holiday. Joni? 'Not Charlie or Joni, no. I'm the grown-up. They call on me.' The phrase 'I'm the grown-up' sounded absurd. 'I *am* the grown-up!' she insisted. Will? Of course not Will.

'Oh dear. I seem to have run out of relationships. That was rather careless.'

A tune arrived in her mind, uninvited.

In the house on Colley's acre Molly's mother sowed a seed

The tune fragmented and bits of it went round and round and came out of her mouth. '*Pearls and jewels gold and silver.* Something else. *In the house on Colley's acre. Nothing could the girl want more.* Please leave me alone. Music, some other music, that's what I need to drive you away you horrid little tune. *Buried there her mother's daughter.* What do I have? *Buried with her daughter Molly.* You can cope with this Gee. You're just a bit tired, that's all. *Pearls and jewels, gold and silver, nothing would the girl want more.* Not surprising. *Sewn inside her little dolly.* Cancer and everything. *Buried with her daughter Molly.'*

She chose 'No More Heroes', a single, and put it on as loud as it would go.

'Whatever happened to – ' she shouted, pogoing the nervousness out of her body, ' – Leon Trotsky?' A drop of wet escaped between her legs and her innards felt insecurely packed.

'Tea isn't working. Wine is the thing. Just until I calm down a bit.'

All the Shakespearos! They watched their Rome burn!

LOOK BEHIND YOU

Over the Downs, up the M5, turn right at Worcester. She must go home, home to her original home. The urge had become irresistible. It wasn't a completely reasonable thing to do, but if an excursion to her own and Shakespeare's birthplace added nothing to her life it would take little away beyond her parking space, which she was about to lose anyway, because the car was coming up to its MOT. In other words, it wasn't completely unreasonable either.

She wanted to go there to try and find out why Maureen and Larry had come in the opposite direction all those years ago, uprooting the family, to replant them in Bristol.

It was half past one. The morning had disappeared and she was still in her dressing gown. She flung it off and switched on the shower, suddenly rushing. She didn't even bother to look up directions, imagining there must be special brown heritage signposts to Shakespeare, probably illustrated with Greek masks. She threw on some clothes, locked the flat and hurried to her 2CV. The windscreen needed a prolonged wiping. The engine started on her third attempt.

But there were several right turns at Worcester and she delayed at every one. She didn't manage to get off the M5 until Bromsgrove, well on the way to Birmingham. She veered off in a kind of nightmarish panic and turned round.

She'd never known that Bromsgrove was anywhere near her home town. How strange that she'd spent the first sixteen years of her life so close to Bromsgrove, yet so ignorant of it! In Geography she'd learnt about Africa, South America and Australia. Columbia's chief exports were oil, minerals, sugar, cocoa, coffee, cotton. Her staple foods were yams, manioc, maize, plantains, potatoes. Georgie didn't even know what a yam was, or notice any imbalance between the two lists. You didn't have to, to get your percentage point. Just as in History they'd gone straight from Cromwell to Hitler without passing 'Go', and learnt nothing about the Cold War, or the Cuban Missile Crisis or Israel or Northern Ireland – things that might have helped her understand the news.

She recognised the Warwickshire countryside as if it had shaped her being. Its gentle hills, its copses and tree-lined hedgerows, which enclosed small parcels of green and reddish brown – the proper green for a meadow, the proper brown for a ploughed field – between which she knew would be streams and footpaths and stiles and puddled gates, around which would be cows and sheds and farms and hamlets – these elements together formed a landscape which, though domestic and timid in comparison to the more rugged and open country surrounding Bristol, was yet to her a paragon of countryside, and no landscape in the world – not the Alps or the Grand Canyon or Victoria Falls – would ever surpass it in loveability, simply because it was the first she had known, the original. But though she sensed this spirit of home, her directional sense was fuddled; the roads were altered and bigger and more, and she arrived in Shottery from an unfamiliar angle, so the topography unravelled unfamiliarly, and didn't pop into place until she was right in the centre of the village, next to the pub in its own little island square. Suddenly she knew exactly where she was. It looked small! She parked the car outside the pub, and decided to have a drink first, explore later. It would allow her to adjust, and steady her nerves; it was going to be hard to see her own house invaded and occupied by strangers.

The pub was one she hadn't used as a teenager, being too close to home. Nevertheless she sensed a change in it – the usual change, from spit and sawdust to plush furniture and carpets. In the seventies, there wouldn't have been a wine list, either.

She took a small glass of Rioja outside, and sat within shouting distance of the only other customer, who put down his newspaper when he saw her.

'Nice day!' he said.

'Surprisingly warm,' she agreed.

'You a visitor?'

'I used to live here, actually. Thirty years ago. Or forty?' She laughed at the absurdity of not knowing. 'Somewhere in between. I just want to see it again, I don't know why. Things seem pretty much unchanged.'

'Oh no, Stratford's changed a lot.'

'You live here?'

'On the estate. We came when it was new. Fifteen years ago.'

'And it's changed?'

'There's more traffic and more buildings, those are the main things. There's too many people here that's the trouble. No room for anyone else, but more are coming. They've got plans for 800 new houses, would you believe it? 800! It's a heritage site! There's plenty of land elsewhere but they want to build them here because, you see...' He put down his pint and began to gesture with his hands. 'For the same outlay, same number of bricks, same amount of work, they can sell them for half a million here. It's the land. The land, you see. It's worth more, they get more profits. Greedy bastards. It's a heritage site! They say it's for young families but what young families can afford half a million?'

'Can't they be stopped? '

'It's happening. Nothing we can do about it. We've tried.'

'It's upsetting.'

'There's no room for any more people. Too much traffic as it is. D'you know, there are eight sets of traffic lights on the Birmingham road? Eight! Sometimes it takes half an hour to go one-and-a-half miles.'

'Might as well walk.'

'How can you walk if you've got to get to Birmingham?' He shook his head, exasperated. 'I'm not colour-prejudiced, not at all, but they've allowed immigration and now they've got to build new houses. It's an excuse. There are plenty of houses.'

'What can you do?' Georgie asked rhetorically, sighing, hoping that would conclude the exchange. She went back to her wine and he went back to his daily news. She drank up, wished him goodbye, and nervously set off to find her adolescence.

Now she looked carefully she could see that there was new building even in the centre of the village; old houses had been renovated, tarted up and smartened. She stared as she walked beside them, failing to recollect any of that lost part of her life, but as she came upon her old home she stopped, transfixed, overwhelmed by a rush of contrary emotions: shock, affection, nostalgia, regret.

There was a four-by-four in the driveway. The front garden was neatly trimmed, with a tidy lawn surrounded by a box hedge. The silver birches had gone. There was her father's study to one side of the front porch, which sheltered an unfamiliar door. It used to be plain, painted blue. This one was panelled and polished, dark wood with a brass knocker and brass letterbox. She looked up at her own bedroom, the latticed casement window, now lavishly adorned with chintzy curtains, the bathroom window in the middle, now glazed with frosted glass, and next to that the guest room, so called, although no guest could have stayed there – another dormer window freshly painted and richly curtained. Nothing could be seen inside. Beyond the house, behind the garage she could see the tops of a group of young trees. It was an old house, but it looked newer now than it had done all those years ago. Had the roof been retiled, bricks and windows been replaced, the chimneys mended or cleaned? As her eyes travelled over its exterior she noticed something she didn't remember having seen as a girl. She wouldn't have been interested, or perhaps it used not to be visible. In the porch roof where two diagonal wooden beams met, there was a carving. She felt a quiver of recognition without consciously grasping its meaning. She walked towards it to see more closely. A ground floor curtain twitched and half a minute later the door opened. A man stood there watching her, grinning falsely. He was a lot older than Georgie – knocking on seventy, she thought, in mustard-coloured cords and a waistcoat.

'May I help you? You look rather lost.'

'Sorry, I was just interested in the carving.'

He screwed up his forehead in confusion.

'In the porch, just there,' she pointed.

He came out and looked up. 'Yes, yes. Lovely thing that. Very old. We think it's original. As old as the house. Are you a visitor?'

'Yes, I suppose so.'

'Well, um. Do enjoy your visit.'

'I used to live here. Actually here, in this very house. In fact, I came to see it again.'

He looked uncomfortable and confused, as though searching for a sequence of words that would extract him from the situation and make her go away. Georgie held on. Normally she would have put him out of his misery and got out of his life. She knew it was her cue. She knew what she ought to say: 'I'd better get along,' or 'Thank you for letting me look. I'd better let you get on with your afternoon.' But she didn't feel like it.

'Well, um, I um. I'd better um,' he blustered.

Georgie endured her own twinges of embarrassment, smiling away.

'It was less obvious, you know, when we bought it,' he explained. 'It was painted, black paint everywhere, all the windows. We stripped it off. Repainted all the rest of course, but we thought we'd leave this bit. It's a tree, there are the branches and there are the roots. Or it could be a wheatsheaf. A highly unusual thing.'

Georgie suddenly realised where she'd seen such a symbol before: on the handle of a silver spoon – a silver spoon in a box called 'Treasures'.

'What does it mean? What kind of people would have carved it, d'you think?' Her intensity seemed to inspire a change in attitude. His expression softened, and he stood aside.

'As a matter of fact, we were interested too. Would you like to come in? My wife's out, but um. Well, I could do you a cup of tea.'

'I'd love that, thank you.' It amazed Georgie how she was censoring all her usual bits of verbiage, like 'but I don't want to be in your way,' or 'but please don't let me disturb you.' It was quite enjoyable to express what you wanted straightforwardly for a change. She entered and he closed the door behind her.

'Michael, by the way,' he said abruptly, immediately turning to show her the way. Georgie introduced herself to his back, as he led her through the hall to the sitting room, a most disorientating and unnerving experience. She felt as though she were entering a parallel reality or a time warp; the floors, walls and doors were in the same relation to each other, but everything had a different colour, and the space was full of someone else's things. In place of the parquet flooring there was a beige wall-to-wall carpet with rugs on top of that. She was pleased to see plenty of books, though they looked suspiciously orderly and unread. And it didn't smell right; it smelt of pets and shepherd's pie. The fireplace now contained a gas fire which only looked like a coal fire, though a brass stand of fire irons stood beside it, and a brass coal bucket full of magazines. Above it the mantelpiece displayed china ornaments, a horseshoe and a framed wedding photograph. Hogging one corner of the room was an enormous flat-screen television encased in its own antique cabinet.

'Let me see now,' he said. 'Do sit down.' He left her to go to the kitchen and she hovered, staring out of the French windows – double-glazed and now leading into a conservatory instead of directly onto the back garden.

'D'you mind if I look at the garden?' she called. She didn't hear him say no, so she let herself into the conservatory and stared through the glass. The summerhouse was still there! There was no sign that there had ever been elms and the swimming pool had simply vanished. Instead there was a curving pathway leading to a line of new trees, bordered by flowers and shrubs. Two of the apple trees had survived, with low branches dragging on the ground.

Her host came in with a tray, a teapot with a tea cosy, two bone china cups and saucers, a bowl of sugar and a little jug of milk, everything edged in gold. She sat down on the sofa while he disappeared again, bringing back plates and a tin of biscuits decorated in boats.

'Thank you, this is so kind of you.'

'We've been here ten years,' he told her. 'I don't think it was you we bought it from?' He went up to one of the bookshelves and looked along the spines, picking out an album.

'No, no, my family was here thirty odd years ago,' she explained.

'Well I never.'

'It's very odd. It's the same and not the same.'

'Lots of people have lived here of course. My wife is interested in the local history. I think she hoped it was related to Mr Shakespeare but unfortunately not. Not that we could find out anyway.' He sat down and opened the album. 'They would probably have known the Hathaways, but it was built after Shakespeare's time. 1670s, we reckon.'

'Really? Not that long after then?'

'We found what we thought was a priest hole, but it's too late for that, and rather too small. Hiding valuables? Nothing in it now, of course, but dust and spiders.'

'How exciting! A hidey-hole? Where was that, then?'

'In the bedroom at the top of the stairs. False roof. Listed building, so we had to keep it.'

Georgie cringed. That bedroom had been hers. For years she had innocently slept beneath a secret cavity. It might have harboured anything – anything smaller than a priest.

Michael showed her a page in the album – a photocopy of a document covered in illegible copperplate handwriting.

'That's the earliest evidence we can find. From, look there, that's Thomas Sutton, sole holder of the deeds.'

A whisper of coldness travelled down Georgie's spine.

'That's my name!' she exclaimed. 'What a coincidence.'

'Oh! Well, there you are then. It's yours.'

Georgie laughed, and he shot her a dry smile.

'But look, do you see? There's that symbol again after his name. So we think it's his. A kind of signature.'

'Is that a normal thing to do?'

'Grander people put coats of arms up didn't they? Perhaps he was a bit of a show-off.'

'Looks a bit masonic?'

'Undoubtedly, that's more like it. Well, we've looked and if it's a secret society we can't find out anything else. It's a traditional freemason symbol, but there were lots of guilds and friendly societies and so on. Not necessarily all documented.'

'A religious thing? Catholics?'

'Anything other than Protestants weren't officially tolerated by the crown. But people got away with it. It's a farmer's, well not much more than a cottage really. He would have had a few sheep, an orchard or two, a cornfield if he was better off, a cow perhaps. One of the more comfortable sort in these parts we like to think.'

'It's funny, I was never interested in anything like this when I was young.'

'No. No. One gets to a certain age and looks back. Nowhere else to go.' He looked wistful.

'Or is it more general than that? We live in a retrospective age?'

Her suggestion was left hanging, and in the silence that followed Georgie pursued the thought; maybe the human race had got to a certain age and there was no future for it. A cold fear came upon her, that she'd borne her children into Armageddon, that payback time was coming. What use would they have for their perfect teeth in the famine and the flood?

He offered her a custard cream with her cup of tea, and she fell to small talk, admiring the china and the garden. She resisted the urge to explore further, because she was beginning to feel oppressed, so as soon as she'd drunk up, she performed the usual politenesses and was shown out. She remembered the day she'd left, kissing the bricks and saying goodbye. She'd got into the back seat of the car, and off they went without a backward glance. Did we leave anything behind, she wondered, apart from dust and hair? Nothing that would still be there, she thought.

A cursory exploration of the area revealed that the Ann Hathaway cottage experience now included an optional five-minute walk and a cream tea, and you could no longer pursue the public right of way along Shottery Brook because it was blocked off by hedging and brambles. Tourists were manipulated into going round the corner on a neatly maintained taster-sized stretch. She set off in the opposite direction to look at the town.

Stratford seemed hardly to have changed at all except that Henley street was pedestrianised and everywhere had the air of a theme park. Falstaff and Mistress Quickly were hanging about outside the birthplace and Shakespeare ice-cream was for sale alongside Devonshire fudge, tartan wool, cashmere cardies and whisky. The town was pretty and petite in a way she was only aware of now she'd seen some of the rest of the world, but her feelings of recognition as she wandered around were bone-deep – in her marrow – not accessible to conscious thought. She knew these streets as she knew her own body, instinctively and with unquestioning love. When she ventured beyond the façades, though, she realised that most of the old buildings had been gutted – scooped out and replaced by a gigantic shopping centre with all the usual chains. Even McDonald's was there, albeit a toned down white-lettered, marginally more tasteful-looking McDonald's, which offered nothing more tasteful in the way of food, however. She treated herself to a restaurant lunch, and was just congratulating herself on having found somewhere genuine and solid when she realised that the oak tables weren't heavy enough to be oak. They were veneered. It's all surface, she thought; everything's all surface, as thin as a screen. You might as well go round it on a computer and save some petrol.

She walked back to the car via the opposite bank of the river so she could take in the recreation ground – the 'rec', as was. Its grass was well-trodden – half mud – and for what she imagined must be reasons of health and safety, the beautiful willows lining the river had been shorn, cut short in their weeping. They were coquettish, mincing. This town has turned into a tart, she thought. But Stratford had been prostituting itself for a long long time. It was more experienced and better at it, that was all.

The weirs smelt less of detergent and didn't froth as they used to. After leaning on the footbridge, nostalgically resting her eyes on the river views, she walked along Mill Lane to the church yard, noting with pleasure some primroses sprinkled amongst the gravestones. To walk on through the backstreets was to witness an unfolding of architectural styles, fast-forwarding through the eras. Georgian, Victorian, Edwardian, then up through the twenties- and thirties-built houses that lined the main roads. Matthew used to live round there somewhere – the innocent foil for her first unrequited flesh-and-blood crush. She walked up and down, racking her brain for the number. It had a gate, a front garden, a porch, she remembered, two upstairs windows, two down, and a facing of red brick and whitewashed pebbledash. She hovered embarrassingly in front of one that looked familiar for no reason she could identify.

She decided to trust her instinct, launched nervously up the garden path and rang the bell before she could change her mind. The wrought-iron house number looked right, though it was chipped and spiderwebby; so did the diamond of stained glass in the door, and the blood-coloured tiles beneath her feet. She wondered if this had been her real goal in coming to Stratford.

It was the wrong time of day for anyone to be home. She pressed her nose on the green and yellow glass, and made out an ordinary empty hall, with a side table, a mirror and a row of coatless pegs. As she turned to leave, a young woman was arriving at the gate. She was trying to open it with her hip because her hands were full – a vacuum cleaner in one, in the other a plastic bucket overflowing with bottles and cloths. She shouted to Georgie. 'Are you looking for the owner?'

'I just wondered if it still belonged to the McGoughs? Or if it ever did?' Georgie rushed down the path to hold the gate open for her. The girl smiled as she negotiated the gap.

'Thanks. Er, no. Helena Butt.'

'Oh well. Thanks. Sorry to bother you.'

'She could have been McGough before she married I suppose.'

Helena. Matthew's little sister was a Helena.

'It's let online. Air b n b. You could find out through that maybe?' She nodded and started up the path.

'Thank you.' Georgie didn't know how to ask politely what age this Helena Butt might be. 'Do you know her?' she called.

'Not really. I'm a student. I just clean.'

She'd put down her tools and was ready to let herself in. She wanted to get on with her work.

'It doesn't matter,' Georgie shouted. 'It really doesn't matter. Doesn't matter at all.'

As she got into the car and turned on the ignition, she felt absurdly happy. A weight had lifted from her heart. It was a laying to rest. Everything that had happened here had happened too long ago to be relevant. The cracks had been filled, the damage rebuilt. Her mum and dad weren't in their old hometown, not even their ghosts. Nor was she. Yet it was still hers, right down in the very middle of her, the place was in her cells. Her own surname was rooted in its soil – in some document in the vaults of the library – and her past was written within her; to her it couldn't be lost. She was pleased she'd come, and just as pleased to be leaving.

All down the motorway she thought about her life, full of gratitude that she'd survived, full of pride at all she'd done, full of optimism about how she was going to make it better and what she was going to do about the house, the garden, relationships, work, money, not necessarily in that order. She'd be seeing Charlie soon, and Joni eventually. How wonderful they were! How wonderful that she'd spawned such a pair! What a privilege! What an achievement!

A phrase from one of the sonnets came into her mind, and

serenaded her for a while. *'Bare ruin'd choirs where late the sweet birds sang'*. It didn't seem appropriate to her elevated mood, though she couldn't remember any other lines. *And trouble deaf Heaven with my bootless cries? And summer's lease hath all too short a date?*

Bare ruin'd choirs where late the sweet birds sang. Bare ruin'd choirs.

Arriving back, she found a card on the hall carpet. It was from Nick, and it said, 'I called but no-one answered'.

She cursed her absence and the fickleness of fate, but was truly delighted that he'd left his phone number and rang it at once. No-one answered. She left an ambiguous message about needing his help, and an over-jolly suggestion that he ring her back.

She'd hardly taken off her coat or put away her keys when she picked up the phone again and dialled a number her fingers might never forget.

'Hello?' he answered in an intimate and suggestive tone, as he used to, as though he knew who she was and had waited all day for her call.

'Kevin. Lovely. I just want to say sorry for everything, and thank you for everything.'

'Whoa. What? Gee. What's the matter?'

'I just want it to be OK between us. I just want the hatchet to be buried and us both to feel fine about it all. We never really resolved anything did we?'

'What do you mean?'

'Well, I mean that I forgive you, and I'm sorry I expected too much of you.'

'You forgive me? I don't need to be forgiven, thank you.'

'We both need to be forgiven.'

'What you mean is that you need to be forgiven. I don't need to be forgiven.'

'Why do you always have to turn everything round?'

'It's you that's turning it around. First you're sorry, then you forgive me.'

'I am sorry. And I'm grateful. And I forgive you.'

'I accept your apology, but I haven't done anything wrong.'

'Kevin, that's not fair. We've both done things wrong!'

'You may have.'

'It's not fair, you're giving me all the responsibility. Why can't you take some responsibility? I've offered to take my fifty per cent. I don't see why I should take any more than that.'

'That's up to you.'

'In fact I'm only going to take forty-nine per cent as you always start it, and I always say sorry first.'

'Oh for fuck's sake, can't we just have a conversation?'

'Why can't you apologise? I'm sick of being the caretaker of this relationship. It's your bloody turn!'

Kevin was silent, and she cut him off without deciding to and without saying goodbye, before he could say anything hurtful about their relationship not being a relationship any more, though a friendship is a relationship, which was all she meant.

There is a world elsewhere, she thought, swallowing her indignation, and turning her attention to that other world before she could regret her rudeness and want to say sorry again.

She looked online for Stratford lettings and located what she thought was Matthew's old house, clicking through wide angle photographs to dwell in the second bedroom for a while, knowing that the curtains and the wallpaper and the bed and the wardrobe and chair and carpet would probably all be different now. You could see a splash of green through the window. The window would be the same as the window Matthew had looked out of, the view changed. The transparent part has lasted, she thought. Unless it broke. Yes, it could easily have broken between now and then, and just as easily not.

She emailed an enquiry.

Dear Helena Butt

I'm writing to ask if you know Matthew McGough – I believe he used to live in the house you now let. I happened to pass by on a recent trip to Stratford, and wondered what had become of him.

Thank you

Georgina Sutton

She got up to look for the sonnets in the bookshelves lining the front room, and found an edition she hadn't seen before, on creamy deckle-edged paper, printed with indentations, a beautiful thing. She flicked to the front of the book to date it. It was a prewar publication, but on the title page, under TT's dedication to WH, there was a dedication to Maureen with love and apologies from Larry.

'Apologies?'

It was dated April 1945.

'1945?' Georgie had no idea they'd met so young. They'd waited a decade before marrying, then! Oh, they were from a more austere generation – delayers of gratification, who'd grown up under the tyranny of air raid sirens and doodlebugs, unlike her own lot, demanding instant everything, and not growing up at all. Still. They can't have been much in love.

She put the book on her bedside table, to be consulted later, wondering what her father had needed to apologise for. The memory of his last words – his last apology – still smarted, and the phrase *it is the father with his child* began chanting in her mind.

'At least he did apologise,' she said aloud, pouring herself a nice glass of red wine.

BREATHE

She opened her eyes. She was shivering cold and wetness had woken her. At first she assumed the hot water bottle had burst, but then realised it was her body that was leaking. Even her knees had sweated. Her legs slithered over one another as she hauled herself out of bed. Sweat ran down her spine. Her scalp was soaked. She turned the mattress once again. The underneath was still damp from the previous night. 'Two sides aren't enough!' All the double sheets were in a stinking heap in the laundry basket so she had to bandage the mattress with a couple of unfitted singles. 'At least I slept a bit,' she yawned. But the clock said two thirty. 'Bugger.' She showered and sat on the bed in her mother's dressing gown, drying her hair. On the bedside table was a heap of reading material, escaping down onto the floor around the bed. Her eye fell on the sonnets. She'd forgotten which one she meant to look up, but the verse now irritating her was another: 'Wer reitet so spät durch Nacht und Wind?' There must be a Goethe somewhere, she thought, or said, abandoning her semi-dry hair to go and search the bookshelves.

She came to it instantly, as if led; her hand falling on the very book, opening it on the very page. Goose pimples rose up along her arms. 'Coincidence,' she said. 'Dad loved the poem, so he looked at it often, so it falls open on this page.' She closed the book and balanced the spine in her palm to see if it would happen again, but as she did so an envelope slipped out from between the cover and the frontispiece and floated to the floor. She stooped to pick it up. Inside she found a locket-sized photograph of a woman with something illegible written on the back, along with documents and newspaper cuttings. The photograph was cut in the shape of a heart. In the front of the book it said *Für Larry mit Freundlichkeit von Karl 1947.*

She took the book and its contents to bed with her. *Molly's mother sewed a seed* sang her brain. 'Fuck off!' she shouted at the tune, and settled into bed with these stained, folded things.

She studied the portrait first. The woman was smiling, but slightly. Her hair was middle-parted and dark. She wore a plain blouse with a curved collar. Georgie shone her bedside light directly onto the handwriting. It looked like Larry's and seemed to say: *Mariya, Parsch '46*

There was an amateurish watercolour painting of a fountain in front of a many-windowed palace, signed *MK, Schönbrunn*. On the back it said *Remember Vienna 1946* in ink, and three names were scrawled in blurred pencil: Laura Varga, Angela Furedi, Mariya Koval.

None of the names meant anything to Georgie. Larry had made friends, she assumed, in the war's aftermath. It troubled her that they were all women. Mariya looked like the favourite. She scanned the newspaper articles, but found no relevant names amongst the German words.

At eighteen Larry had caught the very end of the war, and because he'd volunteered, aiming to have some measure of control over his fate, he'd had to stay in active service for three years instead of the standard one-and-a-half. 'Never volunteer for anything!' was his advice, and, 'wait until you see the whites of their eyes.' He joked about that, but the war was a no-go area. He never talked about it. If Will or Georgie asked about his contribution they'd get a disapproving look from their mother and silence from their father, as if he hadn't heard at all. They learnt to side-step and jump over and crawl under the war. Until Frieda's arrival it was deeply taboo, as bad as sex or God, a dark, horrific place. Then Frieda came, and Larry relaxed, and the war could be mentioned at last. At least, that's how it seemed to her now.

She vaguely remembered visiting Schönbrunn herself. Frieda had infected her with travel fever, and two years on, the condition had reached a pitch. After doing her Art foundation year in Bristol, Georgie gaily postponed her hard-won place at Camberwell and took a year out of her career. It was a novel thing in those days, unless you were bound for Oxford or Cambridge. She'd answered an ad in *The Lady* and aupaired for a family in Salzburg, because seeing Salzburg was what she'd been promised and looked forward to. She planned to go to Venice next, then South America when she'd saved enough, to get the whole trip out of her system. She remembered asking for Frieda's address, with the possibility of visiting. Her request had gone unanswered; she never knew why. During her time in Salzburg, she'd taken the train to Vienna knowing that the family's younger daughter Angela lectured at the university. But Angela had been away on sabbatical. Instead Georgie had seen Klimt, Kokoschka, Schiele. She'd stood within a few feet of Freud's couch. She'd loved Mahler and tried to love Schönberg and not loved most of the Strausses. She'd learnt to cook with garlic and drink Riesling. The boy students wore beards and dressed like mods.

It was supposed to be a gap year. It had turned into a gap life.

She decided to google her questions there and then, in bed, on her laptop.

In 1946, during the Allied occupation of Austria, Schönbrunn palace was where the British Army had been garrisoned, following a short stay there by the Red Army. Parsch was an area in Salzburg. In 1946 a displaced persons' camp had been sited there.

She'd learnt nothing of this on her travels. Her knowledge of second world war Austria starred Christopher Plummer and Julie Andrews, and came with a medley of rousing feelgood tunes.

She found pictures online of tanks and soldiers in the grounds of Schönbrunn palace, and searched hopelessly for Larry's young face in the crowds and ranks, but didn't even know what kind of soldier he'd been. She found photographs of people living in displaced persons' camps too, children mostly, being weighed and measured and given tea, older people stitching boots and playing instruments. The article said that many were from Ukraine. Mariya Koval didn't sound like an Austrian name. Nor did Varga, or Furedi.

It set her thinking again about Frieda. The day she'd arrived out of the blue, with no warning, no introduction. Larry and Maureen hadn't even been expecting her, yet she'd been welcomed and nurtured, in gratitude for some favour her parents had done, so she and Will had been told. What could a presumably youngish Austrian couple have done for a newly recruited, nervous, eighteen-year-old British soldier that demanded such loyal gratitude? He caught the end of the fighting, but the violence didn't stop then. Perhaps they saved his life, she thought, in unthinkable circumstances. Perhaps they endangered their own lives to protect his, or made some other sacrifice which meant that he couldn't do enough for their child.

A horrible idea was weaving itself in her mind. She glanced through her diary, half to distract herself, half in hope of finding the answer.

I saved Will's batmobile. What he actually forgot was that in fact that was my batmobile. It wasn't his to get rid of. Why is he being so goody goody as to give up his room for her anyway? Because he fancies her probably and wants her to like him. Nobody's ever said I could have the summerhouse. I should be the one giving up my room seeing as it is actually clean and tidy. Reasonably. I felt sad when I saw the boxes at the bottom of the stairs with his airfix and action man in there. I suppose I'd better get rid of my dolls.

And:

I have a plain marble in my pocket. It's lovely to look through it. The world is upside down and semicircular and panoramic. I looked outside where there were weeds and ferns of a startling emerald green. The sunshine produced a most dazzling effect.

She heard a noise like the wind whistling through the ivy – whooeeeoooeee! – and stopped reading to listen to it, stock still, cocking her head to one side and suspending her breath. Wheeoeeeooeoeee! Whooaoaeeeooaaoeee! It was a wail, a keening, like the banshee's lament. As she listened, she heard another higher-pitched sound droning in the background, and a muffled low-pitched hum underneath. She heard her own breath wheezing into her nose in a juddery way, slightly too fast, and then the song began to sing in her imagination again. *All a golden girl could need. Pearls and jewels, gold and silver, Molly's mother gave her all.* 'Just the wind,' she said. But it wasn't just the wind, no, it wasn't just the wind. 'And the fridge maybe.' She put the diary on the floor, got out of bed, and wandered round to the kitchen. The fridge was indeed humming. 'But what's that other noise?' It was a faint screaming sound. She shook her head and banged her ears with the heels of her hands. It carried on. She moved from room to room, listening. It seemed not to vary, to come from no direction. 'It's the wires,' she decided. 'There's too much electricity. Or the wi-fi or something. Microscopic reverberations. Can't escape bloody technology. Might as well have a bloody cup of tea now I'm completely wide a bloody wake.'

She filled the kettle, shocked by the fleshy reflections of her own movements in its surface. She'd hardly noticed that she wasn't wearing anything. A sudden banging sound from elsewhere in the flat made her jump and she shrieked. She stopped what she was doing; and held her breath. She went again from room to room, switching on the light, listening, looking with wide eyes. Instinctively she gathered up the hockey stick and clutched it in both hands. She heard the fast padding of feet in the flat above. 'It's just a dog, it's just a dog,' she whispered. She was right. The dog was suddenly barking, loud and hard. At first she screamed in shock, then shouted up at the ceiling, at full volume, 'SHUT UP YOUR BLOODY RACKET! WE'RE TRYING TO SLEEP DOWN HERE!' stressing the word 'sleep' with a mighty crack of stick against plaster.

She switched off the light and as she turned, boiling with rage, still trembling with fear, her peripheral vision was grabbed by the shape of a person in the corner of the room. She gasped, stood still, stared into the dimness. The dog stopped barking, the padding of its feet carried on.

'There's nothing there. There's nothing there,' she whispered, trying to make sense of the shape, not daring to move, even to turn the light back on. She was stark naked. Every cell of her skin tingled with fear. She raised the hockey stick in both fists, her elbows bent, its head cocked.

In the house on Colley's acre.

Slowly she walked towards the apparition, facing it fully, fully ready to strike out and defend herself. But as she approached, her perspective changed, the simulacrum unravelled and was lost. It was nothing but a heap of boxes, an addendum of picture frames, glances of light on a random assemblage of ordinary things.

'What am I meant to find here then?' she quietly asked the air. The vision had gone, but the spirit remained – like the smell of smoke, of burning flowers. 'What are you showing me now, whatever you are? I'll look at it properly in daylight. Will you let me sleep now?'

She heard the dog moaning as if in acquiescence.

'And if you're Mum, please don't scare me by appearing. No, I'm not going mad, and I'm not bloody well going to go mad either. If I were going mad, I wouldn't realise it, would I? No you wouldn't. That's all right then, isn't it? Yes, Gee, it's fine. Get yourself back to bed, have a nice cup of tea, do a little more reading and go to sleep. And don't worry about the melatonin – one more night won't make any difference.'

Now, just as she was calming down, just as she'd switched off the lights and was creeping back, reassured, to the warmth and cosiness of bed, she heard something scuffling in one of the other rooms. Again she stopped. Again she held her breath, not knowing whether to advance and fight, or retreat and hide amongst the boxes.

She heard talking. A male voice. Chinese. Coming from the kitchen. She thought of knives. She began to tiptoe backwards. The voice blared out, shockingly loud, jolting her nerves awake.

Wo shi ying guo ren!

Oh. It was the music system. She rushed to silence it, with

shaking fingers. She must have been clumsy when she was turning on lights. She must have made a vibration that went through the plaster board wall and knocked the equipment against something hard and switched on the cassette player. She fumbled out the cassette. It was Linguaphone Chinese, an eighth of an inch in. Larry must have had prophetic ambitions.

She was thoroughly cold by now; and decided to drink her tea under the duvet. The laptop was still on the bed, still turned on. 'Might as well check my emails. Expect disappointment.'

Oh frabjous delight! Two messages from Joni had arrived!

As you see, Mum, I have the internet here. Would you like to skype? 6.00pm your time tomorrow? love Joni x

Her excitement crashed as she spotted its date. Tomorrow was today. She'd missed her by over seven hours. *I tried but no-one answered,* the second one said, eerily echoing Nick's note.

'Oh Joni darling, are you OK? What's wrong? Is she OK? Why didn't she try Jim? She must be OK or she'd have tried Jim. Maybe she did try Jim! Shall I call Jim? No, don't be daft, he'll be asleep, and she just wants a chat.' Georgie muttered, while strains of the lullaby kept creeping in between her thoughts.

I'm devastated that I missed you, desperate to know you're OK, worried sick about all the terrifying things that could be happening to you my beautiful darling girl, so far away and so unreachable. I miss you so much. I miss you as you are now and I miss the dear baby you were – I miss you as you've been in every changing form and size. I don't know what I would do if anything happened to you. What would my life mean without yours and Charlie's to redeem it? How could I ever love a world without you both in it? I don't know if I could carry on.

Delete.

So sorry I missed you. Hope you're OK. I'll keep a better look out for your next email! Skype soon, lots of love Mum xx

She didn't know how much to breathe. She didn't know how fast she was supposed to breathe. She tried not to think about breathing, but trying not to think about it made her think more about it.

'It's ridiculous! I've been doing it all my life!'

She lay awake, holding her breath, snatching her breath, counting her breath, with an unthought thought nudging about in her mind, in between snatches of *The Sound of Music* and Molly's lullaby, and the squealing of wires and the beating of her heart.

Catching it, she sat up straight, rigid with alarm. Yet it was so clear, so obvious, it seemed absurd that she had missed it.

Frieda's mother was from Ukraine. Frieda's mother might have been a displaced person in Parsch. Mariya Koval might be Frieda's mother. Larry might have been in love with Mariya Koval. Larry might be Frieda's father.

'In which case he couldn't possibly be Mina's father,' she reasoned. She snuggled back down into the warm, satisfied to have exonerated him from the crime of stealing and knocking up his son's love, prepared to accept the slightly less dreadful crime of knocking up someone nearer his age and longer ago, and practically overjoyed to be able to forgive him for being intent on providing her and Will with a long-lost sister. Now she could sleep in peace.

But the words echoed in her mind, taunting her.

They made no logical sense.

And even if Larry wasn't Mina's father as well as Frieda's father, what if he was Frieda's father, and Mina's father was Will?

Oh dear. That still wouldn't be very nice.

In fury she threw off her bedclothes and stood up tall to confront the monstrous suggestion, shouting at full throttle in the direction of the boxes and the heaps of papers and files, the chaos and disorder threatening to swallow her.

'One or the other is all I'm prepared to accept! Promiscuity I can handle. Infidelity I can rise above. Incest I simply WILL NOT HAVE!'

She thought she could hear knocking on wood; she thought it was coming from inside the writing box; and the tune came back to her, bullying and demanding, like a playground chant.

Buried there her daughter Molly. Buried there her daughter Molly.

LET SLEEPING DOGS LIE

Remorse and sorrow wear away the spirit, but of the two, the more corrosive is the first. Time itself may lessen the latter, but guilt may never resolve without confession.

Thus I begin my memoir, one I have long contemplated, ever since my youth ended in that loss of innocence I so deeply regret. Through an upstairs window in my dear father's house I see, now tall and stately, the family of elms I watched him plant and stumbled amongst at three years old when they were but seedlings, smaller than myself. I hear the wind rushing through their summer apparel of greenery, and the bright song of thrushes nesting there. When you discover these words, those trees may yet stand, robust and strong and alive. New birds will fly to them, new people will see them, people who can only extend towards me that neutrality I myself feel for some distant forbear whose company was known and enjoyed and treasured by her contemporaries.

If I have securely hidden these words, I too will be cold and distant now you are reading them. They will mean little to you, and you may preserve or destroy them at your leisure, yet please, dear reader, peruse them to the end, for it is to you, whom I cannot know, that I commend the dark treasure of my soul.

Oh do not judge me! We are all sinners, and I have paid so dearly in regret and sorrow for my crime, which was committed by no evil intention, but in the sway of too passionate a Nature, unrestrained by the edicts of too brief an Education, ungoverned by Parental Influence. My dear nurse loved me, certainly, but from her I gained none of the gracious manners which have moulded my children, and whose impress bore all too late upon my character.

With this humble injunction to you, I, Georgina Sutton, embark upon my memorial confession, on the First Day of January in the year of our Lord Eighteen Hundred and Forty-Five.

'And that's it. Nothing more?' Will flicked through empty pages of stained leather-bound paper. He smelt it and wrinkled his nose before handing it back.

'Weird isn't it? Of course there must have been lots of Georgina Suttons in the world before me, and of course there must be lots of others in the world now, but I got such a shock when I saw my own name there. It's one of my best finds.'

'She's like you, full of intentions. Yes, it's interesting.'

'What could she have done, d'you think? Had a bastard child? Abortion? Infanticide? *Too passionate a nature,* you see. *No manners.*'

'What about trying to sell it? It must be worth something as it's so old. That and the story behind it, someone would love it.'

Georgie pointedly replaced it in the box labelled 'Items relating to Sutton II'.

She hadn't yet worked out how she was going to open the Frieda conversation. They'd already exhausted the necessary topics, such as the wellness or otherwise of offspring, the weather, Will's flight, the fact that he should have let her pick him up and the suggestion of a walk after lunch; but she wasn't yet ready to delve into more difficult territory. She wasn't sure how much to share of what she knew. She certainly wouldn't mention Will's private letter to their parents, for example, and her qualms about implicating their father in any unpleasantness had to do with a sense that admitting the possibility made it more concrete, as though saying a thing could magically make it true, while keeping silent would keep it false. Her best strategy, she thought, would be to elicit as much information as possible, for as little as possible in return.

As he cast his eyes over her work, she watched, ready to point out any interesting titbits which might justify it. Keep was splitting into categories, and spreading out onto the two-foot square of space revealed by a recent reduction in Chuck, Recycle and Sell. She had been getting on with it, in anticipation of his visit. She showed him with her arms how much stuff she'd shifted. 'Three car loads gone. And I've put a few things for sale online.'

'Gee, though.' Will said, thoughtful and not enough impressed. 'Should you be doing this when your health is still an issue? Are you sufficiently back on your feet?'

'Here – look at this.' She handed him a yellowing telegram: DEEPLY REGRET TO INFORM YOU THAT PTE SUTTON WAS KILLED IN ACTION 23RD APRIL. LORD KITCHENER EXPRESSES HIS SYMPATHY.

'Blunt isn't it? His mother, our great grandmother, had to read that. And these. I thought they could go to the Imperial War Museum.'

Will grimaced. 'Private Sutton. It gives me the willies. Who's that then?'

I am directed, by the Honourable Minister of Militia and Defence, to convey to you the enclosed medal for the deceased officer or soldier whose name is engraved thereon, and to express to you the regrets of the Militia Council that he did not live to wear this award. Major-General, Adjutant General, Canadian Militia

'Our great uncle, Dad's uncle. Aunt Ruby's brother. Aunt Ruby is who we inherited this house from. Their brother, Dad's dad, was another Lawrence.'

'How confusing. Why Canada?'

Ah, Will was becoming interested, in spite of himself.

'Emigration. I've got an inventory of his personal stuff too, look, silver cigarette case with name engraved thereon, silver teaspoon, gold ring with black stone, and guess what, I've got some of the actual things somewhere. And what about this – our old house in Shottery has the same symbol over its door as the teaspoon has on its handle. Mum and Dad must have known it was ours, don't you think? And there's the pin box from Bottescote – the Suttons used to be rich but don't ask how.' She waved a hand vaguely over the whole disarray. 'It's history and archaeology both. I sometimes think I could reconstruct our family's whole saga out of all this evidence. I could do it cell by cell, hair by hair.'

'"Officer or soldier".' Will shook his head, in weary despair. 'The ghastliness of war.'

'Especially that one.'

'God, well, I don't know, I think the same sorts of things happen in all of them.'

'D'you remember what Mum said on her deathbed? I'll never forget it. There'd been a thing on the radio. About Iraq I think. And then the deficit and the credit crunch and a bit about some corrupt politician fiddling his expenses. She said "nothing changes". Nothing changes. Oh, dear, even lovely Mummy got jaded in the end. And it was terribly hard for her to say it; she must have really wanted to. And you know Dad's brother didn't go? He didn't go and beat Hitler. He conscientiously objected, then died of asthma. While Dad went all full of fake worldliness – he was only eighteen – and then it finished.'

'He was lucky. We're lucky he was lucky.'

'And did you know that for some reason or other I can't work out, Mum refused to speak to her father? He sent letters asking after us. We didn't know him at all, did we? We didn't know any of them. It was just us, in our funny little Stratford bubble. With a swimming pool.'

Will nodded.

'Why did they give it up, Will?' She was like a cat, she thought, stalking her prey in ever decreasing circles. Inch by inch she was closing in.

'To come here.' His shrug was non-committal, but its vulnerability was endearing. He didn't like admitting to ignorance.

'But why did they come here? They could just as well have sold this place.'

'Gee, your guess is as good as mine.'

'Our shrunken fortunes!' Georgie sighed. Will handed her the papers and she replaced them in their buff envelope. 'Imagine what that house is worth now.'

'It doesn't bear thinking about,' Will said solemnly, shaking his head. But Georgie knew he was thinking of the capital loss, their father's ruinous investments. 'The mortgage was a stretch,' he said with a pouty twitch of his bottom lip, 'and he quit the job because they moved him from Welfare to Planning and he wasn't happy. He had some epiphany about money being nothing but a vast abstraction of numbers. Not real.'

Georgie made a sarcastic noise. 'It's real enough when you haven't got any.' They were on uncharted territory now, so she spoke quietly – treading lightly.

'They would have had to move anyway, soon enough. Imagine the two of them in that huge house alone.'

'They could at least have waited until the eighties.'

Will started laughing raucously.

'I don't get it. I just don't get it,' Georgie said with an over-dramatic sigh, because she had a jolly good idea, in fact.

'If they'd had more they'd have lost more, wouldn't they? It would still have gone tits up. Look, can't we just torch all this crap? Why do we have to know about it?'

'Because it's important. It's where we come from.' Georgie studied his expression, which was amused and affectionate, but betrayed nothing more than mild exasperation.

'Surely where we're going is more important?' he said.

She'd cleared a space in the spare bedroom, where he dumped his case, looking balefully around at the pictures on the walls, smelling the air. She didn't really expect him to stay there with so little in the way of bedding, though she wished it. 'Come and have a cup of tea,' she said. 'How much d'you want to know?'

'I don't want to know anything.'

Georgie was proud of having cleared a comfortable degree of space in the kitchen. Two days' worth of wiping had made most of it more or less clean.

'*In the house on Colley's acre,*' she sang, while she waited for the kettle to boil. 'I've got that bloody lullaby on the brain. Remarkable coincidence. This land here was called Colley Acre. Old Eileen told me. Mum's friend.'

'*In the house on Colley's acre,*' Will sang. 'Isn't it Irish?'

'What's the connection to here? Mummy might have made

it up afterwards, I suppose. But surely she sang it to us when we were little.'

'Or she was attracted to the place because of the song?'

'They inherited the place. It wasn't attraction.'

'Maybe Mum's friend was confused.'

'Eileen. Yes, that's it. Though she told me she thought they were looking for something.'

'Who's they?'

'Mum and Dad. I know it's a stupid idea, but d'you think they could have been looking for the pearls and jewels and gold and silver?'

'I'm worried about you, Pudding. You're being imaginative.'

'Yes, I thought it was a silly idea. Just checking. You're right. It's so great that you've come.'

She brought out the best china. She unwrapped his favourite kind of spiced apple cake, and he grinned, absurdly excited by the prospect of decent tea and tiffin. Now she could no longer avoid the awkward topic that most intrigued and bothered her. She finally asked, as if it had only just occurred to her, and in a light playful manner:

'You know who got her pregnant, don't you?'

'Who got who pregnant?'

'Whom. Frieda. Are you sure it wasn't you, Will?'

The suggestion irritated him. 'No. I've already said so, haven't I?'

Case closed, his eyes meant. Georgie forced herself to press on, as though it were a game of dares.

'You were in love with her, though?'

'I was male,' he said, blankly matter-of-fact.

She stared at him and he stared back, equally inscrutable.

'I have nothing to be ashamed of,' he insisted.

'Who then?'

'I don't know.'

'Who do you suspect?'

'It's all so long ago. It's finished, done with, passé. It's a dead parrot.'

Georgie was silent.

'I don't want to be reminded, Pudding. It was all very painful for me.'

That was an admission, and Georgie couldn't help registering it, but faintly and rapidly. 'It's not over if there was living issue,' she went on, her mouth drying, instantly regretting the pompous legal phrase her embarrassment had chosen.

More silence. Will contemplated his tea. He took out his mobile and laid it on the table, idly tapping it with his fingers, uncertain what to do with it now it was there.

'OK, what have you found out?' he said eventually.

'She had a baby girl. She was called Mina. And someone sent her money.'

Georgie was relieved to have got it out, and with an admirable air of insouciance. She studied Will's reaction. It wasn't a complete surprise to him. He put his elbow on the table, and rested his head in his hand, quietly thinking. If the name Mina meant anything to him, he was masterful at covering it. But then, his courtroom experience had taught him how to act.

'Don't you want to see the evidence?' Georgie asked. Frieda's letters and the polaroid of Mina were close at hand, waiting for the right moment. 'I have thank-you letters.'

'No. Yes. No. It's too long ago to be angry. Water under the bridge. I... I... I... Realise. Yes. It was probably Dad, then, I think.'

Georgie touched his shoulder. Her stomach lurched.

'I had my suspicions at the time but...' Now Will stared at his mobile, his breathing was juddery, his face taut. 'Couldn't he be satisfied with the tarts at the office? Poor Mum! She didn't have a clue, did she?'

The force of his outburst frightened Georgie, and his reference to tarts at the office was outrageous, especially in relation to their father. She modulated her own voice.

'It could have been anybody, though, couldn't it? It could have been Matthew for example. Or any of – '

'Any of my friends?'

'No, I didn't mean that.'

'Dad was besotted with her,' he snarled. 'Everything she did, everywhere she walked, he followed her with his eyes. And his camera. They were always *doing* things together weren't they? Going to the pictures, drinking, shopping. When Mum was off being charitable to someone or other.'

He spat out the words. He was coming undone. Georgie couldn't bear it. She wasn't used to seeing him in any but a calm and reasonable state.

'I remember her being with Mum all the time. Anyway, what if it was fatherly love?'

Will's look was comically incredulous.

'It could have been a fatherly kind of love,' Georgie insisted.

'No,' Will said firmly. 'No, it couldn't. I saw it at the time. Sending her money. That settles it. I don't want to know how you know. I don't want anything more to do with it.'

'If it was Dad then Mina's our sister, you can't – '

'I don't know her and I don't want to know her.'

He left the room. Georgie was bewildered at the way he could simply toss away this potential half-sister, Mina, and equally, how he could arrogantly ignore and refuse and block his full sister's perfectly rational intimations. His reaction – which seemed a bit of an over-reaction actually – precluded any possibility of her saying anything about their father's sojourn in Austria. She was going to have to carry on bearing that particular burden alone.

He returned with a parcel wrapped in gold tissue paper, and a folded piece of paper, which, without ceremony, he thrust into her hands.

'What's this?'

'It came with the will.'

A hot wave of dread rushed up through Georgie's body. She took a deep breath and plunged in.

My Dear William

If you are reading this, it means that I have met my demise (and that you have not!) It constitutes a Letter of Wishes, I suppose, and concerns the property's contents, hereinafter referred to as 'the mess'. I thought I would have time to sort it out, but things have become too difficult rather too quickly, so I'll have to pass on the job.

'The mess' may be something of an adversary. I am sorry there's so much of it, very randomly mixed. My instinct would be for a complete destruction and evacuation – shock and awe tactics – but I doubt if that course will be practicable. In any case, there are one or two good things hidden amongst the bad – a baby in the bath water, so to speak, or at least a respectable rubber duck!

I'm not concerned about who gets what: you and Georgina will decide that for yourselves; but I am concerned that you may discover something distressing. If that is the case, I sincerely apologise – for myself and on behalf of your mother. I hope you will understand, and I'm sure that we all did our best in the circumstances.

Extend this to Georgina if you think it advisable. As the more vulnerable of you, I'd prefer that she be protected from anything upsetting but you must use your judgement.

Needless to say, you two have been our comfort and happiness and more (so much more) than compensated for any trouble that occurred before or since you were born. Similarly I hope that you have been compensated for any trouble inadvertently caused by my actions.

Well, this is an odd post scriptum to what I'm sure was a parting well made, but if for some reason we had not the time nor the luck to say a good Goodbye, I say it now, my dear son,

Goodbye

With all my love

Dad

I wrote so many ifs that Kipling came to mind. The fellow demanded too much of a man, don't you think? We are mere mortals.

Georgie looked up at Will, too confused to speak, so much was jostling for expression. Before she could reread it, before she could marshal her feelings and consider her comment, he'd whipped it from her hands and presented her instead with the parcel.

'Renée sends her love. And Eve and Henri of course.'

She swallowed her objections and postponed her response, obediently opening the gift. Inside its professional wrapping was a silver bracelet, inlaid with turquoise. She eased it onto her wrist, grateful that it fitted, just about. 'It's exquisite! Such taste! Thank you! What a lovely thought. I don't deserve it, though, do I?'

'She wants me to talk to you about the flat.'

Like a clam, shutting at the slightest touch, Georgie resisted. 'I'm doing the best I can,' she said.

'It makes better financial sense to pay a firm to clear it.'

'I don't want to pay a firm to do what I can do myself.'

'We'll pay the firm.'

'And I don't throw things away just because they aren't new. As long as they still work. The music system, for instance.'

'Or we could put it in storage if you must save what Dad didn't want us to see.' Will patted his inside pocket, where he'd put the letter. 'Then you can take as long as you like. Renovate the flat. We can get builders in at all hours while upstairs is empty. And let it.'

'It's not empty. And by the way, I would have liked to read that letter sooner, and may I read it again?'

'Well it looks empty.' He fumbled for the letter and passed it back to her. 'It's for sale, and worth a useful sum, and this place will be as long as we deal with it.'

She slumped in a mock sulk, trying to read but unable to concentrate. The words jazzed about on the page – *baby in the bath, distressing, apologise, upsetting, all my love.*

'We'll finance it and split any profits,' Will went on, more tenderly, more patronisingly.

'This flat does not belong to Renée.'

'It is ours. Just as much as it's yours.'

'It's nothing to do with Renée. We actually lived here. I did, anyway.'

'Everything to do with me is to do with her. She's my wife.'

And Jim's my husband, Georgie wanted to say, but unfortunately he wasn't any longer. She had no parallel reinforcement. She loosened her collar and fumbled off her cardigan, now sweating profusely. 'It's nothing to do with her,' she complained. 'I saw her eagle eyes! I saw euro signs whizzing round in them, wondering how much she can grab out of you.'

Will gasped.

'What if I want to live here?' she went on. 'That's what it's for! To live in! It's just money to you, isn't it? As if you haven't already got enough!'

Georgie had never before been so ill-mannered as to mention the disparity in their circumstances. It was outrageous, and shocked Will into embarrassed stillness and silence. He refused to meet her defiant glare.

'It's not my fault you don't have any money,' he muttered. 'Or anything better to do with your time.'

Heat exploded into Georgie's face. That was the limit. It was his manner that infuriated her, even more than the disgusting insult about the value of her time, which was tantamount to the value of her life. As if he couldn't give a bollocks, and had no conception of what she'd been through, or what she was going through now for both of them.

'I could have been a doctor or a lawyer just as well as you!' she said. 'I could have been an artist! I could have been a writer!'

'You didn't want to be a lawyer. Or a doctor. You still could be a writer. Or an artist. You can do what you like!' he shrugged, pompously reasonable.

'I don't need your say-so!'

'That's what I just said!'

'I don't need you to say it!'

He snatched the letter, got up smartly and went out, returning with his case, his raincoat draped over the other arm. 'Excuse me for liking to breathe. I'll come back when you've calmed down.' He began to walk up the corridor and Georgie shouted after him.

'How am I going to sort through it all if it's in storage? Why have I got to take full responsibility for all this? Why can't you take your half of the burden?'

He turned round, in controlled rage.

'What's the matter with you? It's half mine, all this. If I want it gone, why can't it be gone? You simply can't let anything go, can you?'

Well, that wasn't true: she'd let go of her boyfriend, and her job, and her children, and her best friend and two other friends, and now she was about to let go of her brother; she'd show him how good she was at letting go. As he marched up the corridor she dragged the bracelet over her wrist. It stuck at her knuckles.

'Giving me stuff!'

The door had already slammed by the time she'd managed to wriggle it off and throw it at him.

'I've too much bloody stuff, you can keep your wooden bloody horse! And what about Mina? You don't give a bloody damn do you? She's family! Family! She's our sister!'

She waited, as if he might be coming back.

'Or our niece!'

The words echoed.

'Or both!'

The objects in their piles seemed to be accusing her. She didn't know what they supposed she'd done wrong.

'How dare you get me all worked up about coming and then you go. It's not fair. It's not fair I have to do this on my own!'

She screamed then, as loudly as her body could, a noise that astonished her by its power and fury.

'I could be attacked here and who would know? Who would know if I dropped down dead? I could have a stroke! I could have a bloody accident! Who would bloody care? Who would come and rescue me?'

This thought struck her as so tragic that she threw herself

on the floor and tried to weep. But it was no good, the tears refused to come. She'd learnt too well how to resist them, in the good old British fashion. 'It's your fault I can't cry too!' she screeched. He used to poke her with sticks and pull her hair, and call her 'silly girly baby' if her bottom lip dared to quiver. Once they'd had a competition to see who would break down first, taking it in orderly turns to deliver the pain: Chinese burns, arm twisting, shin kicking, finger bending. And she had won. To her eternal shame and sorrow, she'd made her older brother blub. She'd learnt how to rise above tickling too; even the soles of her feet were immune, even to feathers.

She lay there for a long time, wondering what would happen if she just stayed where she was, motionless and relaxed, refusing to play the game any more of being a human being. She closed her eyes. She heard her heart beating and her breath snuffling in and out of her nose. Other sounds entered and swirled around in her mind – the hum of someone's washing machine, water and air shunting through old pipes, the faint ticking of a clock, a car, another car, a lorry, a car, a siren. 'Has anyone seen Georgina?' people might say. 'Does anyone know where Mum is?' She imagined herself being discovered in a week or two. Furious ringing of the bell and knocking on the door. A pause. Rhythmic pounding. The breaking of wood. Two uniformed policeman make their way up the corridor. 'There she is!' says the first.

'Turn on the light. She's alive!' says the second, more handsome one. 'Call an ambulance!'

Oh no. They arrive too late. Her body is beginning to decompose. Flies and ants and rats all over everywhere. She remembered seeing a calf carcass as a child, like squirming vermicelli carbonara.

Eventually she got up again, bored, hungry, and a little stiff. *Pick yourself up, dust yourself off!* She sang the tune.

'Chid up Geegee. Got to look after yourself. Let's get some ludch. Ooh. I can eat Will's portion too. Lucky be.'

The gas didn't light. 'Bugger.' It wasn't coming through at all. 'Bugger.' The boiler was off and the radiators were cold.

'I've been cut off! Why the bloody bollocks have I beed cut off?'

As executor, Will had dealt with the utility bills. She wondered if he'd arranged for it to be switched off on purpose to spite her.

'Don't be paradoid.'

She'd either have to ring Will, and ask him to sort it, or research a whole forest of gas suppliers, and start again.

'Bugger Will. Bloody barket ecodomy. Where's the copetition, they're all as bastardy as each other. So what? It isn't cold! I can do without.'

As she cleared her nose, congested by emotion and by dust, she thought of Will's parting words: excuse me for liking to breathe.

'Asthma. Runs in the family. Hoarder's complaint, that. It's in the genes. And in the boxes. But I can let go. I can let go! I'm letting go of the gas! See Will? You couldn't let go of gas, could you?

The thought of gas and asthma made her think of suffocation which made her think of smothering and mothering.

'Look how he brings up his children! Nothing but computer games all day! That's her influence, though, to be fair. He'd have got them building things and camping and sleeping in hammocks. Not clean enough is it though, paint and glue and soil? Makes too much mess doesn't it, Renée? Might give you a bad hair minute.'

But why don't they speak English as much as French? she thought. 'Can't help that. Mother tongue. Culture comes down the female line. Language, manners, style, Jewishness. Jewishness? Don't be irrelevant. Mariya Koval, was she Jewish? Names, property, entitlement come down the male line. All the things that think they're important.'

In the house on Colley's acre.

'Like lullabies, mother to daughter, mother to daughter.

How dare you dismiss my ideas, just because I'm younger, just because I'm a girl? Songs have to start somewhere! They have to mean something!'

She'd meant to talk to Will about her own diary. It was lying ready on the kitchen table. Idly she picked it up and flicked through, vaguely looking for clues.

Mummy was in her bedroom for absolutely bloody ages having yet another migraine. We had to wait until about seven o'clock for tea, and then it was only fish fingers and frozen peas. I was famished. Instead of helping us cook which is what you might expect an au pair to do, Frieda was upstairs being Florence Nightingale. They're so lovey dovey all the time. When did I ever get that attention?

'Cook your own meals you self-centred little girl! Poor Mummy.'

Being good at music is a matter of practice, says Frieda. Ich muss üben! She thinks I can get grade 8 in two years but I need to play for at least an hour a day – mostly hard things I can't do well. I owe it to my gift, like a duty, she says. She used to practise at least three hours a day, more sometimes, and she's absolutely brilliant. I wish Mum and Dad had made me.

'Blaming everyone else!' Georgie said, irritated with her former incarnation.

FAIRED DIEFAR IFDEAR DAREFI FEARDI

FRIEDA + N – A = FRIEND thinks I could be as passionately good as Jacqueline du Pré if only I work hard enough. I will work hard. When I saw Mummy listening to Frieda playing my cello I didn't mind any more. I simply determined to make her just as admiring of me. I might even exceed.

Georgie caught her breath. Another horrid idea had slipped across her consciousness. 'No, no!' she said smartly, but the idea was out now and the lid refused to close on it. Anxiety, cold and pervasive, was seeping into her body, into her guts and up her spine like liquid fingers.

'OK then, let's face facts!' she replied firmly to this new presence. 'Mummy and Frieda had a close relationship, so what? Maybe it was even physical. Maybe Will had a close relationship with her too and so did Dad. It's none of my business. Maybe they were all happy. Happy is the important thing. As long as nobody got hurt. Happy is everything.'

After two weeks on my diet I can proudly announce that I have gained one pound. I completely hate school and I completely hate it that Mummy's never here when I get home. Frieda's seen more sights than we have. Will's gone mental and Daddy stays in the office. I might as well be an only orphan! What's the use of a family who's never here? I don't know how I'm possibly going to manage the rest of this year. Atom bombs and pollution and acid rain and whale extinction. The sky is a washed out blue, the sun is diluted. You can feel the emptiness in the air. It seems to be a chasm of nothingness.

She'd written the words, but they felt no more hers than the words of that other Georgina Sutton. When had she changed from the girl into the woman? she wondered. How had such a metamorphosis occurred? 'Cell by cell, hair by hair, by stealth.' Each night the mind shifts and shuffles and reforms; each morning one is a slightly different self. Each moment perhaps a subtle change is wrought. 'True, but some change is catastrophic isn't it? Like dying. What kind of metamorphosis is bloody dying?'

She decided it was time to face a difficult job. She felt so not brilliant now, the difficult job couldn't make her feel any worse. In fact she might as well take advantage of feeling already not brilliant, then it would make feeling not brilliant something to be pleased about.

The wardrobe must be emptied, the clothes given to charity. Her mattress would do as a dumping surface. Mechanically, without allowing herself to think anything, she marched into the bedroom, swung open the wardrobe doors, unhooked the hangers and their dresses and jackets from the rail, and heaped them onto the bed. Amidst a flurry of motes, she slid piles of folded cotton and wool off their polished shelves, and gently, reverently laid them beside the heaps. She slipped everything into thick plastic bin liners, her father's things first; old work shirts, ties, jumpers, suits, belts. Then her mother's. Mechanically she retrieved a tee-shirt here, a cashmere cardigan there, some tights, a skirt that might suit her, making a little Keep pile as she went. Next she emptied the drawers.

'Who wants a dead person's vests and bras?' she asked in desolation.

Suddenly she was consumed with dread, as though the air had thickened and was pressing into her chest, as a kind of answer.

Dead.

She had said the word.

Dead. Cold, final, done.

No breath at all. Thou'llt come no more.

Never, never, never, never, never. She heard it as a stirring of the curtain, a touch of air.

'Who's there?' she whispered. It was broad daylight, but she didn't feel safe any more, not since her energetic screaming had echoed and vanished without notice. There was forever something flitting about on the periphery of her vision, dodging her focus, making her start.

'Is it you, Mum?'

Silence. The daylight was present and kind, as though smiling.

'Or Dad?'

But Larry hadn't believed in supernatural things; he'd never consent to haunting her.

She looked up at the ceiling, as though that were a likelier position than any other in the whole universe for a dead spirit to be hanging. Then, in empathy, she imagined her own spirit floating there above a living body, desperate to be heard, or known or seen, being stared at by the living blind.

'I'm not blind!' she reassured the ceiling. 'I do believe in you, if you're there! I miss you! I love you! Thank you! Thank you for being my lovely Mummy!'

She listened acutely – to a humming and a whistling in her ears, and the strains of *Molly's mother sewed a seed* in her mind.

'And Daddy.'

The pattering of paws from the first floor flat brought her back to reality.

Her parents' shoes were neatly lined up in the bottom of the wardrobe, Maureen's on the left, Larry's on the right. She removed them pair by pair, not wanting to disturb the arrangement. From an empty pair of shoes, invisible legs and a body seem to grow. Shoes are like signatures or gestures, she thought, full of a person's presence; the pounding interface between feet and earth is moulded by that unique and intimate connection. The row of shoes suggested a row of invisible versions of her mother and father standing to attention. She wondered how many miles they'd walked. Then there were the shoes that hadn't walked, that had just been for warmth and show, that had rested on the wheelchair footboard. Tying the laced ones together, and pairing the others with elastic bands, she dropped them respectfully into another black bag.

On top of the wardrobe she discovered a plastic box containing layers of precious cloth, cross-stitch, crochet, embroidered linen, tablecloths and mats, and a matinée jacket and christening dress in which metal hooks and eyes had left orange stains.

A framed sampler emerged from its lace wrapping.

How oft does sorrow bend the head,
Before we dwell among the dead.
Scarce in the years of manly prime,
I've often wept the wrecks of time.
What tragic tears bedew the eye,
What deaths we suffer ere we die.
Our broken friendships we deplore,
And loves of youth that are no more.
Wrought in the year of our Lord 1808
by
Georgina Sutton Aged 12

'Oh look! There I am again. Miserable but jolly good at sewing. That figures.'

Already a Sutton in 1808.

'Oh damn, I must have been a spinster then. Nobody's ancestor.'

A spinster spinning a yarn, like a spider preparing to catch a fly. Or did I keep my surname by marrying a cousin? Why not? Keep it in the family; they used to do it all the time. Fanny and Edmund, Mansfield Park. Georgina and Whatsit, Bottescote Manor. 'Hang on, did I say that or just think it?'

She laid the sampler aside, and kneeling in the midst of these scattered textiles, examined the bottom-most item. It was a huge satin-lined shawl, woven into a complex floral design from different shades of faded red silk, sprinkled with blue forget-me-nots and trimmed with a blue fringe. It was soft and warm. It smelt of plastic and mothballs and age. In places it was worn thin, mended with tiny stitches.

'Who sewed those? Was that you too, Georgina?' She folded it diagonally and wrapped it around her shoulders, shaking out its tangled fringe. It reached down beyond her knees.

'Beautiful.' She moved into the light, in front of the mirror, admiring herself. 'Victorian, this. Must be worth something. But you're not having it, Renée. Ha! It's mine, I tell you! Mine! This'll keep me warm. You can keep your gas, Will. You managed without gas, didn't you Georgina? For most of your life.'

She remembered a similar thing she'd worn as a teenager. It made her laugh, to compare the longevity of this well-fashioned object with some piece of synthetic tat coughed up by the rag trade, tat which had been almost immediately trashed.

'Frieda helped me get that,' she remembered with a pang.

At once, she was reminded of Will's leaving; it was nothing to do with Georgie's bloody-mindedness about the flat; it was her revelation about Frieda that had toppled him.

'Frieda's Dad's!' she imagined shouting at him. 'And I bet Mina's yours, too, isn't she? Bloody irresponsible men, they never own up. They never have to. It's us women have to give birth to everything and live with everything and keep everything clean! Isn't it, Georgina?'

She caught a glimpse of her angry expression, and immediately dropped it and smoothed her creased brow with her fingers.

'Getting old,' she muttered, madly, like the nutter she was becoming.

'I can talk to myself if I bloody like. Who are you anyway, telling me what to do? Oh thou art myself art thou? Well thou canst fuck right off! I've had thee up to here.'

The door creaked. She swung round. The sight of a figure in the door frame made her squeal. It was Nick, his face distorted by concern and bewilderment. Georgie was dumbstruck.

'Sorry!' he said urgently. 'I didn't mean to scare you, I rang the bell. Your front door was open.'

Georgie's body gave an involuntary shudder as she registered the situation.

'I was just passing. I thought you'd like me to look at the garden?'

She gaped at him wordlessly, her mind empty but for the worry that he'd witnessed her strangeness.

'You're busy. I'll come back another time.'

'No. No. I'm. Er. Will must have left it open. Oh, what a shame you missed him! The garden. Yes. It needs attention. Come and see. Would you like some tea?'

They discovered that the electricity was also off, which was why the bell hadn't sounded. Georgie made light of it, as you might brush aside a stranger's concern if you fell over, no matter how it hurt. 'It's rather annoying, but we're too reliant on electricity anyway, don't you think? I'm sure I can manage without. What did we do before we had it? We didn't wither away. Camping stove! I saw one in a box just the other day.'

Nick begged her not to worry, and without too much altercation, she led him into the garden. Cobwebs were glittering in the low afternoon sun, but the ground was still shaded and damp with dew. The garden walls seemed to be crumbling inwards under the sheer weight of dark green vegetation.

'Might need some electricity to get rid of all this ivy,' he said. 'And manpower. It's quite a job: two or three guys and a chainsaw.'

Georgie pouted. It seemed a bit harsh for a mild urban patch of nature. And she was slightly ruffled by his use of the word 'guys'. Why shouldn't a woman use a chainsaw?

'How much?'

'Has to be bagged and dumped too. An afternoon's work? Three hundred as a favour. I'd normally charge four.'

'Blimey. Can't we compost it?'

He merely shook his head. 'It's rooted throughout the... what used to be the lawn.' It was true, the ivy was creeping in towards their ankles. He lifted a thick tangle of ground-level ivy leaves, which clung to the earth with soily fibrous roots.

'I suppose it has to be done.'

'It'll only get worse.'

They fixed a date. As he was leaving he offered to help her carry the bin liners wherever they were bound, and they walked in silence together to a local charity shop, enjoying each other's company and the mild spring day. The sound of birdsong, the fresh sweet smell of the air, the quality and slant of the light as it filtered through a peppering of pale green, this familiar state of the atmosphere connected her with previous such days and for a small window of time she felt completely rooted in the span of her life, a four-dimensional being, in the company of a man who had known her as a young woman. The whole sensation and the whole idea was one she'd had before, and she felt an overwhelming certainty that it would come again one day.

'Please don't put the bras in landfill,' she couldn't help whispering to the volunteer who helped them stow the bin liners behind the counter.

'No, don't worry, we'd recycle any brass.'

Nick winked, assuaging her embarrassment. She felt herself

smiling inside, proud and relieved, as if she'd confessed and been absolved.

'Don't forget to buy candles and matches for tonight,' he said as they parted. For a brief moment she thought he was inviting her to a romantic supper on his boat, until he waved, and shouted after her, 'Happy camping!'

Back home she rescued the bracelet. It had fallen into a Wellington boot and was covered with gritty cobwebs. A text from Will lay in wait on her mobile.

On way home. My fault. Can't bear past. Bad for lungs. We have to compromise, dear Pud. Chin up and cheerio.

SPEAK WHAT YOU FEEL

There are many advantages to keeping one's own company. You don't have to bolt the bathroom door, for example, or even close it. As long as you're not too cold you don't have to put clothes on unless you go out, and when you come back you don't have to take them off again, unless you're too hot, which, come to think of it, you probably are. There's less washing up, and even what there is you don't have to do immediately, or at all, in fact, as long as you rinse off the worst of it, seeing as heating water is a faff. You don't have to cook. You can live on salads and sardines and yoghurt and bananas, all perfectly healthy things. You don't have to clean the bath or the loo, especially as you can't see them, because of the dark, which is the great advantage to having no electricity. You can put the rubbish and recycling with all the other rubbish and recycling and wait until you have a carload or two. You can leave everything until you feel like doing it, because, after all, you're really tired, and there are more important things to be doing, like understanding what went on, like getting to grips with the scheme of things and finding some space in it, like closing the door on the twenty-first century and slipping backwards into better times, where the slow rhythm of night and day governs your movements, and the rhythm of a heart beat marks the time, and the silence lets you think, and in the evening, soft candlelight warms the walls, and enflames your imagination, and sometimes, in between your own thoughts you hear the voice of an extremely great grandmother who might be calling to you all the way from Africa, telling you you'd better get used to the conditions that most of humanity has had to endure, because modern comforts are unsustainable and they're all going to go.

She felt as though her parents somehow knew about her growing sloppiness. If so, were they disgusted, or embarrassed, or saddened, or even that interested? It didn't seem likely that one would care about such mumbling trivia once you were in the exotic realm of an afterlife. How could you have such particular emotions without a body? How could you have any thoughts without a brain? Maureen hadn't understood everything when she was alive, so why should she suddenly understand it all now? Would you even remember your children? You might just be waiting to be born again, waiting to have some other children. Also it was their rubbish she was having to deal with, and if they didn't like the way she was going about it, then they could jolly well be damned. Not really damned. But they ought to have dealt with it themselves instead of dumping it on their offspring, oughtn't they? Didn't they agree? Yes they did, she'd read the apology. So what was she supposed to do about it? Set light to it? Typical! How typical not to communicate, not to simply tell her directly what the hell she wasn't meant to find in all this bloody mess. When they were alive.

'Where did I put that letter? Which letter? The important letter. None of them are important. The blue one. The first one from Frieda. Ah, here it is, yes. Addressed to the old house in Bridgetown. Redirected. 27th Feb 1976. From Salzburg.'

Dear Mr Sutton

I am the daughter of Maria and Karl Lehmann. My mother and father have spoken of you many times and have told me that you were after the war very kind to them.

This year I will visit England and will come to Stratford-upon-Avon on March 24. When we could meet, you could telephone to the youth hostel. I bring a gift from my mother and father. They are hoping that you and your wife are both quite well and with me they send their love and good wishes.

Yours faithfully

Frieda Lehmann

'Maria, you see, Maria. That's Mariya with a different spelling. It's still possible. Mariya gets pregnant by Dad. Karl marries her because he's kind or thinks the baby's his.

'Things relating to Frieda. Things I still don't understand. Well that's more or less all of it.

'Maybe she was Karl's child, after all. Why did I think she was Dad's in the first place? Oh yes – because of Remember Vienna and the heart-shaped Mariya and because he couldn't do enough for Frieda, and because that's the sort of thing that usually happens in family histories.

'Perhaps it doesn't matter.'

The room was darkening, Georgie could hardly read now. She'd been sitting in the same position on the floor for several hours and was beginning to feel stiff. She stood up, windmilled her arms, cricked her neck and did some stretches, sideways, forwards, back, oops not too far, she didn't want to pull anything; then she shuffled into the kitchen in search of sustenance. Having polished off the rest of a tin of beans, she filled the tin with water and left it in the sink, refilled her wine glass, and threw on the pyjama jacket she'd thrown off earlier.

Instead of filing the letter with the other Frieda things, she took it to the kitchen window where there was still some daylight. The garden was now brown, brown walls, brown mud. True to his word, Nick had sent three men and a chainsaw to clear the ivy, and with it had gone the honeysuckle, the jasmine, the brambles, the ferns. They'd carted sackloads of glistening green foliage through the garden and the communal garden, leaving a rambler's track. 'We've killed the stumps, but if you see any new leaves, just pull them off,' the foreman had said, looking at their work with pride. 'It's a blank canvas, you can start afresh,' he'd added, to comfort her horror at its ugliness. 'I'd pave it if I were you.' The ground was still laced with thick roots, encroaching from three sides.

She stared at Frieda's spiky handwriting, willing her eyes to suck up every drop of information it might yield. 'Choice of paper: graph paper, choice of implement: green biro. Generous margins. Generous spaces between words. Long lower loops, long higher loops. Longness and loopiness generally. Slightly on the backward slant. Clear. Not rushed. Paper folded both ways. Smell? Old.' It looked as if it had been read more than once. Larry had seen the Austrian stamp and the Salzburg postmark, opened it, read it, replaced it in the envelope, shown it to Maureen. Or he'd looked at it since, years since perhaps. 'If I'd kept the dust in the folds we could have examined it under a microscope, but I've gone and dispersed it now. It's mixed up with all the recent dust and the ancient dust. I don't know which dust comes from when. And what is it anyway? Skin, I suppose, and fibre. Don't forget your fibre! There might have been some of Mum's face in there. Or her hands more likely. And Dad's. Their skin is all over this place. And mine too, my sixteen-year-old skin might be here! All our DNA!' As she considered this idea, a hot wave of sadness swept through her, a recognition that she hadn't fully appreciated her sixteen-year-old skin. 'DNA is a very stable molecule. Except when you get cancer.' She took off her pyjama jacket. 'Don't be daft! Mites have eaten it and turned it into droppings. Nothing stays the same. Everything turns to shit.'

She lit some night lights and arranged them on a tray which she carried into the hall.

'And shit makes good compost, and that's good for the roses, so let's not moan about it. No, not roses. Food is what we're going to need. Vegetables and trees. Chin up Geegee!'

A loud banging on the door made her gasp so that the tray rattled and all the little flames shuddered. Her heart began to thump violently. She stood still and listened. The banging came again. It must be a stranger with the wrong address. Either that or it might just be Nick, coming for his three hundred pounds. She glanced at the clock, laid the tray of candles on the floor, and, scrabbling around for her dressing gown or shawl, found and donned her raincoat instead, mentally preparing excuses for her state of near nudity. She wouldn't admit that she hadn't got up yet. No, no, it was almost seven.

She could not have been more surprised. It was Charlie, looking solemn and slightly shocked, with longer hair than he'd had eleven weeks ago, beginning to curl.

'Charlie!'

'Mum.'

Georgie's instant joy was instantly confused by Charlie's anxious expression.

'Are you all right? What's happened?'

'I'm OK. What happened to you?'

'What do you mean?'

'Are you ill?'

Georgie yawned dramatically. 'No, no, don't worry. I'm just having an early night.'

'Are you drunk?'

Georgie tutted. 'No. Course not. Come in, come in! How lovely! Why didn't you tell me you were coming?'

She held the door wide open, but Charlie hesitated. 'I've got some stuff in the car. I'll bring it now, it's not parked. Can't park round here.'

'You came by car?'

'Yes.'

'So is Dad here?'

'I don't need Dad. I drove myself.'

Before Georgie could comment he was gone, saying, 'Won't be a sec.' She looked out into the street. The lamps were lit. It was that half-night half-day moment, when the sky is like shining slate, but the ground is darkening and earthly things are blurring. The air was chilly and damp, under clouds that promised rain. She heard a car door slam and Charlie came staggering back behind two plastic boxes.

'What is this?'

'It's your boxes.'

'Well, I don't want them. You'd better take them back.'

Charlie pushed past and laid them on the hall floor. 'I don't want them either.'

Georgie sighed. 'Oh, all right then, it's not much of a percentage difference. Where are you going?'

'There's more.'

'There *are* more,' muttered Georgie.

'There's more stuff is what I meant,' he told her when he returned with another two boxes of similar size. He laid them on top of the two he'd already brought in.

'At least they stack well,' Georgie said, ushering him further into the corridor. He declined her invitation.

'More things in the car. Might as well do it all at once.'

'No, stop it Charlie, this isn't fair! I have absolutely enough boxes here. Why do people keep bloody bringing me stuff? I've got stuff! I've got stuff! I've got plenty of stuff!' She didn't know how to explain any more clearly. 'Do you understand?' She looked at him and he returned her look, unsmilingly. 'Look around. Don't you understand? It's like the whale in *Pinocchio*. Nothing goes out!'

But he was gone and returning now with a hatbox and an armful of carrier bags. Finally he left to park the car, and took so long Georgie imagined he'd abandoned her like everyone else seemed to be doing.

'Why did you leave the door open?' he asked as he came in. He took off his jacket and laid it on top of the boxes because there wasn't any room on the pegs, or on top of anything else.

'Because the bell doesn't work.'

'What's wrong with it?'

'The electricity's gone.'

'Why is it so dark in here? Oh, because the electricity's gone.'

'Whose car are you driving?'

'Mum, are you mad? To have candles out with all this paper everywhere?'

'Does Dad know you're here? '

'It's nuts. If you can't think of yourself, at least think of the people above.' A loud pounding noise came down from the ceiling, and a bark, as if to underline his point. 'And the dogs!'

'I'd quite like the dog to go up in flames, actually,' she confessed. 'How are you? Are you hungry? You must be tired.'

'What happened to the electricity?'

'It stopped. And the gas. It's rather fun, actually, like camping. I've got some tins of things and a stove.' She looked inside the dark, warm fridge. 'Eggs. Bits and pieces of salad. A couple of shops are still open, I could go and buy us a real feast.'

Charlie glanced around the kitchen and spotted the wine bottle. He gave her a look without saying anything.

'It was one glass!' she protested.

'It's too dark in here. Don't you have a flashlight?'

'Somewhere. Dad must have had one. My dad. Grandad.'

'I'll lend you Dad's from the car.'

'No, no, you might need it. Does he know you're here? Don't you have school?'

'We've broken up for Easter.'

'Already? Gosh.'

'It smells.'

'Does it?'

'It's really dusty.' He coughed, to illustrate the fact.

'Why didn't you say you were coming?' But even if he had, Georgie wouldn't have been able to hoover.

'I left a message on the landline.'

'Yes, well. No electricity. I did find an old non-electric phone I could have plugged in but I've lost it again. For future reference, I am trying to keep the mobile charged. Mainly by not using it.'

Georgie pulled herself up to her full height, but he was a head taller, and it was beyond challenging to exert any parental authority in bare feet and waterproofs. She invited him to sit down, cleared a space on the kitchen table for him, and brought all that she had to eat. She gave him the last two inches of wine.

'I don't keep much food in stock because the fridge doesn't work,' she apologised. 'If only I'd known you were coming. Are you staying? You can use the camp bed.'

Charlie looked sorrowful and embarrassed. 'I think I might go back tonight.'

'Are you sure? I don't like to think of you driving in the dark. Or at all. There are such things as trains you know, and buses. It's such a waste of oil, one person per car.'

'How could I bring your boxes on the train?'

'So how are you getting on at home? Are you managing?'

'I've got some bad news.'

Something cold and horrid clutched Georgie's guts. He'd been expelled, he'd been robbed. There'd been a fire, an accident. He'd run out of money. Or worse, something awful about Joni. 'No. What is it?'

'Tania's going.'

Georgie slumped. 'Shit. Why?'

'She doesn't need to be there any more, that's all.'

'Oh bugger it, I'll have to come home and sort out another one.'

'You keep swearing.'

'Sorry. I'm tired.'

'I think you should come home anyway. You said it would only take a couple of weeks.'

'I know, darling, I'm really sorry. But it's not making it any easier your bringing me more, is it? Couldn't you have just put it in my room? '

'Tania's not going 'til the end of May.'

'Well, that's all right then. Joni'll be back soon after that anyway. Have you heard from her? I got a text saying she was out of contact for ten days.'

'I think she's on a trek. '

'And she's all right?'

Charlie shrugged. 'I suppose so.'

'And what about you? Does Dad know you're here?'

'Course. He let me use the car.'

'The insurance must be astronomical isn't it? And it was raining earlier. You drove through the rain? On the motorway? And it might rain on the way back? Charlie, you can't drive in the dark and the rain, please don't. Even I don't do that if I can help it. I think cars are awful anyway. I'm getting rid of mine. Huge waste of the planet's resources.'

Charlie grimaced and carried on chewing.

'I can nip out to the corner shop and get some bread and milk at least?'

'It's OK. I'll get a take-away later.'

'I could get you one now. Something healthy. A vegetable curry or something?'

'It's OK.'

'So how are you getting on?'

'I'm taking drugs mainly. Crack, heroin, meth. Spending all my time on porn and video games.'

'Come on. How are you managing? Do you have enough money? Are you eating enough?'

'Of course. Tania thinks I'm better than she is at cooking. And she's good.'

'And you're getting enough money from Dad? And my bit?'

He nodded.

'And how's school? You must be doing your university application? How are you getting on with the personal statement?'

He grunted and she asked him what he meant.

'Might not be going.'

'Oh dear, why not?'

'I don't want to get into debt. And it doesn't help you with jobs – most degrees don't make any difference.'

'Is it all about jobs now, then?'

Charlie looked at her as if she were raving mad.

'There used to be such a thing as learning for its own sake,' she tried to explain. 'Because you were interested. And the whole university experience.'

'I'm not that interested.'

'Darling, you're intelligent. You won't just waste it, will you?'

'That's why I'm not sure I want to go to university.'

Georgie wondered whether to tell him of her own experience; her faint regret at missing university herself, her whispering suspicion that, after all, she may have wasted her talents. Taking note of his expression, she decided to back off. She must clearly let him gain his own experience, however painful it might be for all concerned.

'So how are your mates? How's Ben? How's Gus?'

'Yeah, they're all right.'

'Rebecca?' she asked with a conspiratorial smile.

He stopped eating, shot her an extremely grumpy glance, and stared at the tabletop, apparently working out how to express something beyond expressibility. He looked like the teenage Will in that pose, and she noticed a hint of red in his cheeks, betraying his sensitivity and discomfort, just as Will used to. But it suddenly occurred to Georgie that she was barking up the wrong tree, that Rebecca was not the object of his desire and never could be. She waited patiently, relieving him of her attention for a while with her elbow on the table and her head in one hand.

'Is there something you want to tell me, darling?' she asked eventually with great delicacy and sensitivity.

Charlie turned his attention back to what was on his plate. 'No.'

'Because... I don't mind, you know, if there is.'

Her words seemed to amuse him, but she was glad they were out in the air. I love you whatever you do, whatever you are, she wanted to say.

'So what do you think you'll do? Have you thought about a career?'

'Yeah. I've been thinking about the RAF.'

Georgie believed him for two seconds and must have looked appalled.

'I wish you'd just trust me to live my life,' he went on. 'And stop badgering me and,' he searched for the right word, 'trying to manipulate everything.'

'I do trust you.'

'No you don't.'

Georgie held her tongue. She hadn't even seen him, let alone manipulated him, for eleven weeks. She changed the subject. 'So what's in the boxes, then?'

He shrugged. 'It looks like old things we don't need any more.'

She groaned.

'I thought you'd be pleased.'

'So there's nothing in there you might want? You give me full permission to throw it all away? Without checking?'

'Yeah. Unless there's anything worth having.'

'But that's just it! Don't you get it? That's the decision! That's the problem, right there!'

'Keep your hair on! It's nothing important.'

'But it might be important, mightn't it? It might be important to you. It might be important to me. Everybody thinks they can decide what I want and what I don't want! I'm sick of everybody telling me what to bloody do! First Dad, then Dad, then Will, now you!'

In the ensuing silence, Charlie pensively attended to his glass of wine. After long consideration he said, 'You can't say anything like well done for passing your test, or thank you for driving sixty miles to come and see you.'

'Charlie, I'm so sorry. I'm really tired. It's absolutely brilliant that you can drive. Of course. And I'm absolutely delighted to see you, I just wish I'd had time to prepare, that's all.'

He mumbled something into his next mouthful of sardine.

'What?'

Silence.

'What did you say?'

'You never say what you mean.'

'What do you mean?'

'It's always guessing what you want and trying to please you.'

'Really? I want the best for you, that's about it. I don't want you to be pleasing me.'

Apparently this was a comment beyond all reason. He shook his head in exasperation. 'It's always nicey nicey smiley smiley and making us feel guilty whatever we do. Why can't you just say what you mean?'

'I just did,' Georgie insisted, noting the 'us' which she hoped didn't include Jim. She sucked in her lower lip as though she thought it was in danger of wobbling.

'What do you actually want?' he asked.

'Ok, then. You're not to go back this evening in the rain and the dark. I don't allow it. It's too dangerous. You don't have the experience, it's too fast a car and Dad should not have lent it to you.'

'I passed first time!'

'You can control the car, but you can't control other drivers! And most people, especially young men, are rubbish! I don't mean you.'

'How long did you take?'

'Exactly! I had hundreds of hours of driving experience before I passed my test! I knew every kind of possible accident! D'you know how I learnt to look in my wing mirror? By being mown down by a lorry on a roundabout!'

Charlie drained his wine glass and stood up.

'But I was safe because the instructor grabbed the wheel!'

'You're off your trolley. I meant what do you want to do, not what do you want *me* to do.'

He passed her on his way out of the kitchen and proceeded up the hall.

'I forbid it!' Georgie commanded. 'You're not to drive! You've drunk!'

'Not nearly enough,' he muttered.

She hared after him, tiptoeing over scattered poky objects, unable to suppress her ululations at the pain.

'Charlie, don't leave on a row! Come on, let's make it up. I'm sorry for whatever I've done wrong.' Each of her conciliatory gestures was accompanied by a ridiculous plasticky noise made by the raincoat. 'I've done my best. If you must demonstrate your independence then you'd better go ahead, I'll bite my lip. But please don't leave on a row?' She tried to telegraph the line she couldn't bring herself to say: what if this is our last goodbye? It's perfectly possible that we'll never see each other again. But he was intent on avoiding her eyes as he gathered up his coat and car keys.

'Drive safely?'

His answering glance was unfathomable. He closed the door carefully, without slamming it, and she howled out in pain. Dressed as she was, she couldn't possibly have offered him a hug, and nor could she pursue him outside in bare feet.

She felt distraught, bereft, and didn't even question the need to ring Jim, though it was a waste of precious charge and precious time. She could have anticipated every one of his responses to every one of her questions. He did know that Charlie was driving the Audi, he did know that Charlie was on the motorway in the dark and the rain, he didn't know anything about anything that was going on at school or anything about anything to do with how well or badly Charlie was getting on at the flat; he hadn't seen him for a week. He knew nothing about Joni either, except that she was on a trek and out of contact. He was letting the children grow up without any meddling and she should try to do the same.

'Without any bothering!' Georgie screamed before cutting him off. 'You and your selfish guzzler of a vanity car!'

She was too tired to regret her shouting, or think about who was right. Only one emotion coursed through her tissues: fright, flight and fight, all together, it was all the same, shaking her about and weighing her heart with doom. That's what darkness brings. Your activity shrinks. Your body contracts. You can't move around freely for fear of bumping into things. Your world is confined to a spherical pool of glimmering firelight, bound by blackness. Time changes too. Space recoils, but time stretches, as if the moment between each tick of a clock is turgid with suspense. And this is when you feel as all humanity has through a million years of night – cold, scared, lonely, stupid. And this is when the souls of the ancient ones come creeping into your body, whispering into your ears and out of your mouth.

'Don't be absurd. It's just a bit bloody dark, that's all.'

She moved the hatbox Charlie had brought into her wobbly patch of yellow candlelight, and peered inside. Here was a card painted in green poster paint, which looked blue in the gloom. It was covered in maroon-seeming sequins stuck with lavish quantities of glue, and two bits of cotton wool that represented a sheep, with four spindly ink legs emerging from it. 'Hapy Mother Day love Charlie' was painstakingly inscribed inside it. 'I do love you Charlie!' Georgie whimpered. She suddenly realised that the bringing of the boxes might have been an excuse; that perhaps he needed her and couldn't say so. She'd missed the opportunity of being any help.

And here was an invitation to the school play. She remembered it, Joni proudly standing in her cardboard crown, wearing a robe cut and sewn from Jim's dressing gown, studiously enunciating the three words she'd been practising at breakfast every morning – 'I bring myrrh' – three breathless seconds after the boy in front had presented his cardboard frankincense. 'Mummy, what is myrrh?' she'd asked afterwards, in her post-performance pride and glory. Georgie regretted not telling her before, and she couldn't remember the response she'd given. 'Did I explain it properly?' she asked herself. 'It's a resinous spice,' she said now, just to make sure. 'Do you know what resinous means? It's sticky stuff that comes out of trees. Myrrh used to be very valuable. You can buy it in little bottles now, and it's good for your gums.' For a few moments she wondered how many thousands of things she'd explained, and how well she'd explained them. Had she explained well enough? What if she hadn't? Could she retake? And if she had, what would happen to her gift for explaining things, now she knew no-one who needed things to be explained?

And here in the next box, amongst dirty and discarded bits of plastic and metal and wood – spare car wheels and Lego figures and felt pens and pencil cases, dusty rubber aliens, dinosaurs, keyrings, torches, fuzzy animals, cap guns, puzzles, stray pawns and Pokemon cards, stamps and stickered notepads, marbles, chains, laces, spacemen, soldiers, badges – amongst all this sticky detritus were Charlie's special favourite bedtime companions. A satin lizard with loose stitches: Wo, by name. And Sharkie, a puppet he had loved the stuffing out of. He was letting go of them; she must follow his example. 'Goodbye Sharkie,' she said, giving it one last dusty hug. Charlie and Joni's toys had not lasted as well as her parents' had done, she thought, replacing Sharkie on the heap of junk. They'd had too many, and they weren't so well made.

And here was a recent addition – a wind-up phone recharger Georgie had given to Joni as a parting gift. She'd left it behind because it was too heavy.

She wondered where Joni was, and what she was doing. It would be four o'clock in the afternoon. She was on a donkey perhaps. Or a llama. Struggling up tussocky hills in the late afternoon sunshine, breathing clean pure mountain air. She was wearing sunglasses and a sunhat. She had companions. She was smiling.

Georgie remembered their parting, which had not been a good send-off. 'Perhaps it's normal to fall out with your children,' she wondered. 'Perhaps I should have fallen out with you?' she said to the ceiling, to her vanished parents.

She'd been too fussy and demanding of Joni while she was packing and getting ready, and Joni had retaliated with sudden rage. 'You'd never ask that of Charlie! You expect far more of me! Just because I'm your first! Just because I'm the girl! It's simply not fair! I'll phone you as and when! I don't need you on my case the entire time! I'm not your child any more! I'm nineteen!'

And when Georgie had tried to calm her down, and tried to explain that Joni was upset and stressed because she was taking a huge brave leap out into the world, and their lives would never be the same but she would always be her child, Joni had said, 'I can't wait to get away from you! I've been looking forward to it for years!'

And here was a school photograph of her, not purchased, spoiled with the letters copycopycopy printed across her earnest gap-toothed grin.

'But you weren't my first,' Georgie murmured. 'And you and Charlie are all I have in the world. The only point to everything. The only laurels I have to sit on.'

(WHEN YOU RUN OUT OF OPTIONS) PRAY

It wasn't late, but it was dark enough to go to bed, and though she didn't expect to be blessed by sleep she was too exhausted for any part of her to be upright. She was already undressed and didn't feel like eating anyway. A pain she had felt developing just to the left of her solar plexus was now intense, prodding her with worry. Liver? Lung? She boiled a kettle-full of water on the camping stove, but decided to forget about washing and used it instead to make chamomile tea. She cleaned her teeth with her eyes closed, avoiding her own reflection because it frightened her, lurching out of the dimness like that, as if from another world. Reserving one flame for the bedside, she blew out the rest as if she were the birthday-girl. The warm waxy smell of candle smoke comforted her. It reminded her of the winter of discontent, that wonderful time when they couldn't watch telly and had nothing to do but talk to each other, and no music but what they could produce themselves and were too embarrassed to. Long before Frieda.

No homework! Hooray! Beans cooked on a camping stove! Extra blankets. No such thing as duvets then, were there? Not in our habitat. Mummy, how did you manage to cook supper for four on a single ring?

Heart? It could be a heart pain. It could be grief.

She must go home to Charlie, she decided, shedding the raincoat and snuggling beneath the duvet. 'Chin up Gee! It'll give me a chance to rest, see things from a different perspective.' It was wonderful to be needed too, she thought, even if the person who needed you didn't know they needed you.

Something was making her dread it. Further information about Kevin would filter through. She might bump into people from work. She might have to think about all that had happened at the end of their love story, and it wouldn't be very nice.

Her mind was frazzled and tired, and like a wireless randomly searching for a station, it hissed and spat, tuning into one cadence after another – musical phrases, snatches of conversation, clamour. Images, too, came to her unbidden, confused and angry, demanding to be acknowledged and processed, as if dreams were exploding into her consciousness, because she couldn't sleep to have them. The guttering candle threw strange shadows on the wall; she let them bamboozle her drifting mind as she lay half-awake and helpless.

How did you manage to boil hot water bottles for all of us as we huddled together in the warm flickering light, talking in whispers in the quiet and the cold and the dark? Even indoors you could feel the earth under your feet, like a presence, holding its seeds and bulbs and biding its time. Crystalline snow smelling of. Cold. Tasting of. Dirt.

What happens when the gas canister runs out?

'You have behaved appallingly!'

She's a child again, wetting her pants, smelling that old school smell of bullies and chlorine.

It's last New Year, she's recalling now. The west coast of Ireland. She's been invited to share Jules and Paula's treasured time away in their special corner of the world with their thirty-year-old student son Linden; to graciously receive the generous hospitality of the boss and the boss's architect wife. Clean grey skies, slanting rain, expansive views. Fine wine, fine Guinness and Atlantic oysters. Too much fine wine and Guinness was the problem. It wasn't all her fault, really it wasn't.

'It was the dynamic of the group,' she insisted, as she lay in bed, turning from one side to the other.

Jules and Paula, this is Kevin; Kevin, meet Jules and Paula. It's love at first sight; everything's going to be wonderful. Jules shares Kevin's passion for the fineness of the wine. Kevin and Paula share a harmless flirtation. Georgie respects Paula too much to flirt with Jules and likes Jules too much for it to be harmless. Paula loves to listen, and Kevin loves to talk about himself. Jules has symptoms.

'I've got some sort of a lump,' he says.

'We've all got some sort of a lump,' says Paula, turning her attention for a moment from Kevin and his latest exhibition, forestalling the cancer conversation which Georgie might have enjoyed. Georgie tries to show an interest in Linden, but Linden doesn't do the older generation, except family.

Kevin hasn't looked at her all day, but now he does.

'Of course Gee doesn't understand these things, not being an artist herself,' he smirks.

Oopsy daisy, here comes Georgie's first bit of unforgivable behaviour. She's up and off on a walk by herself, tired of contradicting him. She's sitting on a rock watching the glimmering sea, listening to the waves slowly coming and going to and fro, figuring out how to escape without spoiling everybody's fun. She imagines treading the path of liquid gold to the horizon, while the sun sinks and the sky darkens.

She's taken too long, they've gone to the restaurant by now, she'll have to say she's ill and then she'll have to prove it by going to bed without any supper. She can't possibly explain the truth of it, that Kevin is taunting her, telling lies about her, flirting on purpose to annoy her. It was her idea to bring him. For five whole days. Because he needed a break.

Now Kevin's back and waking her, grunting into bed. He falls asleep in a tick, snoring fitfully and aggressively, while Georgie lies awake, burning with inexpressible fury. She creeps into the sitting room to use the sofa, where it's quiet but comfortless.

Why did I stay with him so long? What was it I liked?

It's because he riled you and annoyed you and competed with you and teased you. It was for the struggle. It's because he dumped the blame on you for everything, and stole all the attention. You just wanted to win for once, that's all.

The alphabet saucer! She remembers how it broke.

Puddy can't understand the words. Will and Mummy are talking to each other. She doesn't want the cup cake on her saucer. Mummy put it there to make her quiet. A sick feeling creeps into her mouth and a strangling feeling creeps round her neck, squeezing shut the I AM HERE! Oopsy daisy, she picks up the saucer and throws it down with all her might. A sharp dangerous splintery cracky noise makes letters fly apart in little bits. Ah! Now they speak.

'You have behaved appallingly! You did that deliberately!' Now they speak but too loud and scarily. Now they look but with nasty faces. Will sniggers.

'No!' Georgina screams with all her lungs and body. She doesn't know what deliberately means but she knows it's bad.

'Guilty, guilty, jealous, jealous,' Will taunts when Mummy has gone.

Later Daddy patiently sticks the saucer back together.

'There's a good girl.' She's done nothing to be good but sit beside him watching. 'Look, it's almost like new. You didn't mean to break it.'

She's confused. Deliberately. Behave. Mean. Guilty. Jealous. The words don't make sense, but each one is weighted with horrible feelings.

'It's only a thing, anyway. Things don't hurt like people do.'

But when things break, people hurt. And things last longer than people. And now this place is full of things whose owners have completely disappeared.

In the house on Colley's acre No, please don't sing it again, Mummy. *Molly's mother sowed a seed.* Where did she sow her seed? *Molly's mother so deceived!* Did your own mother sing it to you, Mummy? Did your grandmother teach her? Lullabies have to start from somewhere, Will. It's not such a stupid idea!

In a group, which one is hanged and quartered for everybody's sins? Who is cast out alone into the desert bearing the madness of the tribe? Such a painful thing; without the tribe we die.

Is it the strong one, or the one who tells the truth, or the witchy one whose hormones are unreined? Who is that woman standing at the end of the bed, dressed in grey? She's staring at me!

It's because when you hug him you vanish into his chest.

You lose your body in his arms. The pull towards him is intense. You're addicted to his acid smell. It's because he's from a past life, says Sheelah; you have business to resolve. You have to forgive him and let him go.

The dog is pounding the floor above again, flooding her with adrenaline and cortisol. 'That bloody dog is going to give me another bout of cancer!' She actually just shouted that. She is actually still wide awake. This is no dream.

Which was the scapegoat? It was Frieda. Frieda was the scapegoat and it was Georgie's fault. I'm sorry. I'm so sorry. Please forgive me. Smiley smiley nicey nicey doesn't work.

Buried there her daughter Molly how the golden girl would grieve.

Now comes the screaming. The screaming and the shushing. Where's my baby? I want to go home! I've lost my little baby!

Something felt wrong in Georgie's head. The real world was losing reality, she was slipping off sideways, slipping away from herself.

'I don't want to die,' she blathered. Her heart hammered and pain came squeezing hard into her chest and her breathing came too fast. 'Oh please let me stay in my lovely world! Don't take me yet. Not yet. I'm not ready.' Her vision swam, sounds warped. 'If I faint I'll die, so I'm not going to faint. I'm not going to faint. I'm not going to faint,' like a chant.

Her body stands up and puts on the raincoat. Her arm reaches out and opens the French window. Her feet step one by one into the world. A beautiful cool snap of air tickles her hair, strokes her skin. The shoulders drop. 'Lovely ground. Lovely breeze.' It's a whisper, perhaps from her own mouth. The terrace is cold on the soles of her feet. Her legs walk out into the moonlight. Trees are rustling.

She can hear what they're saying!

'It's all right, darn right. Don't interrupt the sorrow.'

She climbs the steps into the garden. The ground is wet, mud, straggling plant life, a mesh of thick gnarled ivy roots. She crouches down to touch it. Gravity holds her safe, streaming through her bare feet, reassuring, calming, encouraging. She grits her teeth, takes a great lungful of air, grasps two handfuls of roots, and pulls, pulls, pulls against Mother Nature's jaws. Slippery and tangled and taut, the roots come tearing up. And now she feels a thousand souls behind her pulling too. 'It has to be done!' the trees are whispering. 'It has to be done. Everyone must play their part! The roots are poisonous. Tear up the poisonous roots.'

For every thing turn turn turn, there is a season turn turn turn.

There is a time for planting and a time for reaping, and a time for sowing and a time for tearing up the roots.

It began to rain, drop by drop, then faster and harder, splashing off the plastic raincoat, and running down her neck. She threw off the coat, to move more easily and because she was already wet. She liked the cold and the rain; they told her she was still alive. Her feet hurt, beginning to numb, mud was creeping up her legs, blood in her hands.

'As long I'm hurting, I'm alive,' she thought. *I'll never go hungry again!*

She didn't know how long she was there, hauling great ropes of roots that stretched from one wall to the other. There were always more. Energy seeped away, her back ached, numbness spread. At last she stopped, knelt and rested her sore hands in the soil. Under her fingers, a handful of bones. She felt them in her fist, and grinding yearning pleading anguish gripped her heart. She thought of the Gorta Mor. Thousands went hungry, children like skeletons were buried where they fell. Clasping her hands together she prayed with all her might, 'Universal Spirit! Or whatever you are! Mother Earth! Father Sky! Oh please please please take care of the children! Please keep them safe!' Suddenly her spine sprang straight. It flicked and curved of its own accord like a whip. She was thrown backwards in a kind of animal ecstasy, as if sparked by lightning. She stayed where she fell then, letting the rain fall after, seeing herself as if from above, half-naked. Her breath was almost non-existent. The pain was gone.

Later, as mechanically as she'd walked outside, she stood up, retrieved her coat and walked back indoors, locking firm the French window and covering it with curtains. 'I'll do the rest tomorrow,' she thought. 'Goodness me, I need a shower.' Her body was frozen numb.

A cold dark shivering shower, blood and mud both black in the candlelight, and little bones dropped around her feet. A rubber bottle full of hot water heated on the stove.

Then sleep. At last.

PASS FOR NORMAL

Daylight needled into the bedroom, and she rose at last from her damp sheets. She wondered how she'd managed to stand living there for so long, and thought about returning to her own cosy home with deep relief.

List of things to accomplish, but really hard to accomplish after a bloody rough night: Wash up, tidy up, clean bath, dry bones. Pay Nick. Fill car with petrol. Recycle and dump – two trips. Lock up.

She hurried through the rain, found the car, and with a sigh of regret at the loss of a good parking space, started the engine. 'Well done, car!' She manoeuvred the steering wheel with her fingertips. 'Power steering! Wonderful invention!' She double-parked in front of the terrace and dashed in and out of the flat, loading up with bin bags and boxes, holding them in her arms to avoid touching them with her hands. Just as she slammed shut the driver door, the engine puttered and stopped.

'Damn.'

She was out of petrol, and double-parked, and a queue of cars was building up behind, waiting for a gap in the oncoming traffic. Heat flew through her. She released the handbrake, 'Ouch!' The bloody thing hurt her hand. 'Drat! It actually is a bit bloody!' She got out of the car, shrugged dramatically at the driver who was top of the queue, and leant her whole weight on the boot of the car, making no difference whatsoever to its position. She set about raising a four-strong team of kind strangers (something she used to manage in a lot less time) who shifted the car, while, with her wrists, she steered it out of the way and onto a double yellow line.

One of the helpers lent her a biro and another gave her half a paper tissue on which to write a note for the traffic warden. Thanking them all effusively, she took her empty canister to the nearest petrol station to buy enough to get the car to it, but when she came to pay, the debit card failed. She apologised and told the girl she'd return with cash. The ATM told her she had insufficient funds. The nearest next ATM was outside her own bank, but though she asked it nicely several times, it refused to part with a single note.

'Outrageous!' she shouted. 'What about the overdraft?' The mini-statement showed her she'd overdrawn her overdraft. She went into the bank but nobody could help because she belonged to a different branch. Sitting in their lobby, she rang the customer service number and waited through five layers of options before speaking to someone who told her that there was no chance of increasing her overdraft limit unless she had proof of regular income. The lodger's rent didn't cover it; in any case payments had stopped. There was nothing that could be done unless she could use a credit card, and he was very sorry and was there anything else he could help her with?

She didn't have a credit card. She only had change. She returned to the petrol station.

'May I have three pound seventeen's worth?' she asked the girl behind the counter. It wasn't possible, apparently, and she must leave the can until she could pay for its contents. 'I beg your pardon but the can is mine!' she protested, so assertively that someone assertively transferred its contents to one of the garage's new ones, and let her go.

'I've no fuel, I've no money, but never mind! Tins in the cupboard. I won't starve.'

All the people she could borrow from were in other towns, she realised, except Nick, and she couldn't borrow from him because she still owed him for masterminding the denuding of the garden. She'd have to get someone to pay cash into her account. Yesterday was Thursday so today must be Friday. Unless she acted fast, she wouldn't be able to draw it out until Monday.

On arriving back at the flat she discovered that the car had been towed away.

'Well, that's one problem dealt with,' she muttered grimly.

*

She refused to ask Will for money. She couldn't ask Sheelah. She wouldn't ask Jim. She thought about asking Charlie. 'Here's something grown up for you to do. I need to borrow some cash. Five hundred? I'll pay you back.' Perhaps not the first sentence, which was patronising and manipulative. But Charlie wouldn't have five hundred pounds, would he? Not unless he'd been dealing drugs or something. In her heightening anxiety, she considered and eventually dismissed the suggestion without enough conviction. No. No. So Charlie would have to ask Jim and then Jim would know, so she couldn't ask Charlie. She couldn't ask work colleagues because she'd left the practice under a slight shadow that she hadn't understood and had successfully avoided thinking about until the last night. All the friends she could think of were too impecunious or not personally close enough in an appropriate enough way.

'There must be some money in this place! Daddy! Where did you chuck your change?' She looked up at the ceiling, as was now her custom when addressing the dead. 'Or was all your money just numbers?' She imagined she was probably not quite meeting him eye to eye, rather as in a skyping session; in any case, no information was transferred.

It was a different kind of looking through the rubbish now. Under the bed. In all the little jars and pots on the dresser, which contained unfranked stamps and rubber bands and dust and paper clips. In the drawer dust. In the dust under the doormat, under the rugs, under the wardrobe, dust balls scanned by the icy beam of her mobile phone.

Under the chest of drawers, a cigar! The universe was bountiful. This was just what she needed, like manna. She tore off its wrapper and breathed in its masculine scent – pungent notes of resin and coffee, in a background of cardboardy staleness.

A flashback. When she first arrived back in London from her foreign jaunts, scruffy, tired, poor, hungry and without shelter, she'd been picked up near Victoria station by a recently divorced, drunk, unshaven, oily-faced man in his forties, who bought her cocktails and took her home and allowed her to sleep in his daughter's room. In the days that followed she'd kept him company while he washed dishes, threw out the empty bottles of Night Nurse, and cooked supper for her. She herself had done nothing but listen to him. His wife had left him for another man. His daughter had gone too. He didn't know what he'd done but work forty-five hours a week to support them. He lent her a key when he returned back to work, and she'd read a couple of his books, listened to his Beethoven CDs, and made herself cups of tea. She washed her clothes in the washer-drier and used his cedar shampoo and bath oils. She signed on, phoned numbers about rooms in flats, and started looking for a job. Every night he kissed her on the forehead before saying goodnight, and she slept, clutching his daughter's teddy bear, grateful and surprised that he hadn't made a pass at her. A week later she said she had to go. She was wearing the rah-rah skirt and frayed jersey she'd been wearing when he met her, but they were clean now, and ironed. He asked her to drop the key in through the letter box. He put down his brief case to hug her, and they wished each other luck.

'It's a good thing you didn't fancy me, isn't it?' she said.

'Of course I did.'

'Oh. But you didn't - ?'

'No.'

'Why not?'

He'd shrugged with a regretful smile. 'I don't know.'

She left him a note with the key, thanking him for being so kind, and asking him to take care, and giving him her love and kisses. She hadn't been able to say any of that in person.

The smell of the cigar was the smell of that flat, as it aired and lost its taint of sickness. It was the smell of that man's life – his books and CDs and good coffee – a smell that stirred her heart. In those fleeting days before AIDS, those last days of free love, she used to expect to be taken care of, while knowing there might be a price on her young flesh. How free love was!

'Perhaps I could stand on a street corner,' she said drily. 'Or sit.'

She imagined herself with the cello and an empty cap, playing 'Full Fathom Five'.

She flicked through books, first randomly, then more significantly, in the hope of finding paper money between the leaves. Shakespeare? The Bible? The Oxford Dictionary? No. Mum's book of Patron Saints? Dad's Bill Brandt and Martin Parr? She could picture a twenty-pound note in such exact detail it was hard to believe that one was nowhere to be found. A clutch of financial self-help books were as helpful to her as they had been to her father: *Live Now Pay Later. Think Yourself Rich. How to Prosper in the Bust.*

There was plenty of stuff in Sell, but selling it required communication technology. I could advertise in the newsagent, she thought. 'I could get on my bike and look for work, if I had one.' The thought of getting on a bike made her blench.

'Jeanette!'

Jeanette would have plenty of money and be only too happy to assist because Georgie had looked after her multitude of cats two summers ago while Jeanette was holidaying in Havana; plus she wouldn't judge Georgie or gossip about her predicament or doubt her paying it back. But when Georgie came to ring her she discovered that she'd run down the mobile and it was out of charge.

Her usual practice since losing the electricity was to recharge it in a café, but she didn't want to waste more than two thirds of all the money she had in the world on a cup of tea. She risked twenty pence of it in the only remaining telephone kiosk in Clifton. It stank of urine and gobbled up the coin without connecting her or apologising or letting her know what she might do about it. From there, she trudged down to the main library, because the local one was shut. En route she avoided the appeals of one beggar, three *Big Issue* sellers and two charity muggers. The beggar wore a shirt just like one of her father's.

Good strong blue cotton. Large metallic buttons. Triangular lapels. It was precisely like her father's shirt. In fact it *was* her father's shirt. He was also wearing a pair of Larry's shoes, and the trousers looked familiar too. In the midst of doom, a gleam of delight. She wondered if that was an example of the so-called trickle-down effect, though given her circumstances it was more of a sideways motion, or at least, downwards at a rather shallow angle. 'I wish some money would come trickling down to me,' she muttered. 'But money's more likely to trickle upwards, isn't it, Georgina? Doesn't often come in this bloody direction.'

In the library she managed to get away with plugging the mobile in behind the photocopier while she lingered nearby, trying to find a book – any book.

'If I found myself penniless in a foreign country,' she thought, 'The British Embassy would help me home. The equivalent here is Britain itself, I suppose.' She felt as though the floor were caving in. If she fell, there was no safety net, and no cushion. 'Which bit of Britain will help me?' she thought, tragically. 'I'm going to be a bag lady!' Or had she said it? She was so used to being on her own that she wasn't sure any more.

'I can always hitch!' Again, her thought might have been out loud. 'Or I could walk. It's only sixty miles. I probably have enough fat stores.'

She retrieved the phone before it had fully recharged and, sitting on a plastic table by empty paper cups in the library café, rang Jeanette. There was no answer. She sent a text. *Got a bit of a prob. Please ring asap.*

'I still have a roof! Or a ceiling at least!' she thought as she hurried back to the flat in the rain. 'And grub and plonk for a night or two. Chin up Geegee! All is well.'

The sensible, properly planned, middle-class solution to her predicament, involving, say, a second mortgage, or selling the flat, would involve Will.

Will could go to hell.

A sodden postcard lay in wait for her, lodged in the letterbox.

We apologise for the interruption to your water supply. Bottled water is provided.

She glanced around, but saw no bottled water. Further along the street was a cordoned-off pit, beside a van, a pump, and a rainwashed man in orange high-viz and a helmet.

'Someone's nicked my water!' she shouted.

He shrugged with both arms and put on a world-weary face, meaning 'what can you do?'

'Well, what can I do?'

'There's a number to ring. Or the supermarket? Won't be long, love. Should be fixed by midnight.'

She didn't want to explain to a perfect stranger that she had absolutely no money, no landline and very little in the way of mobile.

Well, I'll bloody well drink wine until then, she thought. I refuse to go under. I can't flush before midnight, that's all. It's not the end of the world. I won't need to flush before midnight. 'Annoyance I can manage.'

She filled a kettle from the lavatory cistern.

'Despair I simply WILL NOT HAVE.'

'Nick, hello, I'll come straight to the point. I'm in a fix. I'm rather short on liquid assets at the mo and I'm not going to be able to pay you just yet. I should get it to you in a couple of weeks? Is that OK?'

Nick took the briefest moment to answer: 'Yep. That's not a problem.'

His cheerful tone emboldened Georgie, but she came to her next point rather more slowly.

'The other thing is, um... Is it at all possible for you to lend me anything more as I'm stuck in Bristol and I can't sort it out until I get home?' She explained as if it were a huge joke. 'I've got things for sale but I don't even possess the funds to send them to any buyers. I need a train fare, basically.'

'Oh dear. That sounds bad.'

'I could give you something in lieu? A deposit of some

sort. I've found a few first editions here which must be worth something?'

'I trust you Gee. How much d'you need? When shall I bring it?'

Georgie was so overcome with gratitude and relief, that she had to hold the mobile away from her mouth because she was making peculiar noises. He was in the area, he said, and before long was banging on her door.

She greeted him with thankful joy, apologising for the continued lack of doorbell with a gesture which was meant to include every other aspect of the chaos, visible and invisible, which had come crashing into her life. She assumed he must be busy so she didn't invite him in, but waited in awkward expectation as he stood there motionless and expressionless. He asked to inspect the work on the garden.

'Of course!' Georgie blustered. She led him through the corridor, resisting the urge to apologise for anything else – the darkness, the dust, the state of the garden, for example.

He didn't look best pleased as he surveyed the scene outside. It was a swamp, spattering dirt.

'They've left a right old mess. I'll have to say something.'

'At least they didn't destroy the robin's nest!' Georgie chirped.

She ushered him back inside and through to the kitchen.

'Some of it was me,' she admitted. Before he could refuse she was boiling her precious kettle full of water on the camping stove. 'I went a bit potty last night, actually. Really lost it rather. I don't know. A lot of stress. And I had an incredible urge to just go outside and touch the ground, to earth myself, that's exactly it. As if I were full of electricity. I just wanted to plunge my hands into the soil. D'you ever get that? I wanted to plunge myself into Mother Earth.'

Nick smiled, uncomprehending.

'Yes, it is ironic seeing as electricity is exactly what I haven't got, though I suppose it's everywhere these days actually.'

He looked confused.

'In the air. In our bodies.'

The explanation did not enlighten him.

'I mean wi-fi and such.'

Nick nodded and shot her an ironic smile. 'Well, it's no bad thing to plunge yourself into Mother Earth, as long as you plunge in some plants at the same time.'

Georgie laughed. 'Yah. Good idea.'

Here she was saying silly words again. He had this effect on her. He took a wad of notes from his back pocket. 'Hope it's enough,' he said, and Georgie put out her hand. The sight of it seemed to alarm him; he drew a sharp breath, as if suddenly pained. 'Gee! What happened to your hand?'

Georgie looked at both of her hands, as if realising for the first time how red and raw they were. She shrugged it off.

'It's nothing. I just got them a bit bloody and muddy. You know, when I was earthing myself.'

Nick took one of hers in one of his and looked at it, turning it in the light. 'I'd get some antiseptic on that,' he said. 'Doesn't it hurt?'

'Bloody and muddy!' Georgie laughed. 'What a useful rhyme. Must be in a few First World War poems don't you reckon? A bit like womb and tomb.'

He looked amused and concerned at the same time. He laid the money on the counter, covering it with the edge of the now useless toaster as a paperweight.

'Pay me back when you can.'

Georgie was speechless. He didn't even count it out or say how much it was. He sensed the intensity of her gratitude and waved it away.

'It's actually nothing to what you did for me, Gee. I can't spare any more today, but if it's not enough, let me know, I can get a bit more out tomorrow.'

Georgie shook her head, and again was too overwhelmed to actually articulate the words: thank you. It was clear in her expression, she hoped.

'Are you sure you're OK otherwise?'

'Absolutely, yes, fine. It's all rather exciting and challenging here at the mo.'

'I could dress those hands of yours; there's a first aid kit in the van.'

It was difficult to resist his kindness, but he'd probably want to wash her wounds and then she'd have to admit to a lack of water and then he'd feel obliged to deal with that too, and it wouldn't be fair on either of them. She waved him goodbye, grinning ostentatiously to make up for her lack of courtesy.

After he left she counted the money. It was more than she expected; she'd be able to buy some water, survive the weekend, retrieve the car before it racked up any further charges, fill it with enough petrol to drive it to a decent parking space, and buy a train ticket home. All was well. All would be well.

But all wasn't quite well, at least not yet. On opening the lid of the loo she thought she heard a bubbly skittering noise, and as she was turning to sit, saw the cause of it from the corner of her eye – a furious jittery movement in the bowl below. She screeched and banged the lid shut, only just restraining an escapage. Something was alive in there! She listened for a moment, sickened by the noises of frantic splashing. Thank goodness she'd spotted it in time. Thank goodness there was enough left of daylight to see it.

'Maybe it'll go away,' she muttered, in terror. 'Though what comes up doesn't necessarily go down again, does it Gee?'

She secured the lid with two unopened cardboard boxes, in case whatever horrible thing was in there had any idea of jumping out.

It was too cold and too wet to crouch outside for a wee. 'Never mind. In for a penny, in for a pound. You didn't have any plumbing did you Georgina? It didn't kill you.' For a chamber pot she used a shabby aluminium saucepan nobody would now use for cooking. 'Though maybe it did. Cholera. Typhoid. I bet you had something more luxurious than this, though, didn't you? I bet you had a pretty piece of Spode or Wedgwood to wet in. And what about loo paper? When was that invented? About the same time as sliced bread, probably. And best thing since. How on earth did humanity manage all those aeons without loo paper? Rags? Though the Romans used sponges, didn't they? Only the rich ones, of course. And what about hand washing? Which you didn't even know was a good idea! Well, I'll nip out for water when it's stopped raining. Wine for now. Loo flushable by midnight.'

She thought she might as well carry on going through boxes while she was still in the flat. It would help take her mind off the scary noises coming from the bathroom.

World War Two scrapbook.

Museum.

Black-and-white postcards of churches and beaches sent to Maureen's mother from Emily, Aunt Jen, Clare, none of whom Georgie knew anything about. They were brief, like texts. *Will visit next Thursday. Hope you had a lovely day in Stratford. Don't worry about the bicycle.*

Irrelevant and random, yet they seemed to speak to her.

For Charity.

Birthday card: cutesy drawing of a baby, in patch colours, with the legend *Tuesday's child is full of grace*, in Mickey Mouse letters.

Georgie's heart lifted to see her own name inside: *For little Georgina May and her Mummy with love from Daddy.*

'Ah! Thank you Daddy.'

Keep.

'That's odd, though. I'm not full of grace. I'm loving and giving, aren't I? Friday's child.' It bothered her a bit, that she could have got it wrong, and by so many days.

Bank statements. Interesting in their antiquity. Pounds, shillings and pence, how inconvenient, and what tiny sums went in and out!

For shredding or burning.

She looked again at the birthday card – her very first. *Tuesday's child is full of grace.*

'But I'm not full of grace! I am definitely loving and giving!'

The disjunction caught at her mind and wormed its way

to the top, as she carried on sorting. It was no good, it was a checkable fact and she was going to have to lay it to rest.

'How am I supposed to work it out without a calendar or a calculator or the internet? You need electricity for bloody everything!' she moaned.

'No thou dost not. We knew not electricity, yet we haddeth calculus and logs, did we not? All you have to do is to calculate how many days you've lived, divide that by seven, and count how many days are left over.' She mustn't forget the leap years – that was the first task, to divide her age by four and find out how many 29th of Februarys she'd done. Today's date was on her mobile, confirmed by the ATM slip which had told her how broke she was.

After much scribbling and totting and checking she figured out that she'd lived for 18,964 days: 2,709 weeks plus one day. It was Friday today, she was sure of that – it was Good Friday in fact, she thought, so, yes! She was Friday's child! She *was* loving and giving! How could Larry get it so wrong? Fathers weren't as involved then as now, but really! It was sheer neglect! Poor Maureen and her innocent little self had lain in hospital for half a week before he acknowledged them – or else he couldn't give a toss about which card to buy! She bet he hadn't been so careless over Will!

The rain had abated, but it was too late now to go shopping for water. She wasn't thirsty yet and anyway it was going to be on again by midnight. She cleaned her teeth with the swill in the bottom of the kettle after a supper of cold baked beans, nuts and apples. 'Fibre, phyto-oestrogen, polyunsaturated oil, laetrile. Not too bad.'

She lay awake in bed thinking she'd probably already lived more days than the girl in gold was going to, and wondering if she'd make it to 20,000 days, realising it was just as much of an arbitrary figure as, say, sixty years. She imagined all her lost time accumulating in a pile somewhere – the individuality of days blurring. Had she paid enough attention, she wondered, to the individuality of days? How many of them had really been good? From now on, she thought, they will all be good. They will all be better than good.

In the middle of the night she sat up rigid with alarm.

It wasn't me.

She got straight out of bed on wobbly legs, wrapped herself in the duvet, and lit the tray of candles. In their flickering light she examined the birthday card again. There was no clue as to its date except for the quality and kind of printing. Hurriedly she unearthed other samples of Larry's handwriting and compared them. The birthday greeting was more vigorous and better formed than most, but it exactly matched the writing on the back of the watercolour of Schönbrunn Castle.

It was an earlier hand. It was an earlier Georgina May.

She must have died, Georgie thought, and Maureen had simply used the name again. She must have died; Maureen had lost her firstborn child.

'Oh Mummy! Poor Mummy! Why didn't you tell us?'

She knew why. It was so that the sadness over one child didn't flow into her others. Georgie's chin began to quiver.

'Was it an earlier me?' she wondered, hesitating in her grief. That would be Sheelah's solipsistic interpretation: Georgie's own soul had stuck her toe into the river of life, changed her mind and come back to be born again later, when she was more in the mood. She started wondering if she'd done the same thing in reverse the previous night – testing and eluding the river of death? 'I didn't dare to be born and now I don't dare to be dead?' But she hadn't been in any real danger, had she? The danger was all imagined.

Shit shit shit the duvet was on fire. Georgie screamed and leapt away from it, naked. With outstretched arms she shifted it clumsily into an emptier part of the lobby, muttering, 'Blanket, blanket, smother it with a blanket!' She rushed back towards the bedroom before realising, 'We don't have blankets, it IS the blankets!' Coats were on the other side of the flames, and the front door. For half a second she was tempted to run into the back garden and leave it burning. In her confusion the first objection to that plan was the dog! The dog! 'FIRE!' she shouted with all her might, to little effect. She must call the fire service! 'FIRE!' But she had no idea where she'd put down the mobile and couldn't see well enough to find it. She picked up her saucepan of piss, hesitated, threw it onto the fire, and ran into the kitchen, shaking wildly, wildly incompetent in the darkness. The tap grunted and was dry.

'By midnight they said! Fuck! FIRE!'

She ran back with the empty pan and used it to flick one edge of the duvet over the flame, trying to smother it. Smoke puffed out from each side. The damp towel she grabbed from the bathroom seemed to worsen the smoke. She ran through the bedroom with the pan, opened the French windows with flustery fingers, and, naked and barefoot, skeltered over the slippery terrace, to the water butt. She slopped the pan beneath its oily black surface, and pulled it up again with two painful hands and wobbly wrists.

The duvet was only smouldering now but paper, paper everywhere caught and flared, as Georgie doused it with pathetic slops, dashing back and forth from naked heat to naked cold, issuing horrid caterwauls and shrieks which summoned nobody. Now two whole boxes were blazing, blistering, drowning in flames. The knitted teddy bear fell as a martyr into the flames. She saved only its head. She swung the saucepan so thin arcs of water splattered out into the smoke and fire, and watched helpless, as her letters from abroad were consumed, then the scrapbook, the bank statements, old postcards and photographs curled and shrank and blackened and were gone.

At last the room was dark. She stared into it, still holding the saucepan, ready to pounce on any remaining glow. But all was cold and damp and quiet now; the fire was out; she was safe.

Her breathing sounded like a dragon's, so fierce and strong she thought it might restart the fire. It seemed a mad and dangerous thing to do, but she lit another candle, a single one, to cast its trembling light over the scene. Lingering smoke made odd coiling shapes, and there were black shadows on the wall that looked like a huddle of people. She spotted her mobile, where she'd left it on the floor. It was still dry but out of charge.

'You've got to remember where you put things,' she told herself crisply. 'And be more careful in future – you were lucky this once!' She remembered that Larry had taken the battery out of the smoke alarm because he didn't like the noise it made.

Bedraggled and exhausted, she pulled on some clothes and crawled back to bed, her brain fuzzing and buzzing and crazied out again. No sleep, only fitful fancies. Murmurs and suggestions. She couldn't tell whether her eyes were closed or open. She scared herself, closing them, opening them, closing them again. She couldn't tell whether the lady's face was in the room or under her eyelids or only in her mind. She couldn't tell whether the hand she was wringing was her own, now numb, or what the sussurations in her ears were saying or why the air was crying. She thought it might be the echoes of her own distress. She knew only that the throbbing was her own heart.

At dawn she got up to survey the mess. The light was eerie, dirty-looking and flat.

It was odd. Right in the middle of the charred remains lay a perfectly unburnt undisturbed leaflet, as if it had been deliberately put there. She stood staring warily at it before picking it up. St Hilda's Orphanage, Warwick. Indented printing, shiny mottled paper. Poor quality photographs of children in uniform, in the gymnasium, busy, smiling falsely. She could imagine the iron bedsteads, the sad smell of labelled institution linen, corridors reeking of overcooked vegetables, the sound of private crying.

She glanced around at the devastation to see which heap the leaflet had fallen from, and something followed it, sliding out of a gaping file balanced on the bottom edge of a burnt-out box. It was a picture of a candle, on a bookmark-shaped card. She read it: Certificate of Baptism for Georgina May Connor,

1946. And then came a cascade of other things. Pictures of a pretty dark-eyed girl, aged two with fair baby curls, aged three, sixteen, twelve, with pale wavy hair and a familiar smile that touched her to the core. She knew its warmth and friendliness. She knew its secret humour.

She remembered one of the first things she'd found in one of the first boxes she'd opened. Desperately she churned through soggy half-empty boxes and blackened files.

'What's the point of going through all this fucking crap if I can't find anything?'

At last she found her – the monochrome girl on the swing, still wrapped in newspaper, now spotted with water. Georgie ran her nail along the brown paper tape to release the back board. Behind it was a layer of newspaper, in German. She peeled it away and held the back of the photograph to the dim light. In faded black ink it read: Salzburg '55.

The dog began pounding the floor above, over and over again. And instantly there, directly ahead of her, now certainly in the room, in fine clear bright white detail, was the figure of a woman. In shock, Georgie dropped the photograph. In shock she stared ahead, stared hard, as hard as she could. The figure stared back, frozen in an attitude of horror and disgust. Smoke and mirrors, it must be smoke and mirrors.

It wasn't rational. She didn't question whether or not it would help matters. She marched down the corridor, straight through the phantom, screaming at the top of her voice, picked up the hockey stick, and hammered with all her energy at the small patch of ceiling where the noise was coming from. Her smash was stronger than she knew. The plaster cracked. A section of it fell to the floor in a shower of paint and dust, revealing the frayed edges of a rotting lattice work of lathe. A drop of cold fell after it, gently rolling down her hair, bouncing off her body and along the floor, then another, then another, then in twos and threes, then in fast succession, pearls showered down on her like hail.

MAKE DO AND MEND

'I knew it would come in handy!' she shouted, raking through the box of Charlie's old toys to find Joni's mobile charger. She attacked the plastic packaging with a pair of kitchen scissors, selected the correct adapter, plugged it into the phone, and wound. Round and round the handle went, digging into a pain she no longer cared about. It made her wrist and biceps ache. As she wound it buzzed, and the pitch of the buzz went higher the faster she wound. It worked!

'Will!' she said promptly in response to his fuggy greeting. 'It's not an A-plus situation here. I haven't much credit so I might need you to call me back. I can wind it up if run out of charge. I mean "it", the phone, not you or the conversation!' She laughed hilariously.

'Are you OK?' Will yawned. 'What's up?'

'In brief. Um. The trees have been whispering and pearls are falling on my head. Which is peculiar, isn't it? Not normal.'

'What?'

'And I can't get all the roots up, I need some help. And I suppose I ought to give this baby's bones a decent burial. The car's been impounded too and um, Charlie doesn't want to go to university. So all in all it's not... It's not smiley smiley nicey nicey any more is it? Has to be admitted finally don't you think? There are skeletons in the cupboard. Like the cello. The varnish is cracked. Craquelure as they say, which some people actually appreciate.'

'Gee, you're not making much sense.' Will's voice sounded sticky.

'There's another thing. What was it? Oh yes, the worst of it.'

'Gee, I'm not understanding any of it.'

'Frieda. Frieda.'

'Can you keep your voice down? Renée's still asleep. I'm taking you into the sitting room.'

'She's our sister, Will. She's our older sister. Complete, full, whole, total sister. As in Mum's and Dad's.'

Silence.

'Most unfortunate that you didn't know. It might not be anybody's fault. I don't think it's your fault. I just hope Mina doesn't have absolutely hundreds of fingers. This is what worries me. It's not good for evolution, is it, incest? A nice big gene pool is what we need. Coffee-coloured people by the score.'

'Gee, have you been taking any drugs?'

'No! Of course not. Green tea, red wine. And the odd bar of dark chocolate. Green, black and red. That's for Africa isn't it? Does that make sense? Although I suppose the wine is a drug of sorts and you're right, I shouldn't really. The middle age curse. I mean middle class. I haven't even mentioned the rat, which I must say was the absolute last straw.'

There was a pause.

'You mean Kevin?'

'No, no. Rat as in rodent. Though it could be some sort of snake I suppose, or a frog might have jumped in.'

'Gee, listen. What day is it? What's the date?'

'Don't you know? I've forgotten, but I know for sure that I'm Friday's child. Charlie said it was Easter.'

'Do you know where you are?'

'Slightly all over the place. About halfway through, I should think.'

'What's your name?'

'Will, this is you, isn't it? You're not just a recording?'

'Georgina, while you've got some charge, may I suggest you say goodbye to me? Telephone 999? Get yourself to casualty.'

'The NHS! Yes, thank goodness we've still got the NHS! But is it that bad? I'm not physically hurt. Emotionally, yes, a bit.'

'Or just go back to bed and don't do anything. Don't do anything at all, can you manage that? Keep very still.'

'No, no, no, that doesn't work, I tried it before. You have to eat and drink, you see. And you have to go to the loo too. Can't be avoided. Even if there's a rat. You do have to be comfortable. Unless you're dead of course. Yes, then you don't have to do anything any more. Oh, what a relief! Like Mum and Dad, they're all right now aren't they?'

'Yes.' Will sounded serious. 'Yes. Gee, I think you need somebody to be with you. Shall I phone Kevin? Or Jim? Or a friend? Sheelah?'

'No, no, definitely, not Kevin, or Jim, or Sheelah.'

'What about Charlie?'

'Not the children, no, that wouldn't be fair. I am the parent. I'll always be their mother, won't I, whatever happens?'

'Look, can you just pay attention for a second? I'm going to say goodbye and come on the next plane, OK? I'll be there as soon as I can.'

'It's not good for the planet, Will. Your footprint must be gigantic.'

'Just hang on. Listen to some nice music or something? I'll phone you back and let you know what sort of time I'll be there. And I'll be contactable as long as I'm not in the air.'

'Righto.'

'And Georgina. Georgina. I'm so sorry if I've done anything to make it worse.'

'Have you? I hope not.'

'Call someone local if you can think of anyone.'

Georgie couldn't shore up the feelings any more. She held the phone away from her mouth to prevent Will from hearing, for so long that the charge ran out. Weird hollow dry sobs emerged from her chest, unrefreshed by tears.

He says listen to music. That's my singing or the cello then.

In the house on Colley's acre, Molly's mother so deceived, so deceived, sowed a seed! Buried there her daughter Molly. Buried there. Buried with.

Buried for her daughter Molly. All a golden girl could grieve. A golden girl could grieve.

All a golden girl could need. Pearls and jewels gold and silver, nothing could the girl restore.

Pearls.

He says call someone local if I can think of anyone.

She began to recharge the phone but gave up as her hand and wrist and arm were too tired and too much in pain.

The shower was dribbly and unclean and punishingly cold. But it invigorated her, reminding her that she was sensible. Her hands looked OK once they were dry, just a little red and shiny where the skin had peeled, but not so that anyone would notice. 'Thank goodness I didn't burn myself into the bargain,' she cackled. She dressed herself with shaking limbs, ignoring the devastation around her, stopping her ears and eyes against the ghosts, the memories, the carbon, the shit.

She left it all behind, walked out into a crisp grey morning, and found herself knocking on Eileen's door.

Eileen was wide awake, and finely dressed. 'What a lovely surprise,' she chimed.

'It's rather early?' Georgie said tentatively.

'Yes, well, I'm always up and about before other people,' Eileen reassured her. 'It's age, you know. Do come in.'

Georgie entered. She wanted to say thank you, but the words dried in her throat.

'Can I get you some tea?'

Georgie nodded, again not daring to speak in case her voice sounded unusual – it might express the disproportionate gratitude she felt. Tea! Tea! Tea was exactly what she needed. How kind Eileen was! How kind strangers are! She waited on the sofa, wondering whether or not to remove her coat, and was taking it off as Eileen returned with a tray. She thought of offering to help too late to do anything about it.

'You seem a little anxious. Are you all right?' Eileen said, as she handed her a cup and offered her a biscuit.

'I am a little anxious, yes.' The rattling of the spoon in her saucer illustrated the fact. 'I'm waiting for my brother to come. I seem to be breathing too much.'

Eileen nodded gently, seeming to consider her next words

with care, and regarding Georgie with a soft light of intelligence in her eyes, which was in itself reassuring.

'Forgive my asking, but are you going through the menopause yet?'

Georgie nodded.

'Oh that's it then. Poor you. I had an awful time of it, and women don't talk much do they, about their ailments?'

Georgie shook her head.

'So you can feel rather alone. I'd have taken HTM if it had been available at the time. I truly thought I was going mad.'

Georgie questioned with her forehead, feeling it twitching out of control, and her jaw clamping uncomfortably shut.

'Oh yes, one minute I would think that everything in the world relied upon me, and the next I would feel that I hardly existed at all. And then you know, it's all such a relief! I've been a lot happier without any hormones and that's the honest truth. Many women are. They do control one so.'

Georgie gulped down her dry mouth. She forced herself to speak, to explain exactly why she was there, which was only fair. It came out in an outlandish half-swallowed gravelly voice.

'I'm afraid that I'm going to die.'

'I'll tell you a secret,' Eileen lowered her voice and leant forward with a wicked twinkle in her eye. 'You *are* going to die.'

Her humour was a benediction. Georgie sniggered un-controllably.

'I'm sorry, I couldn't resist it. You're not going to die yet dear, you look very viable. And you'll be ready when the time comes.'

'I don't, I don't, I don't know,' Georgie stuttered. 'I don't think my mum was ready.'

A distant look came into Eileen's eyes. 'I hadn't seen her for a while.'

'Or Dad,' Georgie went on. 'Or anyone. Babies die. They're not ready, are they?'

Eileen shook her head, pensively. 'Your mother believed in

God, didn't she? That's a great comfort. It's a pity we've lost all that.'

Georgie put down the cup she hadn't yet managed to drink from and began to groan helplessly, exhaustedly, as Eileen edged closer and awkwardly, but kindly, took one of Georgie's hands in both of her own.

'It's a very good thing to cry, I think. We used to bottle it up and it didn't do anybody any good. There, there. You're all right. You're going to be all right.'

'It's the children!' Georgie choked, hoarse, and struggling.

'We're all children, at heart, I think. We're all just children in many ways.' Eileen stroked Georgie's hand. 'Or maybe I can't help thinking that because most people are so much younger than I am.'

Georgie responded to Eileen's frail touch. Now she was being listened to, now she was in the role of someone 'so much younger', her words tumbled out in a breathless rushing high-pitched panicky torrent, while Eileen simply waited, quietly nodding now and again.

'We've done the living and they'll have to do the paying! There's nothing left for them. We've used it up. Not you. Us. We've turned everything into plastic toys, and screens that are sharper than real life but they aren't going to work when the lights go out or the software's too old, because everything's going to shit, or worse, at least shit rots except for the drugs, but the sewers are already overflowing.' Eileen nodded. 'You can't keep the lid on it any more, can you? If it doesn't come up through the floor it's going to fall in through the ceiling. We can't go on like this. No, we can't go on, because what's going to happen when the numbers crash and everyone finds out that money isn't real? There's not enough food, it's not going to last, it's a great big empty hole of debt and it makes people fight, but what d'you expect if you can't even make peace with your own brother? Because debt turns people into slaves. It turns people into bones. What about China? What about India? We've always had slaves – without slaves, no sugar, and sugar gives you cancer. The world's got cancer, Eileen. We've given it cancer. There's too much carbon dioxide. The whole thing's going to die. The whole thing! Except some weird little sulphur-breathing bacteria under a rock somewhere. D'you think another Shakespeare or Bach or Vermeer will evolve out of that?' Georgie was sobbing and sniffing, and tears at last were spilling from her eyes. 'It's the children. All the lost children. Everything's gone East. War. Slavery. Pollution.'

Georgie released her hand from Eileen's and hugged herself, and Eileen put an arm round her shoulders, quietly waiting until she came to the end of it. Then she patted Georgie's arm and stood up, with a reassuring observation.

'Well, there's no need to worry about China and India. My granddaughter's a perfect little mother.' She disappeared and returned with a wad of paper hankies. 'Maybe there is no God,' she said, in a tone of uncomplicated practicality, 'But we must at least have faith in mothers.' Georgie had thought she was going to say 'faith in money'.

Her further kindness brought on a fresh bout of distress, this time wordless, but eventually Georgie recovered enough to resume the sort of conversation where you take turns. They talked about lighter things for a while – the superior taste of Eileen's tea, the expected rainfall come summer, the regularity and efficiency of Clifton's recycling service. By the end of her visit, Georgie was amazed to realise that she did feel better for crying, and her angst wasn't so bad now she'd owned up to it and shared it. She assured Eileen that she'd helped enormously – was copious in her gratitude.

As she was shown to the door, she saw that Eileen was walking with a pronounced limp and much more slowly than on her previous visit. Georgie had been so caught up in her own chaotic mentations that she hadn't noticed. She drew breath to say something about it – to ask after Eileen's health, to show sympathy or concern – but was deterred by the expression of determined gaiety on Eileen's face. She was reminded of the phrase: 'women don't talk much about their ailments', and wondered if in Eileen's case she preferred it that way. She told herself that the encounter had cheered them both, rather as it sometimes cheered her if Joni or Charlie needed help; but then she wondered who was mothering Eileen? She decided she must come again with flowers next time, and send a card from time to time, before it was too late.

By the time Will arrived, her crisis was over and she was wondering if it was lunchtime. She'd been sitting hugging herself, in the cleanest driest part of the flat, she didn't know for how many hours, after gathering a little pile of what had fallen through the ceiling. She greeted him joyously, and their embrace was prolonged, several seconds of relief that they were both still in the world.

'I was worried,' Will said earnestly, studying her face.

'I know, but you didn't need to be. I'm really glad you're here, though.'

'It reminded me of – '

'I know, but that was very different. I was,' Georgie searched her mind for the word, 'puerperal.'

'I thought it might be similar.'

'Even if it was, you never need to worry about me doing anything silly, Will. It's the opposite, I'm scared to death of dying.'

'Oh, before I forget.' Will released her, fumbled with his briefcase, and took out a piece of paper. 'Renée thought you'd enjoy this.' He handed her an expressive wax crayon drawing of a hideous face. 'Henri drew it for you.'

She exclaimed, in surprise and delight. 'Is it me?'

'Mrs Twit,' he explained, laughing as though she'd been highly witty.

'I love it.' She held it to her chest. 'Come on, come in.'

Will followed her down the corridor. Georgie resumed her little patch on the floor while Will looked around, gobsmacked and desolate, at the soggy piles of charred remains, the mess of half-opened boxes, and the hole in the ceiling.

'What's been happening?'

'Nothing much. I've been on my own, but I didn't feel alone.'

'You had a fire. You put it out. Well done.'

'The electricity stopped. And the gas. And the money and the petrol and the water.'

Will groaned. 'I'm sorry. The gas and the leccy are my fault. I thought we'd be finished here so I wound them up. It slipped my mind.' He tutted, annoyed with himself. 'And what's this about pearls and whispering trees?'

Georgie showed him a handful of the droplets that had fallen through the ceiling. 'They felt like pearls.'

'Lead shot,' Will said.

'They came through that.'

Will examined the edges of the hole. 'That's interesting. They're actually formed by gravity, so it's quite,' he grunted and rested back on his heels, 'in their nature to fall. A Bristol invention, you know.'

'And there were other things up there. Pencils and pencil sharpeners and coins and things. It's amazing what gets in. It's like a sofa.'

'Ah. Well I used to post things into the sofa on purpose. Perhaps it's a boy thing. So a little boy lived up there and found a hole. It's not that strange.'

'What about this one, though?' Georgie showed him another of the objects from her cache: an inch and a half of flat engraved tin soldier, on a little stand. Some of its red paint had come off. It was twisted.

'That certainly looks interesting. Rather Hans Christian Andersen, don't you think?'

'I think it's older. It looks sort of naïve.'

'And the trees whispered? And something about bones?'

Georgie showed him the bones she had saved and cleaned and dried.

'I thought that might be a baby's arm bone. It looks like a baby's arm.'

'It's a chicken leg.'

'Yes. I'm awake but I'm so very very tired, Will. I've been seeing things, hearing things. Look, this is the Frieda file. They're all Frieda, aren't they? But she starts off as Georgina May.'

She passed him the folder and Will, still standing, leafed through the photographs, looking serious and sad.

'There are so many more of me than I realised,' Georgie said.

'Georgina, I don't want to hear that kind of talk. There's only one of you.'

'But do you agree? She's our sister?'

Will took the file into the kitchen and sat down at the table, carefully studying the pictures, reading the documents, thinking. He looked as if he were doing lawyer's work. He said nothing, but Georgie gradually became aware that he was weeping, silently and without moving. He was staring at the leaflet, at the self-conscious uniformed children, who were smiling, but with taut brows and eyes that judged. Oh yes, a year or two in a place like that could fuck you up for life.

She set about making tea, sensing he'd rather be strong than comforted, but then she walked over and put her arm round him, in Eileen's fashion. It was a brave unusual thing to do. Crying simply wasn't *done*, not if you were an adult, not if you were family. So responding wasn't done either. To comfort was to embarrass, because to cry was to admit defeat, to concede, to lose. She had never seen him in so vulnerable a state, even at the funerals. She could feel him sobbing, making no sound.

Eventually the shaking stopped, and he regained his composure. He took a deep breath, and blotted his face with his own handkerchief. 'It's a long time since I've cracked up like that, Gee,' he said, as though to excuse himself for being out of practice, making light of it.

Georgie gave his hand a sympathetic squeeze. 'What a cutie she was, wasn't she?' she said, touching the photographs he'd spread out on the kitchen table. 'Should we look for her? But women get lost in the records; they change their names.'

Will whimpered. 'I've already looked. I found a Frieda

Lehmann who'd lived in Bonn. She was lost in the Boxing Day tsunami. 2004.'

'Oh.' Georgie's heart sank. 'Is it a common name?'

'She wrote for a travel publisher.'

That did seem apposite, for the girl with the tourist badges all over her rucksack.

'Why didn't you tell me?' Georgie said, regretting her slightly whiny voice. He never tells me anything, she thought.

Will shrugged. 'I thought it was better to forget about it. Let it go. It might not have been her.'

'No. Did you look for Mina?'

'I didn't know about her did I?'

Except that I told you, Georgie thought. 'She'd be thirty-odd. No way will she be Mina Lehmann. Frieda might have married, then Mina might have married.'

'Or died.'

'We haven't a hope of finding her.'

'No.'

'What if Charlie meets her and falls in love with her?'

Will tutted, as if it were a perfectly contemptible suggestion. 'First cousins are OK anyway, aren't they, just about?'

'She's a bit more than that though, isn't she? More of a double first.'

'I've told you I'm not the child's father Gee! At least give me credit for that!' He grimaced, as though experiencing the aftertaste of some nauseating medicine. 'It was a long time ago,' he insisted. 'It's dead and buried. How was I to know, anyhow? I was innocent.'

Georgie pressed her lips together, as if to say: That's rubbish, and even if it's an absolutely horrible thing to confront, it's not quite dead or buried, and we have to face it. Will looked away, embarrassed and flustered. Eventually he explained.

'I was literally innocent. Inexperienced.'

His cheeks were glowing a faint pink she knew of old. It convinced her, but the alternative theory was even worse.

'If I'd had conjugal relations with her I'd have had a fighting chance of forgetting her,' he added, with a dry laugh. 'But thank God, eh?'

He seemed to have forgotten his accusations of their father. Georgie didn't know how to mention it.

'Thank God,' he repeated, looking rather sick.

'Hang on,' she said, 'Come and see some other things I found.'

She ushered him back into the hall to find the file of Frieda's thank-you letters, which had survived the inferno because they'd been out of Keep and carelessly left somewhere in the kitchen while it was raging. She handed the collection to Will, and as he read she watched his expression change minutely through a miscellany of negative emotions, by turns shocked, piteous, helpless, outraged.

'You know I never got these,' he said, in self-defence, thoroughly shaken.

'So why did she write them to *you*? And thank you.'

He sighed and bowed his head, as though he were staring into a fathomless hole. Georgie waited silently. When he looked up again, it was with jaded eyes.

'I promised I would help. I would have helped.'

'How on earth?'

'She was going to have an abortion. I argued against.'

'Oh, Will.'

'I was an idiot.'

'You were kind.'

'She inspired me to be kind.'

'Incredibly kind. It wasn't in your interest, even.'

'In a way it was. Some idea about rescuing her, about honour. The knight in shining armour.' He shrugged, ashamed. 'Something about pleasing Mummy?'

He looked down and read again, thinking. 'But who opened them? Dad? Who sent her money? Why? Because he knew who they were from?' He still wasn't twigging to the abominable idea that Georgie had been trying to sleep on for several days. She must get it into the open air; it was festering and mouldy in the dark cell of her mind.

'The point is, Will, we don't know when they got all those photographs of Frieda, do we?' She took a deep breath and pressed both hands against her cheeks, as though to squeeze out the words, and they came out in a strangled monotone. 'We don't know if they knew who she was at the time. When she was here. When, as you say, Daddy followed her everywhere, and as I say, Mummy followed her everywhere.'

Her emphasis had an effect. Horror now dawned on Will's face. Instantly he quashed the idea, shaking his head once and firmly. 'No. You said yourself it was fatherly love.'

'Yes. And you said it wasn't.'

'Why shouldn't he send money to his daughter? For his granddaughter? Or he might have suspected me? He must have done. Oh shit. He suspected me. He was protecting me.'

Georgie gave him a blank look, indicating that she knew no more than he did.

'Oh God, what did he mean "we all did our best in the circumstances". In the letter. In the *circumstances*?'

At last the full horribleness of the worst possible scenario percolated into Will's understanding, with all its upsetting and unpleasant implications and ramifications.

'Well, how can we know?' he cried.

Georgie replied calmly. 'We have to go through the boxes. What's left of them. We have to read all the letters and go through every bloody bit of paper there is. Or else we just try and forget about it and hope for the best?'

'This just isn't fair!'

'I know, it absolutely is not.'

'My vote is that we look for evidence.' Will knelt down amongst the letters Georgie had just disturbed and began to scan them, shuffling through hopelessly with the flat of his hand.

'My vote is that we let it go,' she said, glumly watching his efforts. 'It won't be the first time in human history will it? Nobody's fault. Best left. I want to go home, Will. I want you to put me on a train and sort out the rest of the mess without me. I just want to go home now, what there is of home. I want to sleep and eat and watch the grass grow. I've done my fair share haven't I?'

Will didn't answer. His silence exacerbated the irony of her question, further mocked by the sheer chaos surrounding them, which she supposed she had single-handedly created.

He paused in his frantic searching, looking up at her as though he were a penitent begging for mercy. 'What about Frieda? D'you think Frieda knew we were her family? Whether or not Mum and Dad knew?' He stood up – a sleuth now, with a mission, prepared to treat the case objectively and from all angles.

'I refuse to believe that,' Georgie said vehemently, though it had occurred to her too. Something in the nature of a confession was hovering uncertainly in her mouth. She felt herself breathing too fast again, as though her lungs were urging her to speak whether or not she wished to. So much had been spilled already, she might as well.

Slowly and deliberately she formed the words. 'She told me she loved me, Will.' The revelation seemed to have no effect. 'As if she meant, you know, IN love.'

His expression said 'Really?'

She nodded.

'Me too,' he admitted, in discomfort. 'Oh. I don't like this. Oh Gee, it's not nice is it? Thank God, I didn't...'

Georgie shook her head. She must have betrayed something in her manner of shaking it. She must have looked guilty or upset.

'What's the matter?' he said. 'You didn't feel the same?'

'No.'

'You bloody did. Oh God, it gets worse.'

'No!' Georgie screamed. 'Not like that!' Her strident exclamation seemed to echo in the pause. She began to laugh hysterically, at the sound of her own voice ringing in her ears. Will didn't share in the joke. 'But somehow,' she admitted as she recovered herself. 'Yes. Somehow I did.'

'She captured each one of us, then. Like some titanic...' He looked up at the hole in the ceiling, mulling. 'Spider! No that's not it. One of the big cats. A jaguar!'

'That's not it either,' Georgie interrupted. 'She was more hunted than hunting, surely. But always out of reach.'

'She *knew* me, that's what it was. Inside out. What I wanted and that I was – ' he drew a deep breath, ' – splendid! Or something.'

'But what did *she* want?'

'As though she had a direct route.' He knocked against his ribs with his fist. 'To my core. And when she looked at me, nobody else and nothing else mattered. What a trick. What a predator.' His brow was interrogative, but his mouth tightened in resignation. 'You know, Gee, it's awful to admit it, but nobody ever did that to me again. I looked for it. I never found it.'

Georgie understood. It was absurd, but she felt a touch resentful on hearing him articulate her own experience, as if he'd deprived her of it. It was a bit of a shame to discover that the first and last person to have found her so special had waltzed around finding everyone special.

'I hated her, though, at first,' she said. 'She stole all the attention. Not that I had any to steal – from anyone in the family. Mum. Dad. You. Well, maybe Dad. In an expecting-nothing-less-than-coming-top kind of way.'

It was an important subject and something they might resolve and mend, she felt, but she was still getting no attention. Will had excused himself with a gesture and gone into the bathroom. He pulled the light string and sighed because it didn't work.

'Oh,' Georgie said, 'I forgot to mention, there's an animal in the loo.'

'An animal?'

'I didn't really look properly. A rat. Yes. A rat. I think it is probably a rat. In the loo. You can't use it.'

With a look of dazed and blank bewilderment, he walked pat her and let himself outside into the garden.

'Go ahead! Liquid compost isn't it?' Georgie shouted after him. 'Good for the plants!'

As he came back and was refastening the French windows

she saw that he was laughing, at first a light chuckle, developing into explosions of helpless mirth.

'Oh Georgina! My sister. My little sister. What an appalling mess.' He opened his arms and hugged her.

It was lovely to feel his laughter in her arms. It reminded her of a game they used to play as children, with friends and Maureen and sometimes Larry included. 'What would life have been like with two sisters, I wonder?' he said, quietly. 'Very different I should think. If we'd grown up with an older sib?'

They used to sometimes lie in a circle on the floor, with each person's head resting on another's belly. If one laughed, as one always did, it made another laugh to feel their head jigging up and down. They called it Giggling Tummies. Everybody would catch the infection.

'Right,' he said, as they parted. 'I think the rat's the priority, don't you? Rubber gloves. Bleach. Newspaper. Plastic bag.'

He walked into the bathroom, again pulling the string, again sighing, and then again, laughing.

'And would you bring me a candle, please, I want to see what I'm doing. And don't set fire to anything.'

He shifted the boxes from the loo lid and carried them out of the bathroom, still furiously giggling, so much so that the top one wobbled, tumbled from his arms and opened, spilling paper. Georgie rescued the paper and righted the box, while Will, still chuckling under his breath, searched for a reasonably non-squalid parking space for the other one. Georgie wasn't thinking about it, she was thinking about all the things she needed to fetch, the rubber gloves and bleach and newspaper and plastic bag, but something about its appearance attracted her attention, and made her read. It was the angular continental handwriting, the Salzburg address.

She took it with her into the kitchen and read by the light of the window.

Eventually Will followed her in. 'Yes. It's a rat. Or was. Maybe the rain was too much for the sewers.' He was impatient to deal with it. 'What's up?'

'It's right here,' she said, at last. 'Here. Under our noses.'

Königstrasse 8, den 22. September 1954
Lieber Lawrence

I am finally sure this will reach you and with confidence relate the reason for writing. We found track of you after many years, by chance, from your letter to Time magazine. I know it is you from the style and the opinion. You remember we disagreed on this point – I admit I was wrong!

The publisher has kindly agreed to forward this to you.

We thank you every day in our prayers, dear Lawrence. Without you we would not have lived, and we can never forget how you cared for our son, when we could not.

In 1947 I was fortunate to be invited to England to speak at a Quaker conference on healing and reconciliation. I hoped to find you on that trip from what you had told to us. I knew only of your lodging in Stratford, and your daughter in Warwick. So I found your daughter! But the people at the orphanage would not help me to find you.

This will be a surprise. I hope it will be a pleasant one.

We decided to adopt her. We have raised your daughter as our own in the bosom of our family, with Hans and another, our daughter Angela. We have named her Elfrieda.

If you see her mother again, (did you take our advice!) you may say that her little girl is well and happy and clever and good. You will see from the photograph, she is even pretty. We would wished for your permission, but did not know even that you lived.

We planned to go to America, but, as you see, remained in Salzburg. There was much work for us here.

If you do not reply, we will make no further attempt, and we understand your reticence. We do not let her know her true parentage, for fear she may feel less loved or special to us than her brother and sister.

May God bless you always. It is a miracle that you survived.

Many many many thanks to you

Karl and Mariya

LET GO

'It's ridiculous,' Georgie said. 'Just because someone put their willy in you doesn't make you a different person, does it?'

'It depends,' said Fi.

'Well I'm no different. Except he keeps annoying me now.' She wrinkled her nose and Fi looked compassionate.

They were sunbathing in the rec, right up at the edge of the river opposite the theatre, on a tablecloth laid over brown scratchy grass. It was swelteringly hot. The air was oppressive and thick. Bottles of coke were warming in the girls' matching tapestry shoulder bags. Fi was staring at the sky through screwed lids. She popped her lips to shoo off a ladybird.

'Ladybird ladybird fly away home, your house is on fire, your children are gone.'

'Ladybirds fuck off!' Georgie added, brushing another from her arm. 'Where are you going for your hols?'

'St Tropez,' Fi said, with a mixture of boredom and shame. 'Daddy likes it because everyone goes topless. Mummy likes shopping and drinking gin and tonic on people's boats.'

'Do you go topless?'

'Everybody does.'

Georgie sneezed. 'Whoo! It's so hot. Let's get some shade.'

They moved to a spot under the nearest willow, close to the mud-slaked edge of the river where the grass was longer and less dead. While Fi arranged herself on the rumpled cloth, Georgie sat cross-legged, running her hand through the grass in search of a suitable blade.

'So you've done it too then?'

'Ages ago.'

'Who with?'

Fi smiled and closed her eyes.

'Come on! Who conjugated you?' Georgie plucked the

tallest blade, squeaked out its thin pale stalk and crushed its sweetness between her teeth.

'Rupert Madesley.'

'Gosh. Why didn't you tell us?'

Fi shrugged.

'Did you love him?'

'Not really.'

'Did he love you?'

'Not really.'

'Do you still, then?'

'Conjugate? Sometimes. Not with him, though.'

'Isn't it dangerous? What if you got pregnant?'

'I won't.' Fi sat up and rummaged through her bag, drawing out a foil packet marked with the days of the week which she showed to Georgie who examined it and tossed it carelessly back, as if it were beneath her interest.

'I think it's pointless if you're not in love.'

Fi shrugged.

'Ages ago? So you were fifteen. It was against the law. Technically it was rape.'

Fi turned over. 'Well, I won't tell on him. No-one knows except you.'

'Who is it now, though? Come on, I've told you mine.'

Fi's tanned shoulders and slim back betrayed nothing.

'Oh well. What's done is done, it cannot be undone. Complete disappointment as far as I'm concerned.' Georgie spat out the grass and threw it onto the brown water, where it floated, motionless. 'Are you looking forward to next term?'

'Not really. I won't see you much, will I, if you're doing Science?'

'Guess what? This is a secret. I'm not doing Science. I made a complete bish of the 'O's, and I've had enough of school. I'm not doing anything. I'm going.'

'Rubbish. You always say that and then you come top. You're going to be a doctor.'

'No, this time it's true. The first exams that mean anything and

I've cocked up.' Fi turned round and sat up. 'I've cocked up in every way,' Georgie added, flickering her eyebrows suggestively. They giggled. 'Frieda's taking me. It's all sussed out.'

'Frieda? I thought you hated her.'

'No, no. I like her.' She shrugged her shoulders in false innocence. 'What made you think that?'

'I still think she's got a thing about your dad.'

'How could anyone have a thing about my dad?' Georgie lowered her voice as a group of tourists took up residence a few feet behind them to capture their own unique view of the theatre and the river and the weeping willows. 'What's the opposite to cradle-snatching?'

'Graverobbing?'

'Necrophilia.'

Fi pretended to vomit.

'Exactly. I think she's more into Will, if you want my opinion.'

'Will's into her.'

Georgie picked another blade of grass and focused on pulling its stalk cleanly from its sheath. It required exactly the right amount of grip. 'She's free. She prefers to be free. And that's what I want to be.'

'Ooh, look! Talk of the devil.'

Sure enough Frieda was ambling towards them, peeping over her sunglasses with her usual generous smile. 'Your mother said to find you here,' she called as she approached. 'You worship the shade?'

'It's too hot. We can't bear it, can we Fi?'

Fi made a space for her on the table cloth and she knelt down.

'I thought it was supposed to be all the time raining in England. You made a good summer for me, didn't you?'

She took off her shirt and used it to wipe the sweat from her face and neck.

'It's beastly!' said Georgie. 'I can't bear it. It's so bloody hot and humid, I feel like jumping in the river.'

Frieda needed no more than a hint. She threw off her

flip-flops immediately, wriggled out of her shorts, and strode into the water, into the mud, shrieking with laughter. Georgie loved it – the impulsiveness and sheer heroic bravery.

'Come on Fi, let's go in too!'

'What's it like?' Fi shouted.

'Cool!' Frieda pushed her hands through the water and sprayed it around her in sparkling festoons, threatening to wet the girls on the bank.

Georgie stripped down to her underwear and took a step towards the edge.

'Be a sport!' she shouted at Fi, but then she felt her feet sinking into mud of a horrible consistency and weeds wrapping round her ankles and little stones fiddling between her toes.

'Eeurgh! It's horrible!' she screeched. Frieda was now swimming.

'Come out! Come out!' someone was shouting at them from the side. 'It's not safe!'

Frieda and Georgie looked at each other and burst into giggles. Georgie flopped forwards. She let the water swirl around her, finding the hot cracks in her body as she made doggy paddling progress, still snorting with laughter. It was cool but smelt nasty, and the top was scummed with gungy leaves and dead insects. The level was so low her hands could touch the bottom. She felt like a hippo. 'Mud, mud, glorious mud!' she shouted, staggering to regain a foothold. 'It's revolting. I'm getting out.'

'Poo! It's rank,' shouted Fi, jolting away from Georgie as she hoofed up the bank. She whipped the table cloth out of reach, helpless with laughter.

'Oh come on!'

'No, no, you stink!' Fi shouted back, bending over in spasms of hilarity.

There's a peculiar atmosphere. Maureen is looking at a photograph album. She smiles falsely at Georgie and Frieda as they come in, not seeming to notice their scruffy smeared appearance. They hear a door slamming upstairs.

'We've inherited some things,' she says cheerily. 'Look, there's Aunt Ruby and her little brothers.'

The sound of Larry shouting.

'They died in the Great War, so sad to see them playing innocently on the beach.'

Then Will. Georgie can't make it out. Something about the car. Something about photographs.

There's a noise of footsteps coming downstairs and then the front door slams. Maureen pays extra attention to the pages in the album.

'William's upset with Daddy,' she says eventually.

Larry comes in, looking lost and sad and pathetic in his kaftan and beard. He nods at Maureen and she closes the album and follows him into the kitchen where they murmur for a while. Frieda looks at Georgie, concerned and enquiring. Georgie shrugs.

A few moments later Maureen emerges, followed by Larry. 'We're going for a walk,' she says, as if it's a normal ordinary usual afternoon expedition. 'You two had better get clean, hadn't you?'

It couldn't all have happened on the same day, could it? The day they got muddy. The day Larry and Will had a horrible row. The day Maureen showed her Aunt Ruby's photographs. The day before it rained. She can't remember anything in the right order.

'We mustn't use too much.' Georgie let Frieda go first. She emerged from the bathroom in minutes, and quickly disappeared. Georgie tried to be as efficient. With lemony soap and little squirts of precious warm water she cleansed the Avon slime from her skin, wrapped herself in a towel and went downstairs to find Frieda already dry and dressed with a glass of something alcoholic waiting for her.

'Is this naughty for us?'

'Yes!' Georgie exclaimed brightly, gleefully accepting a drink. 'Chin chin!'

She took a swig. Ice knocked against her teeth. 'Mmm! What's in it?'

'Vodka and lime juice.'

'We deserve it for,' Georgie hesitated, smiling. ' I can't think of anything. Let's drink to travel and experience!'

They clinked glasses.

'To loving and living!' Clink. Sip.

'To not going to university!' Clink. Sip.

'To today!'

'Heute!' shouted Georgie in agreement.

Frieda just raised her eyebrows, and stared at Georgie over the edge of her own glass. She put it down, and with a hand on each side of Georgie's face, she moved her wet hair away, cocking her head, biting her lower lip, as if she were imagining a new haircut, judging whether or not it would suit her. She ran her fingers down Georgie's cheek and across her mouth. 'Du weisst nicht dass du schöne bist. Schwester. Ich liebe dich,' she said.

Because it felt nice Georgie let it happen. She felt Frieda's gentle hands wondering down over her shoulders followed by kisses. She closed her eyes. The towel fell open. Kisses landed on her everywhere, on her arms and breasts and stomach. Such a lightness and sensitivity. Then Frieda's mouth was on her own, pouting and sensuous.

Frieda took her hand, leading her fingers towards moisture and warmth. Georgie pulled away.

'I like boys,' she whispered, breathless. 'I'm sorry.'

Abashed and foolish she picked up the towel and ran upstairs, blocking out the vision of Frieda's bewildered, hurt face. She washed her hands in drips and dribbles. She dressed and sat on her bed, not knowing what to do. Something made her put the cello away.

*

You could tell it was coming; the air smelt of metal and everything went quiet. Clouds gathered and glowered, at first a thin layer, building through the evening to a heavy opaque blanket which cast a dark glare over the world. It started with a light spattering. Is that rain? excited voices whispered. Can it be rain at last? Big fat drops splashed down on the terrace and the mossy pool, on all that had taken up residence in the garden, cushions and cloths and chairs and books and magazines. It came and it came and it came, soddening everything, making channels which ran down beside the concrete tiles and eddied into the drains, mixing with a top layer of dry soil splattering everything brown. Thunder and lightning came too – distantly rumbling at first, then bursting out of the counted pauses in terrifying cracks.

Georgie stood by the window staring through blurred glass at the flashing sky and the creaking shuddering branches of her silver birch. Rain hissed and pattered on the summerhouse roof.

Next morning Maureen knocked on her door.

'You don't know what's happened to Frieda do you?'

Georgie shook her head, instantly attacked by guilt. 'No?'

'She's gone.'

The bedroom was empty, the bed made. Nothing of her was left. No flip-flops or shorts or little bottles of make-up. No rucksack. No dog-eared German paperback by Thomas Mann. Only the faint smell of beauty and a rubber band tangled with fair hair.

She had gone without a word.

TREASURE THE MEMORY

With Will's help Georgie retrieved the car, filled it with petrol and completed her intended journey to the dump, and, after a day of tidying and sorting and drying, and a night in a hotel room insisted on by (and courtesy of) Will, she drove herself home to Salisbury where she was welcomed by the faint smell of cannabis and an atmosphere of intrigue between Charlie and Tania that resonated ominously with recently unravelled memories. But they'd cooked an Easter meal for her, plants were still alive, rent was brought up to date, and Georgie slept as well as she'd expected to in her daughter's room, surrounded by familiar pretty things.

It wasn't long before Tania had to leave, and coincidentally Charlie went back to Jim's, on a sudden frantic decision to apply to university to do History, and try harder to get some 'A' levels. He'd work more at Jim's because Jim nagged him more, he said, sparing Georgie's feelings. She understood. He was freer, at Jim's, to be a seventeen-year-old boy.

So Georgie was alone again for a few days. She got the cello refurbished and enjoyed practising, finding the tunes again gradually and by not trying too hard. In the same almost passive way, as though the music itself had conjured up the idea, she decided to have a certain conversation with Joni when she returned.

It was the end of May. A stunningly cloudless blue sky day. Bright summer light glinted and glanced through the windows, and the outside world was bathed in glory. Joni had announced herself in an email. *See you on Sun 29th, late afternoon, don't know what time. Don't worry about meeting me. I want to do the whole journey by myself!*

Georgie waited, not sure how they would behave towards each other after such a gap, too excited to settle down to anything, but tied to the house because she didn't want to be out when Joni arrived. She looked at her mobile often, worried that something would go wrong at the last minute, to disappoint her or frighten her or ruin her world. She couldn't understand why Joni would send no further message. The simplest explanation, that nothing had gone wrong, didn't satisfy her, and she worried as a kind of duty, as if in the belief that worry itself had the power of preventing disaster.

When the moment came it was strangely ordinary. She heard the key in the lock, the creak of the front door and Joni's light steps in the hall. Georgie hardly had time to get up, and there was her daughter standing proudly before her, real and present, smiling, tanned, five months older, five months tireder, with longer, scruffier hair, in shorts, tee-shirt and flip-flops, weighed down by a gigantic rucksack.

'Darling! Well done!'

They hugged, and Georgie could smell the travelling on her – metallic and slightly musty.

'Oh how lovely to see you! You must be exhausted. How long did it take?'

'It's not too bad, I got some sleep on the plane. But I do need my bed! Can I go up?'

She kept her rucksack on as she trudged up the stairs, and Georgie followed, watching a plastic cup banging rhythmically against its straps.

'It was thirty-six hours altogether, but we stopped in Amsterdam.'

'Goodness. By the way, I hope you don't mind – I had to sleep in your bed while Charlie was home.'

Joni was beaming. 'Oh lovely! Everything is so clean and comfortable-looking. Thanks Mum.' She hesitated a moment, fully appreciating the familiar sight – the floral curtains and walls, the red oval rug, the pine furniture, neatly arranged with precious ornaments and books, dolls and stuffed toys, and everything warmed by soft evening light. Then she flopped down on the bed, eased off the rucksack and began to unpack it. 'I have a present for you from Mama Pacha. Come in, come in. Come and sit down.'

'Mama Pacha. I thought it was Machu Picchu?'

Joni laughed. 'No, Mama Pacha. Or Pachamama. It means Mother Earth. It's their most important deity and it should be everyone's in my opinion.'

The parcel was buried amongst crumpled clothes, which Joni apologetically swept off the bed so Georgie could sit. It was wrapped in brown paper and tied with string. Inside Georgie found a medley of irregular lumps – purple, yellow, orange and blue-black. 'Bulbs!' she exclaimed.

'Potatoes!' Joni corrected her, slightly abashed on Georgie's behalf. 'They have millions of varieties. I thought you could try planting them. Unless you just want to eat them.'

'Thank you, they're really beautiful! All the different colours! They're like jewels!' Georgie picked one up and admired it. 'How surprising that you were allowed to bring them home! Is it legal?'

'No.'

'Oh darling.'

'I didn't know.'

It's no defence, thought Georgie, but she didn't say so. She silently acknowledged her gratitude to whatever force had saved her child from discovery. Pachamama perhaps.

'Why is it illegal?' Joni complained. 'Because they're not McDonald's? If only Raleigh or whoever had brought back a few more there might not have been a famine in Ireland. If you have lots of different kinds they resist disease.'

Joni wriggled up the bed so she was half-lying, half-sitting.

'So did you have a good time?' Georgie asked.

'Amazing. I've so much to tell you.'

'Can I get you anything? A drink? Some supper?'

'I just want to talk for a bit.' Joni held out her hand and Georgie took it in both of her own. Peru was amazing, she said. Tourism was spoiling it but at least it brought in money. She'd been tipping well, too well at first, she'd had to cut it down and not compare everything to English money. She'd hiked from Choquequiraio to Machu Picchu, eleven days, she thought she was going to die, and guess what – there was a bit of it called 'Dead Woman's Pass,' partly the Inca trail but not the one that everyone goes on, which was amazing but actually quite disappointing because she already knew how amazing it was going to be. Not on a horse or a llama, no, the horses carried their packs and tents. Llamas were gorgeous, and alpacas. She saw men spinning too, it was hilarious, someone called them spinsters. The women weave stories into their patterns. Condors and snakes and llamas, amazing gorgeous colours, so bright but it's all done with herbs and cochineal, cochineal's an insect. The scenery was awesome. Some bits of it weren't very nice, she'd got altitude sickness and her feet swelled up like footballs and then it started raining and her jacket sprang a leak and she slipped on some ice it was so high up, but not to worry because the guides looked after her and the cut was healing and didn't hurt any more. The others drank coca tea for the altitude sickness but she didn't like it, had to spit it out. Her Spanish had really come on and she'd learnt some Quechan too, yes they still speak it but they use Spanish for things like fridge and television. She'd lost her phone. But there was no need to worry because it was only three days ago and there were plenty of internet cafés in Lima and she'd already uploaded most of the photographs and no, it wasn't insured, but it wouldn't run up a bill because she was on pay as you go, and anyway, hey it might benefit someone less privileged than she was. She'd stayed with a family in the mountains and helped build irrigation channels. She'd been in the Amazon forest. She'd taken Ayahuasca. It was all right, she was very careful about the people she was with. It was amazing. She saw a vision of what she was going to do with her life. She'd joined a protest march against gold mining in the valley.

'It's a terrible situation,' she said, as she gave in to a yawn. 'The mining must be stopped. It's ruining the environment, because all the poisonous waste goes into the ground water, and the money doesn't get to the poorest people. They're dependent on agriculture.'

'I suppose we all are ultimately.'

'And climate change is affecting them already – their seasons are all over the place and things don't grow right. These mining companies tear down the Amazon forest. We all need trees! We're not going to be able to breathe otherwise.'

Georgie's heart was swelling to bursting point with pride. She reserved any thoughts about the carbon cost of long-haul flights. The issue could be addressed some other time.

'I can't wait till my course starts. I'm so excited. There are so many things I want to do.'

'It's a great thing to know what you want to do.'

Joni stretched back, indulging in rest, gazing contentedly at her mother.

'Did you know? What you wanted to do?'

Georgie thought for a moment. She'd wanted to do hundreds of things, millions.

'I knew I wanted children.'

'Didn't you want a career?'

'I just wanted experience, as far as I remember. I wanted to travel too, and, you know, a bit of everything.'

'And you did?'

'Well. You can't do everything. I thought I might write something one day, if I could think of something to say, but I suppose everyone thinks that.'

'I hope you don't mind, Mum, but I might not have time to have a family.'

Georgie shrugged in an exaggerated fashion, trying to hide a moment of disappointment. There's plenty of time to change your mind, she thought. 'What was wrong with Sam, then?' she asked.

'He was on my case. Not very supportive, you know? About my ambitions. He was a bit of a control freak, actually, it turned out. I was better off without him. I wasn't alone; I met other people.'

Georgie nodded, dumbly, thinking how mature and sensible

her daughter had become, how she wished she had been so, and whether her own experience had anything to do with it.

'Mum?' Joni hesitated, as if searching for the tenderest way of expressing something painful.

'Yes?'

'You know you've always been with, like, creative types?'

'Yes?'

'Well. D'you think it's because you want to *be* creative?'

Oh. Georgie hadn't thought of that. It sounded possible.

'Why, Joni? Do you want to be creative? There's plenty of time to change your mind about what you want to do.'

Joni laughed affectionately. 'I'm talking about you, Mum, not me.'

Georgie was reminded of her conversation with Charlie. What do *you* want to do, he had said, not what do you want me to do.

'And you know how you're always with people who argue all the time?' Joni went on. Georgie nodded.

'Well, why don't you look for someone who agrees with you?'

Georgie laughed.

'Why did you split up with Kevin? He was all right.'

Georgie thought for a moment. 'He wouldn't acknowledge me on Facebook,' was the answer that came first to mind.

'You're kidding aren't you? You don't even go on Facebook.'

'That's one of the reasons I don't go on it. It was an insult – a virtual insult.'

'Not real in other words.'

'It was very real. It went deep. And the further I looked into it... His friends were all sorts of women with breasts.'

'Mum?'

'You know what I mean. Women I didn't know, and didn't know he knew. It made me feel sick. It made me look like an idiot.' Joni didn't seem to be persuaded so, without actually having to use the 'C' word, Georgie summoned up the phrase that always brought sympathy, knowing she was being wicked.

'After all I'd been through.'

Joni's brow crumpled.

'I don't care what anyone says about it,' Georgie went on, feeling a pang of guilt. 'I know I'm right.'

'It's love that matters, though?'

Georgie agreed. She studied her daughter's intelligent hazel eyes, whose honest, straightforward expression was a counterpoint to her slightly exotic beauty. This moment of intimacy was rare – an opportunity for the sharing of confidences. But Georgie decided that Joni was too tired and vulnerable to bear any difficult information. Joni looked suddenly downcast, as if in response.

'I'm sorry I was so horrible,' she said with a quick, embarrassed shrug.

Georgie wouldn't hear of it. 'Horrible? No. You could never be that.'

'I was a bit though. And I am sorry.'

'Forgotten and forgiven. Thank you. Now. I'm going to go and get us something to eat. Do you want a drink of anything first?'

'Yes please.' Joni yawned. 'I'd like some hot chocolate.'

By the time Georgie brought it up, Joni was asleep. She laid the mug quietly on the bedside table. She picked up the pile of dirty clothes and threw it in the washing basket, then fetched the duvet from her own room to lay over her sleeping child, staring as she used to when she was new born, in wonder and gratitude at the soft sound of her breathing.

Let me remember this moment forever.

A shaft of low light had turned her hair to gold. Her skin glowed with health and life. To think that this being – so complete, so individual, so complex, so unknowable, so gloriously vital – had somehow sprung from her own. The ordinary world was full of wonders. Mysteries and miracles. Some sort of magic had dissolved their discord and brought her safely home.

Even though she was asleep, she was smiling.

ONLY CONNECT

Joni wanted to help with the 'family piles', as Georgie now referred to her parents' flat and its abominable contents; so a fortnight after her return, they drove up to Bristol together in a capacious Volvo lent by Sheelah.

Georgie unlocked the front door in trepidation. It was only six weeks since she'd locked it, but the year had turned. It was summer now, light and optimistic, but indoors it was still gloomy. She tried the electricity. It worked. Will had sorted it.

The hall smelt odd, a strange mixture of burning and damp, fire and water. It was cold too. Joni wrinkled her nose.

'I warned you,' said Georgie. 'And here's the mess in all its... Oh, it's not as bad as I thought.'

'It's worse than I thought,' Joni laughed, shocked by the blackened walls, the black hole in the carpet, the loose bits of plaster still hanging from the ceiling.

Georgie explained the different groupings where they were identifiable. Joni's only point was that Think About Later needed to become Think About Now.

As an example, she considered the first object that came to hand. It was a file of drawings Georgie had put together. Joni knelt down and went through them one by one, laughing, and sighing. 'Oh, Charlie, how sweet!' and, 'Mum this is yours! Look at the writing. You were a little girl!' and, 'Here's one of mine! I remember doing this. Look at the glitter and the stars, all over the place. I remember thinking it was perfect!'

Georgie smiled indulgently. 'It *is* perfect.'

'I'm glad you didn't get this finished without me. I like looking at all this.'

'What should we do with it, then? Will suggested a big bonfire in the garden.'

'No!'

'I agree; how could he be so heartless?'

'Let's recycle it.'

Georgie slept where she had slept before, and Joni happily snuggled into her sleeping bag on the canvas and aluminium camp bed Frieda had slept on all those years ago. She had dealt with worse, she said, and preferred it to dusty old sofa cushions or mattresses; and whatever the flat was like it was more comfortable than being in a tent beside a glacier.

They spent a happy week, driving to the dump and the charity shops, sorting, chatting, reminiscing, laughing. They shopped and cooked together. Gradually they created space, and the place became more habitable.

Georgie phoned Will. It would be a good idea to get the flat in better shape, she agreed, but she'd like to be involved with the decisions. Charlie had applied to Bristol University. Perhaps, if he went there, he could live in the flat and let the spare rooms? Perhaps she could live there herself while the changes were being made, to oversee things? They could come to an arrangement. Will's and Renée's offer had been kind. With a mighty effort, she regretted her defensiveness and thanked them both for their generosity. It cost her nothing more than a brief tummy upset.

Joni thought they should buy one big filing cabinet for everything that wasn't going to leave. She designed a filing system and enjoyed putting things into their correct drawer and layer. She was more decisive than Georgie and more practical. As a starting point Georgie had divided Keep into Useful things and Sentimental things. But Joni divided it into Letters, Other documents, Photographs, Trinkets, Tools, Oddments – and there were subdivisions, chronological and alphabetical, so that the sentimental or useful things could be located.

They emptied the lobby before Joni would allow any further boxes to be opened. Her optimism and energy drove the process when Georgie's flagged; Georgie's would drive it if Joni's flagged.

She handed her a letter and its envelope. 'I don't know if I should be reading this. It's very expressive.'

Larry's handwriting.

23 December 1954
My Dear Maureen
I felt so miserable when you rang off, for there were so many things I had wanted to say and had felt unable to say even though they could have been said ever so simply. It was partly the thought of an operator listening in, more the thought that my mother was possibly listening – or at least hearing what I was saying. And there are some things that are very difficult to say to a disembodied voice. So I determined to write to you at the first moment; but I had to finish my game of chess; and since speaking to you had completely upset my equilibrium this took a long time and the game I should have won finished a draw with two solitary kings hurling defiance at one another across an empty board. And then I had to decorate a Christmas tree and then admire a cake and then supper and then bed. And this morning I had to trundle the vacuum cleaner round and then be sociable to my mother's guest and then lunch and then evening in the Cathedral – I have at last a few minutes to myself so that I can write and say what I wanted to say on the phone but didn't dare. And that is simply
I love you
I love you
I love you
I have been trying to think what I mean by I love you but I can't. It isn't just your lips and your breasts and your skin, it isn't just that I want to sleep with you – and lie awake with you too – though I do. I give it up. I must catch the post.
With all my love – darling – darling – darling
Larry x

Georgie concealed a surge of conflicting emotions, all tinged with sorrow. This was the source of her life, and Will's, and Frieda's; one 'I love you' for each of them.

'1954!' Joni said. 'It sounds so long ago to me.'

Georgie gasped.

'The date! The date! Oh Joni! I understand something! I understand something I didn't understand.'

Joni wasn't listening. She was shuffling distractedly through a cache of pocket leather diaries glancing at their front pages.

'It's why we're here. Frieda's father is why Will and I are here. His letter. Oh, never mind, there's too much to explain.'

'Diaries, Mum! May I read? This one's yours, look.1967!'

She held out a Letts Brownie diary, its pages warped and crammed with pencil.

'I don't suppose I had any terrible secrets at that age.'

Joni read the entries aloud, punctuating them with affection-ate laughter. *'Today I played hopscotch with Annabel. For tea we had spaghetti on toast. It did not rain. Today was cloudy. I won the ballet drawing competition. We had beef burgers and mash and peas. Today I got frightened in case there was a cyberman in the cupboard. Today it rained. We played kiss tag with Ian Golding and Timothy Wittingham. It was vastly adorable.'*

'I might have to censor the later ones, though,' Georgie said, taking over.

It suddenly occurred to Georgie as she leafed through this conscientious record of weather and meals, that writing and hoarding might be connected. To keep a journal was to keep the day, to salvage something from the many vanished hours. Nothing is lost if it is written about, every scrap of experience is material, and writing itself could be a hoard – a hoard of memories and ideas and conversations and descriptions, a preservation of the past by which you might extend a life. Reading a letter from her mother or father was like hearing them speak again. Just as to see a photograph was to see them again. They had not completely gone; a tiny slice of their light was captured, a lilt in their voices.

What this hoard required was an editor, she thought. That's what she must be, then; she and Joni must be its editors. She recalled Maureen's poem about tear-off slips, and her posthumous instruction: 'edit'.

'Another birth certificate,' Joni announced. 'It's you.'

She handed it to Georgie.

'Where did you find this?'

'With all these.' Joni showed her the box she'd been exploring. It was labelled *Special Things* in scarcely legible pencil, Maureen's handwriting. 'Wedged up behind the book shelves.'

'This isn't me. It's an aunt of yours who was adopted out.' Georgie pointed out the date and the surname on the certificate: 26 February 1946, Connor, Maureen's maiden name.

'The baby's name was changed to Frieda. We met her, actually. I'll show you photographs.'

'I didn't know I had an aunt.'

'Mmm. Nor did we.' Georgie wondered where to begin, and how to proceed. It would take time to put it all in the right order. 'I'll tell you about it another time,' she said, at once realising that her mother used to use the phrase whenever Georgie asked her about sex or God. An ominous promise.

She rummaged deeper in the box. Under layers of envelopes and papers she found a dark blue oval case, fastened with a metal clasp and stamped with initials too florid to be deciphered. Inside was an arrangement of red beaded jewellery in satin-lined wells, pendant earrings cut into pineapples, two bracelets and a necklace of four strands of beads, joined by a clasp on one side and a cameo of a woman's profile on the other. The fastenings appeared to be gold, faintly tarnished with grey.

'This might be worth a bit,' she said. 'It's coral.'

'Coral like in the ocean? Coral like the reefs that are disappearing?'

'Yes.'

'What a shame there's a strand missing,' Joni said. She was right. There were rings on the cameo and clasp for a fifth strand of beads. 'Was it your mum's? Whoever's it was must have been so cross when it broke.'

'Ah. Maybe that's why it's been overlooked – not so valuable after all. No, this'll be one of the Sutton things from Aunt Ruby. Grandma hardly inherited anything from her side.'

As Georgie was saying so, a recollection was forming in her mind, but so vaguely she couldn't capture it.

The thought almost crystallised when she was showing Joni the photographs of Frieda, and Joni was looking for the family traits Georgie hadn't recognised as a teenager. Suddenly Joni's eyes widened and she opened her mouth in surprise.

'She's wearing the missing bit!' she exclaimed.

'What d'you mean?'

'Look at her beads! It's like the missing bit of the necklace?'

Georgie needed her reading glasses to study more closely. The beads were indeed similar. Allowing for the Kodachrome effect, they were the same colour, perhaps a little paler, and were enhanced, as were the beads of the necklace, by two special-looking beads on either side; which on the necklace were pineapples, to match the earrings. There might be more information on the negative, she thought, if it could be found.

'They are similar,' she conceded. 'But there can't be a connection. What would the connection be? It's a coincidence.'

'Some coincidence. Are there lots of these kind of beads?'

'No, no, it can't be the same. Mum wouldn't have got Ruby's stuff until... It was almost the day Frieda left.'

'Dad doesn't believe in coincidence. There's a thing called serendipity. And what's that other one? Synchronicity.'

'Dad's not very scientific, is he? And none of us are very good at statistics. I found that out when I looked at all the breast cancer graphs. One in ten sounds worse than it is. And there's that thing about birthdays. In a room of twenty-three people there's a fifty-fifty chance two will have the same birthday, would you believe that?'

She looked again at the photograph. Frieda's joyous expression.

'But it is a weird coincidence,' she agreed.

Joni tried on the coral jewellery and Georgie said she could have it, but they should probably value it, and if it was worth something insure it; and if they ever sold it they must split the proceeds absolutely equally between Will's family and hers.

This was a dividing point, she realised. Things could disperse and separate down her own line or Will's. A dividing point, the phrase seemed important.

'I don't want to sell it. I want to wear it,' Joni protested. 'Although, maybe it's immoral, like ivory.'

'I think it's very old, Joni,' Georgie told her. 'Late Georgian, so about two hundred years?'

'Could it be Inca gold?' Joni asked. 'Tons of it ended up in Spain. They melted it down. Isn't it awful?'

Georgie thought for a moment. 'And the coral would be Mediterranean I suppose. It could be Inca gold, but how could anyone ever know?'

Joni put the beads aside and continued investigating the box. She stopped at a portrait of Maureen as a very young child, in a bright white smock, with shining bobbed hair. Again, her mouth opened, aghast.

'Look!' she said.

'That's Grandma,' Georgie explained. 'She must be about four. Photographed in Cork. That's where she's from. Was from.'

'Round her neck.'

'No!' There they were again, a single strand of coral.

'It's like – magic!' Joni said. She retrieved the photograph of Frieda, and they compared the beads. Maureen's were monochrome, but the pineapple shapes were identical, spaced an identical number of round beads apart.

'I suppose she must have given them to Frieda,' Georgie said. 'Or Frieda could have borrowed them.'

Joni raised her eyebrows sarcastically, giving a different complexion to the word 'borrowed'.

Nothing in *Special Things* could be recycled or thrown away or given or sold – not letters, photographs, trinkets, or oddments.

'I'm going to do something with them,' Georgie announced, shutting one of the cabinet drawers in a determined fashion. 'A family memoir. Maybe if I write about them, I can exorcise all these irritating ghosts. They might appreciate their freedom!'

'Free the spirit!' Joni smiled. 'You should, Mum. That would, like, make use of everything?'

Georgie studied Joni's expression – warm and open, expecting a response.

'Joni, I thought I'd never tell you this, but it's better told, so I'm just going to say it, is that OK?'

Joni nodded, suddenly anxious. 'OK.'

Georgie led her to the newly recommissioned sofa where they sat down together. She let out a breath and thought for a while of the best words to use. She'd rehearsed it so many times in the last few days. What a silly she was. It was simple really. Just the facts. Joni quietly waited, looking serious and concerned. At last Georgie launched in, without a preamble.

'You weren't my first child, in fact. You had a twin brother, born a few minutes before you. He died at six days old.'

Joni's face fell. 'Oh!'

'His name was Charles. I have nothing left of him. They did things differently then, you see.'

For a moment Joni was alone with the information, taking it in, imagining herself as a baby, perhaps, abandoned by her older brother. Georgie wished she'd saved it for a better time. How thoughtless it was to dump it on her when she must be feeling so tired, when she'd been so kind and helpful and busy all day. Was there really a good reason to tell her at all? She wasn't sure why she had, and was about to say something to that effect, when Joni put her arms around her, and Georgie made ready to comfort her and apologise.

'Oh, poor Mummy,' Joni said. 'Oh my poor poor Mummy! I'm so sorry. That must have been so hard.'

Georgie was overcome. She laid her head on Joni's shoulder into waves and waves of warmth and love, as unexpected tears sprang from her eyes and flowed silently down to her neck.

'It was my fault Joni,' she stammered. 'I stayed out on the bike too long.'

'No, no, Mummy, it wouldn't have been that. Of course it wasn't your fault.'

'It was.'

She went on and on, deeply quietly sobbing, while Joni contained and soothed her. How different to the frantic sobbing she'd dumped upon Eileen. This was a release, a balm, a blessing. It was as though all the sorrow she had ever felt was pouring out through a weakness in the walls of her heart, split open by the sheer stress of time. Dead dreams, lost opportunities, failed relationships, dead parents, and this was the worst one, buried so deep, locked up so tight that nobody had opened it, at last all flowing out like a great underground sea. The child she had accidentally killed.

'I didn't cry about him at the time,' Georgie explained, dabbing her face with the tissue Joni had produced, 'because I was so grateful for you. Oh, I was lucky with you, wasn't I? I was so lucky with you, Joni.'

Joni smiled, agreeing with ironic enthusiasm, which made Georgie smile too. Suddenly a loud crashing noise came from the kitchen, a metallic avalanche. They looked at each other, shocked, and Georgie went to investigate. A pan had fallen from the counter. She picked it up, looking around to see how it had happened. There was no obvious cause.

As she was falling asleep that night, lulled by the reassuring sound of Joni's gentle snoring, it came to her all at once. Her mind was trawling through the day's experience. The idea of magic had come up and she was thinking about the kind of person who likes to perform conjuring tricks and illusions. Will used to, as a boy. Sometimes he showed her the trick, and usually the thing that seemed to appear from nowhere had been laid well in advance of its revelation, like a seed.

And she was thinking of branches and trunks, trunks and branches.

And Joni had looked up coral on the internet. It had magical properties and used to be given to children as a protective charm. They had noted the contradiction – coral used to protect people, now people have to protect the coral.

The single strand of coral was from her mother's side. The four remaining were from her father's. Their families had a common friend or ancestor who had started off with five. It was as simple as that. Somehow the Irish sea had intervened between the giver and the receiver.

'Or between the owner and a thief,' she murmured to herself. 'Or a loser and a finder.' But she felt sure that was not the case. Deep in her bones she was certain that the beads had been a gift of love from a mother to her baby, just as Maureen had given them to Frieda.

In her hazy mind she heard an echo of Will's phrase: 'it's not that strange'. It might have been a tradition to split a necklace like that; perhaps there were dozens of them made and dozens of them split. And even if there was only one, and the separated parts had to find each other by chance, twisting and turning through the family lines, well, we all have common ancestors, and friends in common too. 'And everyone is family to some extent.'

Then it struck her.

'Beads! Beads! Where have I seen beads before?'

She stumbled out of bed as though in a panic; but the glass photograph was easy to find. It was where it now belonged under *Victorian photos in order of date.* In her excitement, she must have made too much noise, because Joni appeared in the doorway. 'Mum! You're still up?' She yawned.

'Why would anyone on the Sutton side have a rosary?' Georgie asked her, incongruously. 'You look. Your eyes are better than mine. I took the larger beads to be Lord's Prayers and the others to be Hail Marys. Ha! So many ladies to each lord! But mightn't the larger ones be pineapples? And are there only four strands? If it's *our* necklace, she'd already taken the fifth one off!'

Joni shook the confusion out of her head. She squinted at the glass and moved nearer to the light, angling it this way and that to avoid the reflection.

'It's annoying,' she groaned. 'I can't quite tell if they're separate strands or one strand coiled over several times.'

'How many times?'

'Yes. Only four. She's crossing her fingers, look.'

'But the fifth could be hidden in her palm I suppose. Or they could be different beads altogether. It wouldn't stand up in court, would it?'

'Court!' Joni sneered. 'What's the law got to do with anything?'

Georgie gave her a disapproving look.

They decided to compare the photograph with the actual necklace, and as Joni was handling the beads in an effort to mirror those in the photograph, Georgie was re-examining the case and its curlicued initials. She traced them with a finger.

'D'you think this is a G and an S? That's what I want it to be.'

'I suppose so.' Joni hung her head to one side. 'Or it could be an S and a G!' She tutted. 'Why is old-fashioned lettering so unreadable? It's like they didn't *want* anyone to read it.'

She replaced the beads in their case and it snapped shut.

'I think they are the same,' she said softly, leaning over to give her mother a hug. 'And Mum?'

Georgie looked up.

'Did he look anything like us? Like me or Charlie, I mean.'

Georgie caught her breath. 'No. No.' She found herself swallowing uncomfortably. 'He was different.'

'I'm sorry, I shouldn't have mentioned it.'

'You should. Yes, of course you should, Joni. You must ask me anything you want to know, and I'll tell you the best I can.'

She closed her eyes, and searched her memory, the dark part, where she couldn't see much at all.

'He was completely his own little person, you know, with his own smudged-up little face. A tiny thing. Tiny. Yes. Quite a lot of hair, I remember that, that's from my side. But he had his father's mouth. Your father's mouth.' She pouted. 'A bit sulky!' She shot Joni a conspiratorial smile. 'Only I can't see him that well any more.'

'Isn't there a photo, even?'

Georgie shook her head. 'It just wasn't done.'

Joni yawned again, trying desperately not to. 'Sorry. We'd better get some sleep, hadn't we? Maybe we can talk some more tomorrow?' She kissed Georgie goodnight, but seemed reluctant to leave her. 'I want us to have, like, a funeral or something. Like a memorial or something, d'you know what I mean?'

Georgie nodded.

'Are you going to be OK?'

Georgie reassured her, and waited for Joni to go, before taking herself back to bed. She couldn't sleep, no way could she sleep. She didn't want to. She lay wide awake, her mind swimming in ideas.

She thought about the boy, that first little boy. She thought about Jim, and how he must have had to drag her through those first terrible days. About how he'd wanted to call Charlie Simon, and that dreadful time he'd mentioned, 'Charles the first'. She thought about Joni and she thought about Charlie, her almost grown-up Charles the second.

She realised she was crossing her fingers.

It reminded her of the woman and her beads – the intense expression on her face. You could take it differently if you remembered that she'd had to pose, quite rigid, for several seconds. Stern, serious, yes, but was there a glimmer of hope? An entreaty to a lost child, perhaps? Please will you still exist, and if so, please will you know me?

In some hidden place, away from home, had she wrenched one string of coral from the rest, secured it with a ribbon around her darling's neck, and let him go? Him or her. As thousands of women have had to do, before and since.

Since when, what then?

Two centuries of war, invention, birth, love and dying. Heads of state assassinated. Capital accumulated. Species annihilated. Forests devastated. Ozone layer thinned. Climate fucked.

Poor Mama Pacha.

Oh my poor Mama Pacha.

She thought about the next two hundred years.

*

Early next morning she googled 'how grow trees.' Her researches were interrupted by an email:

Georgina how lovely to hear from you. The wonder of the internet – and how on earth did we all lose touch? Yes, I'm Helena McGough. Or was! Matt's sister. Perhaps you don't remember me – I went to the same school as you, but I was two years below. Of course you know that Matt married Frieda Lehmann. Attached wedding photo was buried under mountains of unsorted rubbish, which is why it's taken so long for me to reply. I look terrible don't I (those ghastly 80s hairstyles!) but I love this pic because the parents look as happy as the happy couple. Behind yours are Frieda's adoptive – Mutti and Vati (Mutti still going strong – survivor's genes). I suppose you and Will must have been away or busy – but it was pretty amazing the rest of us made it to Seville as it was. Matt lives in Berlin now (a blessing he's not still in Spain!), still researching for the auto industry and showing no sign of wanting to retire (bit more ethical now though of course – electric cars and so on) with three children a cat and a dog and a grandchild – Minnie (I'm holding her hand in the photo), Stuart, Lawrence, Gracie, Helmut and Dorothee. (Gracie and Helmut are the cat and the dog :-)). Very sadly Frieda died six years ago of breast cancer. Another reason for the delay: I wasn't sure whether I ought to tell you this, as Matty might not, but I think Frieda would want me to and I don't see the harm. You must know how immensely fond she was of you and Will. After she died, I helped to go through her things, and found cards for each of you she never sent. She wanted to be forgiven – what for I don't know. I can't imagine her doing any wrong. She was such a wonderful person. I've never known anyone as kind. She always knew instinctively what you needed. She saw the good in everyone and her only wish was for other people's happiness. She has left a gaping hole in all of our lives.

My mother died last year, and we're letting the house until we work out what else to do with it, so next time you're in Stratford, do drop me a line (mates' rates if you want to stay in the house). I love reminiscing about the good old days! I hope you're well, and Will and your mother and father. You were such a star at school, and so missed after you left. Head girl material everyone said. I'm guessing you've made a terrific success of everything – I'd love to hear your news. Mine: I married, I divorced, and I have a fabulous son Stevie who's about to go off to Edinburgh University! New phase!

CULTIVATE

Family Sketches
for
Joni, Charlie, Henri and Eve

Aunt Elfrieda
A child lost, and found

On 26 February 1946, nine and a half months after VE day, one of the first of the 'baby boomers' was born to your grandparents, Maureen Connor and Lawrence Sutton – a girl, baptised Georgina May. Maureen was only sixteen, and Larry – at nineteen – was serving in the British Army in Vienna. The girl was taken in by a children's home.

By 1950 she was the adopted daughter of a couple living in Salzburg, Karl and Maria (originally Mariya) Lehmann. Given the economic and political circumstances, that was an extraordinary transition; but the even stranger fact that my father had already met these people in Vienna was no coincidence, and they were people who were used to defying tough circumstances.

Theirs would be a fascinating, though harrowing, story. But unless I trouble them for information – and who am I to ask? – they must be ninety-odd – I can only go on general history for clues, piecing these together with the few facts I've been able to glean from scribbles and photographs, and the few things I learnt from Frieda herself.

I know that Karl was a doctor, and Mariya a nurse. I know that Karl was a Quaker, and I know that Mariya was Ukrainian, possibly Jewish (either way, 'sub-human', according to the Nazis). I know that they met before the end of the war – this must be true because their son Hans was a year older than Frieda – and I know they were in Vienna at the end of it. Mariya and Hans could only have survived under protection, and Karl was almost certainly their protector.

I imagine this: Mariya is forced from her home in Ukraine, transported to a labour camp on the outskirts of Vienna. She is rescued by Karl. She is hidden in a basement or attic. Karl brings her food, and takes care of her injuries. They fall in love. Hans is born. As the Russian Army arrives in the spring of 1945, followed by the Americans, the British and the French, their son is only a few weeks old. Their trials are far from over. Mariya now has to evade repatriation, to flee from Soviet rule. There is no Ukraine to go back to. As an Austrian, existence for Karl might also have been precarious. Locals of all ages were badly treated by the occupying forces, even after they were cast as victims and not perpetrators of Nazism.

Soldiers weren't supposed to fraternise with the public, but of course they did, especially with the women. My father spoke German; perhaps this gave him an added sympathy as well as making him useful. At any rate, he made friends. Amidst bombed-out buildings, rat-runs and makeshift graves, amidst disease and hunger, prostitution and black marketeering, there was still music and laughter. Though you might be surviving on a diet of bread and dried peas, under the light of a low-watt bulb you could still waltz. And in the harshest of times individuals may still be kind.

My father did something for Karl and Mariya they could never forget. They say he 'looked after our son when we could not,' and, 'It was a miracle he survived'. Amongst his belongings I found a newspaper article in which I read of troops defying authority by sharing rations, or giving people protection as they crossed borders. I also found a list of Slavic names, and I believe that Karl and Mariya were not the only people my father helped. Moreover, perhaps it was Karl who recruited him and, by doing so, exposed him to danger. What makes me wonder is the level of his gratitude – is it tinged with guilt?

In 1945 Vienna was divided into British, American, French,

Russian and International zones – but, rather like Berlin, it was an island city in a sea of Soviet-occupied territory. Salzburg, under American occupation, was a safer destination for anyone wanting to stay clear of the Iron Curtain; anyone who had hopes of starting a new life in the USA or Palestine, for example.

Somehow or other, with assistance from some kind person or persons, Mariya, Karl and their son Hans found their way to Salzburg, and there they stayed, where their medical skills were in demand. My father kept a photograph of Mariya. I wonder if Karl gave it to him as a means of identifying her, with instructions about her destination: Parsch.

In 1947, Karl travelled to London to speak at an international conference organised by the Fellowship of Reconciliation. During his stay in England he wished to renew contact with my father, but had no idea where (or whether) he was, and nothing more to go on than conversational smatterings of information about his previous life. In pursuit of my father, Karl found Georgina, but that was the end of the trail; either the orphanage had no further information, or they were legally disallowed from providing it. But that was not enough for Karl. He determined to take care of my father's daughter, and by the time he returned to Austria, had cleared the first of what must have been a formidable series of bureaucratic hurdles towards that goal.

I wonder when Frieda discovered that we were her biological family. The rules about adoptees seeing their papers changed in 1975, so it's possible she knew in 1976. I could get in touch with her widowed husband to try and find out, but I don't suppose there's any point in disturbing that bit of dust. If she did know, it would mean she was stranger than I want to believe. Will and I both pretty well fell in love with her, you see, and I'm afraid she did nothing to discourage us.

They called her Elfrieda, which means the strength of an elf. If you look at the younger photographs you'll see how appropriate that name was, and you'll see why Karl couldn't resist offering her a family home. I find the expression on her face heart-breaking – it's a desire to please, mingled with the sheer effort of it, and an intelligence and knowingness which give her the aspect of an ancient soul.

Well, that might have been the end of that, but for a letter my father wrote to *Time* magazine in August 1954. Karl read the letter, recognised the writer's name, and his argument, and swiftly got in touch with Larry through the publisher. Larry gave Maureen the good news: their daughter was safe and happy. There must have been forgiveness, a coming to terms, and a laying to rest. That fortunate outcome of such a bitter business seems to have renewed their relationship. By then Maureen was old enough to make her own decisions. In any case, she married Larry, and they started all over again; so, in a roundabout way, I, my brother, and all of you, have Karl (and *Time* magazine!) to thank for our genesis!

Intermittently thereafter, my parents received news and photographs of Frieda, but Will and I were never told about her. It was normal in those days to gloss over facts and hope that you could dispense with a problem by not mentioning it – a point which in a most uncanny twist happened to be the subject of that letter to *Time* magazine. Sometimes it works, I suppose. Sometimes remembering is too painful. Sometimes you want to shield other people from your pain. But things were more complicated in this case, because Frieda's adoptive parents never tired of mentioning your grandfather, and one day, in the spring of 1976, Frieda arrived on our doorstep like a feather dropped from a passing dove. We thought she was a rather glamorous au pair-come-tourist. We knew only that her parents were Larry's war friends which sounded dreadfully murky and nasty to us then. Especially as he couldn't bear to speak about his army years.

I remember one day in May, quite soon after Frieda had arrived. It was my sixteenth birthday, but the date had another significance. It was a double celebration for your grandparents. They left me and Will to enjoy ourselves, and took Frieda out especially, just the three of them. I imagine the scene. My mother went out to the WI as usual, while my father took Frieda to see a film, (I can't find out whether it was *One Flew Over The Cuckoo's Nest*, or a showing of *Gone With The Wind* – so take your pick!) then the three of them met for supper at a restaurant. I know it from a note in my father's desk diary – *G's B'day Party, Pix w F, Supps w F and M*. I don't think they would have gone for a Chinese or Indian meal, because they'd have wanted champagne, not beer or saki. More likely it would have been a steak house perhaps, with prawn cocktail for starters and schwarzwälder Kirschtorte for pudding. Yes, they would have drunk champagne and got very squiffy, and there would have been candlelight and swirly-patterned maroon carpets and wood-panelled walls. That's what I imagine for them. A blissful evening, followed by an oddness and sadness in not being able to share their happiness with us, or explain it properly to Frieda. 'I so loved your parents,' was all my father could have said, might have said, meaning all the while, 'We so love you.'

At the end of the summer, Frieda went back to Austria, and my parents put aside their own feelings to protect us.

Well, in spite of the mess of it, I'm glad I met her. She inspired me to stop my swottishness, and to see the world, to drop Science and pursue what I loved, which was Art for a while, then travelling, then Jim and the first of you lovely children. My career was very different from the one I might have had, clinking test-tubes or brandishing a stethoscope. Frieda put the first twist into my lifeline. She blunted its edges and corners.

The one regret I have is that our parents never told us, so they never knew that it didn't matter. We would have loved to know our sister *as* our sister! Wouldn't we? And I so wish that they hadn't had the guilt of it.

Georgie read over this first attempt at a Family Sketch and heaved a deep sigh. She scribbled out the bit about herself, put a line through the paragraph about the change in adoption rules, and added a mention of Matthew and the cousins in Germany.

Maybe she could fill in some of the gaps by writing to him. It would be simple – though not easy.

She reconsidered her last four sentences. She didn't want to finish on regret and wishing. She laid a smooth clean sheet of paper on her writing box and stared at it for some time, fiddling with her pen, blinded by the blank.

The empty page reminded her of a conversation she'd had with Nick, a few days after Joni left, several weeks ago, on an evening she'd already remembered many times. They'd been talking about time.

'I see the years as circles,' he'd said, 'spiralling up from the ground. Like a clock. Winter's at the top, at zero; summer's at the bottom of it, half past. Spring is a quarter past, autumn a quarter to.'

Georgie had answered: 'So where are we now? About twenty-five past winter? My favourite!' She'd wanted to talk of summer – the lengthening of days, the furious natural explosions of life and colour, that feeling you sometimes get on a hot afternoon when you can smell thunder and mown gardens and sweating houses, and it takes you back to summers of old, simply because of its rarity.

'Actually, it's all my favourite,' he'd said simply. 'And I seem to feel I'm at the centre of it somehow, at the hub.' Georgie must have made a disapproving face. 'Not because I'm important or anything,' he assured her.

She laughed, amazed. 'To me, time is a ribbon going from left to right, like ink flowing from a pen, I suppose. Indelible ink.'

'I take it you're writing, then? Or are you just reading it?'

'No. I don't know who's writing.' A line of poetry floated up from the depths of her unconscious and rippled out of her mouth, in that mysterious easy way that words used to come to her. 'Nor all your piety nor wit shall draw it back to cancel half a line.'

'Nor all your tears wash out a word of it.'

Georgie smiled, glad that he knew the poem. 'No.'

We don't understand time at all, she thought now. Nobody does. How it might be coiled within us like genes coiled on a string of DNA; how all of living history might be contained in a single cell, connected to every other cell that ever was, vibrating, resonating, spinning an infinity of fractal patterns, repeating over repeated patterns. Ribbons and spirals indeed.

He had taken her hands in his, shockingly. She thought he was about to say something about mourning, about grief; something comforting perhaps, about tears at least washing your heart, or cleaning the wounds. But it was completely different.

'I was wild about you, Georgina.'

How she regretted hearing it in the past tense!

'Hormones,' she said, with a dying fall. Nick looked put out. 'I wish I'd known,' she added, quickly.

'I was probably too shy. Lost the moment.'

He'd looked at her mouth, with an intensity that embarrassed her. She'd pulled away, and he questioned her action, raising an eyebrow.

'I'm scared,' she told him, in puzzlement.

'I'm not scary,' he whispered, 'though I might bite you.'

Oh dear, that was such a sexy thing to say, Georgie felt a tremor in a part of her body she thought had died.

'What if I don't like it?'

'You might like it.'

She had groaned with the struggle of resisting him. 'That's even worse. What if we start something and then it stops and then I have to get over it before I can start something else with someone else, if I actually want to be with someone at all, that is, and I haven't got time! I need someone I can grow old with.' She smiled sardonically. 'Assuming I do grow old. Though I'm already old.'

'I'm quite nice, really, you know.'

'Maybe that's the trouble. It'll make the ending even harder.'

Nick had dropped her hands, and moved away. Quietly,

somewhat mournfully he asked, 'D'you remember the last time we saw each other? When we were young, I mean.'

Georgie said nothing. He measured his words before going on.

'It was 1983. CND march. We went to London on the coach, d'you remember? I lost you in the crowd. I looked for you on the coach home, but you were sitting by someone else. You smiled and said "see you" – so casually – when you left. See you at the Clifton pool in twenty-eight years!' He laughed. 'We'd talked about love. Don't you remember? It made such an impression on me. You said, "do the thing you love, and love the day".'

Frieda, Georgie thought.

'Live. Love. Laugh. That was your advice. And I'd loved that day, and spent the whole journey home thinking what do I love? Who do I love? And I decided I loved you; and I loved gardening.' He sighed and looked away. 'But I suppose it's teenagey to think you can love someone so quickly?'

'I loved the children the moment I felt them kick,' Georgie said. 'Then and forever, I knew it was forever.'

'Georgina.' He shook his head, amused, baffled. 'Why did you sit by someone else?'

She did remember it. She closed her eyes, hung her head, took herself back to that exhausted smoky evening. She remembered that 'State of Independence' had played on her Sony Walkman – her bright shiny red Sony Walkman that some other boy, now irrelevant, had given to her – and she'd been full of the future, of the causes she would support, the places she would see, the people she would meet, the exhibitions she would give, the music she would play, the books she would write, all the fantastic things she would accomplish – all those goals that had fizzled out one by one in failure – sheer unlucky failure – that had accumulated like rust or limescale, gumming the works of her ambition.

Without opening her eyes, because she was ashamed, she said, 'I wanted to be free.' Then she started weeping, foolishly weeping! 'It wasn't fair on you!' she murmured. Nick embraced her. She looked up at him through the blur and saw his tolerant worldly-wise expression, slightly amused, but not cruelly so. No, of course it wasn't fair. Nothing is fair.

And then he kissed her. Oh my goodness, it was wonderful. Together they'd laid her old single mattress on the lobby floor, and spent the whole evening talking. He'd nipped out for fish and chips and they'd finished a bottle of wine. Nick suggested buying another, and Georgie had said, 'Let's not drink any more, because if you drink, you don't last as long,' meaning you die sooner. But Nick had misunderstood.

Hmm.

The memory of it was a physical sensation – his honouring her damaged body, the tenderness and patience of his caresses, the healthy smell of him, his strength and weight, and that blissful moment when she found that the ultra-low-dose bioidentical oestriol, or the herbs, or his touch, or her imagination, or something simply magical, had worked.

Hmm. Hmm.

Yes, on that occasion it was a good thing screaming had failed to summon the emergency services.

She decided to leave the Frieda story to marinade, and turned instead to a pile of papers she'd sorted from Keep, pulling out the two that most intrigued her: a letter, and a newspaper cutting.

3 Sep 1976

Dear Maureen

I enclose this with the rest of the personal effects, because I think it might be as interesting to you as I find it. Yet another 'person of letters' in the family – but published in the local paper at least!

What a summer we've had of it. D'you think we'll remember it? The garden is done for, but Ted is convinced the lawn will come back next year. Roll on spring, then!

Best wishes

Ethel

Dear Sir

Your fascinating article about the basement hoard has prompted me to write to you about my own 'family treasure'.

My grandfather told me that his grandmother told him that somewhere in our family's old business lodging in Bristol – the house in which I myself now live – there lay a fortune in gold and silver jewellery, so we must never sell up. This great-great-grandmother had sewn it inside a rag doll when she was a girl, so the story goes. Her jealous little brother had buried the doll in the garden and wouldn't tell her where it was. It has never turned up though the soil there has been many times turned over. If there is any truth in the tale, presumably somebody found the doll and quietly made off with it! I like to imagine it was during the last war when the ground was disturbed for the planting of vegetables. Instead of cauliflowers and carrots, the hard-working servant must have been rewarded with treasure enough to buy oysters and champagne!

Unhappy families may be unhappy in original ways, but do not most of them carry tales of lost fortunes or royal ancestry? And are not these lost fortunes and connections merely symbols of other normal losses and disappointments which happy families grieve over and eventually accept?

The experience of the family in your article does not necessarily contradict the suggestion – they appear on the contrary to be an exceedingly happy family!

Yours faithfully
Ruby Sutton

Georgie stared out of the window. The rain had gone. The ground looked rich and inviting.

She refiled the papers and recapped the fountain pen, and went to look out the collection of potatoes she had brought up with her from Salisbury, now bristling with shoots. Armed with the trowel and fork Nick had given her, wearing wellies inherited from her mother, she plunged outside into a moist brown world.

Given to me, she thought: it has all been given.

She enjoyed lifting the soil, shifting it to one side and laying the tubers in their little beds, six inches down, six inches apart. She hoped the beds wouldn't become little graves. Sunlight struck the rain-spangled weeds, as if to contradict that suggestion and reassure her. She paused in her labour to look up and let it warm her face. The sky seemed suddenly new to her – a vast canopy of blue and white – rinsed and fresh. She gazed in wonder at the sight of it – familiar yet marvellous, stirring and uplifting – that delicate layer of atmosphere, fragile yet ancient, hanging between the living world and an infinity of lifelessness.

Her earliest memory was of sky. She loved it. She loved the blue. She loved the clouds in all their splendid variety – powdery cotton fluffs, gauzy veils, feathery ripples and frills. She loved the way the sunlight illuminated the birds as they winged across its radiant space and she loved the solid summer green of the trees in contrast to its clean blueness.

She stood and angled herself so that she could see nothing else but this huge, curving, brilliant sky, thinking it had been there for aeons, before the world had eyes to see it. Clouds had already drifted and changed. She saw the particularity of each and the generality of all, the way they transformed and joined and separated so that really there was no particularity, there was only white and light and vapour, dancing and mixing and pulling apart. A whale became a cat, the cat became a face, the face became two, the two became one. Some of that water had been cycling for billions of years, and might have been rivers and sea and slime and sap and tears and sweat. How quickly, how far and wide and thin a single tear might diffuse!

Suddenly she felt that she was the whole world, looking through one pair of eyes at the very top of its mass. And then she realised with a mighty rush of emotion, that she was a part of it all how each cloud was a part of the vapour; but she was a seeing part – she was a seeing part of all that she could see. She started to laugh – in confusion and surprise at the oddity and absurdity of it all. She had felt precisely like this before, she had seen sky like this in exactly the same weather, with the same damp soily smell in her nose, the same cast of light and shadow, at the same angle, with the same breath of a breeze against her face. She had even had the same thought. Where or when, she had no idea, but knowing it made her complete and full and all at once and forever!

What if her last view of the world was the same as her first remembered: a view of this beautiful sky – the source and sustainer of life – which generations of eyes had watched, waiting for the light and the rain, blessed by the air. Her own life might be framed and enclosed by blue and white. That would be pretty. That would be good.

Of course, it might not be blue and white when the moment came.

She shivered. It was growing late. Nick would be arriving soon. Kind, honest, capable Nick, with all his Nickness intact. They were going to discuss a planting project she had in mind. He thought it could work, with a little support and organisation. She knelt down to bury – to plant – the last of her potatoes.

There wasn't really anything missing from her sketch of Frieda – nothing that needed to be told – at least not yet. Just a sentence she could weave in tomorrow to round it off. Something like: *Perhaps they hoped the truth would reveal itself when we were ready, when it could no longer hurt us, when we would understand because we were parents ourselves.* Or a general thing, like the idea that the meaning of things changes with the changing times – or, better still, that idea followed by something about the future – the proper far-off future that didn't contain herself or even the children – just a few of her genes, a few words, perhaps, perhaps a sliver of her light – not the light you throw off in a photograph, no, that didn't count for much – but the sort of spark you generate from within and scatter about you to try and make life a bit nicer, the sort of encouragement or comfort you try and give, or that you might receive from someone else and pass on, perhaps with an extra boost, like the encouragement Frieda had given to her, an impulse that can pass from one person to another to another, even though the source has been lost and forgotten, that could go on for a long long time, growing and dividing, weaving and joining, as though on glistening threads, or in capillaries humming with vital magic, the way sap flows from trunk to leaves, or the other way round, the way it coalesces from roots to trunk, the way milk pools at the nipple and flows into a mouth.

Love. That was it. Of course.

She came indoors and washed the soil from her hands.

She gathered up the pen, the ink, the new pack of paper. She turned the key to the writing box. Simply and silently, and for the first time, it opened like a flower, on every side.

AFTERWORD

I was inspired to write this novel when I was going through the boxes in my parents' house soon after my mother died. My father had died two years before. It was an extraordinary experience. Both my parents liked to keep cards and letters and photographs and trinkets and other bits of paraphernalia, and my paternal grandmother and maternal great aunts did too, so my family had material coming down to us from both sides, and I became involved with history and archaeology spanning almost two centuries.

I have used six of the documents I found, the first being my mother's poem 'Tear Off Slip', which is reproduced verbatim, and, I believe, gave me licence to make small changes to the rest. I credit her here: my mother was Anne Ménage, though her pen name was Frances Cameron – a few of her poems were published in periodicals. There are lots more!

These documents – and a few objects – are the tiny scraps of reality around which I constructed this tale. Apart from the general historical background, nothing of the story is true, except that, like Georgina, I was born and brought up in Stratford-upon-Avon, and went to school in Warwick. My older brother is nothing like Will. My mum and dad were nothing like Maureen and Larry, apart from having boxes. I also have an older sister, a younger brother and two younger sisters – and none of the many relationships between us is reflected here. All events and characters are imaginary, and anything based on experience is not necessarily my own personal experience. I feel it's important to be clear about that, because the autobiographical element is certainly strong.

SJM 2016

STAYING ALIVE

Good relationships with friends and family
Regular exercise in fresh air
Humour
Keep calm
Sleep well/melatonin
Sunshine/Vitamin D
Avoid parabens and other xenoestrogens
Avoid aluminium
Eat fresh food, especially colourful vegetables and fruit
Wash it, peel it, eat organic if possible
Use lots of turmeric combined with pepper
Plenty of omega threes (eg in oily fish, flax)
Use saturated or mono-unsaturated fat for cooking
Might as well include some laetrile
Sugar – cut down or out
If meat, grass-fed, hormone-free, not much
If eggs, free range organic
If chocolate, high cocoa
If caffeine, green tea
If wine, one glass of non-industrial red with supper!

Jenny -> Stuff, Worcester
Jeremy Hem - boat Patishead /Warwick
Sarah   Nicky + Pe
Kate) Chris Hexham
Nick) Banbury / + wife Gill
Joey Bournemall

better & better

Publishing house (more of a flat) Better & Better (so-called because Faber & Faber would not allow its original name, Fabber & Fabber) came about from a combination of vanity and mortality. Having inherited a wealth of excellently written material from both parents, Sarah did not want to endow posterity with her own unpublished work, nor risk its being destroyed or laid to waste. She decided to make it available, in case others might find it useful or amusing.

Better & Better was launched in 2017, and HOW TO MAKE LIFE NICE is its first release. Two further novels are on the way:

THE GLASS GIRL is about a woman in her very late thirties (thirty-twelve) who suddenly decides to have a baby, so needs a man.

LOVE IN A WET CLIMATE is about a love triangle that turns into a love non-convex tetragon.

Sarah has also written two albums of songs, WHO NEEDS A MAN and IN A MOOD. Songs connected to the novels – Love In A Wet Climate, The Glass Girl, They Fuck You Up, How To Make Life Nice and Molly's Daughter – will be released with others on STRIPPED DOWN DITTIES. They are also available as downloads from sarahmenage.com.

SARAH MÉNAGE

Writer and performer Sarah Ménage was born and brought up in Stratford-upon-Avon. She spent her twenties in London, where she studied Medicine for two years and Drama for three, winning her Equity card on the alternative comedy circuit, before fleeing to Bath and eventually discovering the many marvellousnesses of Bristol. She has five siblings, one grown-up son and lots of nephews and nieces.

The name Ménage (which means household) comes from great-great-grandfather John Baptiste (aka Gustave) who bigamously married English girl Naomi Starters in 1839. Since the marriage was illegal, the British Ménages ought really to be called Starters. On her mother's side, great-great-great-grandfather James Cathrow Disney, Somerset Herald and fantasist, believed himself to be a bastard son of George IV. The story has not been proved false. Sarah recently embraced her (Galway and Belfast) Irish ancestry and established her dual nationality and will display her Irish passport with very little encouragement or excuse.